PAGOSA SPRINGS

DENVER CEREAL, VOLUME TWENTY

PAGOSA SPRINGS

DENVER CEREAL, VOLUME TWENTY

Claudia Hall Christian

Cook Street Publishing
Denver, CO

ISBN-13 :   978-1-938057-79-3 (print)
                978-1-938057-80-9 (digital)

Library of Congress: 2020950758

PUBLISHER'S NOTE:
This is a work of fiction. Names, characters, places and incidents either are
either the product of the author's imagination or are used fictitiously.

First edition © December 2020
Cook Street Publishing
ISNI: 0000 0004 1443 6403
PO Box 7247
Denver, CO 80207

WHAT'S HAPPENED SO FAR

Denver Cereal is an addicting, fun, sweet and crunchy serial fiction filled with the tension, drama, and love of urban life.

The best way to catch up is to read *Grand Junction, Denver Cereal* Volume 1-10 and *Fort Garland, Denver Cereal* V11-13. They are very affordable and available wherever eBooks are sold. You can also read *Denver Cereal* chapters online at StoriesbyClaudia.com.

We used to write a section here that gave a synopsis of all of the previous books. Frankly, the synopsis' wasn't very good. More than anything, they deprived you of the chance to hang out in Denver Cereal for a while. We were only be spoiling your fun

You deserve a chance to read all the crazy twists and turns, mischief, and wild adventures of Denver Cereal. These aren't books to be accomplished or checked off a list. They are stories to be savored and enjoys.

Get to it.

We'll be here when you get back.

~~~~~~~~~~~~~

Denver Cereal is provided free online due to the generous support of our patrons and you, the book buyer. This book was created because of your support.

THANK YOU TO YOU, AND ALL OF OUR PATRONS.

CHAPTER FIVE HUNDRED & FORTY-THREE
ENTER THE POLICE

3 days later
Thursday morning — 10:01 a.m.
Navajo Nation Police Station

"No, sir," Blane said.

He was sitting in an interview room, across from Detective Benjie Nez of the Navajo Nation Police. He'd been called in for questioning in the deaths of the Templars.

"We have to wait for the FBI," Detective Nez said.

"Why is that?" Blane asked.

"The FBI has jurisdiction over the reservation," Detective Nez said. "Sometimes we get guys who want to run the whole show. Agent Rodriguez likes to work in conjunction with the Navajo Nation Police."

Detective Nez grinned.

"We like that, too," Detective Nez said.

"I bet," Blane said.

Detective Nez seemed to be trying to keep Blane calm. Blane hated small spaces. This entire situation was uncomfortable and more than a little scary.

"So we wait for the FBI," Detective Nez said with a smile.

The door to the room opened, and a woman wearing a dark-blue suit entered the room. Blane hopped to his feet. She held out her hand.

"Agent Rodriguez," she said.

"Blane Lipson," he said, shaking her hand.

"I apologize for the delay," she said, sitting down next to Detective Nez. She set a file on the table. "This morning, I have received seven phone calls from seven different high-ranking individuals."

She looked at him for a moment. Her cell phone rang. She looked at the caller identification and then back at Blane.

"Eight individuals," Agent Rodriguez said. "Any idea why they would call me?"

"How would I possibly know something like that?" Blane asked.

"They were calling in support of you," Agent Rodriguez said.

"Okay," Blane said.

"You don't seem surprised," Agent Rodriguez said.

"How am I to know who usually calls you or how many calls you usually get?" Blane asked. "Is eight calls a lot?"

Agent Rodriguez looked at Blane for a long moment.

"You did not ask your friends to call me?" Agent Rodriguez asked.

"I only just met you," Blane said. "How could I ask anyone to call you when I've never met you?"

Clearly not impressed, the FBI agent tipped her head to the side and watched Blane. He responded by shrugging.

"How do you know so many high-ranking people in the military or intelligence?" Agent Rodriguez asked.

"I . . ." Blane sighed. He looked at her for a long moment before clearing his throat. "You must know that I cannot tell you that."

"Why is that?" Agent Rodriguez asked.

"I can't tell if you're actually curious or whether you just want to mess with me," Blane said. "And I'm not sure what any of this has to do with what happened to my partner's grandfathers."

Agent Rodriguez gave Blane a hard look. She was silent for so long that Detective Nez shifted uncomfortably. After a moment, Blane shrugged again.

They sat in silence for what seemed like a long time. Agent Rodriguez took a breath and flipped open a file.

"You are a complicated person," Agent Rodriguez said.

"Okay," Blane said.

"Abandoned as a child," Agent Rodriguez said.

"That doesn't have anything to do with me," Blane said. "You should ask my biological mother about that."

Agent Rodriguez looked at him again. After a minute, she continued.

"Foster care, street kid," Agent Rodriguez said. "In and out of trouble — prostitution, drug possession, vagrancy. Taken in by the Marlowe-Lipson clan."

"My father was Sam Lipson's brother," Blane said. "I wasn't 'taken in' by the Marlowe-Lipson clan. My family found me, saved me. If you think anything else, you clearly haven't spoken to any member of *my* family."

Agent Rodriguez made a point of writing that in the file. Blane stifled the urge to roll his eyes.

"Gourmet chef," Agent Rodriguez said. "Worked as a personal secretary to this Jacob Marlowe. He a lover of yours?"

"Cousin," Blane said. "Brother."

"Which is it?" Agent Rodriguez asked.

"Both," Blane said defiantly.

Agent Rodriguez fell silent again. After a moment, she continued.

"And now you're an acupuncturist," Agent Rodriguez said. "Married to Heather. Father of two. And yet you identify as gay."

Blane didn't respond.

"It's quite a history," Agent Rodriguez said.

"Okay," Blane said.

"That's all you have to say?" Agent Rodriguez asked. "Okay?"

"It is what it is," Blane said. "I had a rough start. I've had a variety of careers before finding a passion. My wife and I have made choices for ourselves and our lives that included the choice of having two children."

"She doesn't mind that you're gay?" Agent Rodriguez asked.

"That's really between us, isn't it?" Blane asked. "You don't really care what I do or don't do in my private life. You just want to rattle me, and you think pressing on my sexuality will do it."

Blane shook his head.

"It will not," Blane said. "I am what I am. She is what she is. We love each other deeply. We love our children deeply. We have made our choices based on our love for each other. From that came two children. It seems likely that someday we'll have more. But Wyn is not a year old."

Agent Rodriguez didn't respond.

"I like children," Blane said. When Agent Rodriguez still didn't respond, he added, "Do you?"

"Do I what?" Agent Rodriguez asked.

"Like children?" Blane asked.

Agent Rodriguez looked at Blane for a long moment.

"Are you telling us that you are a pedophile, Mr. . . . uh . . . I see you go by 'Lipson' now?" Agent Rodriguez said.

Blane leaned back in his chair.

"That seemed to get to you," Agent Rodriguez said.

"Disrespect is ugly," Blane said. "You want me to be ashamed of being gay. I am not. You want me to be ashamed of being left by my mother. I am not. You want me to feel like *my* love for *my* wife is somehow wrong and filthy because it doesn't fit within your limited understanding of love. It is not."

The agent looked irritated. But once started, Blane continued.

"You want me to be ashamed of having a rough start in life. Of having to prostitute myself. Of being a drug addict. Of being poor and homeless. I am not," Blane said. "Of being taken in by the Lipsons. Of being married to a woman. You know why I am not ashamed?"

He glared at Agent Rodriguez and continued.

"Because my wife, Heather," Blane said. "That's why. She's taught me that all of these little tiny experiences don't mean anything. That the only thing that matters is how well we love each other."

Agent Rodriguez looked at Blane. His eyes flicked to Detective Nez. The Navajo police officer seemed to be cheering Blane on.

Blane stood up.

"If you'd like to ask me about what happened earlier this week, I will be at our hotel for an hour," Blane said. "Jake is likely to need me out on the site. I will be with him until we finish for the day."

He started toward the door.

"Acupuncture," the agent said.

Blane turned to look at her.

"You didn't mention acupuncture as something to be ashamed of," Agent Rodriguez said.

"Why would anyone be ashamed of being an acupuncturist?" Blane asked. "That's the dumbest thing I've ever heard."

The agent sat there looking at him.

"So you've given acupuncture to all of these people," Agent Rodriguez said.

"I have been called to a variety of places around the world to perform acupuncture for my clients," Blane said. "While I am there, I have worked on other people. When they come through town, they stop in for a treatment and to talk about their options."

"Why is that?" Agent Rodriguez asked.

"They seem to think that I am good at it," Blane said. "More than that, they believe that I listen to them and understand their problems. That I care. They believe that I care."

"And do you?" Agent Rodriguez asked.

"I can tell you that you favor your left arm because you have a torn rotator cuff in your right arm," Blane said. "When you injured your right shoulder, you injured your ribs as well."

Agent Rodriguez didn't respond.

"Sliding into second base?" Blane asked.

Agent Rodriguez blushed.

"You can get surgery, but until you heal these other injuries, you are at risk of another tear," Blane said. He gestured to the door. "Now, can I go?"

"Why you?" Agent Rodriguez asked. "Why do they call you to perform acupuncture? Surely there are acupuncturists all over the world."

"I was in acupuncture school when an old friend of mine's sister, someone I knew by sight but hadn't spent any time with, was injured," Blane said. "Her husband and brother, my friend, were desperate to help her. Jake went to the same high school as she and her family went to."

"Jake is your cousin," Detective Nez said.

"Right," Blane said. "I was just learning. She needed help. I was able to support her healing and learn at the same time. You could say that we did it together. I sought teachers to help me to help her. They are not without resources so they sought teachers for me. She needed real help. I fought through learning Chinese to learn for elderly scholars in the practice. Together, we were able to help her get better. That has become my specialty."

Blane shrugged.

"I can tell you that you will likely need surgery to repair that shoulder," Blane said. "Acupuncture can support your healing as well as support healing your entire side."

Agent Rodriguez didn't move.

"Now, if you don't . . ." Blane put his hand on the doorknob.

"We have some questions about Monday," Detective Nez said. "Would you mind sitting down again?"

Blane went around the table to sit down.

"We have heard from several witnesses that these men were looking for someone," Detective Nez said.

"Dr. Nelson Weeks," Blane said.

"His father is a patient of yours?" Agent Rodriguez asked.

"He and his father were in a train explosion when he was an infant. It's famously attributed to Carlos the Jackal," Blane said. "You can look it up with 'train explosion Carlos the Jackal.' Nelson's father managed to survive but has lived with grave injury."

"Has?" Agent Rodriguez asked.

Blane sighed.

"He is in the process of replacing the joints that were injured," Blane said. "He had his fourth joint replaced last week."

"And he has to do with you because . . ." Agent Rodriguez said.

"Nelson's father has been a patient of mine for almost as long as I've been in practice," Blane said. "I was unaware that they were related because they have different names and they've been estranged. Nelson's father got to me because he is a friend of Seth O'Malley, who is friends with . . ."

Blane stopped talking when Detective Nez made a gesture with his hand. Clearly, everyone in the world knew who Seth O'Malley was and the kind of influence he exerted.

"Why did you go out to speak with them?" Agent Rodriguez asked.

"It was my task to do," Blane said.

"I don't know what that means," Agent Rodriguez said.

"I don't either," Blane said. "That's doesn't make the words untrue. I went out because Nelson and I are close. Because I would not let them disturb my family or him."

"Was this Dr. Weeks there?" Agent Rodriguez asked.

"No," Blane said. "He left before they arrived."

"I see," Agent Rodriguez said.

"Why did he leave?" Detective Nez asked. "By all accounts, he was having a nice time there."

"He is involved in a federalt Trial," Blane said. "He was recalled to Denver because they were talking about a plea agreement."

Blane shrugged.

"It's been on the news," Blane said with a shrug. "Your computer might be helpful again here."

"We are aware of the trial," Agent Rodriguez said.

"You've been in touch with Dr. Weeks?" Detective Nez asked.

"We have video-chatted a few times," Blane said.

"And this guy," Agent Rodriguez said. "This Tres Sierra?"

"What about him?" Blane asked.

"He is your wife's lover?" Agent Rodriguez asked.

"You've really spent a lot of time thinking about our sexual relationships," Blane said, mildly.

"It just all seems a little . . ." Agent Rodriguez looked Blane in the eye. "Hedonic."

Blane burst out laughing. When he realized that the Agent wasn't making a joke, he quickly stifled his laugh.

"It is what it is," Blane said with a shrug. "I can assure you that Tres, me, Nelson, Heather — we don't know anything about why these people came to harm us or what happened to them. Because it seems like you've skipped a step. These people came to harm *us*."

"You are here to . . ." Agent Rodriguez said.

"Our children's school closes a few times a year," Blane said. "They are off this week. A large group of us, myself included, were going to head to Poland for a teaching trip, but the trip was canceled due to political unrest there. Nazis.

"My cousin, Jake, had been asked to help with some water wells here on the reservation. He owns an underground utility. The hotel was empty. We came here. Because the school is a part of the company, a lot of the company came with us."

"And these Templars showed up," Agent Rodriguez said.

"Exactly," Blane said.

"Why water wells?" Agent Rodriguez asked.

The Navajo Nation detective turned in his chair to look at Agent Rodriguez. He shook his head.

"I am sure that Detective Nez can give you the history lesson of how the Navajo Nation was tricked out of the water rights to the river that runs through their reservation," Blane said.

Detective Nez raised his eyebrows.

"Most people do not have running water here," Blane said. "We have a friend whose grandparents asked Jacob for a water well. It just came together that we could do it this week. Once we were here, we wanted to drill as many wells as possible. The need is desperate. Sam Lipson decided to support our friend Gando Peaches in starting his own well-digging company."

Neither Agent Rodriguez nor Detective Nez said anything.

"So far, we've dug six wells," Blane said. "When I am not giving people acupuncture, my focus has been on helping to hire and train one hundred and counting men and women from the Navajo Nation who are looking to gain a skill.

"These are good jobs. Once they learn how to do it, they can work anywhere in the world or stay on the reservation or leave to work in the cities. Hell, they could work for Lipson Construction in Denver. With our support, Gando will be able to provide water to historic areas of the Navajo Nation, allowing people to move back here.

"What is your problem with this?"

"Easy," Agent Rodriguez said. "Forty dead bodies."

"That doesn't have anything to do with me," Blane said. "You know that I was sitting in a room with more than twenty other people when those men died. Nelson was in Denver. The children were in a room together. The adults were with me."

Blane shook his head.

"It doesn't have anything to do with me," Blane said.

With that, Agent Rodriguez got to her feet. Detective Nez followed her out of the room. Blane was alone, in the police interview room, by himself.

Again.

~~~~~~~~~

Thursday morning — 10:01 a.m.
Navajo Nation Police Medical Examiner

"*Oui.*"

Distracted, Pierre Semaines slipped into speaking French. When the attendant didn't respond, Pierre looked up.

"What?" the medical examiner asked.

The medical examiner was about Pierre's size. His skin was the beautiful kind of brown that Hollywood starlets worked hard to maintain. His eyes were intelligent. The wall of the office they were sitting in was lined with degrees from prestigious universities.

Somehow, this man had taken an immediate dislike to Pierre. Of course, it didn't help that Pierre had immediately forgotten the man's name. He silently wished that he'd taken Sam Lipson up on his offer to go with him.

"Yes," Pierre said. "I am able to take all of the remains."

"These folks are a part of some club . . ." The medical examiner looked at his clipboard. He looked back at Pierre. "You sure you can take all of them?"

"I have received permission from the families as well as the Templars," Pierre said.

Pierre pressed across the desk the official form releasing the remains for the families as well as the notice from the Templars that they would like Pierre to pick them up.

"My father is . . ." Pierre nodded his head to the area behind the attendant. "My wife's father . . ."

"I see," the medical examiner said.

The medical examiner's intelligent eyes scanned Pierre.

"You seem..." the medical examiner raised his eyebrows, "*complètement paniqué.*"

Pierre chuckled at the medical examiner saying that he was freaked out.

"My father and I have been estranged," Pierre said. "I ..."

The medical examiner's eyes watched Pierre intently. Pierre blew out a breath.

"I have been very angry with him," Pierre said. "Very angry. I have debated with myself for years — will I go to his funeral? Will I not? Every time my sister calls I think, 'Is he finally dead? Has it finally happened?' But, of course, the next time comes around, and it's a big fucking mess that involves his desire to murder my only son."

Pierre gave the medical examiner a hopeless shake of his head. The medical examiner nodded.

"The Templars still exist?" the medical examiner asked.

"Unfortunately," Pierre said.

"You need help with this?" the medical examiner asked.

Much to his surprise, Pierre's eyes welled up at this stranger's offer for help.

"Probably," Pierre said. "My son's friends are here digging some water wells."

"They're digging a well at my mother's house today," the medical examiner said. "Is that a bribe?"

"Likely," Pierre said with a chuckle.

The medical examiner laughed. He pointed to Pierre.

"You're funny," the medical examiner said.

"Overwhelmed," Pierre said. "I tend to bluff through humor."

"I bet," the medical examiner said. "How are you going to get these bodies home?"

"I'm flying them to Denver," Pierre said. "I'll fly them home to France tomorrow."

"And all of their crap?" the medical examiner asked.

"Crap?" Pierre asked.

"Gear, swords, armor," the medical examiner said. "Knights-of-old crap."

"It will come with me," Pierre said.

"Can't do it," the medical examiner said. "It's still a part of the investigation."

"Then I'll come back and get it," Pierre said.

"Why you?" the medical examiner asked.

"My family is the weapons' masters for the Templars," Pierre said.

"That's what I was looking for," the medical examiner said. "I couldn't figure out why *you* had to take care of all of this. Being a weapons' master isn't a high-ranking position?"

"No," Pierre said with a grin. "We took independence rather than status."

"Why?" the medical examiner asked.

"My family has been making weapons since people first put rocks to metal," Pierre said. "Movements come and go. Weapons are always in demand."

"So you could make weapons for people on both sides of a fight?" the medical examiner asked.

"It has happened," Pierre said.

"How'd you get here to the US?" the medical examiner asked.

"I married the princess," Pierre said.

"Oh, I see," the medical examiner said with a chuckle. "You're not only a low-ranking member of this little club — you pissed off the head of the group."

"The head of the group is sitting in a drawer back there," Pierre said. "My guess is that he's not pissed anymore. At least I hope not."

The medical examiner rewarded Pierre with a quick smile at his joke. Recovering himself, the medical examiner looked down at the paperwork on his desk.

"You know all of these men to make the identifications?" the medical examiner asked.

"Grew up with most of them," Pierre said. "As you can imagine, it's a small club. Some were young . . ."

"Six under thirty," the medical examiner said.

"My sister sent their pictures and identifying images," Pierre said. "I may not have met them, but I know their parents."

"Your sister," the medical examiner said. "She knows everyone?"

Pierre nodded. The medical examiner looked at Pierre for a long moment.

"You get revenge on dear old dad?" the medical examiner asked.

"Not my style," Pierre said. "Plus, I was in Denver recovering from a hip replacement."

Pierre gestured to the crutch next to his chair.

"If I'd known they were going to secretly attack my son's partner and his family, I would have called the police, at the very least," Pierre said.

"And your son?" the medical examiner asked.

"He was in Denver with me," Pierre said. "I am very protective over my son. If they had threatened him, then I might have been involved in protecting him. But he was safe and sound."

Pierre shrugged.

"Yeah, I see that in you," the medical examiner said.

"Plus, my son's partner is my acupuncturist," Pierre said. "I am dependent on him for pain relief."

The medical examiner gave Pierre a blank look.

"Train explosion," Pierre said.

The medical examiner looked like he was going to say something. Instead, he picked up the phone and dialed a number. He spoke into the phone in Navajo for a few minutes and set the receiver down.

"Let's get through identification first," the medical examiner said. "My son and a couple of his friends should be here by then. They'll help you get these bodies to the airport."

"What about Death Sickness?" Pierre asked.

"You a reader?" the medical examiner asked. "Tony Hillerman?"

Pierre nodded.

"Jim Chee was training to be a healer," the medical examiner said.

"That's true," Pierre said.

"We don't go in for that superstitious crap," the medical examiner said. "I am a man of science."

"I'm glad," Pierre said with a smile.

"Plus, I hedge my bets by having a sing every year or so," the medical examiner said. "Gets the family together. Makes my grandmother happy."

Pierre grinned.

"So, don't you worry," the medical examiner said. "My son and his friends will be glad to help. I called Ganny before you arrived. He's already brought a couple SUVs. A couple of his guys should be here soon."

The medical examiner nodded.

"They couldn't pass the drug test to work for the construction company," the medical examiner said. "My son and his friends, too. They have to wait for their systems to clean out. This gives them something positive to do."

Pierre's eyes welled up. He gave a quick nod. The medical examiner stood up.

"One way or another, the Navajo Nation will get you and your family squared away," the medical examiner said. "Don't you worry. We know what it is to lose. We won't fail you now."

Pierre wiped his eyes.

"But first, we need to do the identifications," the medical examiner said.

Pierre got up and followed the medical examiner into the building.

"They really try to kill you with a bomb on a train?" the medical examiner asked. "Got Carlos the Jackal for it?"

"Me, my son," Pierre said. "They killed my wife."

"Families," the medical examiner said, with a shake of his head.

Grinning at the back of the medical examiner's head, Pierre couldn't help but agree.

~~~~~~~~~

Thursday mid-day — 11:41 a.m.
Kayenta, Arizona, at the hotel on the Navajo Reservation

"Hi," Hecate said as she came into the little hotel kitchen. "It's Jeraine, right?"

Jeraine looked up at Hecate. He looked her up and down before scowling. He was mixing a bowl of brownies for the kids.

"Why do you look like our Tink?" Jeraine asked.

Taken back by his demand for an answer, Hecate opened and closed her mouth.

"Truth," Jeraine said. "You her mother?"

"I cannot have children," Hecate said.

Jeraine looked up at her quickly. He gave her a long look before nodding.

"I'm sorry," Jeraine said.

"My parents were cousins," Hecate said with a grin. "It's probably a good thing."

She laughed. Jeraine started pouring the brownie batter into a pan. Hecate reached out to hold the pan.

"Why are you here?" Jeraine asked. "I mean, I heard that you and Heather are friends, but I'll tell you — Miss T and Heather are best friends. They've been together since they were kids. Miss T's never met you."

Hecate sighed. She gave him a long look.

"Everyone whispering about this?" Hecate asked.

"Pretty much," Jeraine said.

Jeraine opened the oven door and started placing the pans into the oven. He looked up at her.

"You know that Heather and I are immortal," Hecate said.

"So?" Jeraine asked. "The pastor at the Baptist Church in my neighborhood says that my soul is immortal."

"You're right," Hecate said. "That's not so different."

"If you say so," Jeraine said.

Jeraine closed the oven and set a timer. He went to an electric kettle. He set a teabag in a mug and poured water over it. He gave Hecate the mug. She smelled the tea and grinned at him.

"How did you know?" Hecate asked.

"Heather loves this tea," Jeraine said. "So does your dad."

Hecate grinned. He looked around the small room until he found a jar of Delphie's honey. He set it in front of her with a spoon.

Curious, she picked up the honey. She looked at it for a long moment before taking off the lid. She seemed to delight and calm down in the same moment. She smiled at him.

"Have you met Delphie yet?" Jeraine asked.

"The Oracle?" Hecate asked.

"Sure," Jeraine said. "The honey is from her hives."

"Nothing better than honey from happy hives," Hecate said.

Hecate took out her teabag. She added a dollop of honey and then put the cup to her lips. After a moment, she looked at Jeraine.

"Let's see..." Hecate said. "I look like Tink because I look like my mother. Tink looks like my mother because she is a descendant of one of my mother's other children, her mortal children. Before you ask, He... uh... Heather did not adopt Tink because she looked like me or her mother. Heather knows that I cannot have children. And, my mother is not necessarily a good or nice person. Looking like her could easily mean that a child is a very bad person. Heather and Blane adopted Tink because she is a wonderful, beautiful person. She is worthy of their love and so much more."

"Makes sense," Jeraine said. "You don't look like Mike or Jill..."

"Titan genes tend to overpower human genes," Hecate said. "My father's children with Anjelika look like him because of his genetic dominance. It's true for all Titans who have children with mortals."

"But not Greek Gods?" Jeraine asked.

"It's more complicated for them," Hecate said.

Jeraine wondered if he cared enough to ask.

"Heather has a child who looks like his father," Hecate said. "She has a child who looks like Olympia. It is not because the first child's father is dominant and Blane is not. Their looks are a mixture of both."

"Oh, I get it," Jeraine said. "Titans tend to just show their look but Greeks . . ."

"They are already a mixture," Hecate said.

"Huh," Jeraine said with a nod.

He started melting chocolate for frosting.

"You asked about why your wife, Tanesha, hasn't met me," Hecate said.

Jeraine looked up at her for a brief moment. He gave her a quick nod and returned to look at the chocolate.

"I will answer you if you tell me what you are making," Hecate said.

"I'm making something called 'brownies.' They are a kind of chocolate cake that you can pick up with your hand," Jeraine said. He imitated eating a brownie with his empty hand. She nodded. "It's a real favorite for this family. Delphie, the one you call the Oracle, makes them almost every day. I wanted to have some ready for when the teenagers come back from work."

"And now?" Hecate said. "Will you pour that on top?"

"This is chocolate," Jeraine said. "It's very bitter."

Hecate walked to the pan and started to put the tip of her finger in the pan.

"No," Jeraine said. "It's hot."

Hecate looked at him and blinked.

"You'll injure yourself," Jeraine said. He put a hand on his chest. "I have seen Heather mad. It is not pretty. If you get injured on my watch?"

Jeraine shook his head. Hecate grinned at him, and he smiled.

"My skin is not fragile to heat," Hecate said. "I won't be injured."

"By all means," Jeraine said.

He held the pan out to her. She dipped the tip of her pinky into the pan. She stuck the tip of her pinky in her mouth.

"Oh," Hecate made a face. "Bitter. What is it?"

"Chocolate," Jeraine said. "It's from a small tree that grows south of here. It is picked and toasted, then ground."

Jeraine had the sense that Hecate was deeply listening to him.

"I don't know this," Hecate said. "You feed this to children?"

Jeraine grinned.

"It is very dry here," Jeraine said. "I'll make frosting to put on the brownies to keep them from drying out."

"Frosting," Hecate said.

Jeraine picked up a jar of sugar.

"Sugar," Jeraine said.

"I know this," Hecate said. "It was a rare privilege."

"They figure out how to make it from beets," Jeraine said. Seeing a look of confusion on Hecate's face, he smiled. "It's very affordable now."

Hecate gave him a distracted nod.

"I will watch you," Hecate said.

"You will talk and watch," Jeraine said.

Hecate grinned at his tone.

"Don't pull that 'I'm a goddess' bullshit with me," Jeraine said. "I've known plenty of starlets, music stars, and even lived with Heather for more than a year."

When Hecate actually laughed, he felt like he'd accomplished something.

"I shall answer your question," Hecate said. "Heather and I have been friends since she was a child."

"You are older than she is," Jeraine said.

"That's correct," Hecate said. "Her grandmother often asked me to watch her. We had such fun. I am unable to have children, and honestly no one knew what to do with this half human, half-god child. So she was given to me."

Hecate smiled.

"Where have you been?" Jeraine asked. "Miss T met Heather when she was a child. Where were you?"

"Good question," Hecate said. "I . . . well . . ."

Jeraine glanced at her and took the chocolate from the stove.

"Well?" Jeraine asked as he got out the soft butter and started mixing it with powdered sugar.

"You know that Heather's mother was able to reset her human body to that of a child," Hecate said.

"Miss T told me," Jeraine said. "We grew up with Heather, but she was really thousands of years old. Like an old soul."

"Like an old soul," Hecate said. "Well put."

"You were going to tell me about you," Jeraine said. "If you're Heather's friend, I want to know about you."

"Why?" Hecate asked.

"Heather and Miss T are best friends," Jeraine said. "We all live together now. Heather and Blane are family to me. Their kids, my Jabari — they are like siblings. They take care of Miss T when I'm on the road and . . ."

Jeraine looked at her and nodded.

"If you're here now, you're likely to move in," Jeraine said. "Just the way things seem to go. I figure I'll get a jump on it so I can tell my brother, Blane, all about you."

"I . . ." Hecate looked at him. She sighed. "I used to spend a lot of time around people and then . . ."

Hecate swallowed hard. Jeraine gave her some space to talk.

"Many of the humans I knew, was close to, died," Hecate said.

"Plague?" Jeraine asked.

"Fire," Hecate said. "Burned alive. Hanged. Tortured. Drowned. Assaulted to death."

"Witches," Jeraine said.

"Right," Hecate said. "I'm responsible for the witches."

Jeraine didn't respond. He kept working on the frosting. A timer rang, and he took the brownies out of the oven. He set them on the counter to cool.

"I used to use drugs," Jeraine said. "A lot of drugs."

Hecate watched his face.

"I'm a singer," Jeraine said. "Popular. I used to do drugs and lots of women. I'd get in front of thousands of people and . . ."

His eyes flicked to her. Their eyes locked.

"It's kind of like being a god," Jeraine said. "Without the immortality and the powers."

"It is an amazing feeling," Hecate said with a soft smile.

"What is?" Jeraine asked.

"Standing in front of a crowd of humans who love you," Hecate said.

"Intoxicating," Jeraine said. "I lost myself completely. Lost my mind. Literally injured my brain."

"I'm sorry," Hecate said.

Her voice was so sweet and kind that Jeraine looked up at her.

"I don't know what that was — spell or whatever — but thanks," Jeraine said. "That felt nice. I am still finding myself."

He shook his head as if to clear it.

"I was going to say that while I was living this high life, I didn't notice that other people were following," Jeraine said. "Then one girl died. Then another. Then . . . Didn't have anything to do with me. I wasn't even there, but . . ."

"All of a sudden, I was in jail," Jeraine said. "My parents had given up on me. Miss T wouldn't take my calls. I had this heavy withdrawal and . . ."

"These women and men died because they believed what I told them," Hecate said.

"They died because someone else didn't like the strength and purpose they got from you," Jeraine said.

"You can see why . . ." Hecate said.

"Withdrew? I withdrew, too." Jeraine cut her off to say. "I hid from the world. I tried to make good with Miss T, but she wouldn't have me, and rightly so."

"What happened?" Hecate asked. "How did you get . . . ?"

Hecate gestured to him now.

"A friend of my father's came to talk to me while I was in prison," Jeraine said. "He sat with me every day for almost two weeks. I don't really know why he did it. He just showed up there and . . ."

Jeraine nodded.

"He probably saved my life," Jeraine said. "He's sober. He definitely got me on the road to recovery."

Jeraine sighed.

"Then I just . . ." Jeraine said. "I ate a lot of humble pie."

"Humble pie?" Hecate laughed.

"It's . . ."

"I can imagine," Hecate said.

"I made my mess," Jeraine said. "I needed to heal it. That became the purpose of my life. And . . . It's not a bad life purpose — to heal those who are hurt by you and the world."

He took the brownies out of the pan and set them on the counter. He looked at the goddess who looked so much like Tink.

"Did you make your mess?" Jeraine asked.

"They came after me! Stupid Roman Catholics! Had to kill everyone because . . ." Hecate said. "I didn't *do* anything! I supported women where they stood for the purpose of making a better world."

Jeraine gave her a sad nod.

"I understand," Jeraine said.

"But?" Hecate asked.

"Did you warn them?" Jeraine asked.

"Warn them?" Hecate asked.

"You knew that people were angry with women and men following your teachings," Jeraine asked.

"Small people, stupid people . . ."

"But people nonetheless," Jeraine asked.

"Are you saying that I caused my followers horrific deaths?" Hecate asked.

"I am not," Jeraine said.

"What are you saying?" Hecate's voice was still defiant.

"I'm saying that we are responsible for those who love us," Jeraine said. "Even if it's just to love them in return. Did you love your followers?"

"I . . ." Hecate's eyes were wild with pain. "I . . ."

"Then didn't you warn them that people were small, jealous, and status hungry?" Jeraine asked. "Protect them or get them to protect themselves?"

Hecate's eyes went wide. They filled with tears as she gasped for breath.

He pressed a warm, frosted brownie into her hand.

The simple gesture was enough. Hecate broke down and sobbed. He negotiated her to a chair. He finished making the brownies and then started in on lunch. When her storm of emotions subsided, he gave her a box of tissues.

"Welcome back," Jeraine said softly.

Hecate, the Titan, gave the human, Jeraine Wilson, her first real smile in a long, long time.

CHAPTER FIVE HUNDRED & FORTY-FIVE
Shifting Wind

Thursday evening — 6:41 p.m.
Kayenta, Arizona, at the hotel on the Navajo Reservation

"Okay, thanks," Kimber said. "I'm just . . ."

"If you feel up to it," Valerie said. "Just take care of yourself, first. We'll be here for a few more days, so that's more days of heat, dirt, and signs."

"Thanks," Kimber said.

She gave Valerie a big smile and walked down the hallway to find Candy, her new mother. Kimber had joined Nash, Teddy, and Noelle to work on the water-well sites. She and Noelle had spent the day directing traffic while Nash and Teddy, because they were older, had spent the day hauling things and cleaning up the sites. They'd worked with a team of Navajo teens about their age. Noelle and Kimber had worked on the sign team with Valerie.

Kimber was covered head to toe with dirt and dust. She was so exhausted that she'd slept in the back seat of the SUV on the way back to the hotel. She was on her way to take a shower and go straight to bed when Valerie told her about a dinner with the sign team.

"There you are!" one of the girls from the pool said.

The other mean girls came up behind the first. Kimber was too tired to even remember their names.

"Hey," Kimber said. "I was just going to find my mom."

"We're heading back out to the pool," the girl said.

"Where you been?" the second girl asked.

Kimber blinked. The girl was white, financially well off, and well educated. Kimber wondered vaguely if she'd sounded as stupid when she was a mean girl.

"I've been working on the sign team," Kimber said. She tucked a piece of hair behind her ear and nodded. Grinning, she said, "*Valerie Lipson* took over the team for this week. We get to work with these fun girls from the reservation. It's . . ."

She stopped talking when she caught a look of disgust that passed between the girls.

"Fun," the girl said with a curled lip to show her disgust.

"Why you have to work?" another girl asked.

"Why can't you speak English?" The question just popped out of Kimber's mouth. She blushed.

"What did you ask me, freak?" the girl asked. She pointed to Kimber, "Ima goin' kick your ass."

Terrified, Kimber took a step back. She felt a hand on her shoulder. She looked up to see that Tanesha had put her arm around Kimber's shoulder. She felt someone come to the other side of her. She looked over to see Jeraine. *The pop star Jeraine and his Miss T.* Kimber took in a quick breath.

The girls stepped backward. Tanesha gave the girls an irritated look and turned to Kimber.

"We were looking for you," Tanesha said.

"I . . . uh . . ." Kimber looked back at the girls. " . . .finding mom."

"She's in the room, waiting for you," Tanesha said.

"Why you looking for her?" one of the mean girls asked.

"Aren't you missing a verb there?" Jeraine asked with a sniff. "My mother would have slapped my mouth if I sounded so ignorant."

The reproach from the world-famous music star was like a dagger through the heart of the mean girl.

"We . . . uh . . ." the girl said.

"We were looking for you, hon, because you were invited to a dinner on the reservation," Tanesha said. "You remember Dibe? She worked on your street today. Her mother wanted to meet you and the other girls."

"What about Valerie?" Kimber asked. "She wanted me to . . ."

"She thinks it's a better offer," Tanesha said. "She and the other girls were invited, too."

"Really?" Kimber asked. "Everyone's going there?"

"Of course," Tanesha said. "Go. You don't want to be late."

Mean girls forgotten, Kimber jogged down the hallway to her room.

"We want to go to the reservation," one of the mean girls said.

"It's only for the sign team," Tanesha said.

Jeraine held out his arm and Tanesha tucked into him. They walked down the hallway to the main room.

The mean girls watched them go. They looked at each other.

"Want to go to the pool?" one girl asked.

The girls looked at each other.

"My dad said I should be ready to go," one girl said.

"My mom's probably waiting for me," another girl said.

The mean girls split off into all directions. Tanesha snorted as she walked away.

"Yeah?" Jeraine asked.

"Nothing," Tanesha said.

Jeraine glanced back at the girls and nodded. They kept walking toward the dining room.

~~~~~~~~~

Thursday evening — 9:01 p.m.
Kayenta, Arizona, at the hotel on the Navajo Reservation

When Blane came into the hotel room, Heather got up from a chair to hug him. Tres was sitting on the couch, with Wyn asleep against his shoulder. Tres got up, gave Wyn to Blane, patted Blane's back, and left the room.

"Did I interrupt?" Blane asked as he looked into Wyn's face. "How are you, sleepy boy?"

Grinning, Wyn put his hand on his father's face.

"Not at all," Heather said. "Tres was asleep before you came in. Early mornings. Late nights. Too much socializing for an introvert."

Blane nodded.

"Where's . . . ?" Blane asked.

Heather stepped aside to show Mack, Maggie, and Jabari asleep on the second bed in their room. With Wyn on his shoulder, Blane went to check on the children. Only Jabari opened his eyes. The boy blinked at Blane, smiled, and then fell sound asleep.

Blane held out his free arm. He held Heather tight.

"How are you?" Heather asked.

"Tired," Blane said.

"I bet," Heather said. "We haven't had a chance to talk since . . ."

"Forever," Blane said with a smile.

Heather grinned at him.

"Do we still have?" Blane gestured to the adjoining room.

Heather nodded. He went through the adjoining door, and Heather followed. He took a spot on the bed, and she sat next to him.

"Do you mind if we talk for a while?" Blane asked. "I really feel like . . ."

"I'd love that," Heather said with a smile. "Any idea why Nelson didn't come back?"

"He left a message saying that he doesn't think it makes sense to come back here," Blane said. We're here for only another day. Plus, he's working on some swords."

"Swords?" Heather asked.

"That's what he said," Blane said. "He's pretty excited about it. I guess his father was there for a while. They made a plan for the blades before his dad came here to get the bodies."

He shook his head.

"He actually has a forge in his garage," Blane said.

"Who knew?" Heather asked.

"Who knew?" Blane repeated.

"He's not going to France with his dad?" Heather asked.

"No," Blane said.

"Is it dangerous still?" Heather asked.

"Seriously?" Blane asked. Heather watched him. "Who fucking knows? I mean, how weirdly complicated does life have to be? I finally get involved with someone, and it's all this complicated, international-intrigue crap."

Heather kissed his cheek.

"It's going to be okay," Heather said.

"The FBI agent really thinks that I killed all of those men," Blane said. "Me! Just unbelievable."

"Any ideas on who did kill them?" Heather asked.

Blane shook his head.

"You?" Blane asked.

"No," Heather said.

"What about Perses?" Blane asked. "He was really chomping at the bit to kill them all. He can bend time."

"Wasn't him," Heather said.

Blane gave a dark shake of his head.

"The police station was bad?" Heather asked.

Blane nodded. Wyn squirmed to indicate that he wanted to be set down. Blane put the infant on the bed between them. Heather gave Wyn a soft smile and then looked back at Blane.

"I just . . ." Blane put his hand to his heart. "I never thought that *I* would be the focus of . . . I mean, *murder*! It's . . . hard."

Heather touched his shoulder, and he leaned his head on her shoulder.

"She went so far as to say that our *situation* was hedonic," Blane said.

Heather chuckled.

"I . . ." Blane sighed and shook his head. "All of my life, I've have to defend my life from someone's ignorance. Never. I never thought I'd have to do that to defend my marriage to a woman and our children and . . ."

Blane shook his head.

"You know how many 'straight' men have gay lovers?" Blane asked. "How many women cheat on their husbands with some dude?"

"A lot," Heather said.

"Every day in the suburbs," Blane scowled. "But set it up so everything is clear and . . ."

"How are you with seeing Tres here?" Heather asked.

Blane looked at Heather and then looked down at Wyn.

"I . . ." Blane started. "Well . . ."

She gave him a soft smile to encourage him.

"I felt like I'd been replaced," Blane said. "Just a flash when I walked in the door. Then I looked at Tres and saw how happy he was to see me. I have known him for . . . ever. I mean he's Enrique's little brother. I watched him grow up. Tres . . ."

Blane glanced at Heather.

"You cannot be replaced," Heather said. "Not by me. Not by our babies."

Blane nodded.

"It was just a moment," Blane said.

"What did you see when you looked at me?" Heather asked.

Blane shook his head.

"No really," Heather said.

"I saw my life," Blane said. "My life really started when I met you and . . ."

Heather smiled.

"So it's weird," Blane said. "Ah, fuck — I'm just tired."

"Do you wish you'd killed the Templars?" Heather asked.

Blane laughed. Heather grinned.

"Hey, I met . . . uh . . . HeeKat . . ." Blane said.

"Hecate," Heather said with a nod.

"Creepy how she looks like Tink," Blane said.

"It's funny because everyone has said that," Heather said. "I don't see it."

"Of course, you don't," Blane said. "Jer says she's moving in with us."

Heather shrugged.

"She's trying out being around people," Heather said. "It's been a long time since she left Olympia. She's fragile. I've been telling her that she could hang out with our friends and be okay. When Perses asked her to help, she decided to try it out."

"Sounds like she'll fit right in," Blane said with a nod.

He yawned.

"Did you eat?" Heather asked.

Blane shook his head.

"Jeraine gave me a plate for you," Heather said.

She got up and took a plate out of the little refrigerator in the room. Using the microwave, she warmed up his dinner. Blane ate it in less than a minute.

"Starving," Blane said.

Heather nodded. Blane yawned again.

"I should shower," Blane said.

"Seems like you need to sleep," Heather said.

"You don't mind?" Blane asked.

"You cannot imagine how people smelled just a hundred years ago," Heather said.

"There's a perspective," Blane said with a laugh.

"Go on," Heather said. "We have a long day tomorrow."

"We're heading home?" Blane asked.

Heather nodded.

Blane shuffled back into the other room. He undressed to his T-shirt and boxer briefs and got in the free bed. Heather picked up Wyn. She changed the infant and set him in the bed bassinette. By the time she got in bed, Blane was sound asleep.

Grinning, Heather turned off the light. Blane rested his head on her shoulder. She fell into a dreamless sleep.

~~~~~~~~~

Friday morning — 7:01 a.m.
Kayenta, Arizona, at the hotel on the Navajo Reservation

After reviewing all they'd done this week, the early-morning leadership crew determined that today would be a day of socializing and packing up to go. Everyone was coming to the hotel for a big breakfast this morning, and then the Navajo crew were taking the Denver group out sightseeing. The crew from Denver would head home Friday evening or Saturday morning.

Jeraine, Blane, and Tres took over the kitchen while Heather, Tanesha, Jill, and Sandy went to the market. The men were so joyful that the girlfriends left them to their joy. By 7:00 a.m., people began to arrive.

Because the dining room was near the back, Heather sent her friend Hecate out to the front of the hotel to direct people toward the dining room.

"Excuse me," FBI Agent Rodriguez said to Hecate.

"Yes?" Hecate asked.

"I'm wondering if you can point me in the direction of Blane Lipson," Agent Rodriguez said.

She pointed to two larger, male FBI agents. Hecate scowled. She didn't know what this "FBI" did but in her experience, anything written in big letters on clothing was not a good thing.

"Are you a friend of his?" Hecate asked.

The agent snorted.

"Just tell me where he is," Agent Rodriguez said.

Hecate reached out and touched Agent Rodriguez's elbow. It was a light touch. The agent didn't notice it.

Agent Rodriguez looked away from Hecate. Her eyebrows furrowed for a moment and then she looked at Hecate.

"Can you point me in the direction of Blane Lipson?" Agent Rodriguez repeated her question as if she'd never asked it.

"Are you coming from breakfast?" Hecate asked.

"He invited us," Agent Rodriguez said. "I've heard he's a good cook."

"He and Jeraine have been working all morning," Hecate said.

"Jeraine? As in the pop star?" Agent Rodriguez asked. "Is Miss T here, too?"

"She's right there," Hecate said. "Tanesha?"

Tanesha looked up from where she'd been directing people to breakfast.

"She would like to have some breakfast," Hecate said.

Tanesha took in the FBI jackets and then gave Hecate a hard look. The Titan gave Tanesha a smile.

"She just asked if you were here," Hecate said. "Miss T?"

Agent Rodriguez looked a little star-struck. Smelling magic in the air, Tanesha gave Hecate a side look. Hecate just smiled.

"Ma'am," Tanesha said. "Let me show you the way."

Agent Rodriguez gestured to the two other men, and they followed Tanesha down the hallway.

Chuckling, Hecate watched them go.

With her eyes on the agents, a human male was able to walk right into her.

She felt him a fraction of a second before he hit her. For the briefest moment, she felt his chest against her breasts. His hips moved against her pubis.

She felt an instant heat inside her core.

She felt a heat rise inside him

Like all Titans, she was immovable. He bounced off her and fell to the ground.

She missed him the moment he was gone. Her entire being longed for him as he fell through the air. She felt his spirit long for her as well.

They were like two ends to a magnet. Instant attraction. Instant repulsion.

Hecate hadn't been that close to a human man in nearly a thousand years.

Curious, she watched him on the ground. She was about to call Hedone to her side when he jumped to his feet and went to her.

"Are you okay?" he said.

Not sure of what to say, she continued to watch him.

"I really creamed you," he said. "I'm so sorry. I was talking to my friend and didn't see you there."

He reached out and his hand cupped her elbow. She felt that heat ignite inside her again.

"Did I hurt you?" His concern was palpable. "Are you injured?"

She felt more than saw his body respond to hers.

The tall thin warrior woman that Hedone had called "Alex," her gorgeous husband, and their two children walked past. This Alex took one look at the man and started to laugh. He looked at Alex but didn't let go of Hecate's elbow.

He did not move away. It was like his hand was locked onto her elbow.

The man looked back at Hecate.

"Who are you?" he asked.

"I am Hecate," she said, evenly. "Who are you?"

"Gando Peaches," he said. Clearly flustered, he said, "I heard that you arrived during that mess with the Templars. To help protect the kids. Right? That's why you came?"

Hecate gave a quick nod.

"You're a friend of Heather's?" Gando asked. "I know them from when I'm in Denver. My brother's daughter lives with . . . Uh . . ."

He stopped talking. His dark eyes looked into hers. For a moment, they just looked at each other.

"We haven't met before," he said.

"I don't think so," Hecate said.

"But you're a friend of Heather's?" Gando asked. "Blane? Tanesha?"

"I have known Heather since she was a child," Hecate said. "I just met Jeraine and Tanesha. Blane, too. While I have seen Heather, I hadn't met their children yet. What a treat! I like them. Do you know them as well?"

Gando nodded.

"What's a 'Gando'?" Hecate asked. "Are you from this place? Or from Denver?"

"I am a member of the Navajo Nation," Gando said. "We call ourselves the Diné."

She nodded. He gave her a soft smile.

"Why don't you have breakfast with me?" he asked. "We can talk."

She blushed.

"Are you Perses's daughter?" Gando asked. "He's my friend Mike's father, too. I've known Mike since the Army."

"In fact, I am," Hecate said. "Different mother."

"You don't look like him," Gando said.

"I take after my mother more," Hecate said.

Gando nodded. He had such beautiful brown eyes that she couldn't tear her gaze away. In his eyes, she saw his ancestors echoing back through time to the first humans. She saw that he was a shaman, a warrior, and a scholar. They looked at each other for a long moment.

"You're sure we haven't met before?" Gando asked.

"I am sure," Hecate said.

The minutes seemed to tick by as their gaze extended. He held out his elbow.

"I would very much like to . . ." Gando shook his head. "Sorry, this is so unlike me. Alex was just telling me that I was 'ripe' for finding . . . That's why she laughed. And then here you are. It's . . ."

"Odd," Hecate said. "Shall we start with breakfast?"

Hecate put her arm through his elbow. They walked toward the dining room together.

"I can't place your accent," Gando said. "It sounds both familiar and also unfamiliar."

"My homeland is near Greece," Hecate said.

As if to protect her from the cold, Gando pulled her a little closer.

She smiled.

CHAPTER FIVE HUNDRED & FORTY-SIX

FORWARD FACING

Friday night — 10:05 p.m.
Private ceremonial grounds, Navajo Reservation

"Thanks for letting me know," Gando Peaches said into the satellite phone. "And really, Jake, thanks for the last week."

"See you in a few weeks," Jacob said.

"Yeah," Gando said. "That will be good."

"Nah," Jacob said. "You're going to be fine. You can always call if you have any trouble. We're not *so* far away."

"Thanks, man," Gando said.

"Oh, Mike said to tell you . . ." Jacob said.

"Fuck off, Ind'n," Gando and Jacob said together.

Laughing, Gando hung up the call. He looked up. Hecate was sitting across the fire circle from him. She was holding a stick and poking at the joyous fire she'd created. The golden-orange light of the fire cast one side of her face in light while the rest of her face was in shadow.

Unfamiliar with telephones, she didn't look up when he finished his call. He was slightly offended the first time she'd done this. Didn't she want to know what was said? Didn't she want to be included in his conversation? She'd laughed away his concerns.

"You have a lot to teach me, young one," Hecate said. "But you may have your own conversations and thoughts. I will never ask. I will never listen in."

"Why?"hHe'd asked.

"If I listened in on everything said to or by a human, even one I care about, I would go mad," Hecate had said. "I would rather listen to the wind, the dance of the stars, the echoes across the water. This planet chants a precious song. It is my preference to hear her melody."

She'd shrugged.

"Would you prefer that I listen in?" Hecate had asked. "Hedone tells me that there are women today who check their partners' phones for texts and other infidelities. How do they have time to listen to the melody of the sun? The decadent sound of the movement of the planets that resonates in the song of your own human heart?"

His heart had squeezed in a way that he'd never felt before.

"If you need this, you will not ever have it from me," Hecate had said, mildly.

"I don't need it," Gando had said. "I'm just . . . acculturated to it."

Feeling his eyes upon her now, Hecate looked up from the fire. Her curious eyes scanned his face.

"Why did you laugh?" Hecate asked.

"Mike," Gando said.

"My brother?" Hecate asked.

"He . . ." Gando pointed at her. "You said you didn't listen."

She gave him a broad smile.

"You laugh every time before you turn off your conversation," Hecate said.

"I do?" Gando asked.

She gave a quick nod.

"What has my brother done?" Hecate asked.

"He tells me to 'fuck off,'" Gando said. She gave him a confused look. "It's a swear word. He . . ."

"He has my father's aggression with his human humor," Hecate said with a smile. "I don't know my father's other family. I am looking forward to getting to know them."

Gando felt a blanket of sorrow come over him.

"What is it?" Hecate asked.

"I want you for myself," Gando said. He lifted a shoulder in a shrug. "Every relationship I have been in — since I was a boy, really — I have been the one who felt smothered. 'Get a life of your own,' I'd say. 'You cannot count on me as your sole source of love.' Or always, 'I need you to have things in your life that you love as much or more than you love me.'"

He paused, watching her watch his face. There was something about her look that felt compelling. He felt her eyes on his lips.

It hit him out of the blue.

He'd never even kissed her. Yet here he was, feeling sad that he would not be her entire universe. He laughed at himself. She gave him a soft smile.

"I don't know what we will have," Hecate said. "I . . ."

"Do you want children?" Gando surprised himself with the question.

"I cannot have children," Hecate said.

"Oh," Gando said. "I can't have children, either. Accident. Military."

Hecate nodded.

"I saw . . . uh . . . *antiqua mater saum*," Hecate said.

Gando translated the Latin to Ancient Mother.

"Abi?" Gando asked. "We call her '*Áltsé Asdzáá*'. First Woman. In the *Diné Bahané*. Uh, the Diné story of creation and the people."

"Your native language is very similar to Abi's original language," Hecate said with a nod. "It would make sense if you were her first people."

"You were speaking of Abi?" Gando asked.

"She was unable to have children," Hecate said. "Most of her life. She has children with her fairy prince. She believes it's fairy magic so . . ."

Hecate shrugged.

"My father is the only Titan who has had children since...
well, many, many thousands of years," Hecate said. "So, I don't
know."

Gando shrugged.

"Did you want children?" Hecate asked.

"I thought that, if I found the right person, I would adopt
children," Gando said. "There are Diné orphans who could use a
loving home. They can be adopted only within the tribe, so there
is a great need."

Hecate nodded.

"Do you . . .?" Gando asked.

He was so ashamed of his need for her that he had the urge to
throw himself onto the fire. He could not meet her eyes.

"Are you asking me if I can have intercourse with a human
male?" Hecate asked. "I can. Have you heard the story of the
women who have so much intercourse with a human male that
the male dies?"

Keeping his eyes on the fire, he gave a quick nod.

"That's a story of my mother," Hecate said with a smile.

"Oh." Gando's head jerked up to look at Hecate. "Really?"

"Most certainly," Hecate said with a laugh.

He laughed. He looked across the fire, and she grinned at him.

"Are you monogamous?" Gando asked. "Or is that a human
thing?"

"Titans are monogamous, in general," Hecate said. "There
weren't human beings when I was a child. We form long-lasting
connections with the right people. Both of my parents have done
this. My father has always been loyal to my mother, still is, even
after she let him go. He deeply loves his current wife, Anjelika."

Gando swallowed hard. He wasn't sure why, but he felt like he
wanted to be her "right person."

"Why do you ask me this?" Hecate asked.

"I . . . uh . . ." Gando said.

For all that he was and all that he wasn't, Gando Peaches was brave, even with his heart. He girded himself for possible rejection and continued.

"I would like to spend what is left of my life, as much as I can, with you," Gando said.

Hecate raised her eyebrows with surprise.

"That surprises you?" Gando asked.

Hecate nodded.

"Why?" Gando asked.

"No human has ever said that to me, I guess," Hecate said. "I am not the one who is usually 'wanted.'"

Shocked, Gando raised his eyebrows in surprise.

"Feared. Hated. Loathed for being powerful," Hecate nodded. "I . . ."

She caught his eye, and they looked directly at each other.

"I cannot promise to spend every moment of every day . . ." Hecate said.

Gando waved his hand.

"I wouldn't tolerate that," Gando said. "I grew up with strong, independent women like my grandmother and my sister. I like powerful women. Admire them. Trust them."

Hecate nodded. She didn't say anything for a long moment. He thought that maybe this was her way of turning him down.

She looked back up at him.

"I will be your life mate, Gando Peaches," Hecate said.

"Do I need to ask your father?" Gando asked.

"Perses," Hecate said.

Perses arrived to stand next to his daughter.

"Daughter?" Perses asked with surprise. Seeing Gando, he hopped over the fire to say "hello." "How are you, Ganny?"

"I find myself wanting to spend my human life with your daughter," Gando said.

Perses laughed. He looked at Hecate.

"You remember me telling you about a human I met who I wanted you to meet?" Perses asked.

"Many times," Hecate said. She looked at Gando. "My father has been trying to get me out of isolation for a long time."

"I have told you about Mike's friend," Perses said. "The one I thought you would like?"

He nodded to Gando and then to Hecate.

"Be happy," he said and disappeared.

"That's it?" Gando asked.

"That's it," Hecate said.

"What about your mother?" Gando asked.

"I'm not sure where my mother is, actually," Hecate said. "She is lost to the world. Many Titans have been killed. My father and I were informed that she was killed. My heart tells me that she lives somewhere — safe and free. But it's possible that this is a fantasy."

Gando gave her a small nod.

"I thought of asking the Oracle," Hecate said. "Surely she knows. The truth is that I don't want to know. I'd rather imagine that she is free and safe."

Hecate gave him a small smile.

"And you?" Hecate asked.

"My grandmother may want a ceremony," Gando said.

"Your grandmother may have whatever she wishes," Hecate said.

"I'm in the middle of this new business and . . ." Gando said.

"I just came back from more than a thousand years' hermitage," Hecate said. "Hedone will never tolerate me hiding out, even in this most precious and sacred spot. You do not wish to enrage Hedone."

He raised his eyebrows in surprise, and she laughed. Hecate got to her feet.

"There are some rules," Hecate said. "But we can get to those. Would you like to consummate our commitment?"

Gando hopped to his feet. She extended her hand, and he took it. He led her to the soft bedding in the sleep area they'd prepared earlier.

~~~~~~~~~

Friday night — 10:05 p.m.
Denver, Colorado

"My own bed," Jill said. She sighed as she lay down.

Jacob slipped into bed beside her.

"The boys were particularly wild tonight," Jacob said.

"They have a lot of energy," Jill said, rolling onto her side.

"From the car ride?" Jacob asked.

"Car ride," Jill said. "The wild trip through the reservation. I think they glean energy from the sheer beauty of the place. Monument Valley was . . . incredible."

"When they're a little older, we should go camping there," Jacob said.

"We were supposed to go camping this week," Jill said, snorting a laugh.

"Okay, okay — I'm an idiot," Jacob said.

She laughed. He rolled onto his side to look at her.

"Thank you," he said. He touched her face. "You were so great about caring for the kids and keeping everything smooth so that I could just work."

"You really did something," Jill said. "You brought water to people who didn't have it. I love that you invited the plumbing group and that so many of them came."

"Just having a well doesn't help anything," Jacob said. "You have to get it into the house. Erik was great."

"Wanda was wonderful to be around," Jill said. "It's such a treat to see her blossom."

Jacob nodded. His hand touched her hair and her shoulder before settling on her waist.

"What?" Jill asked.

"I was just thinking that it's a joy to spend my life with you," Jacob said. "I get to watch your blossoming grow deeper, more intricate. It's the joy of my life."

Jill gave him a soft smile.

"What's next for you, Mr. Marlowe?" Jill asked.

"Get through the weekend," Jacob said. "Delphie has a long list of house stuff to get done. It's going to take all of us to get it done."

"She needs it done now?" Jill asked.

"Some of it is long overdue," Jacob said.

Jill grunted.

"I'm also planning to help get the kids ready for their next term," Jacob said. He shrugged. "You?"

"I need to get ready for my next term at school," Jill said. "Then it's boring stuff — shopping for clothes for the kids, stuff like that."

"Did you have any fun last week?" Jacob asked.

"You mean, did I have fun spending a week with my best friends, my kids, and their kids by a pool in the hot, dry air?" Jill asked. "Dinner under the desert sky? Massages every day? Two pedicures *and* manicures? Meeting the amazing people who saved your life? Seeing that wonderful part of our country?"

Jacob smiled.

"It was perfect," Jill said. "Fun to be there with you to support what you were doing. Fun to be there with our kids and our friends. Fun to see Heather and Blane creep forward in their life. Fun to stand up for us, our family, our world. It was . . . powerful, I guess."

"And getting back to boring life?" Jacob asked.

"I love my boring life," Jill said. "Investing in myself, my children, you, our friends, our family. Enjoying the abundance we've been given. I keep thinking that things can't really get better . . ."

"And then they do," Jacob said.

Jill smiled at him.

"Boring old life is pretty awesome," Jill said. She yawned and closed her eyes.

He leaned forward and kissed her.

"Now that's never boring," Jill said with a sigh.

He smiled. He was about to say something else when he realized she was asleep. Smiling to himself, he fell asleep.

~~~~~~~~~

Friday night — 10:05 p.m.
Denver, Colorado

Heather softly closed the door to the basement apartment they were staying in at the Castle. She took a step into the apartment when Blane came out of the bedroom to greet her. He left the door slightly open so they would hear if Mack or Wyn cried. He helped her out of the backpack she'd been carrying.

Hoping not to wake the kids, they pantomimed whether she needed something to eat. She shook her head. She pointed to the other room, and Blane nodded. Tink was in her room. Nodding, she pointed to the bathroom. She used the bathroom, changed into her sleeping clothes, and came out into the living area. Blane had pulled the bed out from the couch. He was in bed reading when she got out of the bathroom.

She grabbed her tablet computer and climbed into the bed. Blane set down his book. They scooted across the bed so that their heads were close. She turned on the tablet and opened the photo gallery.

"This is the one he was working on when I got there," Heather whispered.

The photo showed a small, ornate sword. It was crusted with priceless jewels on the hilt. The blade was delicate and viciously sharp.

"It's called the 'Fairy Princess,'" Heather said. "I guess there's a great controversy among the swords masters whether it exists. Neither Pierre nor his father believed it existed."

"It's very beautiful," Blane said. "Why is it so controversial?"

"It's imbedded with some kind of life-and-death curse," Heather said. "The blade gives the owner near immortality while ensuring death to anyone the blade is used against."

"Wow," Blane said.

"Mari said that it was a bride present from a minor god," Heather said. "Shiva killed him for using this level of magic for a weapon."

"But not her?" Blane asked.

"Edie worked it out with Shiva," Heather said. "It wasn't Mari's fault that this god had the blade created."

"But she still owns it," Blane said.

"That's part of the agreement," Heather said. "Shiva can call on Mari and the blade whenever, if ever, he needs it."

"Has he needed it?" Blane asked.

"I don't think so," Heather said. "I'm not sure. I have some vague memory of this whole drama when it happened. It was a long time ago."

Blane nodded.

"What was Nelson doing with it?" Blane asked.

"He said it needed tuning," Heather said. "I'm not sure what that is besides sharpening. Mari seemed happy with the results."

Heather clicked the photo and it switched to another picture of a sword.

"This is Edie's sword," Heather said. "He thought it was called the 'Head Remover' or something like that. It's named in Old Norse, so . . ."

Heather shrugged.

"He said that this blade was known for taking the heads of anyone it approached," Heather said. "While I was there, Edie came to get the sword. She told him that she hadn't taken a head in a long, long time. He wasn't convinced. He said that the very essence of the blade was to remove heads."

Blane shook his head.

"Wow," Blane said.

"He personalized the blade for Edie," Heather said. "Added this jewel and colored the hilt to match her colors."

"It's beautiful and terrifying," Blane said.

Heather nodded.

"Where do the jewels come from?" Blane asked.

"Some family collection," Heather said with a shrug. "They are made specifically to go on swords."

Blane nodded.

"How was going through the house?" Heather asked.

While Tink watched the kids, Blane and Jacob had spent the evening going through Nelson's home to see if it might work for combining their families. Mari had gone with them so that she could give them an illusion of what might be possible. Heather and Jill had hung out with Nelson.

"Good," Blane said. He looked at Heather. "There's plenty of space. Nelson and Tres can have their own spaces. We'll have our space. We're not sure if we should have the shared space on the first floor or the second. I'm sure Jill or Jake will ask you about it in the next month or so."

"Pros to first floor?" Heather asked.

"Easier," Blane said. "We can create private access to the apartments so no one can track who comes and goes. More private that way."

"Cons to first floor?" Heather asked.

"Our set up is not exactly 'normal,'" Blane said. "We might want to have a more-public space on the first floor, keeping the shared floors away from view."

Heather nodded.

"I'm just not sure that... well, are we sure that we're not moving too fast? I mean, we just started ..." Blane said.

Heather touched his face.

"What does that mean?" Blane asked.

Heather sighed.

"I think that we have to live — forward facing," Heather said. "We can't hide out in this apartment in the Castle forever. It will take at least six months to rehabilitate his house, and then we need to do the interior design. Nine months from now, we'll be doing endless shopping trips for refrigerators."

"We have time," Blane said.

"We have time," Heather said.

"What if it's not right?" Blane asked.

"Then we don't move in," Heather said, with a shrug. "We figure out something else."

Blane looked off into the near distance.

"What is it?" Heather asked.

"Oh, I don't know," Blane said. "Nothing really. I think I'm so used to there being the next battle, the next trauma that I expect it around every corner."

"Ah," Heather said. She grinned at him. "One day at a time."

"Yes, ma'am," Blane said. "I'll tell you this — I am happy to be home."

"Me too," Heather said.

Blane put his head on Heather's shoulder and fell asleep. Heather read her novel for a while before falling asleep.

CHAPTER FIVE HUNDRED & FORTY-SEVEN
VACATION OVER

Two days later
Monday morning — 5:15 a.m.

"Are you going to be okay?" Tanesha asked Jeraine as she came from the shower.

They were living in a small apartment in the basement of the Castle. Jeraine had spent last night with his sister at the little yellow house. Tanesha had been asleep when he'd come home. Jabari spent the night at Tanesha's parents home.

"Sure," Jeraine said from his perch leaning against the backboard of the bed. "You?"

Tanesha blew out a breath. Her towel dropped. She tugged on underwear and snapped on a bra. She felt his hand on her shoulder. She turned to look into his eyes.

"Are *you* going to be okay?" Jeraine asked.

"Terrified," Tanesha said.

"Of school?" Jeraine asked.

"Second year," Tanesha said. "This is the year that the class starts to separate into 'the best students' and the rest. I *need* to be in the best students."

"Then you will be," Jeraine said evenly.

"It's not that easy," Tanesha said.

She shook her head and turned to the closet. He got out of bed, pulled on a T-shirt and some boxer shorts before going to the little kitchenette to make her some tea.

"Tell me about you," Tanesha said, pulling up her jeans. "You're going with Jammy to Las Vegas today?"

Jeraine had been offered a long-term residency at one of the Las Vegas casinos. It was the first time in the history of Las Vegas that an African-American was going to have a yearlong show. His agent, James Schmidt V, was taking him to Las Vegas to sort out some of the last details.

"We're going to look at the venue and sign some papers," Jeraine said. "I'll be here when you get home."

Tanesha grunted. She pulled on her blue, starched button-down shirt that made her skin look coffee brown.

"How did it go with La Tonya?" Tanesha asked.

"Oh," Jeraine sighed.

He poured hot water into a travel mug and dropped in a teabag. He tucked two more tea bags into her lunch box and zipped the thermal vinyl closed.

She touched his shoulder, and he looked at her.

"How did it go with La Tonya?" Tanesha asked again.

"It went well, I guess," Jeraine said. "I mean, she let me in. I made dinner for her and the kids. Got the kids bathed and in bed. We tried to talk, but... I mean, I'm the fuck-up, right? Not her. It's too hard for her."

"I'm glad you were able to help," Tanesha said. "Did you leave the money?"

Jeraine nodded.

"Three hundred dollars. Cash. Plus the grocery card. On the counter," Jeraine said. "She told me not to leave the money, but Mom said that it was gone when she got there. Hopefully, La Tonya'll get some groceries and stuff."

Tanesha nodded.

"I wondered — I mean, I don't really have a right to ask," Jeraine said.

Tanesha gave him a puzzled look.

"I wonder if Jill might go by and see if she could, you know, heal La Tonya," Jeraine said.

"La Tonya's coming to see Blane this afternoon," Tanesha said. "Your mom's bringing her and the kids. They should be here when you get back tonight."

"And Jill?" Jeraine asked.

"I'll text her," Tanesha said. "She's taking the kids to the orthodontist this morning, but she should be here tonight. I'm sure she'd want to help."

Jeraine nodded.

"It's really hard to watch someone you love suffer so much over something that seems so trivial," Tanesha said.

"Even the tiniest thing can be too much if you're really depressed," Jeraine said.

"Exactly," Tanesha said.

She leaned forward and kissed his lips.

"Thanks for last week," Tanesha said. "It was really nice of you to do all the cooking and making things nice for everyone. I know that Heather is grateful that you helped her friend, our new friend."

"I hope she settles in," Jeraine said with a nod.

She kissed him again.

"Do you have everything?" Jeraine asked. "Lunch, tea, jacket for the cold classroom . . ."

Tanesha looked into her bag and ticked off the things in her bag.

"Laptop, audio recorder, phone," Tanesha said with a nod. "Did you see Fin when you got home?"

Jeraine snorted a laugh and nodded.

"Why did you laugh?" Tanesha asked.

"The brother was decked out head to toe in some kind of silk and jewels," Jeraine said. "He looked like . . ."

Jeraine shook his head.

"You know, he's usually so buff," Jeraine said. "Rippling muscles, testosterone everywhere. 'I am Fin, near fod, fairy prince of macho.'"

Jeraine imitated Fin's Isle of Man accent.

"But I swear he looked so feminine that . . ." Jeraine said. "He appeared, and I laughed out loud. Abi came out from their apartment and laughed at him. He took one look at us and realized how he was dressed."

"Did he laugh?" Tanesha asked.

"For the first time, ever, I think he was actually embarrassed," Jeraine said.

Tanesha laughed.

"Wait a minute," he said. "I'll walk you up."

Tanesha waited while he used the bathroom and pulled on some jeans. He took her bag and walked her up the stairs to the main level of the Castle. For all the quiet of the basement, the main level was hopping with people. Sam and Aden were hustling off to Lipson Construction. Sandy was making biscuits for some kind of biscuit sandwich for breakfast. Valerie had all of the kids' lunches laid out. Abi was sitting at the kitchen table with the twins.

Relieved of his court finery, Fin stood in next to Abi. His dreadlocks were thick and long. He was wearing jeans and a shirt similar to Tanesha. He had a backpack full of his gear at his feet.

"Are you ready?" Fin asked.

Tanesha gave him a stiff nod.

Mike came running out of the upstairs. He was pulling on his shoes.

"I'll take you," Mike said.

Tanesha felt a dagger in her heart. Summer was over. It was time to get back to the work and worry of school. Her eyes flicked around the room. Sandy gave her a firm, flour-filled hug. Jill appeared from upstairs. She hugged Tanesha. Fin kissed Abi's cheek, and they started toward the door.

Heather met them near the door. She gave Tanesha a hard hug and a golden apple.

"Hey!" Fin said when she didn't seem to have an apple for him.

"King Finegal," Heather said while holding out his own golden apple.

Fin shook his head at her mocking. Tanesha gave Jeraine a hug. By agreement, Jeraine only walked them to Mike's truck. Fin got in the passenger seat, and Jeraine opened the door to the back.

"You're going to do great," Jeraine said.

He kissed her and she got in the truck.

"See you tonight," she said.

He raised his hand. They drove out of the Castle parking lot.

"Are you as scared as I am?" Tanesha asked.

"I am King Finegal," Fin said. "Fearless warrior. King of the Fairies."

"Yeah — I didn't ask you that," Tanesha said with a laugh. "I ask if you, King of the Assholes, were scared about school."

"Positively terrified," Fin said. "King of the Assholes? The visual on that is . . ."

They laughed. Mike stopped at the traffic light at 17th Avenue and York Street.

"Are we picking up our friend Cody?" Fin asked.

"We are," Tanesha said.

"Yep," Mike said with a nod.

The light changed and Mike drove them past the Pinacle Towers, where Tanesha had been living with Jeraine when she'd started her first year. She watched the building pass. Smiling to herself, she felt ready to start her second year of medical school.

~~~~~~~~~

Monday morning — 8:35 a.m.

"Noelle! Close the door," Sandy said from the front seat of the big SUV. "We need to go."

"But where's Charlie?" Noelle asked from the middle bench near the door. "Tink."

"Katy," Nash said.

"Tink, Charlie, Katy, and Paddie — if you're keeping track — are at the orthodontist," Sandy said.

"Where's Rachel?" Noelle asked.

Sandy gave a frustrated sigh.

"I don't know, Noelle. What did I tell you a half hour ago?" Sandy asked.

"Rachel and Wyn have to see the doctor today for checkups," Nash said. "Auntie Heather's taking them. Mom's going to meet them after she drops us off."

"Oh," Noelle said, sheepishly.

"Now, *close the door*," Sandy nearly yelled. Everyone in the car jumped with surprise.

"Fine," Noelle said. "Try to *care* about my *siblings* and . . ."

Sandy groaned, which caused Nash to laugh. With Nash's laugh, the little kids —Maggie, Jackie, and Mack — howled with laughter. Ivy patted Noelle's leg in empathy.

"Just be glad it's not your turn," Sandy said. "You and Nash are due to get your braces on soon."

"Charlie's had them forever," Noelle said.

"He should get them off either this visit or the next," Sandy said. "Then . . ."

"It's our turn," Noelle said in a sulking voice.

"Why did Tink go?" Ivy asked.

"She's starting her braces today," Sandy said.

"She gets braces, too?" Ivy asked. "Wow."

"Why 'wow'?" Noelle asked.

"Rich kids get braces," Ivy said with a shrug. "When we were out, we used to talk about what we'd do if we were rich kids."

Noelle's attitude shifted with Ivy's simple reminder of how lucky she was.

"Is Ivy getting them, too?" Noelle asked.

"I don't know," Sandy said looking at Ivy in the rearview mirror. "Ivy?"

"My teeth are all messed because I was out for such a long time when I was pretty little," Ivy said. "They pulled a bunch of my teeth after . . . well, you know."

Sandy nodded.

"When I get all of my permanent teeth, Sam said that I can get implants or maybe porcelain crowns," Ivy said. "Then I'll probably get braces, maybe. I don't really know."

Everyone fell silent. Nash put his arm around Ivy and gave her a slight hug.

"What did I say?" Ivy asked. "Why is everybody quiet?"

"We're sad that you had to suffer so much," Noelle said. "I'm just here being a jerk."

"You could never be a jerk, Noelle," Ivy said.

"I just . . ." Noelle blew out a breath. "Why does vacation have to go by so fast?"

"Good question," Sandy said.

She gave an exaggerated yawn, and the kids laughed.

~~~~~~~~~

Monday mid-morning — 11:35 a.m.
Las Vegas, Nevada

"What am I missing here?" Jeraine asked in a low voice.

Jammy turned to look at Jeraine. Jammy's eyes blinked as he thought. He held up his index finger to Jeraine and turned back to the man behind the desk.

"This is not what we agreed to," Jammy said. "Not even close."

The man behind the desk started talking. Jeraine felt his anxiety start to rise. The words flew fast and furious. Jammy shifted in his seat.

"I'm sorry to interrupt," Jammy said. "I need to speak with my client for a moment."

"Of course," the man said. "There's a lot of language here. I can imagine it's confusing for him."

Jeraine gave the man a hard look. He started to say something but Jammy shuffled him out of the room. Jammy pressed, pulled, and pushed Jeraine into the bathroom. Jammy walked down the stalls to make sure that they were alone.

"What the fuck!" Jeraine said. "Did that man just say that I was stupid?"

"He did," Jammy said. "He thinks you're stupid."

"Why are we here?" Jeraine asked. "You said that . . ."

"I know what I said," Jammy said. "I know what I said. Hell, I know what I have in writing."

Jammy walked down the length of the bathroom and back to Jeraine. He shook his head at Jeraine and walked back to the end of the bathroom.

"Makes my head hurt," Jeraine said.

"I'm furious," Jammy said.

Jeraine watched Jammy walk back and forth in the bathroom.

"I wish Miss T were here," Jeraine said. "She would understand all of this. I wish . . ."

His head was pounding. He wet a paper towel and pressed it against his head. Jeraine's head lowered, and his hands pressed against the marble sink counter. Jeraine was trying to calm down when Jammy yelped in surprise.

Jeraine looked up through blurry eyes to see Hecate. She was wearing a white pencil skirt and a white silk shirt. There was a little red scarf tied at her neck. She had on a pair of white pumps. Her curly hair was up in a French knot. The streak of blue and turquoise looked like a racing stripe.

"How'd you . . .?" Jeraine asked.

"Hedone told me to listen in," Hecate said. "If you needed me . . ."

She put one hand on Jeraine's forehead and another on the back of his head. After a few minutes, his head stopped pounding. The end of pain was such a relief that he was weak in the knees.

"None of that," Hecate said. "Stand strong, Jeraine. We'll get through this."

She turned to see Jammy watching them closely. Jeraine splashed water on his face and stood up.

"Hecate," she said, holding out her hand.

"As in the Titan responsible for witchcraft?" Jammy asked.

"As in a good friend of Heather's," Hecate said.

"Mine," Jeraine said.

"How'd you . . .?" Jammy pointed to where she'd just appeared.

"Some things are without explanation, my dear James Schmidt V," Hecate said, "including why this job has fallen through. Any ideas?"

"Politics," Jammy said. He leaned forward and whispered, "This guy got pressured from people with radical policies that include anti-black policies."

"Anti-black?" Hecate asked. "What is 'black'?"

"My skin," Jeraine said.

"This is an issue?" Hecate asked. "The color of your skin?"

"Last three hundred years or so," Jeraine said.

Scowling, Hecate shook her head.

"Where have you been?" Jammy asked.

"Far from here," Hecate said. "Why are we still here?"

"We?" Jammy asked. He pointed to himself and Jeraine. "We are trying to salvage this deal."

Hecate shrugged.

"Why don't we find something better?" Hecate asked.

"How . . .?" Jammy asked.

"She's . . . Hecate," Jeraine mumbled.

"What is this place?" Hecate asked.

"The men's restroom," Jammy asked.

"The toilet?" Hecate asked. "Why are we in the toilet?"

She shook her head at the men.

"Come," she said.

Jammy and Jeraine followed her out of the restroom. She walked down the hallway to the elevator.

"I don't know how this works, but the Oracle said . . ." Hecate whispered to Jeraine.

Jeraine hit the down button. They stood alone at the elevators. When the doors opened, they stepped inside. The elevator started going down.

"Whoa," Hecate said. "What in the world?"

Jammy looked at her and laughed.

"It's taking us to the ground floor," Jeraine said. He looked at Jammy. "She hasn't been in the modern world."

"Tell me something obvious," Jammy said.

The elevator stopped at the lobby. Hecate stumbled, but Jammy caught her elbow.

"Thank you, James," Hecate said.

"Everyone calls me, 'Jammy,'" he said. "I'm not introducing you as 'Hecate.'"

"What would you call me?" Hecate asked.

"You need a modern name," Jammy said.

"Like Heather," Jeraine said.

"Huh," Hecate said.

She stepped out of the lobby. She started out across Las Vegas. She walked down one street and then turned on another. She walked with such purpose that the men followed her.

"What are you doing?" Jammy asked.

"I am following the scent," Hecate said.

"'The scent'?" Jammy asked.

"Of he who wants us to improve his life," Hecate said.

She stopped in front of the largest, most prestigious casino in Las Vegas.

"Here," Hecate said with a smile.

"They don't have any residencies," Jammy said. "They never have."

"Well, it's time they started," Hecate said. "Come. This will be fun."

She started into the casino. The lights and smells were so overwhelming that she nearly left. Jammy put his hand on her elbow again and gently encouraged her toward the business offices. Once there, Jammy stepped out in front. He told the person at the desk that he would like to speak with the owner.

To Jammy's surprise, the casino owner's son walked out of the inner office at that same moment. He looked at Jammy and then at Jeraine.

"Schmidty?" the casino owner asked.

He held his hand out. Surprised, Jammy just looked at his hand. The men shook hands and then hugged.

"Matt?" Jammy sputtered. "You . . . wait — that's right! This is yours now."

"Well, my dad built it," the casino owner said. "How is Leslie?"

"Good," Jammy said. "Spending the week with her dad. Helen?"

"Running for mayor next year," he said.

"Mayor?" Jammy asked. "Wow. Make sure she hits me up for a donation."

"Of course," the casino owner said. Turning to Jeraine and Hecate, he added, "My father retired recently. I took over last year. I haven't seen anyone since then."

Jammy looked at Jeraine and Hecate and saw that they were both a little stunned.

"We were in the same fraternity," Jammy said.

"Forced to by our fathers," the casino owner said. "Say, you wouldn't happen to be Jeraine Wilson, would you?"

"Sir," Jeraine said.

Jeraine held out his hand, and the casino owner shook his hand. He looked at Hecate and shook his head.

"Surely, you're not Miss T," the casino owner said.

"Miss T started her second year in medical school today," Jeraine said. "This is my friend Hecate."

"Like the witch?" the casino owner asked, holding out his hand for her to shake.

"My mother had a great sense of irony," Hecate said.

The casino owner grinned at her. He turned to Jammy.

"I was just heading to lunch," the casino owner said. "Would you like to join me? Or is there something you need?"

"We've run into a snag with Jeraine's residency at ..." Jammy stopped talking when the casino owner grinned. "What?"

"I told Helen," he said as he looked at Jeraine and Hecate, "my wife. I was telling her last night that I wished we had a chance to book the residency with Jeraine."

Grinning, he looked at Jeraine.

"I may have jinxed your deal," the casino owner said.

"You did not," Hecate said. "Racism did that."

"Of course, it did," the casino owner said. "Bastard."

For his hard word, the casino owner looked positively thrilled. He turned to the receptionist.

"Can you call my secretary?" the casino owner asked. "Cancel the rest of my day."

"Yes, sir," the receptionist said.

"Come on," the casino owner asked. "Let's go through the casino. Figure out where you'll set up shop."

"We haven't worked out the details," Jammy said.

"Schmidty!" The casino owner patted Jammy's back. "Details, details. It's always about the details."

"It is always about the details," Jammy said.

"We'll work it out," the casino owner said. "I really want this, so I'm willing to do what it takes to make it happen."

Hecate grinned. Jeraine shook his head.

"I'm not agreeing to anything," Jeraine stumbled. "Miss T would kill me if I agreed before we talked it through."

"Fair enough," the casino owner said. "Let's find a spot in this casino for your show. We'll take pictures, and you can talk to her about it. How long can you commit to? A year? Let's see. If Miss T is starting her second year, she's got three more years of medical school. Would you commit to that?"

"I'd have to talk to Miss T," Jeraine said. "I know how it sounds, but I have fucked up my relationship a thousand times. I won't do it again. Not for you or any opportunity. She is my world. I won't live without her. And she wants to be involved in these decisions."

"Good man," the casino owner said. "That answers the question I had."

The casino owner looked at Jeraine and then at Jammy. They were so surprised that they didn't know what to do.

"I would love to see this casino," Hecate said. "Find the best spot for Jeraine's show."

The casino owner held out his elbow, and Hecate hooked her hand in it. The casino owner turned to Jeraine.

"Any chance we could get your dad to play?" the casino owner asked Jeraine.

"O'Malley has already agreed to showcase the music he's been working on for the movies," Jammy said. "We've received verbal agreements from most of the African-American pop, R&B, and rock stars. Everyone wants to come and play with Jeraine, but only if we can make it worth our time. Bumpy will play with O'Malley."

The casino owner laughed.

"Why do you laugh?" Hecate asked.

"My dad's going to be so happy," the casino owner said. "We're going to sell out every day."

"Every ticket. Every day," Hecate said. She glanced at Jeraine. "Of course."

"Lead on," Jammy said.

The casino owner started showing them through the casino.

Chapter Five Hundred & Forty-eight

Meet you at the Castle

Monday evening — 5:35 p.m.

Sandy touched Charlie's arm before walking toward the back of the shop. Charlie and Tink were Sandy's last clients before heading home. She usually didn't work on Mondays, but they'd been gone all last week. Plus, she'd wanted to get Charlie cleaned up to celebrate his new, braces-free life. She left the teenagers alone while Tink's deep conditioner worked and Charlie's highlights were processing.

"What do you think?" Charlie asked Tink, who was sitting in the chair next to him.

"About?" Tink asked, looking up from *The Great Gatsby*, a book she was reading for their literature class.

"How is that?" Charlie asked, gesturing to the book.

"Oh, the book?" Tink asked. "It's okay. I don't like him very much. He's kind of . . . I don't know, a jerk, I guess. They live this addict life. They make it seem so glamorous, but then they suffer the downfall of their addiction."

"Like everybody," Charlie said.

"Everyone," Tink said.

"Everyone," Charlie said with a nod. "Thanks."

Tink grinned, and Charlie smiled.

"I don't like the way he treats his girlfriend or wife or whatever she was," Tink said.

"Well, I get it after you," Charlie said.

Tink nodded.

"We can talk about it when you're done," Tink said.

Charlie grinned at her, and she laughed. They both remembered all too well, how, not so long ago, Charlie couldn't read, and Tink was too overwhelmed to bother. Tink went back to her book and Charlie fell silent.

"No," Charlie said after a moment.

Tink looked up at him.

"I meant, what do you think about my braces?" Charlie asked.

He gave her a broad smile. The teeth that hadn't been broken were straightened, and what was broken had been capped. Now, he had a straight, gleaming smile.

"I think you are very handsome," Tink said. "Too good for the likes of me."

She looked back down to read.

"Don't say that," Charlie said.

"Say what?" Tink asked, looking up from the book.

"That I'm too good for you," Charlie said. "You're amazing. I want to spend my entire life trying to be good enough for you."

Tink blushed.

"I don't know what we're going to be, you and me, when we get older, but I know that I will always love you," Charlie said. "I will always be your friend, even when you're a rich and famous whatever you end up being. I will still be working to be good enough for you."

Tink's eyes filled with tears.

"Thanks," Tink said, mildly. "You're amazing, too."

Charlie smiled at her.

"And very handsome?" Charlie asked.

"And very handsome," Tink said with a grin. "Even with all that foil in your head."

Charlie laughed.

"Come on, Charlie," Sandy said, coming out from the back. "I'll wash you out now."

Charlie got up, kissed Tink's cheek, and went to the back, where Sandy's washing bowls were located. Tink looked at herself in the mirror for a moment.

Life was sure different than it was just a few years ago. Tink smiled at her reflection and saw her new braces. Her fingers touched the metal with near-religious reverence. Shaking her head at herself, she went back to her book.

~~~~~~~~

Monday evening — 5:45 p.m.

"You can understand why I am concerned," Jacob said to Nelson's neighbor Mr. Matchel. "I was out of town. My wife and daughter said that you were very angry in their direction regarding my cousin and your next-door neighbor."

Mr. Matchel shifted back and forth.

"Just a bad night," Mr. Matchel said.

"That's what I want to understand," Jacob said. "Because Blane's been over here — every single Thursday this summer — making sure that your grass is mowed and edged. If you think that you'd rather not have 'his kind' around, then he can spend his time doing something else."

Mr. Matchel swallowed hard. His head went up and down.

"Now, Blane, Nelson, and I planned to get after these leaves in your yard this weekend," Jacob said.

"Because you can use them for your own compost," Mr. Matchel said. "For that farm, you're running in the backyard."

"Actually, this is too much for us," Jacob said with a nod. "We've never put your leaves in our compost. We do get them to the city so they can use them."

Mr. Matchel scowled with mistrust.

"So what's it going to be?" Jacob asked. "Are you going to get over this petty issue you've developed with my cousin and your next-door neighbor? Let us help you. Or would you rather sit in your judgments on their lives?"

"Petty?" Mr. Matchel sniffed. "It's in the bible as an offense against God!"

"It's also in the bible that you should love your neighbor," Jacob said. "There's an entire New Testament about that. Are you loving your neighbor when you vent your rage on my wife and child? When you say awful things about my cousin and your neighbor?"

Mr. Matchel shifted back and forth. Before Jacob and Blane started mowing his yard, he was always in trouble with the city for his unkempt yard. The elderly man was simply incapable of keeping up with his yard and house.

"Is hate so important to you?" Jacob asked.

"It's not like I hate Blane," Mr. Matchel said.

"Then what is it?" Jacob asked.

Mr. Matchel blinked at Jacob for such a long time that Jacob nearly gave up. After a moment, Mr. Matchel took a breath and then another. Jacob glanced behind him and saw Heather standing at the fence of the Castle.

"I just get so angry these days," Mr. Matchel said, finally. "I didn't mean to scare your little girl. It just came out of me."

Jacob nodded in understanding.

"Seems like maybe you haven't had a chance to meet Nelson," Jacob said.

Mr. Matchel shook his head.

"He's coming to dinner tonight," Jacob said. "Why don't you come over? Do you have dinner plans?"

"Me?" Mr. Matchel asked. "Just what they bring from the service."

"Why don't I ask Nelson to come get you?" Jacob asked. "You can come over together. Share a meal. We can get to know each other better."

Mr. Matchel gave him a distrusting look but nodded.

"Good — then it's settled," Jacob said. "You'll like Nelson. His family is one of France's oldest families."

"I was in France in the service," Mr. Matchel said.

"See? Something in common already," Jacob said.

Mr. Matchel nodded. Not sure of what to say next, Mr. Matchel closed the door. Jacob walked next door to tell Nelson the news. Nelson simply nodded. Smiling, Jacob went back to the Castle.

Passing Heather, he said, "Thanks."

"Don't thank me yet," Heather said.

Jacob laughed.

~~~~~~~~~

Monday evening — 5:45 p.m.
Between Las Vegas and Denver

"They're going to have AA meetings during the day in the space," Jeraine said, on his cell phone. "He said it was something he'd always wanted to do. 'Can't service one side of addiction and not the other.' That's what he said, anyway."

"What did Jammy say?" Tanesha asked. "I'd hate it if we got excited again and . . ."

"Nope," Jeraine said. "I mean, Jammy stayed to work out all the details and get the signatures. He's not sure that the other guy will let me out of my contract."

"But he won't put on a show, either!" Tanesha said.

"Yeah," Jeraine said. "You know how they are."

Tanesha snorted.

"Now don't get all mad," Jeraine said. "This is a really good thing. If all the details line up . . ."

"That's right," Tanesha said.

"I'll be heading a show here until you're done with medical school," Jeraine said. "This guy, man, he wanted something like this for a long time. His wife came by with his kids. She told me that he'd talked about it for years. He wanted a mix of styles and people, you know, like we talked about."

"I . . ." Tanesha started.

"Oh, and he's going to give me an apartment in the hotel," Jeraine said. "We get childcare when Jabari is there, if we need it. But it's available to me. I can even take the hotel jet back and forth."

"And the pay?" Tanesha asked.

"I did like we'd talked about," Jeraine said. "Same flat salary with a percentage of the door. Hecate said we should sell out every night."

"Wow," Tanesha said.

"We get medical insurance too," Jeraine said. "Because I'll be an employee of the hotel. He said the insurance isn't perfect, but it's okay. I could cover you and Jabari."

"Great," Tanesha said. "It sounds just great!"

"Right," Jeraine said. "We need to talk to Nelson because I'm going to be there more. We need a more than a spot for you and Jabari."

"I think he's coming to dinner tonight," Tanesha said.

"Great," Jeraine said. "We should land in about twenty minutes. I'll be home for dinner. You?"

"I'll be there," Tanesha said. "Listen, I'm really excited for you, for us. I hope this works out."

"Me, too," Jeraine said. "But you know, whatever happens, it's going to be okay. If the last year taught me anything, as long as you're by my side, everything is going to be okay."

"Tsk," Tanesha gave an embarrassed sound.

"Just the truth," Jeraine said. "So I'll see you soon?"

"I'll be there," Tanesha said.

"You didn't tell me how school was," Jeraine said.

"It was okay," Tanesha said. She gave a heavy sigh. "I have a lot of work ahead of me."

"Me too," Jeraine said. "But what else are we going to do?"

"True," Tanesha said. "Love you, weirdo. See you tonight."

"Love you, Miss T," Jeraine said. "See you tonight."

Smiling to himself, Jeraine looked over at Hecate. Her face had been pressed to the window as soon as they'd taken to the air.

"We're going to land in a bit," Jeraine said.

Her face marked with awe, she turned to look at him.

"What happens then?" Hecate asked.

"There's a big bump and we roll to a place where we can head home," Jeraine said. "I called for a car, so they should be there waiting for us."

Hecate gave him a distracted nod and turned her face back to the window. Smiling at her, Jeraine closed his eyes to meditate until the plane landed.

~~~~~~~~~

Monday evening — 6:15 p.m.

"How was it?" Ares asked Hecate.

Much to Jeraine's surprise, the God Ares was waiting for them when the plane landed. Ares had grunted at Jeraine and turned his attention to Hecate.

"Jeraine?" Hecate asked. "Have you met my nephew, Ares?"

Jeraine nodded.

"So, how was it?" Ares asked in an impatient and excited voice.

Jeraine grinned. The great God of War seemed exactly the excited nephew that Hecate had introduced him as.

"A-*maz*-ing," Hecate said.

Ares tucked Hecate's arm into his elbow, and they walked off down the terminal. Jeraine scowled at their retreating forms. The Titan and Greek god stopped to wait for Jeraine. He put his bag on his shoulder and walked toward them.

"You could see everything," Hecate said. "Clouds, birds, air, blue, so-very-blue sky. And the land. Acres and acres of gorgeous hills and rivers. And . . . this really is the best planet, you know?"

Ares nodded rather than respond.

"Was it like flying?" Ares asked. "Hedone says it's like flying but also not like flying because you're up so high up."

"Right," Hecate said. "It's like flying at many thousands of feet."

"Wow," Ares said. "All while you were safe and warm."

Hecate nodded.

"I could see the land and the animals and the clouds and ..." Hecate gave a happy sigh. "Have you been?"

Ares shook his head and gave Jeraine a hard look.

"How is that *my* problem?" Jeraine asked. Heather had told Jeraine to give Ares as good as he got. "If you want to go, you could ask."

Ares gasped.

"Really?" Ares asked.

The Greek god's face lit up so brightly that Jeraine had to hold back a laugh. If Ares, God of War, had ever been a child, he must have looked just like this.

"I have been in something called an 'S-U-V' and, let me tell you, Hecate, it was incredible," Ares said. "We went over the land at such a speed. The 'S-U-V' is on rubber tires. No horses. All mechanical."

"I took a 'taxi,'" Hecate said. "We went from one place to another — *across* the land, not through time."

"Yes, this 'S-U-V' did the same," Ares said. "We were up in the mountains on some kind of black track. Just incredible. Not with ten horses could you go as fast or as far."

"We were in the city," Hecate said. "Then we came to something called an 'air-port.'"

"Yes, that's what *this* is," Ares said.

"Oh," Hecate said on an exhale. She looked around. "We are not in the air?"

Ares shook his head and looked at Jeraine again.

"*Air*-plane." Jeraine pointed to the monstrous tubes of aluminum out the windows of the terminal. "*Air*-port. Where you port airplanes?"

"Ah," Ares said at the same time Hecate said, "Very smart. Makes perfect sense now."

Groaning to himself, Jeraine continued down the terminal. The Titan and her Greek god "nephew" chatted back and forth. Jeraine put his ear buds in to listen to music from his phone. After a moment, Ares put his hand on Jeraine's arm.

Jeraine took an ear bud out.

"What is the difference between an 'S-U-V' and a 'tax-ee'?" Ares asked.

"They are the same kind of vehicle but different types," Jeraine said. "A taxi, or at least the one we took in Las Vegas, was a car."

Jeraine nodded.

"A car," Hecate said with a nod.

"Technically, a sedan," Jeraine said. "It's a kind of automobile."

"Ah," Ares said. "It moves automatically?"

"Instead of horses," Jeraine said. "That's the 'auto.' There is a big engine, which moves the car. Ask Mike when we get to the Castle. He'll show you."

"I will do just that," Ares said. "And an 'S-U-V'?"

"It's a type of automobile called a 'Utility Vehicle,'" Jeraine said. "It's set up to be more rugged for difficult roads, thicker tires, bigger. Jake has a couple to get around town in bad weather and carry the children."

"I see," Ares said with a nod. "It always was such a big deal carting everyone around."

"No family we know gets along," Hecate said.

Ares laughed out loud.

"So true," Ares said. "So true. But everyone loves Hecate."

Hecate blushed.

"You might need one of these 'S-U-V's," Ares said with a nod.

"She would have to know how to drive it," Jeraine said.

"Watch yourself young man," Ares said in a low, threatening voice. "You are speaking to your betters."

Jeraine gave him a mildly irritated look. He put his other ear bud in and started toward the bridge to the main terminal. He was mildly surprised to see that Ares and Hecate had followed him all the way to his car.

"What's this?" Ares asked, his boyish glee apparent.

"This is a kind of sedan," Jeraine said.

"A sedan is a kind of automobile," Hecate nodded.

"A sedan is the kind of automobile where the nephew sits in back," Jeraine said. "And the lady sits in front."

Ares howled with laughter. Jeraine clicked the automatic locks and opened the passenger door for Hecate. When he turned to look, Ares was bent over, looking at the door handle.

Jeraine flicked it, and the door opened. Ares inhaled quickly at the unexpected event.

"Very clever," Ares said. "Very clever."

"Get in," Jeraine said.

Ares got into the back seat next to one of Jabari's car seats. Ares pointed to it.

"This is to lock children in so that they don't bother you while you operate the auto-mobile," Ares told Hecate with a nod.

"That is a safety device," Jeraine said from the door of the driver's side, "for small children so they are safe while you drive."

"Oh, yes. Small human children are so fragile," Hecate said. "Makes sense."

"Now, I have to operate this machine," Jeraine said. "Please watch, but don't interrupt. It can be very dangerous."

"As you wish," Hecate said.

Jeraine looked at Ares in the rearview mirror.

"Of course," Ares said.

By some miracle, they managed to get out of the airport and onto the highway. Hecate and Ares' faces were pressed against their windows watching the world go by. Jeraine took the Colorado Boulevard exit from the I-70. In a few minutes, he was at the driveway to the Castle. He clicked the gate opener and saw that his passengers were completely fascinated.

He pulled into his parking spot and let the gods out of his sedan.

"That was fantastic!" Ares said. Seeing Heather waiting for them, he rushed out of the vehicle and to her side. "We rode in a sedan."

Heather shot Jeraine a mildly amused look and escorted her grandfather into the Castle. Hecate waited for Jeraine.

"Thank you for sharing all of this with me," Hecate said. "It is a rare gift for us to be able to see all the wonders of the modern world, let alone experience them. We are the envy of all of Olympus."

Jeraine grinned and nodded. They walked to the door of the Castle.

"Dinner can be crazy here, so . . ." Jeraine said.

He pressed open the door for her. She went in the side door, through the entryway, and stopped short.

Sandy's cat Cleo was curled up in a ball in an armchair.

"Mother?" Hecate whispered.

The cat opened its eyes slowly, sleepily, and looked at her.

"She was injured when I finally found her," Heather said. "I searched high and low for a long, long time. When I found her, she was more dead than alive. Clinging to life. She had transformed into this form because it is so resilient. But . . ."

Hecate looked at Heather's face.

"She's stuck in this form," Hecate said.

"She's regained great health in the years she's been here," Heather said. "It may take millennia to return to her former self — if she ever can. She is whole only in Olympia but can go there for only short periods of time — ceremonies and the like — when Perses is there."

"She has always drawn strength from father," Hecate said.

"Even then, she is really more illusion than anything else," Heather said.

Rachel Ann walked into the living room and picked up Cleo.

"She has been my friend Sandy's cat," Heather said. "Even in her weakened state, she's given much love."

"The more she can give, the stronger she will become," Hecate said.

"That is Sandy's daughter," Heather said. "She is Rachel Ann's champion."

Hecate nodded. She looked down to see Rachel Ann holding Cleo out for Hecate to see.

"This is Cleo, my cat," Rachel Ann said. "You can hold her. I think she'd like that."

Hecate took the cat from Rachel Ann and the little girl ran off. Hecate kissed the cat's head and hugged her close.

"Oh, mother — I'm so very glad that you are alive," Hecate said.

Cleo the cat purred.

Chapter Five Hundred & Forty-nine
After Dinner

Monday evening — 8:25 p.m.

"My beloved is calling for me," Hecate said. Standing up from the dinner table, she lifted Cleo from her lap. "I must be going."

Hecate kissed Cleo's head. She leaned down to kiss Heather's cheek.

"I will return," Hecate said.

Hecate took a few steps away, to where she could speak with Cleo in private.

"That was fast," Jill whispered to Heather.

"You mean, Gando Peaches?" Heather asked.

Jill, Tanesha, Sandy, and Aden nodded.

"She's always been like that," Heather said. "It's part of her magic. The appropriate partner is drawn to her the moment she enters the world. It's just how it is. She can grant this as a blessing or a gift."

Heather shrugged.

"Too fast for me," Heather said. "But don't worry. They will live out his life very joyfully."

Hecate threw Heather a smile and kept walking.

"Thank you," Tanesha said as she passed.

"My pleasure, dear one," Hecate said.

Tanesha blushed, and Hecate smiled. Hecate grabbed a cupcake from the tray that Jacob was holding.

"Take two," Jacob said. "Ganny likes the chocolate. The dark one."

Grinning, she took a chocolate cupcake and walked out of the dining room.

Pierre Semaines, Nelson's father, watched Hecate go. He was sitting with Nelson and their neighbor Mr. Matchel. He glanced at Nelson's neighbor. Rough around the edges, the elderly man had been a pleasant-enough dinner companion. Pierre was glad that he'd been there for the frank conversations about sexual "preference." It was awkward and, at times, uncomfortable, but they had all survived. It seemed like the elderly man had actually enjoyed his dinner, and the barrier was defrosting. Mission accomplished.

"Dessert?" Jacob asked. He set down a tray of cupcakes in the center of the table. "We have chocolate and vanilla."

Jacob glanced at Sandy, and she nodded.

"I should study," Tanesha said.

Tanesha nodded to Fin, who stood up. Tink, Charlie, Noelle, and Nash stood at the same time, each taking a cupcake with them. They left for the study room down stairs. Jill touched Katy's shoulder and she nodded. The little girl had told her mother that she wanted to spend more time with the older kids to figure out what it would be like to be older.

"I have to do my reading," Katy said, as she slid off her chair.

She ran after the older kids. Edie had taken the infants upstairs to the loft, and Honey's daughter Maggie was having a sleep over for all of the toddlers. So, Honey and the "wild bunch," as they were fondly called, were in her apartment. The remaining adults had a chance to relax over their coffee and dessert.

"I wonder if you would mind helping me home," Mr. Matchel said to Nelson.

"Of course," Nelson said.

Nelson glanced at Blane, and Blane got up. Blane helped the elderly man to his feet.

"I'll see you tomorrow for your acupuncture treatment," Blane said.

"At my house?" Mr. Matchel said. "You're sure?"

"It's easy," Blane said. "Just a walk across the street."

"For you," Mr. Matchel said, with a chuckle.

The elderly man shook Blane's hand. Nelson took his elbow, and they started toward the door. Sam jumped to his feet as they approached.

"Thank you for coming, sir," Sam said. "You are welcome any time."

Embarrassed or possibly overwhelmed, Mr. Matchel simply nodded. Nelson and the elderly man shuffled out of the room.

"That went well," Sam said.

Pierre raised his eyebrows to Sam, and they both laughed.

"Prejudice is just a way of saying, 'I don't know you,'" Jeraine said.

"That's good," Aden said. "Are you quoting someone?"

"The great songwriter Jeraine Wilson," he said. He sang the line from the song. "Know him?"

Aden shook his head as if he'd never heard of Jeraine, and everyone laughed.

"Come in," Delphie said.

As she did every night, Delphie encouraged the dinner stragglers to move closer together now that the children, studiers, and others had left. Because her school didn't start for a few more days, Jill was able to stay. She moved with Valerie, Mike, and Jeraine closer to Delphie. Pierre picked up Nelson's tea and cupcake, as well as his own, and carried them across the room to where Delphie was sitting. Jill, Sandy, and Aden moved in closer as well. Heather and Blane sat next to Nelson's empty chair. Jacob came in with a pitcher full of water and a thermos decanter of decaffeinated coffee.

They filled their cups. Jacob returned with hot water and a selection of tea bags. He sat down next to Jill.

"I believe that Pierre has something to tell us," Delphie said.

Surprised by her words, Pierre looked at Delphie. She gave him an even smile.

"I wondered how you were doing," Sam said. "Burying your father could not have been easy."

"Well . . ." Pierre said.

"Going back to France for the first time since your wife was killed," Blane added.

"That was harder," Pierre said. "Yes. Uh . . . Well, as you can imagine, I was welcomed with open arms and ready knives. A kind of 'Glad you're here — when are you heading back?'"

"Why is that?" Heather asked.

"Oh," Pierre said with a sigh. "As the husband of the heir to the head of the order, I technically can take over the Templars."

"Do you want that?" Valerie asked.

Pierre gave her a long look. He shook his head and didn't respond.

"You aren't sure?" Heather asked.

"Oh, I know that I don't want to be head of the Templars," Pierre said with a laugh. "I just . . . well, there's Nelson to think of. If I walk away completely . . ."

"I am capable of making my own decisions," Nelson said as he walked into the room.

"You want to be the head of the Templars?" Pierre asked.

"Not a chance," Nelson said with a laugh.

Everyone laughed at his tone and quick reply. Pierre smiled.

"What is on your mind, Pierre?" Delphie asked.

The room became very quiet. Nelson sat down next to his father. He reached for the hot water to warm his tea.

"There is a lot," Pierre started.

"English, Papa," Nelson said softly.

"Oh, I am sorry," Pierre said. "I have been so wound up . . . But you don't need to burden your life with this. Please . . ."

"This is how we do it," Sam said. "We make an effort to talk through things. If anyone has a difficulty or decision to make, we sit here and talk it through. I can assure you that if any of the people who left wished to speak, they would be here."

"You talk through everything?" Nelson asked.

"Not everything," Jacob said. "*Anything* is a better word. Anyone wants to speak about anything can bring it up here. Please, Mr. Semaines . . ."

"Pierre, please," Pierre said.

"Don't feel like you need to bare your soul to us," Jacob said.

"Actually, it might help me quite a bit," Pierre said. "But first, I was instructed to ask the Oracle . . ."

"Oh God," Delphie said.

"Exactly," Pierre said. "I was instructed to ask if the Oracle could see a divine future for the Order."

Delphie looked at Pierre. She squinted and looked down at her hands.

"I can go get your cards," Nelson said.

"She doesn't need the cards," Jill said. "They are just a prop. She is a true Oracle. What comes to her just comes."

Nelson looked at Jill, and Jill nodded. They looked at Delphie.

"Are you able to see?" Pierre asked.

Delphie squinted at Pierre and then looked at Blane.

"Do you still have it?" Delphie asked.

Nodding, Blane got up. He looked at Heather.

"Hall closet," Heather said.

"Oh, sorry — that sword?" Sandy asked.

Blane nodded.

"I moved it to the basement closet," Sandy said. "I know it was in a bag and wrapped with protective stuff but we have curious kids. I didn't want anyone to get hurt and . . ."

"Tidying?" Heather asked.

Sandy blushed. Sandy's favorite thing was to go through closets and clean out the junk. It was a regular occurrence to find something you loved moved to somewhere more "appropriate." Valerie laughed. She'd been on the receiving end of the moving object more times than she could count.

"I can . . ." Sandy said.

Heather blinked at Sandy, and a long, thin black bag appeared in her hand. Blane took it from her.

"Parlor tricks?" Aden asked.

"I am a *goddess*?" Heather asked, laughing. "Where is your respect?"

Sam cleared his throat to speak. She pointed at him before he could remind Heather that they made every effort not to use powers in the house.

"Point taken," Heather said. "I was showing off."

"Well don't," Sam said.

"Where's my respect?" Heather asked with a laugh.

"My house," Sam said. "My rules."

"Actually . . ." Delphie said.

Everyone laughed. Shaking his head at them, Blane unwrapped the sword and held it out to Delphie. She gestured toward Pierre. Blane held the sword out to Pierre.

Still laughing at Delphie's joke, Pierre blinked a few times before he really saw the sword in front of him. Nelson looked at the blade and then up at Blane.

"Where did you get that?" Nelson asked.

Pierre hopped to his feet.

"Have you touched this blade?" Pierre asked. "Actually touched the metal?"

"I have," Blane said.

"Anyone else?" Pierre asked.

Blane looked at Heather, and she shook her head. She looked at Sandy, and Sandy shook her head. As if called, Abi walked through the doors. She looked at the sword and each of the people in turn.

"Where is your grandfather?" Abi asked Heather.

"He went back to Olympia," Heather said. "Something about something."

Abi raised her eyebrows.

"Mostly, I think he went to brag," Heather said with a nod. "Do you need him?"

"Absolutely not," Abi said. "I would send you away, but . . ."

Abi snapped her fingers, and the door to the dining room closed. She pointed to Jill.

"You can either call your father now, or he will not be able to come here," Abi said.

"Do we need him?" Jill asked.

"This is an object of power," Abi said. "He will know about it."

"I'd like to hear what he has to say," Pierre said. He looked at the blade and then at Jill. "His father commissioned the blade."

"Perses," Jill said.

The Titan God of Destruction appeared. He was fully armed and dressed in the armor of a Titan warrior. His broadsword was in his hand. He looked at Jill and then walked to the sword in Blane's hand.

"Is this what I think it is?" Perses asked.

He looked at Pierre, who shrugged. He looked at Blane.

"How is it that this human can hold the blade?" Perses asked.

"It's coated," Blane said.

"I didn't want anyone to injure themselves," Heather said.

"I wore gloves when I took it," Blane said.

Abi looked at the Titan directly.

"I see," Perses said.

"Is this Uranus's blade?" Nelson asked.

"It is Gilfand's," Abi said. "He had it made after Uranus and Gaia had all those children."

Jill shook her head as if she was confused.

"My grandparents," Perses said. Seeing everyone's confusion, he sighed and added, "My grandparents had six children. They almost immediately had eight others, including me."

"An infestation," Abi said.

"Gilfand created the blade so that they couldn't use their magic against him," Perses said. "Couldn't take over from him and Abi."

"You didn't need something like that?" Heather asked Abi.

"I would never give children a weapon that could destroy me," Abi said. "I was only in danger of being annoyed. But Gilfand isn't as strong as I am."

Abi sighed and shrugged.

"We have that in our line," Pierre said. "We are immune to magic."

"Imagine that," Perses said, mildly.

"What are you saying?" Pierre asked. "Speak directly."

Not used to speaking to humans, Perses shrugged. He brushed at Pierre as if he were brushing an ant off his arm. Heather stood in support of Pierre, but Abi walked to Perses.

"Lord Perses," Abi said. "Why does Pierre's line hold the same as this weapon?"

"If they don't know . . ." Perses said.

Abi touched Perses' arm, and the Titan looked deep into her eyes. Everyone watched in rapt silence. Something was happening — they just weren't sure what. He seemed to sigh. After a moment, he broke Abi's gaze.

"Excuse me," Perses said. "Abi was reminding me of something dear and important to me."

Perses nodded.

"Your ancestor is a child of the creature that goes by 'Gilfand,'" Perses said. "Direct descendant. He refused to make the sword if he and his line weren't covered by the properties of the sword."

"It's called 'Cronus blade,'" Pierre said.

"It wasn't always," Perses said with a shrug. "Where did your father get it?"

"I ..." Pierre said. He shook his head. "I'm not sure. I thought that the sword was never given to the person who had it made — or, possibly, two were made."

Abi shook her head.

"Gilfand," Abi said.

Gilfand appeared before her. He was wearing silk finery and looked like he'd been resting. He looked at Abi and then saw the sword.

"Hey!" Gilfand said in his distinctive accent. "My sword!"

He held out his hand as if he expected Blane to set the sword into his hand. Abi rolled her eyes at him.

"We were discussing how you lost this sword," Abi said. "I thought you might tell them."

For the first time, Gilfand noticed the others in the room. He nodded to Heather and Perses, but his eyes glided over the others. He touched Delphie's shoulder.

"Did my ancestor make two swords?" Pierre asked.

Gilfand snorted at Pierre.

"I'll take that as a 'No,'" Pierre said. "Did he steal it?"

Gilfand gave Pierre a defiant look. Abi rolled her eyes.

"My darling Gilfand and your ancestor were tricked out of the blade by Bernard of Clairvaux," Abi said. She nodded to Nelson. "Your ancestor, Nelson. You look like him, only you are bigger, stronger, and gratefully, saner."

Gilfand gave Nelson an appraising look. Pierre looked at his son, and Nelson nodded.

"We always believed that the blacksmith was deceived by the order," Abi said.

She gave Gilfand a side look.

"Yes, but he kept the sword," Gilfand said.

"That was the thing," Abi said. "Gilfand ordered the sword, and endued it with certain powers to deal with our annoying children.

When Bernard discovered the purpose of the blade, he decided the order needed the blade to protect them."

"From magic?" Pierre asked.

"A side effect of the charm on the blade is that the owner is immune to the repercussions of his actions," Perses said.

"Totally unintended," Gilfand said.

"No weapon or blade has carried this charm since this blade," Perses said.

Pierre nodded.

"How did you get it?" Nelson asked.

"I took it from your father," Blane said.

"Oh," Pierre said. He fell back into his chair. Looking stunned, he said again, "Oh."

"Oh?" Perses asked.

"As long as the order held complete possession of the blade, they were immune to the repercussions of their actions," Abi said.

"Everyone was killed because I took the blade?" Blane asked Abi. "Why didn't you tell me?"

"It's not your fault," Abi said. "You did what was needed to save your family and many others from sure doom."

"But Alex was there!" Jill said. "She and her husband, and Dad and Hecate, and Heather, and ..."

Perses and Abi shook their heads.

"We are no match for the protection wielded by this sword," Heather said in a low voice.

"That's why they came with only forty guys," Blane said.

"And swords," Aden said.

"What happened in that garage?" Blane asked.

"The repercussions of their actions came out upon their heads," Delphie said.

"Some were really gruesome," Blane said. "I mean, they showed me the pictures because they said it was my fault. More than a few of them were cut apart alive."

"Many of them had more current actions," Delphie said.

"But why should they have to pay for what their ancestors did?" Nelson started.

Delphie shook her head.

"These were not what you might call 'good people.' They knew that they were free from . . . repercussions," Pierre said mildly. "They used this to create large empires of violence and cruelty. This is one of the reasons your mom and I left the order. We couldn't stand worshiping one set of rules and practicing another because we were 'immune.'"

"And now?" Heather asked.

"They are all dead," Delphie said. "*If* the order continues, it will be clear of this criminal stain."

Her eyes flicked to Blane.

"You have cleansed the order," Delphie said.

"Have I endangered my family?" Blane asked. His eyes went to Pierre. "Are they coming after you?"

Pierre's eyes went to the blade. Perses' hand dropped onto Blane's shoulder with a thud.

"You have possession of this blade," Perses said. "You cannot feel the repercussions of this action."

"But I don't want that," Blane said, his voice rising. "Live or die, I stand in the glory of my actions."

He nodded to Sam.

"You taught me that, Sam," Blane said.

"There is only one thing that can be done," Delphie said.

As if she were making a decision, she looked at Heather and then at Perses. She shook her head before looking at Gilfand.

"I'll do it," Abi said.

"If you destroy the blade . . ." Blane said.

"Trust me," Abi said.

She took the sword from Blane's hands and disappeared. Everyone in the room held their breath. After what seemed like an age, Abi reappeared.

Heather pointed to Gilfand.

Abi held out her hand and blew.

"What was that?" Jill asked.

"No one can follow Abi's trail, now," Perses said. "She has hidden the blade either in time or in space. Will you look for it?"

"I haven't actually missed it," Gilfand said. "Especially since the Titan purge."

Perses nodded. Gilfand shrugged.

"Is that how Maughold got the Sword of Truth?" Heather asked.

"Are you asking me if I might have given Queen Fand's child — a child, I might add, who had been stolen at five years old by the Romans and brutally abused by Patrick all of his life — an object of power to help him find his way?" Abi asked.

No one said anything in response. After a moment, Jill spoke up.

"He wasn't very nice to Katy and Paddie," Jill said.

"He wasn't," Abi said. "I am sorry for that. He felt that he had to test them to see if they were strong enough to carry the weapon."

"It wasn't his to give," Pierre said.

Abi rolled her eyes at Perses and he looked every bit the annoying child.

"I *gave* it to him," Abi said. "Are you saying that it was not mine to give?"

Perses cleared his throat. Abi raised her eyebrows and he shook his head.

"Maughold used the sword to clear his mind of his traumatic experience," Abi said. "Once his mind was clear, he was to find a suitable recipient. I believe he has found such a recipient."

Abi raised her eyebrows to Pierre. He looked at her for a moment before nodding in agreement.

"I'm sure you're right," Pierre said. "Paddie is so young."

"By modern standards," Abi said. "True. But many of the Templars went to war at five or six years old. Plus, Paddie and Katy are more than they seem. Together, they could easily conquer the world."

Jill snorted a laugh. Abi looked at her.

"And, they are just small children," Abi said.

Everyone grinned.

"Unless you need me?" Gilfand asked.

"You may return to your pleasures," Abi said.

Gilfand and Abi hugged. He disappeared.

"Will the order continue?" Pierre asked.

"That is another question," Delphie said.

"Wait — what happened in the garage?" Jacob asked. "I ask because I know that Blane is going to feel bad about it."

Jacob looked from face to face. No one seemed to know what had happened in the garage.

"I can tell you only what I see," Delphie said.

They fell silent and waited for her to continue.

CHAPTER FIVE HUNDRED &FIFTY

A SWORD, A GHOST, AND SOME TEMPLARS

"You're sure you want to hear this?" Delphie asked, looking up at the adults before her. "It's pretty gory."

"Just an outline," Sam said in defense of Delphie. "Will that suffice? Or do you really need the gory details?"

Jacob tipped his head back and forth as if he was deciding.

"I've already seen the gore," Blane said, pressing the palms of his hands away from him. "I don't need gory details."

"No, I don't need the gory details," Jacob said with a nod. "I was kidding."

He gave Delphie a wide, boyish grin, and she chuckled.

"The easiest place to start is this: We know that objects hold energy," Delphie said. She looked up at the group. Seeing confusion, she added, "Science tells us that everything in our world is made out of the same substance."

Abi shifted uncomfortably but said nothing.

"Electrons?" Aden asked.

"Exactly," Delphie said. "The difference between a stone and the meal we just ate is the manner in which these electrons were put together."

Abi picked up a fork from the table.

"A fork," Abi said. She turned her hand over. "A stone."

Everyone gasped at the magic.

"Same material makes both objects," Abi said blushing. "Every configuration of the same matter has its own energetic signature."

"Every object has its own energy," Delphie said.

This time when she looked up, everyone was nodding.

"Intense moments — emotional scenes, violent acts, tense moments — they all release a certain amount of energy," Delphie said.

"The reason we energetically clean our apartment every week," Sandy said with a snort.

"Too much teenage-drama energy," Aden said with a laugh.

Everyone smiled at their joke.

"Exactly," Delphie said.

"These swords have been used in some of history's most intense and violent times," Delphie said. "The older blades — like the one Blane took — have been used to kill and maim people for a thousand years."

"More," Abi said.

"Or more," Delphie said.

"I worked on a blade this week that is a head stealer," Nelson said. "It was ... intense. It sparks with power."

"Who possesses that blade?" Perses asked.

"Princess Edith," Nelson said.

"Really?" Perses asked.

"She says she took it from a Viking," Nelson said.

"There's a story that the Vikings landed on the Isle of Man but were repelled by a vicious fairy army," Pierre said. "The blade Nelson is referring to was with the Viking raiding party."

"But these swords were made in France?" Jacob asked.

"Emphasis on 'Viking raiding party,'" Pierre said. "They stole it from its original owner."

Delphie watched all of this conversation with a kind of smug satisfaction. If they chattered about swords and objects of power, she wouldn't have to relive the events that happened in the garage. The only person who appeared to notice her satisfaction was Jacob.

"So what you're saying is that, every time these swords were used, they took on the energy of what they were used for," Jacob said, shifting the conversation.

Everyone in the room turned to look at Delphie. She looked overwhelmed and shook her head. Abi took over.

"We live in a cause-and-effect world," Abi said.

"Every action has an equal and opposite reaction," Jill said. "Newton's Third Law."

"That's correct," Delphie said, finding her ground again.

"The energy couldn't discharge because of the power of that other blade," Jacob said.

"Exactly," Delphie said. "You have cause, but no effect — no equal and opposite reaction. Unbeknownst to anyone, these swords stored the energy of their actions."

Everyone fell silent, digesting the information.

"Like ghosts," Delphie said softly. "What are ghosts but life energy that is not dispersed by death?"

"What happened when the order was released from the protection of the blade?" Blane asked. A reflection of his anxiety and guilt came through in his voice.

The emotion in Blane's voice caused Delphie to look up at him. For a moment, the room was silent again. No one dared to move.

"First, you should know," Abi said, breaking the silence, "there were powerful beings watching these Templars the moment they reached the reservation."

"Gando Peaches and his vet group," Jacob said.

"No," Abi said. "I mean, yes — Gando and his friends were there. You should know that that region of the world has its own protectors. They are the ones who woke Gando to the danger from these strangers."

"Naayé'neizgháni and his brother, Tóbájíshchíní," Delphie said.

"I thought I saw them there," Perses said. "I was surprised that they were not taking a more active role."

"What are we talking about?" Aden asked.

"The Diné Gods — Naayé'neizghání and Tóbájíshchíní," Delphie said. "Naayé'neizghání is called 'the Slayer of Ancient Gods,' and Tóbájíshchíní is called 'Born of Water.'"

"Were you threatened by them?" Blane looked at Heather and then Perses.

They shook their heads.

"They don't mean us or Abi," Heather said. "In fact, Abi helped them find a region where they would be happy . . ."

"The area of the four sacred mountains," Jacob said. "The Navajo Reservation."

" . . . when they came to this planet," Heather nodded in agreement with Jacob.

"But . . ." Blane said.

"It's just a name," Perses said.

Abi and Heather nodded.

"Naayé'neizghání and Tóbájíshchíní were there in the garage," Delphie said. "They wanted to hear the plan and intervene if they could. Their vision has been shared with me."

"And what do you see?" Jacob asked.

"I see spirits of people coming out of the swords," Delphie said. "They easily overcame the person wielding the sword. It was as if the person holding the sword was paralyzed or simply incapable of fighting back. The whole thing happened very, very fast." After a moment, she added another, "Very fast. Very bloody."

Delphie nodded.

"Naayé'neizghání and Tóbájíshchíní stood there and watched," Delphie said. "They would have happily taken the blame for the deaths, but they wanted to share what they had seen with me, in case I wanted to share it with Abi and the rest of you."

No one said anything for a moment.

"Then I will tell the order that . . ." Pierre said.

"Naayé'neizghání and Tóbájíshchíní killed the Templars," Abi said with some finality.

Pierre nodded.

"And the police?" Blane asked.

"They already believe that Naayé'neizghání and Tóbájíshchíní killed the Templars," Delphie said. "It's just taking them a while to get around to it."

Blane nodded.

"So, again, if the order continues, it will be clear of this criminal stain," Delphie said with a nod. "Do you wish the order to continue?"

"There is a question about this wealth or prize or maybe treasure that only Nelson can get," Pierre said. "People have heard about it for a long, long time. They aren't likely to forget it, especially now that they know there is an heir."

All eyes turned to Nelson. He was leaning backing in his chair. His arms were crossed, and his eyes were rolled to the ceiling. In one sudden movement, he sat up. He pointed to Delphie.

"What is this 'treasure'?" Nelson towered over Delphie. His raw frustration made his voice loud and aggressive.

"Watch your tone," Sam said, standing in defense of Delphie.

"Dad," Jacob said with a shake of his head. "He's just upset."

"No, he's right," Nelson said. "I am angry. I don't need to take it out on our Delphie. I am sorry, ma'am. I am just getting . . ."

"The life you've always dreamed of," Delphie said with a nod. "And now this."

"This bullshit that doesn't have anything to do with me," Nelson said. "My mother's life was taken for it. My father has lived in terrible pain for . . . nothing, something that happened more than a thousand years ago. I am not an immortal being. I have only one life. I want to live it and . . ."

"Shackles," Delphie said. "Yes. You feel shackled by the past and your connection to events that have nothing to do with you."

At this truth, Nelson gasped a breath. He sucked in another breath. Nodding, he let out the air.

"I think you'll find that almost everyone in this room understands how you feel," Delphie said. She nodded to Perses. "He didn't ask to be born into a barely formed world. He was assigned his first wife. She ..."

Delphie gestured to Cleo the cat, who was standing on the table in front of Perses.

"You've known," Heather said.

"Who else could she be?" Delphie asked. "She's always been welcome in my home and will be for as long as she wants or needs to be here."

"Thank you," Perses said.

Cleo picked her way across the table and slipped onto Delphie's lap.

"Everyone here has made their own choice," Delphie said. "Some, like Heather, have taken on their parents' burden to save their parents and the world. Others, like Jacob, have taken on the responsibility and transmuted it into something that will benefit everyone who works there."

"I rejected mine completely," Aden said. "Sandy walks a line between caring for her father and creating her own life."

"I can love my mother in my heart, because she sacrificed her life for me," Sandy said, in a low tone. "From my birth to her death, she did it for me. As yours did. That has to matter. I try to live my life to its fullest in reflection of her sacrifice. As do you."

Sandy and Nelson's eyes caught. Nelson nodded at this shared truth.

"I change my mind on a daily basis," Valerie said, when Nelson looked up again. "Some days, I am working to be here in Denver and live the life my mother couldn't live. Other days, I'm out doing my own thing — achieving, becoming, growing my own way."

"You asked what the treasure is," Delphie said looking at Nelson. All eyes turned to her. "Right now, the 'treasure' is this question — who am I? You've learned tonight that you have an ancient ancestor who is a direct descendant of Gilfand. Your ancestor took up an anvil and a hammer to become a blacksmith. Your family has continued in this tradition."

"Your mother's family have always been scholars," Delphie said. "She was a promising PhD scientist. Your father is, as well. You are a mixture of them and became a medical doctor and a forensic scientist. You will always feel the pull between your need to beat metal and your desire to understand. The scholar; the blacksmith — your treasure is to decide what you wish to do with it."

"Is there an actual treasure?" Pierre asked.

Delphie shook her head.

"What does that mean?" Nelson's voice rose with desperation.

"You don't get it," Delphie said. "This is the problem with orders such as the Templars. They get so focused on gold and jewels that they miss the real treasures available in this temporal, short life. Would you give up your new life for a few trinkets?"

"But there are trinkets?" Pierre asked.

Delphie raised her hands in frustration, and Pierre laughed. Delphie shook his head, and Pierre blew her a kiss.

"What is in this 'treasure' that you want so badly?" Abi asked, in a soft, low tone. "You expect us to believe that jewels, gold, paintings, books . . . anything material . . . is a *treasure* to you?"

Pierre's head jerked up to look at Abi. With their look, the entire room could see the treasure Pierre longed for — his wife, Nelson's mother. She was wearing a white chemise that was nearly see-through. Barefoot and her hair free, she looked like a free spirit of the 1970s. She smiled at her son. Pierre's eyes flicked to the apparition. Nelson fell into his chair.

"You may speak," Jacob said.

"You?" Pierre looked at Jacob.

Jacob pointed to Blane. Blane held one hand to his mouth and another hand open.

"You may speak," Delphie said.

For a long moment, Pierre just looked at his beloved.

"I don't know what to say," Pierre said to Delphie.

"Ask her about this treasure," Delphie said. "What is it? Should you find it?"

The apparition leaned down and held out her hand. Pierre held out his hand to her.

"What is it, my love?" the apparition said in Blane's voice.

"The Order has ordered our son to find the treasure," Pierre said. "This is the only way they will leave him alone."

The apparition gave a slight shake of her head.

"Of course, they do," the apparition said.

"My father, yours, are dead, and they still . . ." Pierre dared not take his eyes off her, or she would disappear again.

"Yes, I am aware," the apparition said, quickly.

"This treasure could . . ." Pierre said.

"Treasure!" the apparition said. "You know how many people have died in service of this treasure?"

"I do," Pierre said.

"What is the treasure, Mom?" Nelson asked.

"Oh child — what did Bernard love most?" the apparition asked.

"Power," Pierre said.

"Gold, jewels, finery," Nelson said.

"What would he put in his treasury?" the apparition asked.

"The bodies of those who knew where it was," Delphie said softly.

Horrified, everyone turned to look at Delphie. The apparition nodded in agreement.

"What do I do?" Pierre asked.

The apparition simply smiled at him. Pierre began to cry.

"Are these the things you value most, son?" the apparition asked. "Money, power, jewels, silence, secrets?"

"No," Nelson said.

"Then this is no treasure for you," the apparition said. She turned to Blane, "Let's let them think for a while."

Blane closed his hand, and the apparition disappeared.

"Why do you cry?" Sandy asked Pierre in a kind voice.

"We had this plan," Pierre said. He looked up to the spot where the apparition had been. "Once we were away safely, we were going to tell the British Museum or possibly the Museum of Antiquities about the treasure and where we thought it might be. The treasure would be revealed to the world as the order wanted. The order would not have access to the treasure. We would be free."

"Why does the order want this treasure so badly?" Aden asked.

"They want to expand," Pierre said. "They feel that this is a time when the world would be receptive to them again. The decline of the Catholic Church makes it less dangerous for them. The call against Islam and Islamic countries gives credence to their mission. They believe that, with the proper funding, they could take back Jerusalem."

Shocked, everyone turned to look at Pierre. He held up his hands as if he were being accused.

"It is not *my* plan, nor that of my beloveds," Pierre said.

"No one ran that shit by me," Nelson said. He crossed his arms. "There's no way I would participate in that shit."

"They said there is only one other way in which they will leave you alone," Pierre said.

"And that is?" Sam asked.

"If he breeds with Olympia," Pierre said, nodding to Heather.

Heather blushed, and Blane scowled. Everyone else looked disgusted.

"Now I am a prized heifer?" Nelson asked. Shaking his head, he repeated vehemently, "No. This is stupid. No."

"We should find this treasure and give it to the museums," Sam said.

"Do you know where it might be?" Abi asked.

Nodding, Pierre grunted.

"Has it occurred to anyone that the swords you hold in your home are worth more than any treasure trove?" Blane asked. "I assume you will receive the others when the police are done."

"It is my position in the order," Pierre said.

"They are trying to finance a war," Jacob said. "You need to get rid of what you have."

Pierre looked up at Jacob. He didn't say anything. He simply blinked.

"It would mean truly leaving the order," Delphie said.

Pierre nodded, looking down at his teacup.

"You asked me about the future of the order," Delphie said. "I will tell you this, Pierre Semaines."

Pierre looked up at her.

"You do this thing — give or sell the swords to museums, find the dragon's hoard, and turn it over to be studied by museums, participate in real academic research into the order — you will do something no one else has been able to do," Delphie said.

She paused to catch her breath.

"Which is?" Nelson asked.

"You will bring an end to the order," Delphie said. "You should know that now, before you start on this road, because you will need allies to make it happen."

"Who?" Pierre asked. "You're an Oracle. Your kind has advised many a general. Who would I need on my side to bring about the end of the Templars?"

Delphie looked up at Pierre. After a long moment, she shook her head.

"No one," Delphie said. "Everyone. I don't know them to tell you one person over another. But I will say that many involved are, right now, wishing the end of this order. No one dares come forward, for fear of death."

"How do I find out who?" Pierre asked.

"You can bring me a photo," Delphie said with a shrug. "Sometimes that works. But . . ."

Delphie's eyes flicked to Nelson.

"What?" Nelson asked. "Just say it."

"The bravest way would be to have your son publicly say that he will not participate in the order," Delphie said. "The biggest way to do that is to, as Blane and Jacob suggested, sell or give the swords to a museum."

Clearly conflicted, Pierre looked away.

"You don't want that," Delphie said.

"I don't want my son to risk his life," Pierre said.

"My life is already on the line," Nelson said.

Pierre looked at Nelson. After a moment, he nodded. Pierre's shoulders dropped with the weight of the gravity of this situation.

"Then, what is it?" Delphie asked.

"These weapons . . ." Pierre said. "Ancient. Deadly. So dangerous. I have felt as if I were saving the world from them. Now, you're telling me to let them out into the world, where they could . . ."

Pierre shook his head.

"Think about it," Delphie said. "Your elder sister is on a plane to Denver right now. She would like to speak with you in private."

"Really?" Pierre asked.

"She brought the swords in her collection with her," Delphie said. "She will be here by the time you leave for work."

Delphie looked at Nelson.

"You should go with him," Delphie said.

"I'll call Ava to see if I can have the day off," Nelson said.

Delphie nodded as if something had been decided. The room held the heavy energy of fate and expectation. They finished their dessert and slowly made their way to their apartments. With Sam clearing the last of the dishes, Jacob was filling the dishwasher, while Blane cleaned up the kitchen.

"You okay? All of that takes a lot out of you," Jeraine said. He hadn't said anything through the entire event. Delphie looked up at him and nodded. "Why don't I help you back to your apartment?"

"I'd like that," Delphie said. "Thanks."

Jeraine helped Delphie to her feet. With his arm around her, he led her to her apartment.

YOU ARE NO FUN!

Monday evening — 8:40 p.m.

"You guys okay here?" Tanesha asked.

She was standing at the door to the basement room that they used as a study room. Charlie, Tink, Nash, Teddy, and Noelle had picked their favorite spots. Ivy slid in under Tanesha's arm and took her place next to Noelle.

"We're fine," Nash said in a bored tone.

"We need to finish this up," Teddy said, more brightly.

Not a fool, Tanesha knew that there was something going on. Her suspicions were confirmed when Katy slid into the room with her big chapter book. Tanesha scowled at Katy.

"I have to finish my reading," Katy said.

She held up her book and gave Tanesha a big grin. Charlie slid over on the couch, and Katy went to sit next to him.

"Are you coming?" Fin's irritated voice came from the meditation room next door.

Tanesha scowled in his direction.

"I can feel it when you scowl," Fin said. "You can always use your magic for this."

"I need to go," Tanesha said. She pointed at the teenagers. "Whatever you're up to, just know that I know that you're up to something. And . . ."

"We're just studying!" Noelle said. "Gaah! We go to school. You know that we go to school. We have *work* to do in school!"

Tanesha took a breath and then sighed.

"If you run into trouble, we're just next door," Tanesha said.

She grinned at the children and closed the door. She stood at the door for a moment to hear if they would start to talk. Remembering that Katy was there, she shook her head and went into the meditation room. Fin was sprawled out on the meditation mat. The electric kettle clicked off. Tanesha made tea in mugs. She gave him his Irish Breakfast, seven sugar cubes, and sat cross-legged next to him.

"You ready?" Tanesha asked taking out her flash cards.

"How do you get those made so fast?" Fin asked.

"I did them this afternoon while you were playing Prince and looking for sweets on campus," Tanesha said. "Applying yourself to the task — you should try it."

"Then when would I play Prince?" Fin said.

Tanesha grinned at him. He glanced over at her and gave a big laugh.

"Did you figure out what they were up to?" Fin asked.

"No," Tanesha said. She shook her head and sighed, "I guess I have to trust that they are good kids and . . ."

"Trust?" Fin asked. "Bah. Why not use your magic to listen in?"

Tanesha held up the flash cards.

"Well, I already have," Fin said.

"You already have what?" Tanesha asked.

"Listened in," Fin said.

"How?" Tanesha asked. "You're not a time walker."

"This is true," Fin said. "They spoke of it as soon as you left from behind the door."

"What are they doing?" Tanesha asked.

"They are wrapping up final details for that military team to go to Poland," Fin said.

He wiggled his eyebrows.

"Fun!" Fin said. "Why aren't we going?"

"Because . . ." Tanesha held up her thick stack of cards.

Fin snapped his fingers, and sparks flew.

"You're funny," Tanesha said. "There you're going to be, standing in front of one of your precious children, and they are dying. You're going to be like — *What was that thing I should know but I cheated?*"

Tanesha gave him a hard look, and he acquiesced.

"I am a role model for my people," Fin said.

"Sure," Tanesha said, with a grin.

Their heads turned to the wall when they heard the teenagers next door laugh.

"Should we . . .?" Fin asked.

"Nah, let's leave them to their secrets," Tanesha said.

"I couldn't agree with you more," Fin said.

"Okay," Tanesha said. "Statistics for Scientists . . ."

"Oh, Gods. This class is going to kill me," Fin said.

"Why?" Tanesha asked.

"Numbers?" Fin asked. "Fairies don't do numbers."

"Because you're cheaters," Tanesha said in a chiding tone. "And anyway, we found out about the cooking thing. No one taught you to cook, so you don't know how."

Tanesha waved her cards in his face.

"Here's some teaching for you," Tanesha said. "You can learn."

He pointed at her.

"Exactly right," Fin said with a laugh. "I will learn."

"Be the wannabe-King we know you to be," Tanesha said.

Fin groaned and lay back to stare at the ceiling. Tanesha started going through her cards by herself. After a few minutes, he sat up.

"You're right," he said.

"I know I'm right," Tanesha said. She gave him half of the pack of cards. "Here — you quiz me."

He picked up a card and read one side. He turned it over to see the back.

"What is a percentage?" Fin asked.

Pretending to be him, Tanesha groaned, put the back of her hand to her forehead, and fell back.

"This will kill me," Tanesha said. "Numbers — why are you so mean to me?"

Fin snorted a laugh. The more she hammed it up, the more he laughed.

"Ah, fuck it," Tanesha said.

"Yes, my dear, let's get to work," Fin said.

He made a whip with a lightning bolt of magic.

"That better not be for me," Tanesha said.

Fin laughed. Tanesha shook her head.

"I cannot believe that I actually *missed* you this summer," Tanesha said.

"I am thoroughly charming, aren't I?" Fin asked.

Tanesha laughed, which caused him to laugh. When their laughter died down, they just looked at each other.

"I am so lucky to have a granddaughter who is leading our people into the modern world," Fin said. "Many fairies are jealous of this assistance."

"And my cookies," Tanesha said, wryly.

"That goes without saying," Fin asked. "Say, how is it that no other fairies besides myself and my siblings can enter the Castle or the Castle grounds?"

"The house got sick of them being around," Tanesha said.

"The house?" Fin asked raising his eyebrows.

"That is what I was told," Tanesha said.

"By whom?" Fin asked.

"Delphie, the home's owner," Tanesha said.

"Huh," Fin said. "She'd know. Why can Abi and I come here?"

"Abi can go where she likes," Tanesha said. "You should know that. Gilfand, as well."

"Me? Edie?" Fin asked.

"You are considered family," Tanesha said. "Your sisters, as well. Mari will be here tomorrow."

"Good," Fin said. "That is very good. No more annoying fairy envoys."

"Vying for your cakes and cookies," Tanesha added to his statement.

"Very true," Fin said. "I make no measure to hide that. Now . . ."

He nodded to the flashcards.

"Carry on," Tanesha said.

They settled down to work.

~~~~~~~~~

Monday evening — 8:45 p.m.

"Finally," Noelle said when Tanesha closed the door.

The kids laughed.

"What are you doing here, freak?" Nash asked.

"You need my help, jerk-face," Katy said.

"Whoa," Teddy said. "When did you start calling Katy 'freak' and she calling you 'jerk-face'?"

Nash and Katy turned to look at him.

"He started it," Katy said.

"That is not very nice," Teddy said to Nash.

Nash shook his head.

"He's just mad because Nadia lives so far away," Noelle said.

The kids looked at Nash, and he shrugged.

"Leave me alone," Nash said with a sneer.

Katy ran across the room and hugged him. The other kids got up to hug him as well. They stayed up for a few minutes before falling over. They laughed.

When Nash finally got free, he pointed to Katy.

"Why are you here?" Nash asked.

"You can't make a plan without me," Katy said.

"I can, too," Nash said with a sneer.

"You need me to tell you where the booby traps are," Katy said very slowly, as if she were talking to her younger brothers.

Nash swallowed hard. He sneered at Katy.

"You know, Nadia misses you, too," Katy said. "You could say that it's harder for her because she's so beautiful. There are lots of men who want to be her beloved. She wants you."

Nash blinked at the six-year-old girl.

"Sometimes, you really freak me out," Nash said.

"Good," Katy said with a grin. "Now, let's get to work."

Tink pulled the country map from her backpack. Nash and Teddy set up their computers. Charlie got out the topographical map for the region.

"Don't we think that Auntie Alex will have all this worked out?" Ivy asked.

"She doesn't have me," Katy said with a nod. She pointed to Ivy. "Or you."

Ivy's hand instinctively went to her chest in a gesture of "Me?"

"Are you ready to stop pretending?" Katy asked.

The other kids watched the interaction with intense interest. Ivy looked terrified. She looked around the room.

"It's just us, Ivy," Charlie said. "Why would you be afraid to be yourself around us?"

Ivy looked at him for a long moment.

"Okay, Pan," Ivy said.

"Come sit by me," Tink said.

Ivy crossed the room. Tink made space on the couch for the small girl.

"Ready now?" Nash said, with a return of his irritability.

"Go through it," Charlie said. "Start at the beginning."

Nash nodded to Teddy. He got up and went to the board to explain the plane. For the next half hour, no one said anything. When Teddy stopped talking, he looked at Katy.

"Well?" Teddy asked.

"Let's get to work," Katy said.

"She scares the fuck out of me," Nash said under his breath.

Katy grinned at him.

~~~~~~~~~

Tuesday afternoon — 3:45 p.m.

"So, you'll never believe what Zeus said!" Ares said.

Nelson looked up from Mari's sword, the "Princess Blade." Nelson had been working on the blade when Ares showed up. Nelson was standing next to his wide worktable under the big hood.

"He did not believe that we could travel so far in such a short time," Ares said.

"He was in the Sea of Amber for a few centuries," Nelson said, looking back down at the blade.

Ares tipped his head back and laughed. He looked around the shop.

"This is amazing," Ares said. "In my day, smithies were brutal disgusting places."

He took a breath.

"How do you keep it so clear of gasses and dust?" Ares asked.

"That's a vent hood," Nelson said, pointing to the black hood over his work table. "It draws air from the room and through the hood. There's a dedicated chimney over the forge, but this one takes care of the rest. It has heavy environmental pads on it to cover the smell of the smithy inside and outside. I get the pads cleaned every month or so, depending on how much I use it. There's an air monitoring system in the corner that I check once a month to make sure the particulates aren't too high."

"Vent hood." Ares said the words and shook his head.

The God of War looked up at the large black metal hood that took up most of the center of the garage's ceiling.

"Put your hand under it," Nelson asked.

Ares gave him a distrusting look but complied.

"I can feel the air flow!" Ares giggled with glee.

Nelson grinned. Ares gave him a saucy look.

"No. I've told you this before," Nelson said. "I'm not going to have sex with my new partner's wife's grandfather. That would be just wrong."

"But I am Ares, the God of War," he said.

"You're a nut case," Nelson said under his breath. He gestured to the sword. "Now if you don't mind . . ."

"What is wrong with the blade?" Ares asked.

"The sword itself is true to form and holds a point," Nelson said. "So, technically, there is nothing 'wrong' with the blade."

"Then, what?" Ares asked.

"This jewel keeps falling off," Nelson said. "I've done everything I can think of to reattach it. It says for a while and then falls off."

"Have you cleared the magic from it?" Ares asked. "It *is* a fairy blade. It's possible that the magic is crimped at that location."

"I've done what I can, so far," Nelson said. "In the middle of the night, I realized that I hadn't checked the leveling at this spot. That's what I'm checking right now. What would you do to clear off the magic?"

As if to keep safe, the Great Ares pulled his hands into himself and lifted a corner of his lip.

"It *is* a fairy blade," Ares said with a sniff. "Ask them."

Nelson chuckled. He set the blade down and went to a metal cabinet. His head was in the cabinet when he heard someone open the door to the garage. He scowled at Ares, who regularly forgot to close or lock doors. Nelson grabbed a soft cloth from the stack of them and his smallest level.

When he turned, a woman he'd never seen before was moving into the smithy. Ares was looking at the newcomer in the way a lion looks at a lamb ready for the slaughter. His clear delight at having a new human to destroy was written all over his face.

"Is there something I can do for you?" Nelson asked.

"Guy?" the woman asked, in heavily accented French. "You must be Guy because you look . . ."

"I go by 'Nelson,'" he said. "Who are you?"

"I am your aunt," the woman said. "Your father's sister, Martine. Your aunt."

Remembering that some relative from the order was due in Denver, Nelson raised an eyebrow at her. He gauged her to be a few years older than his father. Her hair was cut short. She was a few inches shorter than Nelson but had a strong, wiry look. Her eyes were ice blue.

"What can I do for you?" Nelson asked.

He picked up the sword. She opened her mouth and then gasped.

"Is that?" Martine asked. "The 'Fairy Princess.'"

Nelson looked down at the blade.

"And if it is?" Nelson asked.

"It's . . . legendary," Martine's strong hand went to her chest. "I . . . It's so beautiful. Incredible detailing. My God — the 'Fairy Princess' actually exists!"

As if she couldn't stop herself, she reached out for the sword.

"*Don't touch*!" Nelson said, quickly rotating the blade away from her.

Her hand brushed the hilt of the sword, and Nelson groaned.

Mari appeared. She was wearing her modern full fairy armor. She was holding a traditional long bow with an arrow ready and pointed at Martine's head.

"You touched my sword," Mari said.

Martine gasped and jumped back. Mari checked the room for intruders. When she got to him, Ares gave her a little wave. She shook her head at him and stashed her bow. She sneered at Martine and went to Nelson.

"Is this human bothering you?" Mari asked.

"She appears to be a relative," Nelson said with a shrug.

Mari whipped a long, curved blade from her belt.

"I'll gut her for you," Mari said.

"Whoa, Mari!" Nelson said. "Take it down a few notches."

Mari mouthed the words and looked at him in confusion.

"We've talked about this," Nelson said.

"Sorry. I forgot," Mari said, and tucked the blade away.

She held her hand out.

"Princess Marigold of Queen Fand's Queendom," Mari said. "Isle of Man."

"A fairy?" Martine gasped and stepped back.

"Oh, *now*, you have to let me gut her," Mari said.

Nelson tapped the blade against the table. A high-pitched, bell-like sound rang from the blade. Martine stopped moving. Ares started laughing hysterically. Mari looked at Nelson.

"I have no idea why she's here," Nelson said.

With her knife out, Mari walked around the woman.

"She wishes to kill you," Mari said. "Some business about the 'order.' Why don't you let me . . .?"

"No," Nelson said.

"You are no fun," Mari said.

"Says one who doesn't ever clean up her messes," Nelson said.

Mari looked a little guilty but nodded.

Nelson pointed to Ares and demanded, "Stop it."

"The little fairy is hilarious!" Ares said.

Mari sniffed at the god. Nelson stopped the blade from ringing. Mari was putting her blade back when Martine took a breath.

"What just happened?" Martine said.

"Nothing," Nelson said.

"You consort with fairies?" Martine asked.

Ares stepped forward and held out his hand in the manner that Blane and Nelson had taught him.

"Hi," he said. "I am Ares."

Martine looked at the god's hand and looked terrified. Nelson scowled at this Martine.

"You may as well shake his hand," Nelson said. "He won't eat you."

"Not yet," Ares said.

Mari laughed.

"He's just learning his modern social cues," Nelson said. He punched Ares in the shoulder to get him to stop laughing. "Just shake his hand."

To her credit, Martine shook Ares' hand.

"Why are you here?" Nelson asked. He set the Fairy Princess on the table. He nodded to Mari. "Princess Mari says that you are here to kill me."

Martine took a step back.

"Why would you wish to kill a total stranger?" Nelson asked. "A relative, no less."

"It's the order," Martine said mildly. "It must continue."

Ares and Mari groaned in unison. Nelson raised an eyebrow to them.

"You really should . . ." Mari started.

"No," Nelson said.

"What does the tiny fairy wish to do?" Martine said with a sniff.

"Don't antagonize her," Nelson said. "She's ruthless by nature."

Martine gave Mari an assessing look and fell silent. Nelson went back to look at the blade. Martine nodded to the sword.

"That yours?" Martine asked.

"I *am* a fairy princess," Mari said. "Use your keen mind to work that out?"

"It's said to have mythic properties," Martine said.

"That sword?" Ares asked.

He walked over to the sword and looked at it. He shook his head.

"There are a lot stronger blades," Ares said.

"Oh, and I guess *you're* an expert," Martine said.

"He's the Greek god of war," Nelson said, mildly.

Martine's eyebrows shot up in surprise. She instinctively took a step backward.

"He has seen and reviewed every sword and weapon, at least once," Nelson said. "How does this blade compare to others?"

Nelson held up the sword.

"It's powerful, but..." Ares said with an appraising nod. "Woman's blade and..."

Nelson gave the sword to Mari. Her hand went to the grip. The sword emanated a bright, hot light. The air became stifling. Nelson's clothing started to smoke. The overhead vent increased a notch for the increase in noxious chemicals released by the light.

Nelson grabbed the sword back from Mari. The light ended and the room descended into darkness. It took everyone a moment to adjust.

"Well, that's a different matter," Ares said. "Isn't it? Is that a property of the blade?"

"It was made for Princess Mari by our family on contract for a semi-deity," Nelson said. "She's not sure that he even knew that he had that gift. Although, we've looked up the record, and it appears he was fairly ruthless."

Nelson looked at Martine.

"He was killed by Shiva before they could wed," Nelson said.

Martine blinked at Nelson.

"Yes, *that* Shiva," Nelson said. "Now, you're here to kill me? How were you planning to do that?"

Mari and Ares started laughing.

CHAPTER FIVE HUNDRED & FIFTY-TWO

DREAM A LITTLE DREAM . . .

Tuesday afternoon — 3:45 p.m.

Sitting in the passenger seat of a Lipson Construction truck, Rodney looked over at Jacob and then back to the road. Jacob had arrived at the job site just after one. He'd goofed around, played big man, and then asked Rodney if he would be willing to take a drive with him. There was something Jacob wanted Rodney's take on.

Rodney had jumped at the chance. With all of the weird stuff going on — and, really — when wasn't there? — Rodney hadn't had time to discuss his idea of starting a place to help the men released from their marijuana sentences. He was never going to get a better chance to talk to Jacob than now.

Rodney looked out the window.

They'd been driving for more than forty-five minutes. He hadn't said a word. Every time he tried to speak, he felt a well of innate shame.

This was a wealthy young man.

He was just . . .

Then his logical mind kicked in. Because of his wrongful-incarceration settlement, he actually had a lot more money than Jacob.

More than that, Rodney had everything he'd ever wanted in his life. Who did he think he was to . . .?

Rodney stopped the thought.

"Who did he think he was . . .?" was the theme song of his own inner jail. He could spend days in a loop of this thought. He'd given up years of his life thinking that this was "wisdom."

"Rodney Smith was a free man— in thought, mind, and deed."

Pressing his head against the cool glass of the passenger window, he repeated his mantra in his head.

He felt like a child.

Why the hell couldn't he talk to this young man? The worst he could do is say "No." Then, like he'd practiced with Tanesha, he would ask Jacob if he could help connect him to people who could make this happen.

One way or another, Rodney Smith was going to make this a reality for himself and his community.

That's what Tanesha told him to think. Yvonne had just given him her soft, loving look.

"You'll know what to do when it's time," Yvonne said, softly. "You always do."

Rodney sighed. Yvonne was really the best thing in his life. To gather his courage, he spent a half hour or so thinking about Yvonne.

He glanced at Jacob.

No matter the logic, Rodney couldn't get the words out.

"Wasn't," he corrected his inner diatribe. He *wasn't* getting his words out.

He nodded to his reflection in the window. He wanted to beat his hand against the passenger window, and he would have!

But then he'd actually have to tell Jacob what was going on with him.

As if Jacob could hear Rodney's thoughts, Jacob looked over at Rodney. All Rodney could do was smile at the young man and continue to grumble at himself inside.

Jacob pulled the truck off the highway. They drove along a frontage road for a mile or so.

For the first time this trip, Rodney wondered where they were going. He searched his memory for any project — past or present — that had been done in this area. He couldn't think of anything.

Truth be told, Rodney reasoned with himself, Jacob probably wanted him to look at a job. After the mess with the state, Lipson Construction had grown financially strong. They were taking — and winning! — bids from all over the state.

This was probably just another job.

Jacob turned off on a dirt road and drove to a gate. He gave Rodney the key. Rodney unlocked and opened the gate. He closed the gate after Jacob came through. Walking to lock the gate, Rodney looked around for the first time.

They were in the near mountains, not far from town. He glanced up the road. It seemed to go up a slight depression. A few hundred feet from there, the road disappeared.

The air was brisk and clean. It was beautiful in that dry Colorado way. Stands of trees clung to the mountains. There were scar marks from some large construction site that had been here at some point.

Rodney looked at the highway they'd gotten off of.

Probably from building that highway.

For the first time, Rodney actually wondered why Jacob had asked him here.

He locked the gate and jogged back to the truck. Getting in, he held out the key to Jacob.

"Why don't you hold onto it?" Jacob asked. "You can help us get out of here."

Rodney nodded. Jacob gave Rodney a grin.

"You're waiting for me to ask you what we're doing," Rodney stated. He rolled his eyes at himself and laughed. "What the hell are we doing out here?"

"I thought you'd never ask," Jacob said.

In pure Jacob fashion, the young man didn't say anything else. They drove up the slightly steep road a bit. At the top, the road headed down into a wide . . .

Rodney wasn't sure what.

"What is this?" Rodney asked.

"That's a good question, my friend," Jacob said, with a grin.

"Tanesha told you," Rodney said.

"Tanesha, Jill, Sandy, Heather, Blane . . ." Jacob looked off into the distance. "I believe I heard from Fin and . . ."

Jacob nodded.

"That's a lot of people," Rodney said.

Jacob gave him a broad smile.

"But that doesn't answer the question," Rodney said.

"Yvonne asked me if I would keep my eye out for property where you could build a place to help reintroduce some young men to the world," Jacob said.

"She did, did she?" Rodney asked with a scowl and a sniff.

Feeling hypocritically betrayed, Rodney scowled. He glanced at Jacob, and Jacob laughed at him. Rodney couldn't help but grin.

"I picked out five or six places from the listings," Jacob said. "We spent a couple of weeks looking at places all over the state. This was her favorite."

"*Her* favorite," Rodney said.

Jacob didn't say anything for a moment.

"And how the hell did she do that while she was supposed to be rehabbing that knee?" Rodney asked.

"This was before she hurt her knee," Jacob said. "Before the Marlowe Mine."

Rodney didn't say anything for a long moment.

"You've been talking about this for a couple of years," Jacob said mildly. "We've been looking for about three months."

Jacob looked at Rodney.

"Want to take a look?" Jacob asked.

"It's pretty far from town," Rodney said.

"There's a bus stop at the highway where we got off," Jacob said. "The buses run up and down I-25. We can also run a shuttle into town, if we need to. One thing..."

Rodney turned to look at Jacob.

"There's going to be a lot of work that needs to be done around here," Jacob said. "We have to assume that these men won't know how to do anything. So, they will be trained in a skill while they help us get this place together. Just that will take up most of their work time for the next year or so. By the time this place is cleaned up and ready to go..."

"Wait," Rodney said.

"You said 'they,'" Rodney said.

"I did," Jacob said.

"Who is 'they'?" Rodney asked.

"Your charity took possession of five young men about a week ago," Jacob said.

"What men?" Rodney asked.

"The top five from the list you keep in your wallet," Jacob said.

"My ... what?" Rodney's hand went to his chest. "Did you say something about a charity?"

"You know — the one Tanesha and her mom set up?" Jacob asked with a grin.

"Tanesha and her mother..." Rodney sounded out each syllable. "You're serious."

Jacob nodded.

"Come on," Jacob said. "I'll show you."

Rodney's eyes scanned Jacob's face. Jacob pointed ahead.

"Yvonne's waiting for you," Jacob said.

"Yvie?" Rodney asked. "But I ..."

He shook his head.

"I knew there was something screwy with that new job of hers," Rodney said.

Jacob smiled.

"She's really excited about it," Jacob said. "If you don't like the site or decide that you don't want to do it, I'm okay with that. We'll head back to Denver and either pick a different location or . . ."

Rodney took a breath. He paused and then took another.

"Who owns this land?" Rodney asked.

"Uh," Jacob said.

"Yvonne," Rodney said. He squinted. "That big check? It wasn't to secure her knee surgery, was it?"

"Down payment on the land," Jacob said. "And really, the land is owned by your charity. Dad and I helped to secure the loan. You know, used our — what do you call it?"

"Whiteness?" Rodney asked.

"Privilege?" Jacob said.

"Like I said, 'whiteness,'" Rodney said. His words were hard, but he was smiling. "What is that great smell?"

"Cedar fire," Jacob said. "One of the men found a wild pig caught in the fence. It was too injured to survive so they are smoking it. They watched some videos on YouTube and are making bacon, too."

"Caught in the fence?" Rodney asked.

"You can imagine it was a tense moment," Jacob said.

Rodney nodded.

"Who . . .?" Rodney asked.

"We have a small staff here," Jacob said. "Most of them came with the place, but . . ."

Rodney looked at Jacob. Jacob's dad, Sam Lipson, pulled up next to them. Sam waved at Rodney and drove on.

"Dad's been here," Jacob said.

"I was wondering what he'd been up to," Rodney said mildly. "He was so happy and positive, ready to start that business on the Navajo Reservation."

"Why don't we take a look?" Jacob asked. "You'll feel better."

Rodney grunted.

Grinning, Jacob put the truck in gear. They went over the rise. The road became just two ruts in the mud for the tires. They drove past a falling down barn and a more modern shed. On one side was a kind of bunkhouse or maybe a hotel with what looked like ten single rooms.

The doors faced the outside. On the porch, there were a variety of boxes and chairs for people to sit on.

"This place is a dump," Rodney said.

Jacob looked over at him. Rodney was grinning from ear to ear. They pulled up to a large hall or, possibly, an old church.

"What was this place?" Rodney asked.

"It's been a lot of different things," Jacob said. "Most recently, the owners were trying to make it a dude ranch, but they got in over their heads. The former owners have stayed on to help get this up and running."

A hippy-looking middle-aged man and woman came out of the hall and waved at them.

"Why would they . . ." Rodney started to ask.

"They love the spot," Jacob said. "They've invested every penny they had into this property simply because they loved it. They were happy to see it used in some 'good' way. Plus, they're flat broke. The sale paid off the loan, but they . . ."

Jacob nodded to Rodney.

"They need a new start as well," Jacob said. "The wife's mother is the cook. Their youngest child will be the cleaner. Everyone's excited and on-board."

Rodney looked at the couple for a long moment.

"They are stoners," Rodney said.

"Exactly," Jacob said. "Incensed by the drug laws."

"They going to smoke here?" Rodney asked.

His voice rose with anxiety. His head started to spin.

This! His dream! It was spinning out of . . .

Yvonne stepped out of the building. That woman only ever made him smile. He gave her the same stupid grin he'd given her since they were children. She waved for him to come inside.

"To answer your question," Jacob said, "they've agreed to stay on to see how it goes. If they are uncomfortable or need to be high, they've agreed to leave. They love this place more than they love weed. Or so they said. And, like I said, they need a fresh start, too."

Rodney nodded.

"Jury's out," Jacob said. "This was an old meeting hall. Quakers. It's *beautiful* inside. Simple. Strong. Profound. There's a kind of stillness . . ."

Jacob nodded his head.

"Honey's already filed the paperwork for it to be on the historic register," Jacob said.

"Honey's good with paperwork," Rodney nodded. "Wait, I've been signing a lot of papers for . . . She said that they were insurance papers for Yvonne's knee."

Jacob nodded.

"I was buying this place," Rodney said.

"Honey is good at paperwork," Jacob said. "Ready?"

"It's going too fast!" Rodney said.

"Life does," Jacob said. "Don't you have some saying about that?"

"Life goes by fast," Rodney said, by rote. "You can either sit on the bank of the river or just jump in and see where it takes you. Either way, the journey will be over soon enough. That's kind of my life mantra."

"Yeah," Jacob said. "That's it. Good mantra."

They sat in the truck for at least another full minute. Jacob looked up to see Yvonne shaking her head and scowling at them.

"The truth is that it's a stupid idea. Really dumb," Jacob said. "I mean — *look* at this place! These men! Those hippies! Us! What do we know about doing this kind of work? Exactly nothing."

Rodney's head jerked to look at Jacob.

"I think it's going to work!" Jacob said.

Sighing, Rodney started to get out of the truck.

"What if we fail spectacularly?" Rodney asked.

"We'll bulldoze the entire place and build some houses or apartments," Jacob said. "This gives us a chance to hold on to the land until we see how far the city is going to grow."

Rodney nodded.

"What if it succeeds?" Rodney asked, almost to himself, but he really *was* hoping to get an answer.

"Then we'll advertise the hell out of it," Jacob said. "Put the plans online. Let other people around the country see it. These men might have marijuana offenses, but there are lots of people who get out of prison and have no idea what to do with their lives or how to live them. When all these pot-offense people have moved on, we'll still have stadiums full of citizens who could use a place to learn to live."

Rodney didn't say anything. Jacob nodded his head to Yvonne. She was just starting out across the uneven mud toward them.

"Don't make her walk across this mud with that knee," Jacob said. "I'll never hear the end of it."

"Oh!" Rodney jumped out of the truck to meet Yvonne.

Jacob sat in the truck for a few minutes to let them talk. Yvonne waved to Jacob, and they all went inside the hall.

Chapter Five hundred & Fifty-three

Tuesday afternoon —4:15 p.m.

Sitting in the tile-lined, cold hallway, Jill looked up at the clock and then at her advisor's door. Her advisor was late.

Jill sighed. She'd felt out of sorts and spacy all day. She had to check everything at least twice.

Katy was at school. The boys were at school. Jacob was . . .

Her phone "dinged" to indicate she'd received a text. Yvonne had been sending out mass texts of photos of Rodney and his new project. Jill smiled at an image of Rodney and Sam standing inside a Roll-Off dumpster. They were up to their elbows in the destruction of the day — plaster, trash, old clothing, appliances, and what Jacob called "unusable construction crap." The men were filthy. They looked incredibly happy.

Glancing at the clock again, she slipped the phone into her purse.

A thought struck her out of the blue.

Her pulse quickened.

What if I'm pregnant?

She loved kids, but the boys were such a handful. Katy was at such a precarious age. Half of the time, she was just a little girl. The other half, she was more Titan than anything else. Jill was pretty sure that Katy would just be an adult if Jill would let her — which she would not. The children she had right now needed as much as she could give.

Of course, she would have the child, but the pressure of having another child — how could they handle that? And, Jacob was just taking his "gap" year — which was turning into him going around with his dad and starting businesses for other people.

Another child would just be . . .

Reality hit.

She'd had her period last week. There was no way she was pregnant. Plus, she was on birth control.

Why was she so spacy today?

The door opened. A red-faced, weeping woman rushed out of the office. Jill's heart went out to the poor woman. When she caught the woman's face, Jill realized that she knew her from those big military parties at Katy's best friend, Paddie's, house.

"Jill?" her advisor asked. "You can come on in."

Jill picked up her purse and her school satchel. The advisor stepped back. Jill shuffled sideways to get into the small office. Her advisor was a smallish woman with blond-grey hair up in an easy knot. She wore what Tanesha called "the middle-income uniform" — black boots, a straight skirt, some kind of plain shirt, with a lovely floral silk scarf.

"I'm sorry about that," her advisor said. "Her husband is in the military. He was just killed in Iraq. She's not sure she'll be able to stay in school. It's so sad because school has really been the thing that has carried her through her husband's deployment. Now, she'll have to give it up."

As her advisor slid into her chair at her desk, Jill's heart clenched for the poor woman.

"It's a crazy thing," her advisor said. "She needs only a few thousand dollars — three, I think. But . . ."

Jill set her bag and her book satchel down.

"I'm sorry. I probably shouldn't have said all of that," her advisor said.

"I'm glad to know," Jill said. "What an awful thing!"

"So many people don't even remember we're at war," her advisor sighed.

Jill nodded.

"So." Her advisor took a breath and smiled at Jill. "This is a little happier appointment."

Jill nodded.

"You've done well in school, Jill." Her advisor pulled Jill's file out of a stack on her desk. "You've met all of your basic requirements. It's time to declare your major and move forward into your profession."

"I want to be an interior designer," Jill said.

"Of course," her advisor said. "I remembered that. But I like to talk to every student at this moment. It's good to be clear and focus on what you want. At the same time, life is long. You may want to take a minor or a more general major so that you can have a broader base. Twenty years from now, you might need another skill and would draw on those skills."

"Oh, I see," Jill said. "If I focus in on just interior design, I might limit myself in the future."

"Exactly," her advisor said. "You're already good at interior design, Jill. You and your husband rehabbed a friend of mine's home. It was stunning. Truly beautiful."

Her advisor caught Jill's eyes.

"Why not learn something you don't do as well?" her advisor asked. "Going to college is such a great honor. It's unlikely that you'll take this kind of time later in life to just learn. These last two years are a great chance to dive deeply into other topics. I've seen it really change lives — maybe not at first, but later, as your passion for your career matures."

"Why not...?" Jill asked. She stumbled a bit in her mind. "Well, I don't..."

Jill's eyes caught the date on the "Quote-a-Day" calendar on the advisor's desk.

"Is that the date?" Jill asked.

The advisor looked concerned for Jill. She nodded.

Jill felt the ground come up under her. Her feet were on solid ground again. She was steady again.

Trevor had been killed three years ago tonight.

Ha. That's what was wrong with me!

"I'm sorry," Jill said. "You must think that I'm a complete nut. I've been really spacy today, and I couldn't figure out why."

The advisor silently tracked her words.

"My ex-husband was killed on this date," Jill said.

"I'm so sorry," the advisor said.

"It's a mixed bag, really," Jill said. "I would never be here if he were still living. I mean, you don't want to celebrate in anyone's death."

"I understand," the advisor said.

"So, what would you recommend that I spend time studying?" Jill asked.

"Oh."The advisor dug around on her desk for a moment. "Good question. I always think that people should study something near their profession but a little off from it. That way, you would know enough to lead a team of people who do this or start a business on your own. For you, that would be . . ."

The advisor turned her attention to her desk. For a moment, Jill simply stared at the date. She smiled at herself.

Somehow, some way, she was living her dream life.

The advisor came up with the catalog and set it on top of other things. For the next ten minutes, they went through possibilities for Jill to either minor in or possibly major. The advisor thought manufacturing would be good, but Jill couldn't imagine anything more boring.

Looking at the catalog this way, on this day, Jill saw that she had every possibility open to her. Instinctively, her eyes followed the path of the grieving widow.

"So, you have some things to think about," the advisor said.

"When do I have to decide?" Jill asked.

"You need to declare a major this quarter," the advisor said. "But we can always change it."

The advisor looked at Jill and nodded.

"But?" Jill asked.

"Well," the advisor sighed. "Taking some time *now* will help you for the rest of your time here."

The advisor gave an impish shrug.

"That's all," the advisor said.

"Absolutely," Jill said. "Thank you."

Jill got up from the advisor's desk.

"When you know, let me know," the advisor said. "I wouldn't take too long, though. The term starts next week."

"Let's schedule for next Monday," Jill said. "That will give me a week to think about it, go over it with my friends and husband."

The advisor beamed.

"Good," the advisor said. "That's really good!"

They made an early Monday morning appointment. Jill left the small office. Outside the door, she passed the next student, waiting in the hallway. The student shot Jill a hard look, as if Jill were the reason the advisor was late. Jill smiled at the other student and continued down the hallway. She walked down to the payment office.

There was no one at the front desk. The smell of brewing coffee was coming from somewhere in the back.

"Hello?" Jill said in a loud voice.

"I'll be right there," the clerk said from somewhere in the back.

Jill took out her credit card. For a moment, she simply tapped it on the counter. Her heart of hearts told her that, no matter how long it took them to pay it off, Jacob would agree with this.

Plus, she thought it was a great way to celebrate the bittersweet passing of Trevor Guinsey.

"May I help you?" the clerk asked.

"I wanted to pay off the tuition for . . ." Jill said.

She gave the name of the woman whose husband had been killed.

~~~~~~~~~

Tuesday afternoon —5:05 p.m.

Standing in his living room, Nelson poured an inch of whiskey into a tumbler. He gave it to his father.

This was one of the things they'd practiced when Nelson was a child. If his father drank the whiskey, even just a sip, there was nothing to worry about. If Pierre set the drink down, Nelson should be on guard.

Pierre nodded to Nelson but set the drink down.

"Whiskey?" Nelson asked his aunt. "This is made right here in Denver."

Martine nodded to Nelson. He poured an inch of the amber liquid into a tumbler and gave it to her.

"You are not drinking?" Martine asked.

"I don't drink," Nelson said. "I never really developed a taste for alcohol. Blane is sober, so it's pretty easy."

"Blane?" Martine asked. She looked at Pierre. "Do we know this Blane's family?"

Pierre gave Martine a vague look before nodding. He glanced at Nelson to see the angry set of his son's eyebrows.

"He is the consort of Hedone," Pierre said.

Martine's eyebrows rose in surprise. She took a drink of her whiskey.

"Father to her children," Pierre continued.

"I had heard that Eros found his Psyche." Martine looked at Pierre and then at Nelson. "He gave his assignment to his daughter."

Because his father's drink sat untouched, and only because of that, Nelson didn't respond.

"You have nothing to say?" Martine asked.

"Are you asking something?" Pierre asked.

Martine didn't respond for a moment.

"Why are you here?" Pierre asked.

"I came to drop off the swords," Martine said.

"And to kill my son," Pierre said.

"Those were my orders," Martine said. She gave Pierre a vague smile. "It appears that he is well protected."

She took a fast step toward Nelson, and Mari appeared in front of him. Mari sneered at Martine. This time, Martine stood her ground. After a moment, Martine sighed and turned away from Nelson.

"Yes, the little fairy," Martine said. Switching to French, she said, "You consort with fairies, Pierre?"

"My son has many friends," Pierre said, mildly, in French. "Some of them are my friends. Some I've just met."

Pierre nodded to Mari. She gave him a wide, beautiful smile that sent sparkles around the room.

"Have you ever wondered why there is a ban on fairies?" Mari asked in French. "Why do the Templars hate fairy-kind?"

"They've met them?" Nelson asked mildly.

Mari laughed, and Nelson chuckled.

"I was serious," Mari said. She looked at Pierre. "Why is there a ban on fairies?"

No one replied.

"They are not creatures of God," Martine said finally.

"How would you know?" Mari asked. "Fairy-kind was here long before your order or Bernard or even Olympia. We were here long before humankind crawled her way out of Africa."

Martine looked uncomfortable. She glanced at Pierre. He shrugged.

"She is correct," Nelson said. "I've run her DNA. It's similar to a part of the backbone of human DNA, which makes them likely to be an ancient ancestor. At least, the line of Fand."

"Your Bernard kept a fairy consort," Mari said.

"How dare you!" Martine said.

Mari shook her head.

"Why are we wasting time on this person?" Mari asked.

"She came to kill my son," Pierre said. "If she's unable to accomplish this task, they will send another."

"Who will fail," Mari said.

Mari walked toward Martine until she stood just inches in front of Martine.

"Why do you wish to kill your kinsman?" Mari asked.

"I . . . Uh . . ." Martine said. "The order must continue."

"Why?" Mari asked. "There were thousands and thousands of years of human existence before there was an order. There will be thousands and thousands of human existence after the order has ended."

Pierre looked at Mari and then at Martine.

"Who are you to determine what is of God?" Pierre asked. His voice was hard. He stood up. "I am the head of the family now. I am the head of the order now. Isn't that up to me?"

Martine turned her cool eyes to him.

"My orders should supersede any order you received," Pierre said.

Nelson and Mari shifted in such a way that they were a little behind Pierre.

"And what are your orders?" Martine asked.

"I have ordered the entire armory shipped to the United States," Pierre said. "To me."

"I've brought what we have," Martine said.

"You're funny," Pierre said.

He nodded to Mari. The fairy just grinned. Martine's mouth dropped open.

"You didn't," Martine said with disgust.

"We have everything from the armory in France and England," Pierre said. "Including the lesser work you brought. In spite of the efforts to go around us, we will take possession of the swords in New Mexico, my father's sword, and the rest."

"Our father," Martine spit at Pierre. "He was killed . . ."

"Attempting to murder my son, his family, and his friends," Pierre said.

"They are all dead," Martine said. "Have you bothered to ask yourself 'Why?'"

Martine gestured to Nelson.

"This abomination . . ." Martine started.

"They were killed because two Navajo gods wished it," Pierre said. "Or at least that is what I was told."

Martine gave him a dark look.

"And you know this . . .?" Martine asked.

"I was informed by Perses," Pierre said.

"The Titan?" Martine asked.

Pierre nodded. Martine looked to Nelson and then to Mari for confirmation.

"It's my understanding that the French government has discovered the oversight which has granted the order possession of the Templar land," Pierre said. "I was notified this morning that they demand that the land to be returned to France. I have agreed to comply. You will be allowed to live out your life in your home. Upon your death, your farm and land will go to France."

"And our father's home?" Martine asked in horror. "The head of the order's home?"

"France has already filed for possession," Pierre said.

Martine sputtered.

"You should also be aware that the protection from our father's sword has been broken," Pierre said. "New evidence has come to light that you made and planted the bomb that maimed me and killed Nelson's mother."

Martine turned in place and started toward the door.

"They will be waiting for you when you land," Pierre said. "If you stay here long enough, the Denver Police will come to get you."

Martine stopped at the door. She turned to look at them again.

"You must know that it wasn't personal, Pierre," Martine said. "We didn't know about the child and . . ."

"It was personal to *me*," Nelson said.

He opened his mouth to say more, but nothing came out. Martine looked him. Pierre held out his hand. Nelson walked into his father's arms. Martine watched them for a moment and left Nelson's home. Mari watched Nelson and Pierre for a moment before disappearing.

Pierre and Nelson hugged each other for a long moment. Pierre gave Nelson a hard kiss on the cheek before letting him go. They were just separating when they heard someone come to the door.

"Hello?" a woman's voice called from the front door. "Nelson?"

Recognizing the voice, Nelson grinned at Pierre.

"You'll never believe it," Nelson said. He called toward the door, "Coming."

He jogged down a few steps to the entry of his home. Honey Lipson-Scully was sitting outside the front door. Maggie was on her lap.

"Oh, Nelson," Honey said, with relief in her voice. She saw Pierre and said, "Mr. Semaines."

Pierre looked at Honey and then back at Nelson.

"You remember Honey, don't you, Dad?" Nelson asked. "She's married to Michael Junior. He goes by 'M.J.' now."

"Really?" Pierre asked. His eyes asked Nelson the obvious question.

"We've worked it out," Nelson said with a nod.

Glancing at his son, Pierre knelt down to Honey.

"Who do we have here?" Pierre asked.

"This is Maggie," Honey said. She looked at Nelson. "I'm so sorry, Nelson, but Maggie is sick. She has been asking for you. I wondered if you'd mind keeping an eye on her. She has strep. Is that okay?"

Nelson picked up the little girl from Honey's lap. Red faced with fever, Maggie looked at Nelson and then at Pierre. Her large blue eyes blinked at Pierre.

"My father," Nelson said softly to Maggie.

The girl smiled at Pierre before collapsing into Nelson.

"It's strep," Honey repeated.

"That's okay," Nelson said. "Is M.J. traveling?"

"He's here," Honey said. "But I have that doctor's appointment. You know, the one we talked about?"

Nelson gave Honey a quick nod.

"Heather's on school pickup today," Honey said. "She said that she could take her if . . ."

"Maggie is welcome here," Nelson said.

Pierre silently watched his son's face.

"I assume that, if Maggie, is sick then . . ." Nelson said.

"Yes," Honey said. "The rest of the Wild Bunch are sick, too. Val and Mike are taking them to the pediatrician."

"They are welcome here, too," Nelson said.

"Oh, good to know," Honey said. "Only Jabari isn't sick. Maybe. That child is so hardy that you never know if he's sick or not."

"The doctor will sort it out," Nelson said.

"Let's hope so," Honey said. "I just . . . You're sure you don't mind?"

"Not at all," Nelson said.

"Thanks," Honey said.

She turned in place to go.

"Good luck," Nelson said.

Rather than respond, Honey sighed and started out the door.

"You've really connected with . . ." Pierre said.

"Let's just say that you're not the only person I had to forgive," Nelson said.

"Oh, yeah?" Pierre asked with a chuckle.

Nelson looked at his father for a long moment.

"Once I forgave myself, it was all pretty easy," Nelson said.

Pierre hugged Nelson. After a moment, Maggie made a sound.

"You're squishing me," Maggie said in a hoarse voice.

"Yes, I am," Pierre said. He rubbed his hands together. "It's been a while since I had a sick infant to care for. Do you have popsicles?"

"I'm not an inf'nt," Maggie said. "I'm Maggie."

Completely charmed, Pierre grinned.

"Why don't you get comfortable?" Pierre asked. "I'll set everything up?"

He gave Nelson such a big smile that Nelson dropped an eyebrow in "What?" Grinning, Pierre shrugged. Nelson went to the couch and sat down. He closed his eyes for a moment and opened them.

"It's really a great life," Nelson said softly.

CHAPTER FIVE HUNDRED & FIFTY-FOUR
ONE WRONG STEP

Tuesday evening — 6:10 p.m.

"Come on, you guys," Sandy said from the door of their apartment. "It's time for dinner."

"What are we having?" Noelle asked as she walked toward Sandy.

"Stew," Sandy said. "I made a couple loaves of bread to go with it. There's a cake for when Honey comes back from her doctor appointment."

"That's today?" Noelle asked.

"Right now," Sandy said with a nod.

"Salad?" Noelle asked.

"I think so," Sandy said. "There usually is."

Noelle nodded and moved out of the apartment. Sandy looked down at the basket by the door. The house rule was to leave your cellphone at the door when you entered the apartment. The kids spent so much time on their phones that, if they didn't leave them here, they'd never sleep, eat, or do almost anything else. Sandy flipped through the phones that were there.

Her phone, Noelle's, and Charlie's were there. She wasn't sure Charlie's phone ever left this basket.

"Nash!" Sandy yelled. "Teddy!"

Looking like they'd been asleep, they tumbled out of the hallway and into the apartment living room.

"Phones," Sandy said.

She held out the basket. Both boys looked mildly embarrassed. Teddy held out his phone.

"I wanted to keep mine with me," Teddy said. "You know, because my dad's on a trip."

"Your father is on a skiing trip," Sandy said. "To Crested Butte."

She gave him a firm look and shook the phone basket. Grumbling, he put his phone in the basket. Nash started out the door.

"Nash?" Sandy asked.

Nash took off down the hallway.

"You little shit!" Sandy took off after him.

Out of the corner of her eye, she saw Teddy pick up his phone from the basket. Turning ever so slightly, she missed the top step. Her ankle twisted and gave a sharp "pop."

Sandy tumbled down the stairwell.

She hit the hard edge of one wooden stair and then the other.

Her head hit. Her nose mashed. Her back. Her leg.

Down the stairs she went.

Bam, Bam, Bam.

She landed in a crumpled heap at the bottom of the stairs.

Sandy felt completely and totally alone.

How long had she been lying here at the bottom of the stairwell?

A month? A second? She felt the floor underneath her. She wanted to open her eyes. She should open her eyes. But . . . She tried to scream.

"*I'm at the bottom of the stairwell!!*"

No sound came out.

Why had she been coming down this stairwell? She couldn't remember.

And still, no one came in her direction.

No one said a word.

It was as if she were on a planet all by herself.

She heard a sound.

A scream echoed against the walls of the hallway.

Was that her voice? Why couldn't she get up or . . .

She was caught up in the atmosphere of the planet she'd somehow fallen onto.

No one could hear her.

She was utterly and completely alone.

It wasn't much — or anything. Really.

She'd experienced this — exactly this, lots of pain followed by absolute aloneness — over and over again as a child.

Whenever something horrible happened, she was completely alone. It was up to her to deal with what happened, to deal with herself.

Now, it was up to her to survive on this hostile and cold planet. She faded out.

Sandy felt hot, so hot when she awoke.

She felt wet, like wetness was pouring out of her. Why was she so wet?

A cool hand touched her shoulder.

She opened her eyes and looked into a strange woman's face. The woman sort of looked like Tink or that Hecate. She also looked like . . . a goddess. Sandy wasn't sure which one, but this woman was most certainly, at the very least, a goddess.

The woman had long dark, curly hair brushed into gorgeous waves. There was a pure white streak through her hair — not the grey of age, but the purity of white. Her skin was on the dark side of tan, which reminded Sandy of Perses. In fact, almost everything about this woman reminded Sandy of her best friend, Jill's, father, Perses.

The woman was beautiful in the way of a statue or a monument. There was something incredibly hard and permanent about her features, as well as something fragile. When Sandy looked into the woman's eyes, she saw eyes as familiar as her own cat's, Cleo's, eyes.

For some reason — and maybe it wasn't real, after all — she remembered seeing this woman on the lonely planet of her childhood. She felt a well of love for this face, this creature that had been by her side always.

"You have been badly injured," the woman said as she leaned over Sandy. "I am here to hold you while the doctors help."

"Will I survive this?" Sandy asked.

Somehow, Sandy was now standing. The woman was standing just to her right.

"If you wish," the woman said. "If I had my wish, I would say 'yes.' But it's not my gift to give life or death."

"Where am I?" Sandy asked.

"You are with me," the woman said. "This is Delos. It belongs to me."

"Cleo?" Sandy asked.

"Yes, Sandy," the woman said. "I am Asteria, mother of Hecate, wife and cousin to Perses, and your Cleo."

Sandy reached out her hand, and the woman rubbed her face against Sandy's hand. Sandy smiled.

"My body?" Sandy asked.

"You're in the ambulance," the woman said. "Would you like to wake?"

"Can I go to the sea instead?" Sandy asked.

Asteria gave her a soft smile. They were standing on sand the color of a sunflower. The sky was the same warm, yellow sky. In front of them was a warm, yellow sea. Asteria held out her hand, and Sandy took it. They walked to the edge of the sea.

The warm sea lapped against Sandy's ankles.

"This is a favorite place of Hedone's," Asteria said. "It is her power and will that give it this color. When I am stronger, it won't have this color. But for now, she graciously powers this home. It is where she found me before she brought me to you."

"I won't tell her that we came here," Sandy said.

"She knows," Asteria said. "She will be here as soon as she can get away."

"I feel very tired," Sandy said. "If I go to sleep, will I die?"

"No," Asteria said. "I will hold you until you are ready to return."

"But Hecate said you were not strong!" Sandy said. "Oh, Cleo! You are so beloved to me. Please don't injure yourself for me."

"My husband and my daughter have lent me their strength," Asteria said. "Plus, I am my strongest here. Do not worry, Sandy. You and I will be safe here."

"You promise?" Sandy asked.

"You have my solemn promise," Asteria said. "I will not let you down."

Sandy walked across the warm sand until she found a place to lie down. She lay on the sand for only a moment before falling into a sound, but dreamless, sleep.

~~~~~~~~~

"How does this happen?" Aden asked.

Or maybe he *hadn't* asked it out loud. No one turned in his direction.

He'd just walked into the Castle. He was pulling at his tie when . . .

How did it start?

Oh, yeah. It had started with Nash.

He caught the guilty, thrilled look on Nash's face as he ran out of the stairwell, clutching his phone.

"Nash?" Aden had yelled after his son.

He heard the sound.

Was it a grunt or the sound of her ankle breaking? He took two long steps to the stairwell just in time to have his beautiful, precious wife tumble out of the stairwell.

She landed in a heap at his feet.

The sound of a high pitched ring began to chime in his head.

He was in the process of bending down when someone . . .

Could it possibly have been that pompous ass, Fin? That didn't make sense to him!

The fairy moved like a burst of water from a hose. Aden's butt hadn't hit his foot before Tanesha was calling 9-1-1.

Fin flicked open his hands and sparks flew.

Tanesha was yelling at Fin, but Aden couldn't make sense of it. He turned his head to see that Delphie was standing behind him. She pointed to something.

Sandy was bleeding. Blood was pooling fast from her. Badly. From her ankle?

Fin made a kind of bandage with the sparks and wrapped up the wound.

Fin pointed his fingers to the sky and, gently, so gently, Sandy straightened out on her back.

Sound came back to Aden with a jolt.

"Her ankle has a compound fracture," Tanesha said, pointing to the source of the bleeding.

"Nose," Fin said.

"Cheek," Tanesha said.

"Head," Fin said. "Lots of blood from the head."

"You have the light," a voice came from behind them. Aden looked up to see Abi. "Put it on her head."

"How?" Tanesha asked.

"Put one hand on one side of her head and the other on the other side," Abi said. "Your light will help the swelling until . . ."

"Ice," Tanesha said. She pointed to Teddy who came down the stairs. "Get me ice packs."

The boy blinked at Tanesha.

"Go," Tanesha said. "Now."

Tanesha clapped her hands, and Teddy jumped into action like he'd been spanked. Shaking her head at the boy, Tanesha dropped down to Sandy's head. She closed her eyes and put a hand at each side of her friend's head.

Aden saw Sandy's hand was lying right in front of him. He picked it up.

So warm.

So cold.

"Sandy?" he whispered.

There was pounding on the door.

They were so close to the hospitals here that the ambulance was there in less than five minutes. He watched Tanesha update the EMTs. They set to work stabilizing his wife.

His wife.

His beloved Sandy.

The love of his life. The one he had waited for.

Sandy was dying.

Aden felt someone drop down next to him.

Nash.

The boy was still holding that stupid phone in his hand. How many times had they argued over that phone?

Aden looked at his son and then at the phone. Nash swallowed hard.

Aden wanted to be the parent who said: "It was just an accident. It could have happened to anyone. She clearly broke her ankle and fell. She just fell. It happens."

But at this moment, he felt only wrath.

Nash winced at his look.

The EMTs loaded his wife on to a stretcher.

Without giving a second thought to anything or anyone else, Aden walked out to the ambulance with her.

It was a short trip to the hospital.

One minute? Two?

He was running alongside his wife's stretcher. They went through a set of doors and ...

Aden was standing in the waiting area. A financial person waved him over, and he was signing papers and filling out forms.

One form.

What if Sandy dies? Was it possible that she might die?

"Do people die from falls down the stairs?" Aden whispered.

"All the time," the clerk said.

Aden was surprised by the fact that the clerk had answered. He blinked at the clerk.

"Why do you ask?" the clerk asked.

"My wife just fell down the stairs," Aden said.

The clerk swallowed hard and turned his focus to reviewing the papers.

"They'll call you when they know something," the clerk said.

The clerk stood up, so Aden stood up.

"You can wait out there," the clerk said.

Aden nodded. He wandered out to the lobby and sat down.

What just happened?

Aden had no idea.

He dropped his head into his hands. A few minutes later, Blane slipped into the seat next to him. Blane hugged Aden and kissed his cheek. Jeraine sat down on the other side of Aden. Jacob appeared out of nowhere. Jill and Tanesha were there.

"What's happening?" Charlie asked when he and Tink arrived.

Aden shook his head.

"Listen, Nash feels really bad," Charlie said.

"What happened?" Aden asked.

"He wouldn't turn over his phone," Charlie said. "She took off after him and fell."

Aden shook his head. His shock and helplessness turned to rage. He crossed his arms and thought about what he would do to Nash.

"Don't worry," Charlie said with a grin. "Abi zapped his phone. Teddy's, too. She said it was retribution for their selfishness."

Charlie nodded.

Staring straight ahead, Aden didn't have anything to say.

They settled in to wait.

~~~~~~~~~

Tuesday evening — 6:10 p.m.

"Okay, little man," Dr. Bumpy said to Jabari. "You've got to tell me . . ."

"I don't *got* to tell you nothing!" Jabari said.

Heather winced. She'd forgotten how surly Jabari could be. She looked at Dr. Bumpy, and he was grinning at Jabari.

"What?" Jabari asked with a scowl.

"You are so much like my son," Dr. Bumpy said.

Dionne came into the examination room.

"Like *you*, you mean," Dionne said.

Dr. Bumpy grinned. Jabari burst into giggles.

"He's developed a rash," Heather said. "It's hard to tell because his skin is so dark."

Dr. Bumpy looked at Jabari.

"Where is this rash?" Dr. Bumpy asked.

Jabari crossed his arms and shook his head. Dionne picked up the boy. In quick, efficient moves, she stripped him down to his underwear. She pointed at the boy's stomach and bottom.

"You are not my first sick Wilson boy," Dionne said.

Jabari looked at his grandmother with big eyes. He nodded.

"I feel sick," he said in a soft voice.

Dionne swiped a thermometer across the child's forehead and held it out to Dr. Bumpy.

"Well, every one of your friends is sick," Dr. Bumpy said.

"I should take care of them," Jabari said.

"It's okay to be sick," Dr. Bumpy said. "Open your mouth. I want to take a look at your throat."

Jabari opened his mouth. The child allowed Dr. Bumpy to take a look at his throat. Dionne did a quick swab for a strep test and left the room.

"Looks like strep," Dr. Bumpy said.

"And the rash?" Heather asked.

"Scarlet fever," Dr. Bumpy said. "Son, have you been sick like this before and not gotten treated?"

Jabari thought for a moment and then nodded.

"He's probably had a low grade infection for a while," Dr. Bumpy said. "You can put his clothing back on."

Heather nodded and started to dress the young man. Jabari's arms were up in the air, and Heather was holding his shirt, when it hit her like a lightning bolt.

Sandy.

Stairs.

Heather blinked. She needed to go.

Dionne came into the room.

"Heather?" Dionne asked. "Are you all right?"

Heather shook her head and looked at Dionne. The woman nodded to Jabari. Heather put his shirt on and picked him up.

"Something has happened," Heather said. "Can you call the hospital for me?"

"Of course," Dionne said. "What . . .?"

"My friend Sandy," Heather said. "She changed her name to Norsen, but it's Delgado-Norsen."

"I'll call," Dionne said. "I've called in the prescriptions for the children."

"Jabari can't take pills," Heather said. "He just throws them up."

"Family trait," Dionne said. "I got the liquid for all of them. Would you like us to take the children to our home?"

"I . . . uh . . ." Heather said.

She looked out into the waiting room. Valerie and Mike were surrounded by toddlers. Their two children, Jackie and Eddie, were sick. Her children, Mack and Wyn, were ill. Jabari. Rachel Ann was sitting on Ivy's lap. Ivy was sitting next to Valerie. Maggie was . . . *Where was Maggie?*

The door to the doctor's office opened, and Pierre Semaines appeared.

"Honey said that the children were ill," Pierre said. "Maggie is at my son's home. Nelson said that you can bring the rest of the children there. I came to see if I could be of assistance."

"What about that crazy woman who's trying to kill Nelson?" Mike asked, looking up from his son Eddie.

"She is no longer a problem," Pierre said. "Now, how can I help?"

In quick order, with Pierre's help, Valerie and Mike ferried the children into the car.

"I'll tell you what," Dionne said. "Why don't I head to the pharmacy? Where does Nelson live?"

"Right across from the Castle," Heather said. "Have you had a chance to call the hospital?"

"She's just arrived at the Emergency room," Dionne said. "I called someone I know who's on shift today. She said that Sandy needs emergency surgery for her ankle. She said that, somehow, Fin and Tanesha were able to get early intervention."

"What does that mean?" Heather asked.

"There's hope," Dionne said. She put her hand on Heather's arm. "You go. I'll take care of this. I'll stay with Nelson until you're able to pick up the children."

Heather hugged Dionne. She went to the SUV to kiss Mack and Wyn. Her children were sound asleep. Of course.

"Don't worry," Pierre said. "We've got this."

"Thanks," Heather said.

She watched the SUV pull away. She felt torn in two.

She should be with her children! She promised Tanesha that she would help Jabari!

But Sandy!

Heather did something she hadn't done in a thousand years. She teleported herself to the Castle. She noticed that Cleo the cat was sleeping on their bed. Lying down next to the cat, Heather set her body down.

She stepped out as Hedone. She went to Delos to be with her friend.

CHAPTER FIVE HUNDRED & FIFTY-FIVE
A BIG CELEBRATION FOR TWO

Honey rolled into her apartment from the Castle driveway. She knew from the driveway that no one was here. Jacob had called her when they were just leaving the doctor's office.

Sandy was battling for her life at St. Joe's.

Honey understood. She really did.

It's just that tonight was *her* night. It was *her* night to be the center of attention. It was *her* night to share the fancy champagne M.J. had brought home from France. It was *her* night to celebrate.

Honey's procedure was scheduled! She was going to walk again, maybe!

There would be no celebration for Honey. Not tonight, probably not ever.

M.J. had dropped her at home before going to check on Maggie at Nelson's house. He was now heading to the hospital to see if he could help.

Honey had nodded at his suggestion. She'd even made mouth noises that said she was absolutely fine to be alone. She was going to take a bath and go to bed early.

After all, today had been a big day.

She was leaned over the bathtub when a thought came to her.

Sandy would have made her cake long before she fell down the stairs. In fact, Sandy told me this afternoon that it was ready and waiting in a secret hiding place that only Sandy and Honey knew about.

"In case those fairies come back," Sandy had said over the phone. "We want to make sure that you have some cake."

Honey's eyes welled with tears.

"Oh Sandy — I love you," Honey whispered.

Somehow, she knew that Sandy had heard her. She knew what Sandy would say — eat the cake while you can!

"And drink some champagne," Honey said out loud. "To celebrate Sandy's triumphant healing and my new adventure."

Grinning at herself, Honey rolled her way to her little apartment's tiny kitchen. She took a bottle of champagne from the refrigerator and went out into the Castle.

The building was so eerily quiet that Honey almost went back into her warm apartment. She rolled into the main Castle living room. In this light, this room — now empty of all inhabitants — looked every bit the creepy medieval Castle. She was midway through the living room when Abi stepped out of her apartment.

Abi grinned at Honey. With a snap of her fingers, a fire started in the large marble Castle fireplace. Suddenly, the room was bursting with energy and light. It was such a happy greeting that Honey smiled automatically.

"You're not at the hospital?" Honey asked Abi.

"Oh," Abi said. "I set off digital devices on a good day. I love Sandy, so it's likely that I am likely to burn the place down today."

Abi grinned at Honey.

"Plus, I wanted to be here to help you celebrate," Abi said.

"Is Edie here, too?" Honey asked.

"Edie has taken the babies to her home on the Isle of Man," Abi said. "They will be out of mind there, which will allow everyone to heal."

"She took your babies too?" Honey asked.

"Oh no," Abi said. "Zoe and Zaidy are asleep in the room."

Abi gave Honey a knowing grin.

"You must be worried about Maggie," Abi said.

Honey nodded.

"I want to hold onto Maggie, hold her tight," Honey said. "But she's so bright and sparkly. She wants to run and meet everyone. She believes everyone loves her because she loves everyone. She's..."

Honey's eyes became a little misty.

"It's hard on us when they are so independent," Abi said.

Honey nodded.

"I understand there is some cake?" Abi asked.

Honey tipped her head to the side.

"Are you a fiend for sweets, too?" Honey asked.

"A fiend?" Abi asked. "You mean like the fairy envoys? They really did eat a lot of sugary things."

Honey nodded. They fell silent.

"To answer your question, I am not," Abi said. "I wanted to celebrate with you — although, I am not sure that I understand the celebration."

"Let's get some cake first," Honey said. She held up the bottle. "And we have champagne!"

"Sounds like a plan," Abi said.

"M.J. brought it all the way from France!" Honey said. "It was for ... well ..."

Honey's face dropped. She didn't want to feel disappointed, but she did.

"I'm so sorry, Honey," Abi said. "It's only me."

Honey smiled.

"You are enough," Honey said. She smiled. "I can always go hang out with Nelson and a bunch of sick kids."

Abi grinned at Honey, and Honey actually started to feel better.

"Shall I get the cake?" Abi asked.

"What?" Honey asked. "Do you know our secret hiding place?"

"Of course," Abi said.

"But ..." Honey started.

Abi lifted a shoulder and smiled. Honey grinned at her smile.

"I'll get the glasses if you get the cake," Honey said.

"Deal," Abi said.

Honey spun in place and went to the counter. Using her hands, she pressed up on the counter to get glasses from the cabinet. She collapsed back into her chair. When she turned around, Abi was sitting at the table.

The cake was in front of her.

"Hey, that's not fair!" Honey said.

"I would have gotten the glasses too, but you said that you would," Abi grinned. "I did not wish to get in your way."

Shaking her head, Honey wheeled her way back to the table. Abi cut a generous piece for each of them and set them on plates that appeared out of nowhere. Honey struggled with the champagne bottle. She gave it to Abi, who opened it easily. They were soon eating cake and drinking champagne.

"This is lovely," Abi said. "I am so delighted to be here to celebrate with you, dearest Honey."

The cake had white frosting and was white cake on the inside. Sandy had placed raspberries between the layers along with some of the raspberry jam they had made together last summer. The cake was magnificent.

"Do you know — will Sandy survive?" Honey asked.

"I don't see why not," Abi said. "No one can be sure, of course. Life is precarious in even the strongest among us. But Sandy . . . I believe that she will be fine."

Honey nodded her head.

"And Nash?" Honey asked.

"He has some things to learn, as does his friend Teddy," Abi said. "It will be fine. You will see."

Honey nodded and turned her attention to her cake.

"You care a lot," Abi said.

Honey nodded.

"I didn't have much family growing up, certainly not anyone who really cared about me," Honey said. "My mom was always busy with her men. My sister was cruel — evil, really. And . . ."

Honey shrugged.

"This is the best family I've ever known," Honey said. "They cared for me when I was injured. I don't think I would have survived it without Jake and Sam, and then meeting Jill and Sandy and Tanesha and Heather!"

Honey nodded.

"I love M.J., more than I can say," Honey said. "But it's those women — you, Val, and Delphie, included — who make my life work."

Abi smiled at Honey's words.

"Will you explain to me what we are celebrating?" Abi asked. "Please go slowly, as all of this is very new to me. I don't understand it. I didn't understand it when Jacob told me about it."

"Jake told you?" Honey asked.

"He was excited to celebrate with you," Abi said. "I know that he's disappointed not to be here."

Honey's eyes welled with tears, which she swiped away. She smiled at Abi.

"Well, I was injured," Honey said.

"How were you injured?" Abi asked. "I know that I should know this information, but somehow, I do not."

"Oh," Honey said with a nod. "Okay. Um . . . Let's see. Jake and Jill had just gotten together. Valerie had returned from LA and decided she really wanted to be with Mike. Jake had been injured but had healed up. Val wanted to have a party to show off Mike and celebrate her renewed life here in Denver. Jake invited me."

"Of course," Abi said.

"Well, it wasn't as clear then," Honey said. "Jake's dad, Sam, was in the fake marriage with my mother."

"Really?" Abi said, leaning back in her chair to listen.

"Crazy, right?" Honey asked. "He had just ended it. My evil older sister was with Jill's ex-husband."

"The one killed by Perses," Abi said.

"That's the same night," Honey said.

"Oh," Abi said.

"They planned to steal Katy — kidnap her — for some crazy reason or another, I can't remember," Honey said. "But Paddie's auntie and her team — M.J.'s on that team — were here to stop them."

"Sounds like a wild night," Abi said. "Where were you in all of this?"

"I . . ." Honey said. She blushed. "Jake gave me a credit card and told me to get a 'really nice dress.' That's what he told me. So, I did. It was super expensive, but he said he didn't care."

"It was blue . . ." Honey said with a sigh. "My hair was up, and I even put on make-up! I danced with some of the movie stars who were there and some Lipson people. I . . ."

"It sounds wonderful," Abi said.

"It was," Honey said.

"What happened?" Abi asked.

"My sister," Honey said softly. Her emotion welled, and her eyes filled with tears. "She . . ."

Honey pointed to the landing just below the long stairs to Jill and Jacob's loft.

"Right there," Honey said. "She tried to kill me. She almost did, but Jill . . . I would have died . . ."

Honey sighed. She cleared her throat.

"I was in the hospital for a long time," Honey said. "Paralyzed. She'd cut right through my spine. My sister, that is."

"Oh, dear," Abi said. "How awful. I have seen this before. It's a terrible injury."

Honey nodded. She ate some cake to avoid looking at Abi.

"I've been like this since she hurt me," Honey said, looking up at Abi.

Abi nodded.

"About a year ago," Honey said, clearing her throat again. Tears began to fall down her face. "I was invited to join a trial for a promising technique to reconnect my spine. I could walk again!"

Honey smiled at the idea.

"I had to do the work," Honey said. "I had to learn to control my legs again — as much as I could. I had to be sure to make that connection. And I did it! Every day. Oh, it was so hard!"

"What happened today?" Abi asked.

"Today, I met with the doctors," Honey said. "They say that I'm ready to have the procedure done. Since the time that I was admitted to the program, three other people have undergone this treatment, and all three of them can walk again!"

Speaking in a rush of language, Honey continued on.

"I've felt so conflicted," Honey said. "I love the wheelchair community. I haven't really hated being like this. I finally decided that I was going to be like this for life, and, so, I may as well get used to it. So, I invested in the community. Got to know people. And, I mean it took a long time, but I'm okay being wheelchair bound."

"Then this came up . . ." Honey looked at Abi. "It was a hard decision to make, but, now, I really want to walk again. So, I have a chance now. I mean, it's not 100%, but . . . We scheduled a date to start the treatments. I might be able to walk by the end of next year."

Abi's eyebrows dropped with concern.

"What is it?" Honey asked.

"I never knew this was something you wanted," Abi said. "That's all. You've always seemed so . . ."

Honey nodded.

"That's just it," Honey said. "I think that I should want to stay in the chair. But the idea that I could walk again? It's like a dream come true. I mean, M.J. and I would have another child or two and . . . I could truly be over it.

"I mean, this thing happened, and my life turned upside down and I . . ." Honey shook her head. "It probably doesn't make any sense."

"You make great sense," Abi said with a nod. "Would you really want to be 'over' this argument with your sister?"

"What do you mean?" Honey asked.

"Oh, I don't know," Abi said. "In my experience, humans don't really want to 'get over' things. They carry around their pains and resentments for all of their life. Look at this scar — it was his fault. You must know this."

Honey gave a slow nod of her head.

"I know what you mean," Honey said. She took a bite of cake and savored the taste. "This is good cake."

Abi nodded. They ate in silence for a while as each woman sorted through their thoughts.

"Why did you ask about my sister?" Honey asked. "I mean, me."

Honey gave a frustrated shake of her head.

"Why did you ask me about 'getting over' my sister?" Honey asked.

"I can fix this little problem with your spine," Abi said.

Honey scowled at Abi.

"With some fairy magic?" Honey asked.

"I am no fairy," Abi said.

Honey shook her head and sneered.

"I would rather have real science," Honey said with a sniff. "Then some . . . wait — you're not a fairy?"

"I am not," Abi said.

"What are you?" Honey asked. Her hand flew to her mouth. "Oh, sorry. I don't mean to be rude, I . . ."

"It is a fair question, Honey," Abi said. She smiled. "You have heard of the 'First Mother'?"

"The Navajo thing?" Honey asked.

Abi gave a quick nod.

"I know something about it," Honey said. "It doesn't make a lot of sense to me."

"You've heard of an Earth Mother," Abi said.

Honey pointed to Abi, and Abi nodded.

"What does that mean?" Honey asked.

Abi gave her a bright smile.

"I'm sorry — did I offend you?" Honey asked. "My mom always says that I offend people with my stupid questions."

"I think you are wonderfully practical," Abi said. "After all, what does all of that mean?"

Nodding, Honey looked a little relieved.

"I am the Earth," Abi said. "The Earth is me."

Honey leaned forward and whispered, "Really?"

Abi nodded.

"How cool," Honey said. "How come you're . . ."

Honey gestured to Abi.

"I mean, you look so human," Honey said.

"I wish to look like this, so I do," Abi said.

"Were you a dinosaur?" Honey asked, her voice filled with wonder.

Nodding, Abi laughed.

"Wow," Honey said. "I mean . . . wow!"

Abi grinned.

"You are every bit your daughter's mother," Abi said.

"She's so magnificent," Honey blushed. "I'm just . . . well . . ."

Honey thought for a moment and then leaned forward again.

"Will you show me?" Honey whispered.

Abi held up her human hand so that the palm faced Honey. She put her hand onto the table. In a moment, her hand joined the table. Her hand was gone. It now looked like Abi had no hand. Instead her wrist went into the table at a right angle.

"Wow," Honey said.

Abi shook off the table, and her hand returned.

"Have you joined the Earth before?" Honey asked.

"I have," Abi said. "I was here for a long time by myself."

Abi pointed to Honey.

"You will not tell anyone what I tell you," Abi demanded.

"Never," Honey said.

"Gilfand believes we are twins," Abi said.

"You're not?" Honey asked.

Abi shook her head.

"I was so lonely that I wanted to rejoin the Earth," Abi said. "She was molten then. No land. No water. The Earth would not allow me to return. I am separate, so that I can advocate and care for her."

"Do you do that?" Honey asked.

"I do what I can," Abi said with a nod. "I have saved her a few times. I have missed a few more. I was in the Fairy Queendom when the world slipped into danger with this climate change. I missed it. I trusted humans to care about their home. That is my oversight. I can only work now to do what can be done to save the human race. Long after you are gone, I will be here."

Abi nodded. Honey fell silent.

"What would you do to me?" Honey asked.

"I would rearrange your molecules," Abi said. "Your scar, both inside and out, is horizontal, about three inches wide."

Honey nodded.

"I would return you to whole," Abi said. "Your body wishes to be whole. Your body is like the Earth. You are made up of the entire universe. The entire universe strives for wholeness. I will tap into your body's own desire to be whole and return your body to health. But . . ."

"But?" Honey asked.

"It only works if you are ready to let go of this thing with your sister," Abi said. "Give up the burden of this injury. Embrace your wholeness. I cannot fight your human will. You would have to align yourself with your body's and mind's desire for wholeness."

Honey tipped her head to the side and looked at Abi.

"I don't know how," Honey said, emphasizing every word.

"You just let it go," Abi said. "I have to let go of my form to embrace another."

"Shape shifting?" Honey asked.

"It's a kind of shape shifting," Abi said. "Akin to that skill. But instead, we are taking the cells, healing them, and reorganizing them."

"Show me," Honey said. "Fix my hands."

"I cannot until you're ready to change," Abi said.

Abi picked up her fork and took a bite of cake.

"But isn't that what we're celebrating?" Abi asked. "That you are ready to embrace change?"

Honey squinted at Abi for a moment. Then Honey closed her eyes.

"It's too much of a burden to carry," Abi said, in a soft, kind voice. "No one can heal and carry the rage — appropriate or otherwise — at the one who injured them. It's like being pulled in two directions. It is unlivable."

Honey nodded. She sighed.

"I am ready," Honey said. "Can you take the rage from me?"

"No," Abi said. "It doesn't need to be taken from you by magic. You just need to set it down — like luggage set on the side of the road. It's time to set it down. The trick then is not to pick it up again."

"I am willing," Honey said.

"Good," Abi said. She clapped her hands together and gave Honey a bright smile. "Let's get started."

CHAPTER FIVE HUNDRED & FIFTY-SIX

HONEY'S TURN TO HEAL

"Will it hurt?" Honey asked.

"It might," Abi said. "You let me know if it is too much, and I'll stop immediately."

Honey nodded.

"Let's start with your hands, as you suggested," Abi said. "I know that Liban did an excellent job giving you 'more' flexibility, but what if they were whole again?"

"That would be great!" Honey said.

"Good. We'll do one hand at a time. You can stop at any time," Abi said. She gave Honey a warm, reassuring smile. "Now, close your eyes."

"Have you done this before?" Honey asked.

"A few times," Abi said.

Honey wasn't sure if she could ask for examples, so she didn't say anything.

"For a man who was at war for more than 3,000 years, my darling Fin has few physical injuries," Abi said.

"He's a fairy," Honey said with a shrug.

"He cannot use fairy magic to put on an arm or a leg," Abi said with a grin.

Honey nodded.

"I will stop at any time," Abi said. "You say the word, and it's over. You can use your science. Deal?"

"Deal," Honey said. "Can I watch? Ever since I was a child, I've had trouble closing my eyes to people."

"Yes, I see," Abi said. "Hmm . . ."

Abi snapped her fingers, and Honey's head dropped forward as if she were sound asleep. Abi gave a nod.

"Mari," Abi said.

The fairy Mari appeared.

"She has chosen to let me help her," Abi said. "I will need your assistance."

"Of course," Mari said.

Abi grinned at Mari. Abi and Mari had spent thousands of human years trapped in Queen Fand's Queendom. They were fast friends.

"She does not trust fairies," Abi said.

"It's those fairy envoys," Mari said.

"They've really soured these humans to your entire kind," Abi said. "Even to Fin and Edie. I will speak with Fin, but it's something to be aware of and change, if possible."

"Yes, Nelson has made a few remarks as well," Mari nodded.

"I told her that I would work on her hands first," Abi said. "Would you get them for me?"

Mari went to where Honey was sitting. She laid Honey's wrist out onto the table. In attempts to get some movement out of her hands, Honey had had a number of surgeries on her hands. Abi clucked at the scars.

"When you're ready," Mari said.

"Let's start," Abi said.

Abi's hand went over Honey's wrist and arm. Honey's arm became soft, like butter. It swelled to nearly grotesque proportions. Abi pointed her finger to Honey's wrist, where it was closest to her pinky finger. Spinning from some unseen screwdriver, a screw came out of her wrist. And then another. Abi moved down Honey's wrist, clearing it of screws. She pulled a long, thin plate from the hand, which she set on the table next to the ten screws. One at a time, she set them onto the table in front of where Honey was sitting.

"Please stand behind her," Abi said. When Mari moved, she added, "Put your hand on the base of her neck."

"As you wish," Mari said.

Abi turned over Honey's hand so that her palm faced up. Abi placed her hand over Honey's so that the palm of her hand touched the palm of Honey's hand. A minute past and nothing happened. Mari took a breath to say something when Honey's entire hand and arm started to jerk.

Honey's hand and arm pulsed with seizure-like jerks twice more.

Abi took her hand from the palm of Honey's hand. The swelling in Honey's arm dropped immediately. Honey's hand looked completely normal.

"Back away — I'm going to wake her up," Abi said.

Mari nodded and moved to where Honey would not be able to see her.

"Honey?" Abi asked.

Honey opened her eyes and looked at Abi. She blinked.

"You nodded off a bit," Abi said with a soft smile.

"What happened?" Honey asked.

"I used the opportunity to work on your hand and wrist," Abi said. "I took these screws out of your wrist and this metal plate."

Honey turned to look at her hand. She closed her eyes and opened them in disbelief.

"It looks . . . I mean . . ." Honey said. She leaned forward as if to whisper, "Normal."

Honey nodded, and Abi grinned.

"Of course," Abi said. "Try it. Make sure it works."

Honey opened and closed her fingers. Her thumb made and an easy journey into a fist. She rotated her wrist with ease and without any pain. She shook her head in disbelief.

"But the nerves!" Honey said. Her hand moved instinctively to her neck.

"Yes," Abi said. "I woke them up, as well. They had forgotten that they needed to heal," Abi said. "You may have some spasms or fleeting moments of pain. They are rejoicing in the opportunity to function."

Honey nodded. Her hand went to her face. It tried to pick up the fork, but the implement fell through her fingers.

"It may take a while for your hand to regain some strength," Abi said. "I am sorry."

"Who cares?" Honey asked. "Strength will grow!"

Abi grinned at Honey's words but Honey didn't see her. She was too caught up in looking at the movement in her hand.

"Just incredible," Honey said. "Can you do the other one?"

"Of course," Abi said.

"*But . . .*" Honey said. She gave Abi a knowing look. "Can I control when you put me to sleep?"

Abi looked a little embarrassed.

"And, can Mari come out?" Honey asked.

"How did you know?" Mari asked as she moved forward.

"You are wearing the perfume we gave you," Honey said. "The one M.J. got in Africa that smells like limes."

Mari mouthed "Sorry" to Abi. But Abi shrugged.

"We should not have tried to fool you," Abi said.

"I understand why you did," Honey said.

"I am here only to help," Mari said. "I'm not doing anything. At all. Just holding you up."

"Thank you for that," Honey said. "Okay . . ."

She put her other hand up on the counter.

"I'm ready," Honey said.

Abi snapped her fingers, and Honey was asleep again. She leaned forward to look at the hand.

This was clearly Honey's non-dominant hand. Honey had had no surgeries on it. The hand was locked in a fist.

Abi touched Honey's hand with a feather-light touch. The hand naturally opened. Not understanding what was wrong with this hand, Abi shook her head.

"Show me," Abi demanded of the hand and arm.

A red light shone at Honey's elbow. Abi turned Honey's arm over and saw a straight scar. Honey's nerves had been severed. There was nothing any human could have done to help her regain function in this hand. Abi nodded.

"Anything else?" Abi asked.

"There's a light at her neck," Mari said.

Abi got up and walked around to look at Honey's neck. She touched Honey's neck.

"Will you remove her clothing?" Mari asked.

"As you wish," Mari said. With a snap of Mari's fingers, Honey was naked from the waist up.

Both women gasped. Mari's hand instinctively traced the lines of scars and surgeries.

"What are you doing?" M.J. asked from the doorway.

He had a handgun in his hand that was pointed to the ground.

"Honey has asked for my help," Abi said. "She wants to be whole again."

"We've just returned for a meeting that would do that," M.J. said, evenly.

Abi looked at M.J. and returned to look at Honey's back.

"Answer me," M.J. demanded.

"Do you have a question?" Abi asked.

"What are you doing?" M.J. asked.

"I have answered that," Abi said. She walked around Honey again. "Now, you cannot kill me. Mari can be killed, but she comes from a line of warriors who have been at battle for thousands of years. They move like air. You will never see her coming. She will likely kill or maim you before you get a shot off."

Abi looked at M.J. for a brief moment.

"Do put the weapon away before you hurt yourself," Abi said.

M.J. gave Abi a kind of trance-like nod.

"Now, you are welcome to watch," Abi said.

"What are you?" M.J. asked.

Abi sighed with irritation. Mari stepped forward.

"She is the representative of the planet," Mari said. "She is creation and holds the power of the planet."

"Like those cherub things that healed Jacob?" M.J. asked.

"Let's say that they work for her," Mari said.

"At my request," Abi corrected.

Abi touched Honey's back.

"She has asked for help and healing," Abi said. "She is ready to let go of what happened before and move to wholeness. We have already worked on her hand."

Abi gestured to Honey's healed hand. As if transfixed, M.J. moved forward to touch the hand. He held it up to his eyes and scanned the skin.

"The scars!" he whispered in awe.

Mari pointed to the screws and plate.

"You took those out of her?" M.J. asked in the same whisper. He pressed on her palm, and her fingers curled.

His face made a "Wow!" expression.

"You did this?" M.J. asked.

"The weapon?" Abi said.

"Oh, right," M.J. said. He put on the safety and set it on the kitchen counter. "May I watch?"

"You may watch, but do not interfere," Abi said. "I did not realize that she had such an extreme injury."

"She hides it well," M.J. said.

"Jill must be very powerful to keep her here," Abi said.

"Honey's very stubborn," M.J. said. "She'll take the tiniest gift and grow it into a fortune."

"She is amazing," Abi said. "I may need your help holding her up. That is what Princess Mari is here doing."

"Not eating cake?" M.J. asked.

"I was celebrating with Honey," Abi said. "We had cake and some champagne."

M.J. nodded.

"Okay," M.J. said. "I'll do my best."

"That is enough for me," Abi said. "Shall we begin again? This hand should function. There is a scar at her elbow?"

"She broke her elbow when she was a kid," M.J. said. "Or her dad broke her elbow. It got infected. She didn't have insurance, so she was really sick. I took her to the free clinic, and they installed a drain. She took her pills, and I cleaned it every day."

"This makes sense," Abi said. She nodded to the elbow. "There is infection there."

"Oh," M.J. said.

Abi looked up at him.

"She has an underlying infection," M.J. said. "They've never been able to figure out where it is coming from. She takes a lot of antibiotics. Every day. Her biggest fear is that Maggie will get sick. She freaked out when Maggie had a fever."

M.J. nodded.

"What do we do?" M.J. asked quickly.

"You could hold up her elbow," Abi said. "Bend her forward."

Mari bent Honey forward so that her head was on the table. Abi put her hand on the elbow. The skin opened, showing the bone. She ran her hand over the bone. A tiny speck of yellow formed near the bone. It began to grow in size.

"I am picking up pieces of the broken bone," Abi said. "Now, I'll ask them to rearrange themselves into wholeness."

Abi smiled when the elbow became whole.

"These bacteria," Abi said softly. The yellow speck was now the size of a quarter. "Yes. Thank you for your service."

She snapped her fingers, and the yellow disappeared.

"Are they dead?" M.J. asked.

"I sent them home," Abi said. "There's still . . ."

Abi pointed as another yellow pool began to grow.

"Where is it coming from?" M.J. asked.

Abi didn't respond, so M.J. looked at Mari.

"From pockets in her body," Mari said. "She has a lot of metal inside?"

M.J. nodded.

"Holding her back together," M.J. said.

Mari nodded toward Abi. She released another quarter-sized yellow pool. This continued for two or three more rounds. When no yellow appeared, Abi ran her hand over Honey's body.

"I believe it is gone," Abi said. "At the very least, these antibiotics should clear up whatever remains."

"The bacteria will die," Mari said.

"They knew the risks," Abi said, mildly.

Mari and M.J. gave Abi a long look. Clearly, when Abi spoke, the entire world should respond.

"Okay," Abi said. The skin on Honey's elbow reattached. "If you can hold her at the neck."

Abi placed her hand over Honey's. Honey's hand began to seize and jerk.

"What are you doing!?" M.J. asked.

"I am restarting her nerves," Abi said.

"Healing them," Mari said.

"You've seen this before," M.J. said.

"When she gave me back my hand," Mari said.

"Your . . ." M.J. said.

Mari held up her hand and wiggled her fingers.

"We need to wake her," Abi said. "Our agreement was just for her hand. Please back away. It's too much for her to wake to you."

"But!" M.J. said.

"Both of you," Abi said.

Mari touched his arm, and they moved away. Abi woke Honey. Groggy, Honey opened and closed her eyes. Abi saw something and snapped her fingers again.

"Hey!" M.J. said.

Abi pointed. There was a puddle of bacteria on Honey's tongue. Abi snapped her fingers and the bacteria disappeared. She woke Honey again.

"What happened?" Honey asked.

"Your husband came in," Abi said, nodding in M.J.'s direction. "He was concerned."

"M.J.?" Honey asked. Her head rotated so easily and freely that she could only whisper, "Wow."

She glanced at Abi, who smiled, and then she looked for M.J. He leaned down to kiss her. She rotated her head in his direction and he grinned. They kissed.

"How is Sandy?" Honey asked.

"Out of surgery," M.J. said with a nod. "Her head hasn't swollen as much as they thought it might. So, she doesn't need to have the skull surgery. The plastic surgeon is coming to see her for her nose and cheek. She'll have more surgery tomorrow."

"This is great news," Honey said.

"Jill has been with her since she got out of surgery," M.J. said with a nod. "Her dad showed up. You know, O'Malley. He had her moved to a private ICU. You would have laughed. They've been kind, but pretty gruff with us. He showed up and was like, 'This is my daughter!' and suddenly everyone is scraping and bowing."

"Why would that be?" Abi asked.

"He's a big donor to that hospital," M.J. said. "He's donated money for the new hospital and then held a big fundraiser. They were going to name a building after him, but he thinks that's dumb. Maresol brought these wonderful pastries and coffee. They took Charlie and the teens back to their house. Delphie, too."

"Maresol and Delphie are lifelong friends," Honey said.

"Yes, I just learned that," M.J. said with a grin.

"So Sandy is well?" Abi asked.

"As good as can be expected," M.J. said. "There's no guarantee, but it seems like she will heal completely."

"That is wonderful news," Abi said. "Those hospitals are wonderful."

Honey reached up with the first hand Abi had healed. M.J. did something he hadn't been able to do well since they were children. He took her hand.

She giggled.

"Try your other hand," Abi said.

Honey looked down at her hand and blinked.

"It's perfect," Honey said.

She opened and closed her hand. Letting go of M.J.'s hand, she clasped her hands together. She wove her fingers together and held them out in front of her.

"Wow," M.J. said.

Honey simply beamed.

"I apologize that you were out for such a long time," Abi said. "You had a fairly severe infection."

"Yes," Honey said. "They don't know what that's about."

"Your elbow," M.J. said. "Remember when your dad punched you and you fell? Broke it? Got infected?"

Nodding, Honey looked up at him.

"It was still broken there," M.J. said. He nodded to Abi. "She fixed your elbow and cleared out the infection. Try to move your elbow."

Honey slowly bent her elbow so that her hand moved toward her. She then moved her elbow to straighten her arm.

"Wow," Honey said. "That's just amazing."

Abi nodded.

"That is probably enough for one session," Abi said. "Especially the first session. I know that you have to be up early to get to work. Why don't you two take the rest of the champagne and cake? You can see how those hands work a bit in private."

Honey blushed, and M.J. gave her a sly grin. They made polite talk until Abi told them to go.

With the cake on her lap, Honey took one last look at Abi before rolling into her apartment. She felt such overwhelming gratitude for the creature named Abi, who had helped her, *and* for her life. She sighed.

"You okay?" M.J. asked, putting a cork into the champagne.

"Just grateful," Honey said.

M.J. tucked the champagne into their refrigerator. He took the cake from Honey and put it next to the champagne. He pointed to the smaller bathroom, and Honey nodded. He always got ready in the other bathroom to allow Honey to get ready in the bathroom off their bedroom.

She rolled into the bathroom and hefted herself onto the toilet. She marveled at how well her hands worked. When she finished, her now working hands easily flushed the toilet.

Laughing to herself, she brushed her teeth with abandon as her hand could now hold a toothbrush. She went out into the bedroom. Her hands easily worked to undress her and put on her night shirt. She was almost done when she heard M.J. gasp.

"I know!" Honey said. "Look at how great these hands work."

She turned to look at M.J.

"You're standing," M.J. whispered.

Honey looked down at her legs so fast that she almost lost her balance.

"Can you . . .?" M.J. asked. He held out his arms.

Honey easily walked into them. They laughed until they cried.

Chapter Five Hundred & Fifty-seven
Needing Comfort

Wednesday early morning — 1:15 a.m.

Blane looked at his watch.

It was late.

Nelson had said he should come by when he was done at the hospital. And, anyway, Wyn would be up soon and need his bottle.

He winced at his own rationalization.

What he really wanted — needed, maybe — was comfort.

He never got used to how life could change in a moment. One moment Sandy was trying to get the kids to dinner, and the next, she was intubated.

No one besides himself, Fin, and Tanesha knew how close she'd come to dying right there at the bottom of the stairs. They'd seen Abi grab Sandy's soul from the air and push it back into her body.

Fin and Tanesha were fairies.

Blane's new "senses" were newly forming from his work with Abi.

He watched in dumbstruck awe as Abi stepped between the seconds to make this happen. As far as everyone else was concerned, Abi was sitting in the dining room serving dinner.

It's okay to want some comfort.

He would go home to Heather, but he knew that she had stashed Sandy somewhere so that her body could heal. He groaned at himself and put his key int the lock of Nelson's front door. The door swung soundlessly open.

He took one step inside, and Mari the fairy appeared. She held her finger to her lips and gestured. He followed her up to Nelson's living area. The Wild Bunch of toddlers were asleep on the couch and the floor. His son, Mack, was lying on his side with his best friend, Maggie, in front of him. Lying on the couch, Jabari opened his eyes when Blane entered the room. Blane put his hand on the boy's stomach, and the boy went back to sleep.

Nelson's father, Pierre, was sound asleep, leaned back in a recliner. Sandy's daughter, Rachel Ann, was lying against him. Jackie and Ivy were on the other end of the couch.

His son, Wyn, was... Blane didn't see him. He gave Mari a questioning look.

Mari gestured toward the kitchen with her thumb. He followed her into the kitchen.

"What are you doing here?" Blane whispered.

"I'm still protecting Nelson," Mari said.

"If you are protecting him from sick toddlers, you have failed miserably," Blane said with a grin.

Missing his joke, Mari shook her head at Blane.

"His crazy family is still in play," Mari said. "Pierre thinks that he's taken care of it."

Mari shook her head.

"Igh," Blane said. "Where is Wyn?"

"Wyn's with Nelson," Mari said. "We ran out of space out here. Nelson said that Wyn eats in the middle of the night. We didn't want to wake the others."

"He's still pretty little," Blane said.

"He's not that little," Mari said with a pointed shrug.

"Point taken," Blane said.

"There is no biological imperative for humans or fairies to sleep through the night," Mari said. "The little Olympian god is going to be hard to convince that he should do what *you* want him to do."

"He is very sweet," Blane said. "Neither boy is defiant. I've never seen either one of them turn down a request from us. They like to get along with everyone."

"Family trait," Mari grinned.

"Hedone?" Blane nodded.

"Yours," Mari said.

Blane chuckled in earnest. With his laugh, a door opened off the kitchen. Nelson came out carrying Wyn. Nelson's hair was mussy, and he was wearing the flannel pajamas that Heather had given him. Blane held out his arms, and Nelson set Wyn into his arms.

"Da," Wyn said in a croak. "Froat, Da. Hot."

"Poor Wyn," Blane said.

Blane put his son's head on his chest. Wyn pressed his warm body into his father's chest. Blane could smell Nelson's fancy shampoo on his hair. He looked at Nelson.

"You bathed him?" Blane asked.

"All of them," Nelson said. "The little ones went into the bath together. Easy. Drying them off was a trick, but Papa helped."

"Not Mari?" Blane asked.

"She was helping Abi get Honey walking again," Nelson said.

Nelson gave a quick shake of his head, and his eyes went to the ceiling to indicate that he had no idea what that meant. Blane gave an almost imperceptible nod of his head.

"I'm glad you've come," Nelson said.

He reached out to touch Blane's arm.

"I knew Wyn needed his bottle," Blane said.

"Liar," Mari said with a snort.

Shaking her head, she walked out of the kitchen, leaving them looking at each other.

"It's hard to . . ." Blane said.

"Ask for what you need?" Nelson asked.

"To need," Blane said. He sighed. "Anything."

Nelson nodded. He leaned forward and kissed Blane's cheek.

"I'm glad you're here," Nelson said. "What can I do?"

"Hun-gy," Wyn said. "Mommy?"

"She's in Olympia," Blane said.

"'S'okay, Da," Wyn said. "Love you."

Wyn patted Blane's chest. The wise old man faded, and the baby Wyn whimpered. Wyn pressed his face into Blane's chest.

"Val said that she brought . . ." Blane said.

Nelson pulled a bottle of breast milk with a little oatmeal out of the refrigerator. He made quick work of warming it. Wyn took the bottle and settled down in Blane's arms.

"Come on," Nelson said.

He gestured to the room he'd come from. Blane followed him into what turned out to be a small guest room off the kitchen. Nelson sat down with his back against the backboard of the bed. He patted the space in front of him.

"What about Wyn?" Blane asked.

"You can hold him," Nelson said. "I'll hold you."

Nelson shrugged. Blane felt his internal homophobia rise.

What if Wyn saw them? What if his son knew that he was gay?

His self-rage grew.

Why am I like this? God, I'd give a million dollars just to be . . . I can't have what I want. I can't be who I am. I can't. I can't. I can't. And this gorgeous man, who says he loves me wants to help me, and I . . .

As if she were standing next to him, he heard Heather's voice:

"What will happen if your son sees Nelson holding you when you're in pain? Then our son will see love in action. He will know that comfort is available — for him and for you. He will know that his father is loved, that his father loves. I can't imagine anything better for him to see — every day, all the time."

His self-rage drained out of him. He took a breath and then another.

Nelson patted the bed again.

Holding Wyn against him, Blane crawled across the bed until he was sitting near Nelson. Nelson reached out and pulled Blane backward. Blane set Wyn down on the bed between his legs.

"Lean back," Nelson said.

Blane did as he was told. Nelson wrapped his arms around Blane. After a moment, a tear ran down Blane's face.

"What is it?" Nelson asked in a soft voice.

"Just life," Blane said. "So fragile."

"Sandy?" Nelson asked.

"So crazy," Blane said. "Stupid. And she almost... She almost..."

Blane let out a sob. Nelson kissed Blane's cheek. Blane leaned into Nelson. They lay like that until they fell asleep.

Nelson's father tapped on the door at six in the morning. Pierre opened the door.

"Your alarm is going off, and I don't know how to turn it off," Pierre said, in French. "I have tried."

"*Oui, Papa*," Nelson said.

Blane leaned forward so that Nelson could get out.

"I'll take the child," Pierre said continuing in French.

Unsure of what he meant, Blane blinked at him. Pierre held out his hands and leaned over the bed. Blane picked Wyn up from the bed. Blane set Wyn into Pierre's hands.

"Baby Wyn needs a diaper change," Pierre said with a dramatic whiff, indicating that Wyn smelled.

"I'll get..." Blane said

"I would advise you to take a shower while you can," Pierre said. "These babies will need breakfast and medication. They are still very sick. Dionne will be here at seven."

"In English?" Blane asked.

"You will need to learn," Pierre said in English while wagging his finger at Blane. "No love of my son's will be non-French speaking."

Blane grinned at Pierre.

"Go shower," Pierre said. "There is a shower in there. The children are ill and need food. The nurse will be here at seven."

Blane nodded.

"Come on, Wyn," Pierre said. "Let's get you a new diaper."

Pierre gave Blane a nod and pulled the door closed.

"That went well," Blane said to himself.

He went to shower.

~~~~~~~~

Wednesday morning — 6:15 a.m.

For the last several hours, Nash had been staring at the ceiling of Seth O'Malley's den.

He knew that it was his fault that Sandy had fallen down the stairs. No, it was his fault that *she'd nearly died*! He sighed.

How can you love someone and hurt them so badly?

And the way his father had looked at him?

A tear ran down the boy's face.

The last time they'd fought over his phone, his father had told him that if he didn't like their rules, he could go live with his mother. His mother was *dying* to have him come to live with her — and get her hands on child support for him.

He swallowed hard.

He'd argued that Sandy was his mother. His dad had said: "If that's the case, then why don't you follow Sandy's rules? Why don't you trust that she's doing this for your own good?"

Why? Why? Why?

He had no answer to any of the "Why's."

Why hadn't he just left his phone and gone to dinner?

He heard movement in the kitchen. Using his nose, he tried to do what his martial-arts teacher had told him to do — identify the person through his senses.

He had no idea who was there.

He was drawn out of his blankets by the idea that there was someone to keep him from his dark, desperate thoughts. He crept past Teddy, who was sleeping on the floor next to him. A lighter sleeper than even Nash, Noelle opened her eyes and leaned up on her elbows.

Nash put his finger to his lips and whispered, "It's early. Go back to sleep."

"Any news?" Noelle asked.

Nash shook his head. Noelle nodded and lay back on the couch.

"I'll come and get you if I hear anything," Nash said.

Noelle nodded. Nash went past the couch and across the ten feet or so between the den and the kitchen.

No one seemed to be in the kitchen.

He was so disappointed that he nearly cried. Then Delphie stood up. She closed a low cabinet and set the electric teapot on the counter. She lifted the kettle and turned to fill it with water from the filter.

She startled.

"Sorry," Nash said in a low whisper.

His mood continued its plunge.

"I didn't see you. That's all," Delphie said with a smile. "Would you like some tea?"

Nash gave a slow nod. Delphie filled the pot from the filtered-water tap in the sink and turned it on. She took a few quick steps and hugged Nash tightly. Nash gasped a breath, but she held on. After a few minutes, she stepped away. She set out two cups and placed tea bags in them. When the pot clicked off, she poured the water into the cups.

Seth's father, Bernie, appeared with a stained mug that looked like it had been made by a child. He held it out, and Delphie filled it with warm water and a tea bag. He set the mug on the cabinet and took half-and-half from the refrigerator. He set the cream on the counter.

Nash was sure that Bernie hadn't seen him. Certainly, the elderly man had never spoken to him. The man turned to look at Nash.

"You must feel horrible," Bernie said, mildly.

Nodding, Nash had to bite his lip to keep from crying.

"I understand," Bernie said. "I am a man who has always tried my very best. I am also a man who has hurt those who love him the absolute most."

Nash grunted rather than respond, which made Bernie grin.

"Who made your mug?" Nash asked.

"My son," Bernie said.

"Seth?" Nash asked with a laugh.

"Saul," Bernie said, looking at the mug. "He made this when he was three. He was an incredible artist, truly magnificent. If you'd like a real treat, ask Seth or Maresol to show you his paintings. That's his sculpture in the side yard. Don't tell anyone, but his ashes are buried there, too."

Bernie winked at Nash, and Nash nodded at the seriousness of what Bernie had said. Bernie squinted as if in pain.

"Had he lived, I'm sure he would have risen to the level of the masters," Bernie said. He looked at Nash. "War will make corpses of us all."

He touched Nash's shoulder in a kind way that somehow made Nash feel better.

"I love that book," Nash said, referring to the *Lord of the Rings*.

"Book?" Bernie asked. "Most boys your age would just have seen the movie!"

"Sandy wouldn't . . ." Nash sucked in a breath.

"Let's watch it together this afternoon," Bernie said. "Maresol makes the best popcorn. Seth will be playing. Ava's at work. It's a perfect time."

Nash gave him a numb nod.

"Dale and I sometimes dress up when we watch movies," Bernie said. "Dale says that it's very popular among young people now. I think it's a gas! I usually dress up as Gandalf, although last time I dressed up as Wormtongue."

Bernie laughed. Nash looked at the ninety-something-year-old. Bernie took out his tea bag, liberally doctored his tea, set the half-and-half in the refrigerator, and walked out of the room. Nash watched him go. Thinking about Bernie, Nash looked after him.

He startled when he realized that Delphie was standing right in front of him. She grinned.

"Come," Delphie said. "Let's sit in the pool house."

"But it's so cold out!" Nash said.

"Maresol built a solarium off the south side," Delphie said. "It's warm and private. You'll love it."

Nash gave her a numb nod, and she smiled. She gave him a metal tin. He tucked the tin under his arm. They walked across the grass in the bracing cold until they reached the pool house.

The pool house had once been a garage behind Seth O'Malley's stepfather's home. When his stepfather had broken his hip, Seth had this lap pool put into the ground back here. During her remodel, Maresol had added an apartment for Dale on the main floor, remodeled the four upstairs apartments, and added a sun room and greenhouse.

After the frigid cold of the back yard, the air in the pool house was moist and warm. It hit Nash like a wave. For the briefest moment, he felt everything — exhaustion, terror, self-rage, and overwhelm. Then, as he always did, he packed it away. When he looked up, he noticed that Delphie was watching him.

"This way," Delphie said.

She made the little cackle that used to make him laugh when he was a little boy. He managed to stay glum through one cackle, but the second one had him giggling like a five-year-old. She smiled at him. They walked past the pool and down a hall. Dephie gestured to a door.

"That's where Dale's room is," Delphie said with a nod. "It's really nice."

"He showed it to me and Charlie," Nash nodded. "It was really nice of Maresol to make it."

"O'Malley wouldn't have it any other way," Delphie said.

"Oh?" Nash asked. "He said it was all Maresol."

"Of course, he did," Delphie said. "But you know how things really are, don't you Nash?"

The words hit him like a brick wall. He stopped walking.

Truth was that he did know how things really were. He always knew the truth. He could pick it out of the air.

But lately . . .

"Can you get the door?" Delphie asked.

He had to jog to catch up with her. He opened the glass door and followed her into a kind of greenhouse garden. It wasn't very big, but the space was used efficiently. Along one wall, there were vegetables — tomatoes and other summer foods. Some plants he recognized and some he didn't. There were orange, lemon, and lime trees scattered around. The citrus trees were all in bloom.

"Who's the gardener?" Nash asked.

"Me," Delphie said, with a grin. "And Bernie. Maresol helped me set this up. Bernie hadn't had a garden in almost forty years. We tend it together. Now that you know about it, I'm sure you can take a shift."

Nash nodded.

"It sounds like . . ."

"Bees," Delphie said. "Yes, they have access to the plants in here. There's a hive in the wall over there."

"Does it make good honey?" Nash asked.

"Really good," Delphie said with a nod.

"Are there pot plants?" Nash asked.

"In the back," Delphie said. "I don't use it, but Bernie finds it helpful for his aches and pains."

"O'Malley?" Nash asked.

"He hates the stuff," Delphie said.

"That's good, because he's an addict," Nash said.

Nash knew all about addiction and addicts from the classes and groups he and Noelle went to because both of their parents were addicts. Delphie gave Nash a mild look.

"Let's sit over here," Delphie said.

She gestured to a couple of chaise lounges that looked out onto the trees that separated O'Malley's yard from his neighbor's. For the first time, Nash noticed the garden built around the statue on the side yard. He realized that it was a memorial garden to both of Seth's brothers.

"And his mother," Delphie said, finishing his thought.

"O'Malley is a nicer than I would have ever given him credit for," Nash said. "Sweeter."

Delphie nodded. They sat in silence for a minute.

"I can hear something . . ." Nash said.

"Fish," Delphie said. "The vegetables are a kind of aquaponic. There is a fish tank with Tilapia. They live in a big tank at the end. Their water fertilizes the plants."

"Wow," Nash said.

"It's very high tech," Delphie said. "And also something done thousands of years ago."

"Really?" Nash asked.

"Really," Delphie said.

"How's your heart doing?" Nash asked.

"I'm well," Delphie said.

"Any word about those fairy queens?" Nash asked.

Delphie just looked at him.

"That's not really why we're here, is it?" Delphie asked.

"Will you tell me?" Nash asked. "One minute, they are ready to destroy the planet, and the next . . ."

Delphie sighed and just looked at him.

"Please?" Nash asked.

"The four queens are on retreat," Delphie said. "The fourth queen . . ."

"The one Jake rescued?" Nash asked.

"Yes," Delphie said. "She has put a kind of spell on her sisters. They do not remember their queendoms or the world outside."

"Why did she do that?" Nash asked.

"I told her to do it," Delphie said. "Well, I told Abi to tell her to do it. She complied with Abi's order."

"Why?" Nash asked.

"Because the fairy queens were never meant to build their own warring queendoms," Delphie said. "They were to rule together, but they were separated during the shift to a more masculine, patriarchal society. They don't remember this, of course. But I do."

"What will happen to their queendoms?" Nash asked.

"They will unite," Delphie said. "Fin is working on the structure right now. Most fairies are relieved to not be fighting each other anymore. There are still some who have a high sense of their uniqueness."

"Couldn't they just be like states or countries in the EU?" Nash asked.

"That's the hope," Delphie said.

"Who will lead them?" Nash asked.

"Edie," Delphie said. "At least until they are through the transition."

"Edie?" Nash asked. "The baby nanny?"

"Yes," Delphie said with a grin. "She is extremely powerful. She's wise and kind. She wants to have an elected person from every fairy state. Right now, the fairy states are so used to being ruled that they want a queen. It's going to be a journey for them."

Nash nodded.

"Are you ready to talk about something that matters?" Delphie asked.

"Excuse me for caring about the state of fairies!" Nash said in an offended voice.

When she looked at him, she saw that he was smiling. Delphie grinned back.

"Why are Saul's ashes over there?" Nash asked.

"You don't want to talk about . . ." Delphie started.

"Just warming up," Nash said.

Delphie grinned at him, and he shrugged.

"What do you know about Saul?" Delphie asked.

"He was in a concentration camp, and Seth found him," Nash said.

"Mr. Seth?" Delphie asked.

"He told me never to call him that," Nash said. "'If you can't call me 'O'Malley' like everyone else does, then leave it at 'Seth.' That's a direct quote."

"It does sound like him," Delphie said.

Nash nodded. They were silent for a moment before Delphie sighed.

"Saul was Seth's older brother," Delphie said. "You've never had an older brother."

"Charlie?" Nash asked. "But I know what you mean."

"You've met Bernie," Delphie said. "If you took the best of Bernie — his intelligence, wit, crazy courage — and added Seth's mother's good looks and hardy bone structure, you'd get close to

Saul. He was gorgeous to look at *and* had such a beautiful soul. He could light up a room. Any room. When Seth had been at the school for two years, Saul told their stepfather that he was going on a school field trip. He took the train across the country to check on Seth. They spent a riotous week in New York City, before Saul went home. Seth gave him money for his brothers and their mother."

Delphie nodded.

"Saul never touched a penny of that money," Delphie said. "Even though that meant that he needed to get a job to pay for football, his clothing, and anything else he needed. Saul gave the entire sum to their mother. She used it to care for Silas. But Saul wouldn't take a dime."

"Why?" Nash asked.

"He wanted his mother to have it," Delphie said. "Saul didn't mind getting help from Seth. He just knew that his mother has no other way to make money. He was young and strong and . . ."

Delphie sighed.

"That's how he ended up in Special Forces early in the war in Vietnam," Delphie said.

Unable to continue, she nodded.

"What happened to him?" Nash asked.

"It's a good question," Delphie said. "Most aren't sure."

"But you know," Nash said with surety.

"Yes," Delphie said with a sigh. "They told his mother that he was 'lost,' MIA. That's what they told a lot of people, but I was Maresol's good friend."

"You and Maresol go back a long time," Nash said. "Maresol worked here then?"

"As soon as Seth had any money at all, he hired someone to help his mother with this big house," Delphie said. "Maresol was little more than a girl. Her husband had been killed, and she had four children to care for. She leapt at the chance to work here."

Delphie nodded and fell silent.

"What did they tell Seth's mom about Saul?" Nash asked.

"I . . . uh . . . ," Delphie said. "Well, the military told her that he was 'lost.' I will tell you that it nearly killed her to 'lose' him. Day in. Day out. It started to wear her down, so Maresol brought her to me."

"And?" Nash asked.

"For the longest time, Saul was hiding in the jungle," Delphie said. "He was cut off from anyway of getting home. He just endured and survived — nearly a year and then he was picked up."

Delphie nodded and fell silent again.

"You had to tell his mother that?" Nash asked.

"I couldn't," Delphie said. "Seth was out of the Army by then. Mitch, too. His mother had kept this situation from Seth while he was in Vietnam."

"Tunnels of Chi Chui," Nash said.

Delphie nodded.

"When Seth got back, he . . . well, he just did his Seth thing," Delphie said with a chuckle. "He shook hands until he found someone with the connections to help him look for Saul."

"General Hargreaves," Nash said.

"Now, you are not supposed to know that," Delphie said.

"Sensei Colin told me," Nash said with a shrug.

"Seth doesn't talk about what happened or how he found Saul," Delphie said.

"Did you help him?" Nash asked.

"As much as I could," Delphie said. "But he had to do a lot of the groundwork while he was in Vietnam, in the middle of a war. It was dangerously crazy."

Delphie nodded.

"He wasn't able to bring his brother's body back because of the war," Delphie said. "He paid the Buddhist monks to cremate

Saul's body. The military had already put up a grave for Saul at Arlington. So, Seth brought him home."

"So he could have his brother close to him?" Nash asked.

"I don't think Seth ever dreamt that he would live in this house again," Delphie said with a shake of her head. "He brought Saul's ashes here for his mother."

Nash nodded and felt like he understood.

Nash took a breath to ask another question, but Delphie cut him off.

"Would you like to talk about what happened yesterday?" Delphie asked.

Nash swallowed hard and shook his head.

"You mean, 'Would you like to talk about killing the only person in the world who loves you?'" Nash said with a sigh.

"She's not dead," Delphie said.

"If we lived in a normal house with normal people in it, she would be," Nash said.

"If, maybe, might," Delphie said. "Plus, she is not the only person who loves you."

Nash looked at Delphie.

"I know, it's just that . . ." Nash said with a sigh. "I . . . I mean . . . It's all my fault."

He put his hand to his chest and repeated, "My fault."

"Teddy has a bit to do with it, too," Delphie said.

Nash grunted.

"Teddy always wants to do what he's told," Nash said. "He's so . . . good. I . . . He was . . ."

Nash took a breath to try to stop the storm of emotions. Thinking that he was winning, he took another breath and then another. But sorrow overtook him like a tsunami. He began to weep.

Delphie sat with him. She'd sat with him any number of times when his mother had "forgotten" to pick him up. She'd listened to him rant when he'd argued with his father. She'd seen him through the rough nights after their mother had broken Noelle's cheekbone.

She didn't try to soothe him. That's not really what he needed.

She sat with him in the middle of his emotions, showing him that she had great confidence that he would survive these feelings. When he stopped crying, she got up and went into the other room. She returned with a box of tissues and a large glass of water. Nash used the tissues and drank the water. They sat in silence for a while.

"What can you tell me about your phone?" Delphie asked.

"My . . . what?" Nash asked.

"It seems like you and your parents have been arguing over your cell phone," Delphie said. "I wondered if you might talk to me about it."

Nash took the cell phone out of his pocket and held it up to her. The screen was smashed. The plastic was bent. There was a putrid odor coming from it.

"It's fried," Nash said. "Abi did it. I can't even blame her, it's just . . ."

Delphie didn't respond. She knew that Nash needed to talk about this *thing* he carried around, even now that it wasn't working.

"Tell me about it," Delphie said.

Nash's mouth opened and closed. He squinted at her and then shook his head.

"I know my dad says it's *bad*, but what does he know?" Nash asked with a sneer. "He has *no* idea."

"About what?" Delphie asked, keeping her voice neutral.

"About . . ." Nash scowled again.

He looked at Delphie and tried to determine what she wanted him to say so that he could be off the hook.

"What doesn't your father know?" Delphie asked. She put her hand on her heart. "I would be happy to inform him. I'm just not sure what he doesn't know."

She gave him a kind smile.

"What is it that your father has no idea about?" Delphie asked.

"I . . . uh . . . hmm," Nash scowled. He leaned toward Delphie as if someone could hear him. "I'm not normal."

"How so?" Delphie asked.

"I . . ." Nash sighed. "I don't have anyone who really gets me. You know?"

"Hmm," Delphie said.

"I have this weird relationship with Nadia — who, don't get me wrong, is amazing. But . . ." Nash sighed. "I can't even drink, let alone . . . And she's in New York. She's really rich — rich like rich-people-want-to-be-her kind of rich. And I . . ."

Nash lifted a shoulder in a shrug.

"I'm a weirdo," Nash said. "*Unique.*"

"Sounds lonely," Delphie said.

Nash nodded.

"Teddy is my best friend," Nash said. "No question, but he's so . . . sure of himself. He loves Noelle. Noelle loves him. I'm his friend. That's it. He doesn't need anything else."

"And you do?" Delphie asked.

"I want to belong," Nash sighed. "Somewhere. Anywhere."

"Yes, I know what that feels like," Delphie said softly. "Is there a place where you feel like you belong?"

Nash raised the burned-out phone.

"I play games with people all over the world." Nash's voice rose in tempo and delight. A smile broke across his face. "Nadia can call me anytime. I have friends — people who are like me, really get me. They like what I have to say and what I do. I'm enough for them. I don't have to be smarter or richer or older or . . . Just being me is okay — no, *better* than okay. Being me is good."

Nash nodded his head.

"I feel *good* when I'm on it. Really good. Normal, even cool," Nash said. His voice turned hard and he added, "I'm not just the *freak* who goes to the freak school with all of the other freaks."

He held up his phone.

"I'm friends with artists and athletes all over the world," Nash said. "I'm friends with other people who do martial arts, and we talk about martial arts. They really *like* me, cheer me on."

He shook his hand with the phone in it.

"This is the best friend I've ever had," Nash said. "It's always there for me — day and night. If someone's mean to me, I just block them. Trolls. I tell my friends, and no one says, 'What did you do?' They understand that the other person was a troll. There are lots of people who are just like me. They don't live in stupid Denver and aren't stupid fifteen years old."

Delphie didn't say anything.

"Dad just doesn't get it," Nash said.

"Oh, I think your father gets it more than you think," Delphie said.

Nash turned to look at Delphie. He didn't say anything for a moment and then asked, "What do you mean?"

"I'm going to repeat back to you what you said — and you tell me," Delphie said. "Let's pretend your father was saying it."

Nash didn't respond. Delphie raised her eyebrows, and Nash nodded.

"Whiskey is the best friend I've ever had," Delphie said. Nash gasped, and Delphie continued, "It's *always* there for me — day and night. If someone's mean to me, I just block it out. But better than anything, when I go to the bar there are lots of people who are just like me. They don't ask anything of me. I just have to . . ."

"Drink whiskey," Nash whispered along with Delphie.

He gave Delphie a long look.

"I want to say that I'm not addicted," Nash said. "That it doesn't have anything to do with me."

He shook his head.

"I don't do drugs or alcohol," Nash said. "That's Dad's and my stupid mother's *issue*."

"The scientists tell us that we get the same high from these phones and social media that we get from drugs and alcohol," Delphie said. "They are highly addictive."

He held out his burned and reeking phone to her.

"This has never cost me anything," Nash said. "I haven't lost a job or a friendship or custody of my child or . . ."

"And Sandy?" Delphie asked.

Nash didn't respond. He didn't dare look at her.

"Your relationship with your father?" Delphie asked.

"My father is an asshole," Nash said.

Delphie grinned.

"Come on, Nash — you *know* this stuff," Delphie said. "What was the last thing you did with Teddy?"

"Uh," Nash said. "Um . . . He wanted to ride our bikes out to the gully but I was on Snapchat and . . ."

He looked at Delphie for a long moment.

"Shit," he said. "I really love my phone. Love it. I feel like it was the best thing that *ever* happened to me."

"It's not living, Nash," Delphie said. "It's just a *thing*. What you get out of it comes from you and you only. It cannot give back to you."

"That's what Abi said, but she doesn't understand," Nash said. "I mean, how could she? I have *real friends* here."

"Realer than Sandy?" Delphie said, softly.

Nash's mouth dropped open.

"This is how all addicts feel," Delphie said. "They feel lost and alone when their drug — the thing that works — is no longer available or they can't use it. They *love* their drug or alcohol."

Nash looked dumbstruck.

"But it doesn't love them back," Delphie said. "It is a thing that will take your entire life away or that of those you love with all your heart."

"But . . ." Nash started.

His eyes filled with desperation; he looked at Delphie.

"You didn't realize that addicts love their drugs?" Delphie asked.

Nash shook his head.

"Drugs work," Delphie said. "That phone *works* for you. You don't have to figure out how to meet your own needs, find your own confidence, talk to Nadia about how you feel, or even stretch to find what you're good at because . . ."

"It's always there for me," Nash said. "Ready. Willing. Able to fill the gap."

Nash sighed.

"I didn't think it would be like this," Nash said.

"Everyone says that," Delphie said with a nod. "We all think it will be bigger or more consuming — that's why it's so dangerous."

Nash numbly looked away from her.

"You know how the cigarette companies made their cigarettes more attractive to people — right?" Delphie asked.

"They put extra stuff into cigarettes to make them more addictive," Nash said.

"That's what the companies who make the phone and social media and apps do," Delphie said. "They intentionally make it addictive. You know that scroll feature?"

Nash nodded.

"It's the same motion as using a slot machine," Delphie said.

"But what am I going to do?" Nash asked. "I can't . . . I just . . ."

Delphie didn't say anything. She trusted Nash to come up with it himself. He gritted his teeth and looked at her.

"I have now paid a consequence I am unwilling to pay," Nash said.

"Sandy nearly dying so that you could have your phone?" Delphie asked. Her question was hard but her voice was neutral.

Nash nodded.

"I just... I mean..." Nash said softly. "I'm going to miss it so much."

"Well," Delphie said. She leaned over to him and touched his leg. "What will you fill the void with?"

"Fill the..." Nash said. "Oh. Right. The void. I could... uh... I don't know."

"We'll figure it out as we go," Delphie said. "Are you ready to do the work?"

"I'm not willing to hurt someone else that I love," Nash said. "I just won't do it. I won't."

"Even if that person is you?" Delphie asked.

"Me?" Nash asked.

"I know that you and your father talked about you living with your mother," Delphie said. "You told him that you'd rather live with her than lose your phone."

Nash gasped. With her words, he remembered this situation more clearly. He *had* told his father that he would love to live with his crazy, stupid mother if it meant he could keep his phone. Nash let out a breath and started to cry again.

Delphie leaned back in her chair and waited.

Nash had finally realized what was going on. Now the work began. It was okay to feel a little sad about the work you have to do to rebuild your life. It was okay to be sad that you've hurt people, including yourself. She waited a few more minutes, before she cleared her throat.

"Suck it up, buttercup," Delphie said in an imitation of Nash.

Nash gasped and looked at her.

"Isn't that what you usually say to addicts?" Dephie asked. "What else do you say? Something like..."

"No one cares about your regrets," Nash said, his numb voice still thick with tears. "All that matters is what you *do* about it."

Delphie nodded.

"What are you willing to do?" Delphie asked.

She held out her hand and Nash put the phone into it.

"So we start," Delphie said. She gave Nash a soft smile. "I love you, Nash. I will do everything I can to help."

Nash threw himself at Delphie. They fell off the chaise lounges and landed in a heap on the floor.

Delphie held onto the boy while he cried for himself and the start of his journey.

CHAPTER FIVE HUNDRED & FIFTY-NINE

AFTERNOON TEA

Wednesday mid-morning — 11:20 a.m.

"Don't get distracted, Jeraine," he said to himself as he walked into the Castle. "You just need to grab a tin of cookies, fill some water bottles, get some snacks . . ."

He repeated his words like a mantra.

"Don't get distracted, Jeraine . . ." He took a breath to continue.

He stepped into the kitchen.

"What the . . .?" Jeraine asked.

Abi was sitting at the kitchen table, with her back to the kitchen. There was a large man — both thick and tall — with dark hair and medium-dark skin. He was wearing heavy clothing that covered most of his body. His hair was dark and long. He nodded to Jeraine and looked back at Abi. There was another other man who was white skinned and beautiful. His hair was yellow, the color of fresh corn. He had eyes that were the bluest blue, beautiful lips, and a gorgeous smile. He was wearing an expensive business suit and seemed to be about six feet one or maybe six feet two. He smelled like . . .

"Jasmine on a warm day," Jeraine whispered. He shook himself. "Don't get distracted, Jeraine."

The blond-haired man gave Jeraine such a seductive look that Jeraine's entire body responded. Until this moment, Jeraine had never been interested in men.

"Knock it off," Abi said.

The man shot Jeraine a smirk and looked back at Abi.

"Who . . .?" Jeraine started. "What?"

His lip curled with disgust.

"Fairies," Jeraine said with a sniff. "I don't have time for your nonsense."

"Mr. Smith doesn't like the fairies," the dark-skinned man said. His voice was low and deep, firm and equally entrancing. "That's unusual for humans."

"How do you know *my* name?" Jeraine asked. His hand pressed against his chest.

The dark-skinned man's dark eyes scanned Jeraine in an assessing look. He did not reply.

"The fairy envoys were here for a long time while the fairy queens were in conference," Abi said. "They wore out their welcome."

one side of the beautiful man's lips curled in a smile.

"I *told* you to knock it off," Abi said to the other man.

He looked back at Abi and gave her a fond grin.

"This is Hades," Abi said, gesturing to the dark-skinned man with the deep voice. "He is the Greek God of the Underworld."

"Oh?" Jeraine asked. He took a step backward.

"This is Lucifer," Abi said.

"I *knew* it!" Jeraine said. He looked up at the ceiling and shook his head. "I fucking *knew* it!"

"What did you know, Jeraine?" Lucifer said in his seductive voice.

"That the Devil was a good-looking white man," Jeraine said with a grin. "I knew it."

"Now, Jeraine, we've had this conversation," Abi said. "Are there white men?"

"No, but . . ." Jeraine said.

"There are just men," Abi said. "One human race. Human men."

"Yes, but . . ." As if he were a child, Jeraine pointed at Lucifer. "He's a white man."

Jeraine nodded.

"I *knew* it."

Abi sighed and looked at Lucifer.

"Show him," Abi said.

"Oh, come on," Lucifer complained. "You have to admit that this is kind of fun."

"Now," Abi said.

Lucifer looked disappointed, but Abi was firm.

"I am not playing with you," Abi said. "Do it. Now."

"Fine," Lucifer said.

The gorgeous blond, blue-eyed white man disappeared, and a voluptuous, light-skinned woman appeared.

"Whoa," Jeraine said.

A moment later, he transformed into the most alluring dark-skinned woman Jeraine had ever seen. Jeraine took a step backward.

Lucifer transformed into a tall, strong, dark-skinned man, and then what looked like an Asian business man from Japan, and then China, and then Mongolia, and then . . .

"Stop!" Jeraine said holding up his hand to block the sight of Lucifer. "I get it! He's a shape-shifter, like the cat."

"The cat?" Hades asked.

"Asteria lives here in cat form," Abi said.

"That's a relief to me," Hades said. He nodded to Abi in thanks. "My wife believes that she 'lost' her. She will be greatly relieved to know that she is all right."

Abi nodded.

"What would you like me to look like?" Lucifer cut in to turn their attention back to him.

Jeraine took his hand away from his eyes and immediately regretted it. Lucifer looked like a unicorn with a rainbow emanating from his long horn.

"The Devil can take any form," Jeraine said, closing his eyes.

There was a noise, and Jeraine opened his eyes.

The traditional demon shape of The Devil stood in front of him. Even though he knew that he shouldn't be, Jeraine was terrified. He yelped with fear and covered his eyes.

"Knock it off," Hades said.

He heard a demonic laugh.

"Enough," Abi said with finality.

"If he's not a shape-shifter, what is he?" Jeraine asked, still not opening his eyes.

"He's an archangel," Abi said. "Show him."

Jeraine opened an eye.

Lucifer gave her a long look before turning back to Jeraine. Lucifer transformed into the brightest, most beautiful light.

"This is what they look like when they aren't in form," Abi said. "They take the form that the other being *expects* them to take. This is the only way they can interact with a physical being. It is a great honor to see an archangel in energetic form."

"Thanks?" Jeraine said mildly. "Hey, is that why Tanesha and her mom glow?"

"That's right," Lucifer — as a light — said. "You are my brother Uriel's grandchild's husband. We are family."

"No, no, no." Jeraine shook his head. "I don't think so."

Lucifer — as the light — laughed. It was truly the most beautiful sound Jeraine had ever heard. He looked at Abi, but she looked angry.

"Knock it off," Abi said. "You injure him in anyway, and I cannot predict how this house will respond."

Lucifer — as the light — seemed to wince.

"How did you get in here?" Jeraine asked.

"It was not easy or pleasant," Lucifer said. "I will honor the rules of the house."

Lucifer gave Abi a little nod. His form became that of an older, medium-skinned man in casual clothing. As if he was having trouble keeping up, Jeraine shook his head. Lucifer raised his hands in acquiescence, and Hades laughed.

"While it's horrifying to meet you both," Jeraine said, "I am here on a mission for Miss T. I won't let you distract me. I just won't."

"What does she need?" Abi asked.

"Food, water, blankets," Jeraine said. "Comfort for her and her girls. They are with Sandy in her room. Everyone except Heather. She's in Olympia. The other girlfriends are... this thing is... well, it's very hard on her and the other girlfriends."

Abi gave a succinct nod of her head.

"It is done," Abi said.

Jeraine swallowed hard. He looked from Hades to Lucifer and back again.

"Surely, you all aren't here for me." Jeraine's voice came out in a squeak.

"They are not," Abi said. "But since you are here, you might help me."

"Uh," Jeraine said. His eyes went from Hades to Lucifer. "Remind me why I'd like to do that?"

Hades laughed. Lucifer smirked as if he'd predicted Jeraine's reluctance.

"I have broken an ancient agreement," Abi said. "When this happens, I must make tea for Hades and Lucifer."

"Wha... uh... what did you do?" Jeraine asked.

"She stole a soul from me," Hades said.

"I thought every soul was hers," Jeraine said. "No insult meant."

"That is correct," Hades said. "She wanted to live with the little fairy prince, so she asked me to take care of the dead. It was my great honor to be of assistance. Since then, there has been an order to things. Stealing a soul might be her right, but she has disrupted the order of things as well as our agreement."

Jeraine looked from Abi to the God of the Underworld to Lucifer. The archangel — as a middle aged, casual looking man — nodded in agreement.

"But Sandy cannot be going to hell," Jeraine said. "She's the sweetest, nicest human being in the world. Why would she need to suffer eternal damnation?"

"She would not," Lucifer said. "But that is not what I do."

Jeraine looked at Lucifer and blinked. He wondered if he should actually ask the archangel what he meant or if he should just nod and head back to the hospital.

"Would you be willing to help?" Abi asked.

"Uh," Jeraine said, keeping his eye on The Devil. "You?"

"Yes, me," Abi said. "They have asked me for . . . mmm . . ."

"Favors," Hades said.

Hades looked at Jeraine, and Jeraine was surprised at how kind this god seemed.

"I am too full up to do anything else," Abi said.

"What can I do?" Jeraine asked.

"Could you make some tea?" Abi asked.

"I would love a biscuit," Hades said. "Ares has been bragging about some kind of biscuit that has chocolate in small form that he called a 'chip' inside a salted butter biscuit. I . . ."

The God of the Underworld stopped talking when he noticed that Abi, Lucifer, and Jeraine were looking at him.

"Why are you more afraid of him than me?" Hades asked Jeraine. "I am death."

"Yeah, but he's damnation," Jeraine said.

"Him?" Hades asked.

Hades laughed.

"He's not?" Jeraine asked.

"That is a common modern interpretation," Abi said.

"Oh?" Hades asked. "I wasn't aware of that."

"What is he, if he's not damnation?" Jeraine asked. "Decades of torment for sins on Earth? Retribution on a soul level?"

"If I tell you, will you get me one of these biscuits that Ares has talked about?" Hades asked.

"I want to try them as well," Lucifer said. "My brother Uriel says you have something called 'pears'? From trees?"

"They are out of season here in Denver," Jeraine said. "Our trees are dormant right now."

"What a shame," Lucifer said.

"We usually have some in the refrigerator," Jeraine pointed to the refrigerator. "They are grown in warmer climates and shipped here."

"What a luxury!" Hades said.

"Refrigeration," Jeraine said, lifting a shoulder in a shrug.

"What is a 'refrigerator'?" Lucifer asked, but it was clear that Hades wanted to know.

Jeraine pointed to it. He opened the door.

"It's cold inside," Jeraine said. "Ideally, 45 degrees. Helps food last longer."

"Ares is correct," Hades said. "This really is a world of wonder."

Lucifer nodded. Jeraine went to the electric pot, filled it with water, and turned it on.

"Please make the tea I like," Abi said.

"Not the one Miss T drinks," Jeraine said, with his eye on Hades and Lucifer.

"No," Abi said.

"What is this luxury?" Hades asked at the same time Lucifer said, "Why can't we have it?"

"It weakens her powers," Abi said. "Magical and angelic. When she's not on the tea, she and her mother can light things on fire with a look or a touch."

"Good skill to have," Hades said.

"But not tea you'd like?" Jeraine asked.

"No," Abi said.

"Very well," Jeraine said. "I'll make a pot of English Breakfast tea, because it's very common for people to drink it."

"What is this tea the mother likes?" Hades asked.

"She likes Chai tea or a Hot Cinnamon Spice tea," Jeraine said. "We have it in tea bags, so I'll give you water, and you can make what you like."

"Most of those words are new to me, young Mr. Smith," Hades said.

"To me, as well," Lucifer said. "Please go ahead."

"Might I watch?" Hades asked.

"Knock yourself out," Jeraine said. "But I don't know what would injure you, so just keep back."

"Good thinking," Lucifer said.

While Abi was rooted in her chair, the men stood together at the end of the kitchen. Jeraine warmed the ceramic teapot and took out a fine mesh tea strainer. He put a couple of teaspoons of their English Breakfast tea. When the electric kettle clicked off, he picked it up.

"What is that?" Hades asked.

"This boils water very quickly," Jeraine said.

He opened the top to take off the lid. Hades moved to put his finger in.

"Don't burn yourself," Jeraine said.

"Thank you for your concern," Hades said. He put his finger in. "It is very hot."

With the God of the Underworld on his shoulder and the creepy archangel at his side, Jeraine poured out the warm water from the tea pot, placed the tea strainer into the pot, and poured the hot water into the pot. He set it at the end of the counter so that Hades and Lucifer could look inside.

He filled the electric kettle again and turned it on. He set out mugs and got the cream from the refrigerator.

"You have to wait three minutes," Jeraine said.

The God of the Underworld blinked at Jeraine, and Lucifer shook his head. Jeraine pointed to the digital clock on the stove.

"Hours," Jeraine said, pointing to the hours and then to the minutes. "Minutes."

Hades and Lucifer went to the stove to touch the clock.

"Wait for three of these to pass, and we'll try the tea," Jeraine said.

He turned away and went into the pantry. He took out the ladder and climbed up to just under the rafters.

"What are you doing?" Hades asked.

"Getting your cookies," Jeraine said. "We make them in batches and put them in tins so that we always have some. But we have three teen-aged boys, so we have to hide them."

"Why is that?" Hades asked.

"They will eat through these tins and anything else." Jeraine passed Hades the tin of cookies and then another. "Ginger and chocolate chip."

The God of the Underworld nodded. A thought occurred to Jeraine. If they knew what an amazing woman Sandy was, they might not be upset that she was staying on Earth.

"You might like to try some cake," Jeraine said. "Sandy makes the best cakes. That's the woman whose soul was stolen from you."

The God of the Underworld grunted. Jeraine put the ladder away and went to the refrigerator's freezer. He took out an already-prepared chocolate cake.

"This is frozen," Jeraine said.

"Frozen?" Hades asked. "Like lakes in winter?"

"Like in there," Jeraine said.

Hades and Lucifer looked inside the freezer. They opened and closed the door a few times to see how it worked. In the meantime, Jeraine took out a large knife and began to cut the cake.

"Now, you both said you work for Abi," Jeraine asked.

"We have taken over some of her duties," Hades said. "My brother, Poseidon, has taken over the seas from Abi's brother, Gilfand."

"And what does Lucifer do?" Jeraine asked.

His eyes flicked to Lucifer and then back to Hades. He gave Hades a quick nod to encourage him to speak.

"Do you know of people who live in great shame? Great self-loathing?" Hades asked. "These people can barely take a breath without feeling as if their very existence blots out the sun."

"They are depressed," Jeraine said.

"Come now, Mr. Smith," Hades said. "You know better than that."

Jeraine gave the barest nod.

"This kind of thing had not been seen in other species," Hades said. "The single-celled creatures and early invertebrates had none of it. It did not exist in the creatures you call 'Dinosaurs.' Not in most of the creatures on this planet . . ."

"Add a humanoid brain," Abi said from the table.

"Yes," Hades said. "As soon as a creature can think about himself, we see this kind of self-torture."

"Doesn't it come from being abused?" Jeraine asked. "It's not really self-torture."

"It is often started in abuse — torture at the earliest ages," Hades said. "Certainly, in a humanoid brain, the torture is internalized. The self-rage grows and grows. For a moment of abuse, there can be decades of self-torture, self-rage, and self-loathing. This kind of thing does great damage to the soul."

"I take care of them," Lucifer said.

"What does that mean?" Confused, Jeraine wrinkled his nose and shook his head.

"I take care of those souls who cannot love themselves," Lucifer said. "They are broken, sorrowful. They weep and cry. I am their caregiver."

Lucifer gave a nod.

"His ruler, the one you call 'God,' was asked by Abi for help," Hades said. "Lucifer is the most beautiful, cleverest, and loving angel. He was willing to love these poor souls back to soul integrity."

Jeraine blinked at Hades and then Lucifer.

"What about the levels of Hell?" Jeraine asked.

"They are things the souls do to themselves," Lucifer said. "I care for them until they are able to stop injuring themselves. You see, Jeraine, the soul holds the energy of the universe and in that way *is* the universe. It knows how to be whole, complete, unbroken."

"Abi says that the body wishes to be whole," Jeraine said.

"The body is a reflection of the soul," Lucifer said. "If you care for the body, your soul will heal. It takes time, but it can be done in this realm through therapy and other modalities. If a person dies in, or particularly from, this state of self-loathing, these poor souls come to live with me."

"Some souls are never able to heal," Hades said with a sad nod.

"No matter what I do," Lucifer said.

"But most work their way out of their broken place and come to live with me in the Underworld," Hades said. "We welcome them with open arms. They see their families again, those who love them. They share the knowledge of what their self-loathing had done, as well as how they healed. Everyone grows."

Lucifer nodded.

"Human civilization has become more kind and more peaceful over time," Abi said from the table.

"Am I going to remember this?" Jeraine asked.

"If you wish," Abi said from the table.

Jeraine pointed to the clock — more than five minutes had passed. He took the tea strainer out of the tea pot and carried it to the table.

"Can you . . .?" Jeraine nodded to the mugs.

Hades picked up the mugs. Lucifer picked up the cream. They carried them to the table where Abi sat. Jeraine set the containers of cookies on the table and went back into the kitchen to warm the cake.

He stood on the other side of the barrier while the God of the Underworld and The Devil he'd feared opened the cans of cookies and marveled at their first tastes of tea. If anyone had asked him, even a year ago, if he'd be warming cake for the terrifying monsters of his childhood, he would have said "No."

But here he was – making sure the cake was delicious and getting ready to sit down with these creatures and share some tea.

Jeraine shook his head.

Life really was amazing.

And in that moment, he understood what Lucifer was saying. His own soul had been damaged by self-rage from his addiction, his feelings of inferiority to his sister, and his abusive relationship with himself.

Lucifer looked up at him. He held up his tea up and nodded.

"To you, Jeraine Smith," Lucifer said.

"To Jeraine!" Hades and Abi said.

Somewhere deep inside him, he felt some teeny-tiny portion of his soul move toward healing. It felt so good that he promised himself to try to stop the self-rage that had injured his soul.

"Come, share tea with us," Abi said.

Jeraine brought the cake to the table and sat down next to his friend and mother of all, Abi.

CHAPTER FIVE HUNDRED & SIXTY

GOOD FRIENDS

Wednesday afternoon — 3:42 p.m

"Isn't he the one who raped the daughter of . . ." Jill asked.

Jill looked at Tanesha, and she said, "Demeter. Tricked her into having to stay with him by feeding her pomegranate seeds."

"That's what I said," Jeraine said. "He groaned and dropped his head into his hands. Lucifer shook his head and laughed. Then Hades asked me if I had a mother-in-law. I just shrugged because Yvonne is such a joy, but . . ."

"That's a story that Demeter tells," Heather said as she walked into the small family room next to Sandy's hospital room where the girlfriends had camped out in. "Gods know why anyone believes it."

"Heather!" Jill and Tanesha said in near unison. They got up to hug their friend. "We were kicked out because they thought . . ."

"Sandy should be awake," Heather said with a nod. "It's going to take some time, but she's going to be okay."

They'd been scolded so many times by the nurses that they didn't dare cheer. Instead, they beamed at Heather.

"Jeraine met Hades and Lucifer," Tanesha said to Heather. "They kept calling him 'Jeraine Smith.'"

Heather grinned.

"He was too intimidated to correct them," Tanesha said.

The women shot laughing looks at Jeraine.

"Okay, okay," Jeraine said. "I dare any of you to stand in front of those two and not be intimidated."

"They are powerful," Heather said with a nod.

"Will you tell us about his wife?" Tanesha asked.

"The story Demeter tells is that Persephone can escape the dark for half of the year," Heather said. "That's why spring and summer are only half of the year."

"On one side of the globe," Jill said.

"Exactly," Heather said. "The Greeks were world travelers. They knew better; they just . . ."

Heather shrugged.

"Let the mother have her story," Heather said.

"What's the real one?" Jill asked.

"You know about Kronos eating his children?" Heather asked.

"Zeus is supposed to have freed them," Tanesha said with a shake of his head. "I can't imagine that man tying his shoes without help."

"No one really knows what happened," Heather said. "It is what Zeus *says,* and he was the only one there to tell the story. Anyway, Hades is the eldest and the last freed. When he came out, he wanted to travel the world. See what he had missed. He is handsome, powerful, and deeply kind."

"He has the power of truly kind people," Jeraine said with a nod. "You just want to be decent around him."

Heather nodded.

"While he was traveling, he ran into Demeter and Persephone," Heather said. "Persephone traveled with her mother as a child. Her mother lived a rather lonely life, and Persephone is lovely. It was really nice for Demeter to have her daughter with her."

"Seems kind of selfish to me," Jill said.

"That's because you have a powerful daughter," Heather said. "You've chosen to let her thrive as herself rather than keep her love and power with you. Demeter didn't want to give her daughter up.

"Anyway, Hades and Persephone met in a field." Heather nodded. "They just fell for each other. Hard. Demeter was afraid that her daughter might leave her. They snuck around for a while, but Demeter caught them. One of the reasons Hades took the honor of caring for the souls of the dead was to get away from her wrath. Of course, Persephone became so despondent without her lover that Demeter relented."

"Those pomegranate seeds?" Jeraine asked. "He looked at me and said, 'It wasn't pomegranate seeds I implanted in her' and then laughed."

"They have children," Heather said. "Most of them live in the world. If you'd like, you can meet them. They are as lovely as their parents are."

The women and Jeraine fell silent thinking about the story they'd heard.

"Did he think Zeus was crazy?" Tanesha asked Jeraine.

"Oh, yeah," Jeraine said. "I said something about Zeus raping everyone, and he said, 'I can't imagine how he did that from the Sea of Amber.' Then he and Lucifer laughed."

"Everyone knew that Zeus was a problem," Heather said with a nod.

"Why do you think the stories are so different from what happened?" Jill asked.

"Stories are stories," Heather said. "It's only in modern time that we confuse stories with fact. Look at the news now. We get stories about facts in newspapers and on the television. Stories about facts are not facts. They are carefully edited to make them interesting."

Heather shrugged.

"What in life makes sense?" Heather asked. "Look at Sandy's situation. Nothing about it makes any sense."

The women and Jeraine nodded. Jeraine poured more tea from the thermos he'd brought.

"Life is life," Heather said. "We're not meant to understand it all. We are meant to live it."

Lost in thought, no one responded. A few minutes later, the nurse peeked inside the room.

"She's awake," the nurse said. "She's very weak. Is her husband here?"

"We sent him home to rest," Jill said.

The nurse looked at Heather and said, "Oh, hello."

Heather smiled.

"Do I know you?" the nurse asked. "I feel like I know you."

"I get that a lot," Heather said. "I'm Heather Lipson."

"Nice to meet you. I met your husband," the nurse said.

"Blane," Heather said.

"Nice guy," the nurse said. "Sandy did ask for her husband. When she heard that he had gone home, she said, 'My friends are here' with great confidence. You must be good friends."

"The best," Jill said.

The nurse looked at Jeraine.

"Not offended," Jeraine said.

"Okay, two at a time," the nurse said. "For five minutes, no more. Then she must rest. She was very near death. It's going to take time for her to come back fully. So, don't wear her out now."

"Of course," Heather said. She nodded to Tanesha and Jill. "You two can go. I'll call Aden."

"I can call Aden," Jeraine said. "Maybe the nurse will . . ."

The women turned to look at the nurse.

"Oh, okay," the nurse said, a little intimidated. "But do not upset her. Only happy, joyous faces."

"Of course," Jill said.

The nurse led them into the private ICU where Sandy was staying, and Jeraine went to call Aden.

~~~~~~~~~

Wednesday afternoon — 4:17 p.m.

"Did you hear something?" Noelle looked up when Nash came into the room at Seth O'Malley's house.

She and Teddy had been lying around in the den, reading old mystery novels.

"Dad called the house," Nash said. "Sandy's awake. They think she'll make a full recovery. He said that we should expect that it will take a . . ."

Nash's voice caught, but he continued, " . . . long time. A long time."

"That's wonderful news," Noelle said.

His eyes filled with tears, Nash nodded. He cleared his throat.

"Listen," Nash said. "I wanted to say . . . well . . ."

He had spent the last few hours preparing what he would say to them. Now that he was there, the words just seemed too dumb. He looked down.

"What's going on?" Teddy asked.

"Ihaveaproblemwithmyphone," Nash said the words as if they were one word. "Addiction.Sorry.Sosorry."

"Tell us something we don't know," Noelle said with a sniff.

Nash looked up at her. He blinked and then blinked again.

"You knew?" Nash asked.

Both Teddy and Noelle nodded.

"I have struggled with it myself," Teddy said. He nodded. "Sandy fell because she turned to look at me."

"What?" Nash asked.

"I was joking or . . . maybe not," Teddy said.

"Sandy turned when Teddy took his phone back," Noelle said.

"That's why she fell," Teddy said.

"No, it was me," Nash said. "She was chasing after me."

"It was both of us. Combined," Teddy said. "I didn't mean for her to get hurt."

"*I* didn't mean for Sandy to get hurt," Nash said, his hand pressed against his chest.

"But she did," Noelle said. "Is that a consequence you can live with?"

Nash's eyes welled with tears. He gave a barely audible, "No."

"I feel the same way," Teddy said. "It's just hard. I tell myself that I keep the phone because Dad's in the military and my sister's not all that well and . . . But mostly I use it to play games and . . ."

Teddy's eyes flicked to look at the wall. No one said anything for a long moment.

"We've decided to do what Charlie does," Noelle said.

"Not carry a phone," Nash said with a sigh.

"Charlie has a phone," Noelle said. "He just has a pay-as-you-go phone."

Nash looked up at Noelle.

"I don't think that would work for me, either," Nash said. "I'd just probably blow through it really fast and . . ."

"I wasn't sure for myself," Teddy said.

Nash nodded.

"I haven't told Nadia," Nash said. He took a breath and let it out. "I have to do what's best for me. And . . . I don't talk to her that much, anyway."

Nash gave a determined nod. Teddy got up, and the boys hugged.

"I have to find other things to do," Nash said.

"That's why we were reading these books," Noelle said. "Seth had thousands of them. Maresol said we can read them as long as we don't mess them up. So, we're being careful."

"How are they?" Nash asked.

"Crazy," Teddy said at the same time Noelle said, "Like little museums."

Teddy looked at Noelle.

"The books are from the 1940s and 1950s," Noelle said. "They are like looking at a museum of that time."

"It's a lot like today," Teddy said.

"But really different," Noelle said. "I bet you'd like them."

"Did Dad say if we can see Sandy?" Nash asked.

"Not for a while," Noelle said. "They are restricting her visitors to adults. Dad said that they get a few minutes at a time and that she's mostly asleep."

"So, we just have to fill up today," Nash said.

Noelle nodded.

"I don't know how I'll ever learn Ukrainian," Nash said.

"You were learning on that phone app," Teddy said.

For a moment, the three teenagers fell silent.

"I apologize," Bernie said. "I was listening in."

They looked up. Bernie was dressed in a red robe with a plastic crown on his head. He seemed not to notice his attire.

"I didn't mean to eavesdrop," Bernie said. "I came to see if you'd like to watch the movie with Dale and me."

He gave the teens a broad smile.

"I am King Theoden," Bernie said. "Want to watch?"

"I would," Teddy said.

"Who will you be, young Theodore?" Bernie asked.

"I was thinking of being Legolas," Teddy said.

"Great choice," Bernie said. "And the lass?"

"Eowyn," Noelle said. "I like how strong she is. Plus, Ava's sister is called 'Eowyn.'"

"Indeed, she is," Bernie said. "Another good choice."

He turned to look at Nash. In slow Ukrainian, he said, "And you, Master Nash?"

Nash blinked and blinked again.

"You know Ukrainian?" Nash asked in Ukrainian.

"I know a number of languages," Bernie said, returning to English. "My Ukrainian is a little rusty, but it worked fine when we were there a while ago."

Bernie winked at Nash.

"You know, in my day, we used to rely on learning things from people, not machines," Bernie said.

"Oh," Nash said. "Would you mind helping me?"

"It would be my pleasure," Bernie said. "Seth told me about those dark arrows and the lovely Nadia. I knew her father."

Nash looked up at Bernie.

"He was an evil sod," Bernie said. "But, his choice of a wife was brilliant. Nadia was a lovely child. I haven't seen her in a long while, but I have every confidence that she's an amazing adult."

"She's . . ." Nash said and blushed.

Seeing Nash's reaction, Bernie put his hand on the boy's shoulder.

"We'll get you speaking Ukrainian in no time," Bernie said.

"Thanks," Nash said, his voice cracking with emotion.

"Now, onto more pressing matters," Bernie said. "What would you like to be today?"

"Can I be 'Boromir'?" Nash asked.

"Of course," Bernie said. "Might I ask why?"

"I like that he was never really affected by the ring," Nash said. "I mean, in the movie, he more does his duty than is under its influence."

"Boromir is one of the few incorruptible characters in the book," Bernie said.

"I'd like to be that," Nash said. "Incorruptible."

"Then we shall talk about how to do that," Bernie said. "All with time. You know, I heard your talk about giving up your phones."

"I nearly killed Sandy," Nash said.

"Hmm," Bernie said. "I will tell you that one way to fill time enjoyably is to learn new things. I can teach you piano or the violin. If you ask really nicely, Maresol might teach you some of what she knows about cooking. My son is a walking encyclopedia of murder and mayhem. He can talk your ear off about solving cases, but more than that — he really knows his villains. Dale is an incredible young man. He can tell you all kinds of interesting things. He also had a problem with phones for a while."

Bernie nodded.

"I want to know about Chi Chui," Teddy said.

"Let's see if we can get Seth to talk about it with us," Bernie said.

He looked at Teddy and then at Nash.

"People are our greatest resource," Bernie said. "Those phones give you only a *sense* of being connected. They are not a substitute for actual human connections. That's how they are like drugs or alcohol. Drugs and alcohol substitute for the feeling of being connected. Soon all you have is your drug or alcohol."

He nodded.

"Or phone," Bernie said. "Seth knows this firsthand. He can talk to you about it. But if you really want to give up your addiction . . ."

Both Nash and Teddy nodded. Noelle nodded in support.

"Then you need to fill your life with real connections," Bernie said. "That's people, knowledge, art, exercise, joy, tragedy — life is big and wonderful. If you want to beat addiction, you must open yourself to the glory and pain of life."

The boys nodded.

"You're going to be with us until your mom is well," Bernie said. "Let's see if we can't make a stab at changing things a bit."

"We have to go back to school tomorrow," Noelle said.

"That gives us evenings and mornings," Bernie said. "We're going to have so much fun."

When the children gave him a worried look, he laughed.

"But first, we need to get you dressed," Bernie said. "Come along!"

He moved across the den.

"We have our costumes in here." He opened a non-descript trunk. "Take what you like. I'm going to start the popcorn."

Teddy was on his knees, looking at the amazing things inside the trunk. Nash was standing over the trunk, ogling the odd clothing.

"Where did you get this stuff?" Noelle asked.

"Here and there," Bernie said mildly. "Your brother, Charlie, called from work. He's going to join us midway. Tink went to the Castle to see her friend, Ivy. I guess Ivy's been ill."

"The toddlers have strep throat," Noelle said. "Ivy caught it, too."

"Good that she's taking care of herself," Bernie said. He gave them a wide smile. "We start in fifteen minutes!"

Smiling at the children, he went into the kitchen to make popcorn. Nash and Teddy pulled odd clothing items out of the trunk. Noelle picked up a wooden sword for her costume. Teddy found a child's toy bow. Nash picked up a plastic shield. They were laughing and putting on clothing in no time. Noelle stepped into a tulle skirt.

Bernie watched them for a moment and then smiled. He turned his attention to the popcorn.

~~~~~~~~~

Wednesday evening — 6:10 p.m.

Even though he had a key, Blane knocked on Nelson's door. Nelson opened the door and stepped back to let Blane in. Nelson's hair was wet, and he was just tying his tie.

"I just need a minute," Nelson said.

Blane lifted his hands to show that he was carrying two grocery bags.

"I wondered if you might be interested in staying in," Blane said. "I thought I could cook something, and we could talk."

Nelson's cheeks flushed with color, and his eyes welled. He gave a quick nod. He let Blane pass into the kitchen.

"You don't wish to be seen in public with me," Nelson said, softly. "After what happened at the gym . . ."

"No. Not at all." Blane scowled and shook his head. He set the bags on the counter. "I just didn't want the Baeckcoffe to go to waste."

Nelson's mouth fell open.

"You made my favorite dish?" Nelson asked. "I can't believe you remembered. But it takes two days . . ."

"I started it yesterday between things," Blane said. "I thought I'd make it to thank you for taking care of the little ones. Then you talked about going out for dinner and . . ."

Blane gave Nelson a bright smile. He took two warm baguettes from off the top of the bag and carefully pulled a covered casserole dish out. He turned on Nelson's oven.

"Surprise!" Blane said when he turned back to Nelson.

Nelson laughed. Blane opened the lid of the covered casserole, and Nelson swooned a bit.

"It's been cooking all day," Blane said.

"But Jeraine said that Hades and Lucifer were over! Didn't they . . . ?" Nelson asked.

"The Castle has a kitchen in every apartment," Blane said. "I used Sandy and Aden's. They have the most complete kitchen."

"Makes sense, since Sandy bakes so much," Nelson said.

"Exactly," Blane said. "I also made some cookies and a few other things for the kids and Aden. To help."

"How are the Wild Bunch?" Nelson asked.

"The toddlers are still sick, of course," Blane said. "Now that Sandy's out of the woods, their mothers have set up a rotation to care for the children as well as, Sandy. Plus Val's back from her trip to LA."

"Heather set that up?" Nelson asked.

"Jill," Blane said. "Jill is the hyper-organized one. Well, second to Sandy, that is."

Nelson nodded.

"The tweens and teens are at O'Malley's," Blane said. "I checked in on them this morning when I gave O'Malley a treatment. They are . . ."

"Upset?" Nelson asked.

"Teenagers," Blane said with a smile. "Morose, angry, feeling sorry for themselves — the usual."

Blane shrugged.

"I also made . . ." Blane said. He took a covered pie pan from the bag. " . . .a clafoutis."

"But how?" Nelson asked.

"I cheated a bit," Blane said. "We froze cherries after our trip to the Eastern Slope in early spring last year. It looks good, though."

Blane took the cover from the pie pan.

"Oh, wow," Nelson said. "Just the smell . . ."

Nelson grinned at Blane, and it was Blane's turn to blush.

"I just . . ." Blane said. "I . . ."

He sighed. Nelson's intense ability to listen caused Blane to continue.

"I don't know if I'll ever be able to speak to you about love," Blane said. "I say 'I love you' to my children. Sometimes, I'll say, 'Love you, too' when Heather says that she loves me. Sometimes. The words *hurt* me."

Blane put his hand to his heart. Nelson opened his mouth to say something, but Blane held up his hand.

"But I can cook," Blane said. "For you. I made this *for you*."

Blane nodded.

"Last night, I really needed . . . comfort," Blane said. "You were lovely. Exactly what I needed. The children were so happy to be here. You and Pierre — you were real family to them. I am grateful. And . . ."

Blane sighed.

"I see what you are, and I . . ." Blane grimaced and shook his head. He managed, "Am grateful."

Nelson hugged Blane. For a moment, they just stood there. Blane sighed and stepped back.

"Are you hungry?" Blane asked.

"Famished," Nelson said. "Dad was able to stay today, so I went into work this afternoon. I missed lunch and . . ."

"It's all ready," Blane said with a smile. "Let's eat."

CHAPTER FIVE HUNDRED & SIXTY-ONE

PAST MEETS PRESENT

Thursday early morning — 4:29 a.m.

"I thought you'd be there," Jacob said as Blane came out of Nelson's house.

They were dressed to take the dogs for a run around City Park. Jacob had Sarah and Buster on leashes and Mack in a sport stroller. Jacob nodded to Mack.

"He's still really sick, but he insisted on going," Jacob said. "Heather couldn't deter him."

Jacob and Blane looked up as Nelson came down the stairs to join them.

"I'll take him," Nelson said.

Still sucking his thumb, Mack looked up at Nelson.

"Can you go really fast?" Mack asked around his thumb.

The child gave a little cough. Blane knelt down to check to see if Mack was warm enough. The child had about five inches of clothing on, a hat, and a warm fleece blanket.

"Really fast," Nelson said with a nod.

"Okay," Mack said.

Nelson grinned and went to stand behind the stroller. Blane got up. Jacob gave Blane the leash to Buster the ugly dog.

"Now, I want no fighting, no showboating . . ." Jacob said in a mock official tone. "And . . ."

Jacob took off. Laughing, Blane and Nelson easily caught up with him. They fell into a vigorous pace as the men shot up Sixteenth Avenue. They stopped at the lights and then crossed into the East High Esplanade.

"Did you go here?" Jacob asked Nelson.

"Yeah, I was a couple years after you," Nelson said.

"You didn't go to the Catholic school?" Blane asked.

"I went there a couple of years, but Michael Junior started," Nelson said. "I couldn't deal, so Dad transferred me to East."

Blane nodded.

"You?" Nelson asked.

"Here," Blane said.

He gave Buster's leash to Nelson and took off down the Esplanade with Mack. Mack squealed with delight.

"What did I say?" Nelson asked.

"He was in the park during high school," Jacob said. "Doing drugs and servicing men. You know, prostitution? Addiction?"

"Oh," Nelson said. Nelson stopped running. "You mean this crap about him being an addict and a prostitute was when he was a kid?"

"Fourteen to sixteen," Jacob said. "Come on. He feels like an asshole enough already."

Nelson ran along with Jacob. They watched Blane and Mack head into the park.

"And anyway, if you can't fucking handle it, then maybe you should head home," Jacob said in a gruff voice.

Nelson ran right into a wall of psychokinetic energy. He hit the wall and slid down to the sidewalk. Buster walked right through it.

"What the . . .?" Nelson asked.

"Go home," Jacob said.

"I didn't know you could do that," Nelson said. "I thought you were human."

Jacob stopped running to turn and look at Nelson.

"What's it to you?" Jacob asked.

"I mean, I knew your boys had . . . skills," Nelson said. "I guess I thought it came with being the grandchild of a powerful Titan. But you . . . What are you?"

"Pissed off," Jacob said. "What's your problem?"

"My problem?" Nelson asked. He jumped to his feet and looked at Jacob. "Wait — what are we talking about?"

"You clearly have some problem with Blane's past," Jacob said with a snort.

"Oh, that's why you . . ." Nelson pointed to where the energetic wall had been. "Do you know how rare that skill is?"

Jacob gave Nelson an irritated shake of his head and snatched Buster's leash.

"Go home," Jacob said.

"Wait," Nelson said. "Now, just a minute."

Jacob turned to look at Nelson.

"I don't have any problem with Blane or his past," Nelson said. "Not one. So don't make up some bullshit."

"Why did you ask about Blane and high school?" Jacob asked.

"I didn't know," Nelson said.

"You said, 'You mean this crap about him being a prostitute was when he was a kid?'" Jacob said.

"I was surprised," Nelson said. "Enrique made such a big deal out of it, like it had happened just yesterday."

"What's up with that?" Jacob sneered.

"With what?" Nelson asked.

"You being friends with Enrique," Jacob said. "Repeating anything the asshole said."

"I was friends with Enrique because I fell in love with his partner," Nelson said.

"Oh," Jacob said mildly.

"It's supposed to be something with my family line — my mother's and my father's," Nelson said. "We fall for people immediately and completely. There's nothing that can change it. It's why my ancestors became crusaders — to keep from acting out their love for someone unattainable or to get away from the angry husband or king after being caught."

"Did Enrique know?" Jacob asked.

"What do you think?" Nelson asked. "He thought it was hilarious. Tried to get me into a threesome without Blane knowing."

Saying nothing, Jacob started running again. Nelson ran beside him.

"We'll never catch him," Nelson said.

"He and Mack run a loop down to the arches and back up to the Martin Luther King statue," Jacob said. "If we're not there, he'll come up to the Thatcher Fountain."

"Oh," Nelson said. "He didn't go on without us."

"He did go on without us," Jacob said with a laugh. They stopped at the light. "He does that when he gets emotional. It's a primal response. But he's learned to come back. He used to do that only with me, but it's Heather and his children that really cemented it in him."

"How do you know?" Nelson said. "He might not want to be here because of what I said."

"No," Jacob said. "If he was upset by something you said, he might run away. But he'll always come back. Well, always now."

Jacob pointed as they crossed the street. Blane and Mack appeared beside the Thatcher Fountain.

"He's right there," Jacob said.

"That's fast," Nelson said.

"He's really fast now," Jacob said. "We've had to modify the stroller."

"Now?" Nelson asked.

"Since he's been working with Abi," Jacob said.

"He's been working with Abi?" Nelson asked.

Shaking his head, Jacob continued running to where Blane and Mack were standing. Looking windblown, Mack was laughing. Blane was bent over, catching his breath.

"Hey, I'm sorry," Nelson said. "I didn't know."

"Didn't know?" Blane looked confused.

"That you were in the park instead of at high school," Nelson said.

"Group home," Blane nodded. "They wanted the fee for having me there but didn't want to have to deal with me."

"I can't believe that Enrique made such a monumental deal about something you did in *high school*," Nelson said. "And people believed him. That's incredible to me."

"Wealth," Blane said. He looked Nelson straight in the face. "The wealthy never hesitate to make the poor feel as if being poor is some moral failing."

"I'm sorry," Nelson said.

"Oh," Blane grinned. His eyes flicked to Jacob. His eyebrows went up. "I saw you run into the wall."

Blane pointed at Jacob, and Jacob nodded. They laughed while Nelson gawked at him.

"You two are like Jacob's twins!" Nelson said, with a slow shake of his head.

"Celia made me finish high school at an alternative school," Blane said. "I also got my GED."

"Mom was crazy for education," Jacob said with a nod. "He lived with us until Mom got sick."

"What happened then?" Nelson asked.

"Mom bought her best friend this falling-down house on Race Street and moved in there," Jacob said with a snort. "They sold their house in Crestmore and split up the business. Val was at college. I moved in with them."

"I moved into an apartment," Blane said.

"He wanted his 'space,'" Jacob said. "It wasn't very far. He ate meals with us and Dad . . .'"

"That's a mess," Blane said with a grin. "Let's run."

"Run! Run! Run!" Mack croaked.

They started running again. They ran down toward the Martin Luther King statue.

"So, Jacob . . ." Nelson started.

"What?" Jacob asked.

"These powers of yours," Nelson said.

"What about them?" Jacob asked.

"Where do they come from?" Nelson asked.

"Who knows?" Jacob shrugged.

"Abi says that Jacob is nearly a direct descendant of Gilfand," Blane said. "Fin and Jacob are something like third cousins."

"Huh," Nelson said. "Gilfand has a lot of children. Most of them don't have powers."

"Go figure," Jacob said. "Sprints?"

"Faster! Faster!" Mack cheered.

Blane took off. Jacob and Nelson sprinted after him.

~~~~~~~~~

Thursday morning — 10:24 a.m.

"No," Heather said. "You are *not* coming with me."

She pulled her Subaru into the Marlowe School parking lot and parked.

"Go home," Heather said to her grandmother.

"But Hedone," purred her grandmother, Aphrodite. "No one knows more about this topic than I do."

Heather turned and pointed to her grandmother.

"No," Heather said.

Turning forward, Heather turned off the car.

"Why?" Aphrodite asked.

"Why?" Furious, Heather turned to look at her. "Where should I start?"

Aphrodite pressed her hand to her heart and looked away. Heather scowled.

"Oh, you're right," Aphrodite said. "I shouldn't help you give a little talk about the six types of love as defined by . . ."

She put her finger to the side of her lips.

"Who was that again?" Aphrodite asked.

Heather rolled her eyes.

"You can't 'help' me," Heather said. "Go home."

"I want to try that tea!" Aphrodite said. "Persephone said that Hades brought her some lovely cookies and tea!"

Aphrodite looked deflated.

"How come I don't get tea and cookies?" Aphrodite asked.

Heather groaned.

"Little bits of chocolate," Aphrodite said. "Why does Persephone get something that I do not? Me! The one who worked out her little problem with her crazy mother."

"By being crazier than Demeter," Heather said under her breath.

Aphrodite laughed.

"You know me so well, my dear," Aphrodite said.

"I know you well enough to tell you to go home," Heather said.

Aphrodite didn't move. Heather let out a pained sigh.

"You won't let me torture your mother anymore . . ." Aphrodite said in a mild reprimand.

Despite her anger at her grandmother, Heather laughed. Aphrodite smiled.

"Fine," Heather said. "But!"

"'But'?" Aphrodite asked.

"You cannot go in there looking like a goddess," Heather said.

"Why not?" Aphrodite asked.

"Because a lot of women spent a lot of money in attempts to look the way you look now," Heather said. "You will look like a cheap knockoff of yourself."

Aphrodite's visage shifted to a middle-aged human woman. Heather was surprised at how much she looked like Honey's mother Tiffanie — after Tiffanie's recent remodel, that is. Heather shook her head.

"Oh, fine," Aphrodite said. "But you know that I cannot be human."

"I do know that you do not have even one iota of human in you," Heather said.

"That's exactly right," Aphrodite said with a sniff.

Heather groaned, and her grandmother laughed.

Aphrodite shifted to looking a little heavier, a little more life worn. She was still a shockingly beautiful woman. She just looked more like her genuine self and not some magical entity.

"You are beautiful," Hedone said.

Aphrodite sniffed. The "women" got out of the car and went into the school. They checked into the office. Aphrodite was silent through the "vapid conversation with the imbecile at the front desk" and when the "ugly gnome" (hall monitor) walked them down the hallway. Heather didn't need to hear these judgments from her grandmother. She had heard them enough times over the years that she could repeat her grandmother's ridicules in her head.

Heather stole a look at Aphrodite. Much to her surprise, the goddess gave Heather a soft, kind smile rather than the nod of agreement at the judgments that had gone through Heather's head. Heather had only a moment to process this change because the hall monitor stopped at the upper-grade students' room. Heather gave her grandmother a stern look at the door and opened it.

They stood on the edge of the room for only a moment. Noelle noticed them first. She jumped up from her seat and ran to Heather for a hug. Nash, Teddy, Ivy, Tink, and Charlie were right there.

"Is there news?" Charlie asked.

"Oh, dears," Aphrodite said before Heather could answer. "Your Sandy is healing. Don't you worry. She will be home very soon. She is strong and well loved."

The goddess's voice was like a salve to some deeply hidden wound. For a moment, the teenagers stopped moving. When Heather and Tink exchanged a wide-eyed look of irritation, the others started moving back to their seats.

"See," Aphrodite said. "I know more than my fair share about love."

Heather had to fight rolling her eyes like a twelve-year-old. Her grandmother gave her a laughing grin.

"Quiet! Quiet!" their history teacher yelled over the din. "Take your seats!"

Heather and her grandmother made their way to the teacher while the students wandered back to their seats.

"Heather Lipson," she said, shaking the teacher's hand. "This is my grandmother, Agnes. She was a professor in Greek History."

"Heather," the teacher said with a nod. "Agnes. I am so glad you could make it. When Noelle told me that you were an expert in all things historic Greek, I jumped at the chance to have you come to talk to us. It's so good for the students to hear this material from many different voices and angles."

"Happy we could help," Heather said with a nod. "We were told that you wanted us to go over the six types of love as defined by the Greek culture."

"Sounds great!" the teacher said. Leaning in, he added, "This is such a smart and lively group of kids that you can expect lots of interesting questions."

"Who are you?" a sneering tween in the front row asked.

"Now, Joey..." the teacher started. "Let's not start off like that."

"No, it's okay," Heather said. "I understand. I'm Heather Lipson. My husband is Blane. He has worked at Lipson Construction for a long time."

"So you're here because you're married to a relative of the owner?" The boy asked.

"Joey!" the teacher said.

"I am here because I'm an expert on ancient Greece," Heather said. "I speak a number of ancient and dead languages, including ancient and modern Greek. I have read most of the source material as they were written."

"What about her?" Joey asked.

"My grandmother has a PhD in a number of Greek specialties, from Greek Literature to Greek Archeology. She's been on most of the significant archeological digs. She is the reason I am so familiar with all of these dead languages."

Heather pointed to her grandmother and said, "It's her fault."

The children chuckled.

"I have a question," Jill's sister, Candy's adopted daughter, asked.

"Yes, Kimber," Heather said.

"Why are Greek goddesses so hysterical?" Kimber asked.

"This was my friend Tanesha's complaint about Greek goddesses," Heather said with a smile.

"How are goddesses hysterical?" Aphrodite-disguised-as-"Agnes" asked.

"They're always upset with their cheating guys," Kimber said. "They take it out on the other women rather than kicking that cheating asshole to the curb. That Zeus, for example. Why didn't someone stop him from raping their daughters? I mean, they are goddesses — with powers and shit."

"Don't swear," the teacher said.

"She gets what I mean," Kimber said.

Heather and her grandmother looked at each other. Heather nodded to agree that her grandmother would answer the question.

"My first response is to ask you why you think that they *didn't* stop him?" Aphrodite-disguised-as-"Agnes" asked.

Kimber started to speak, but Aphrodite-disguised-as-"Agnes" held up her hand.

"Men wrote the stories," Aphrodite-disguised-as-"Agnes" said.

"Men knew how to write, so they did the writing," Aphrodite-disguised-as-"Agnes" said. "It's as simple as that. They didn't see the brutality of some behavior because it didn't affect them directly. They saw any action by a goddess as 'hysterical' or 'jealousy' rather than natural logical consequences."

Aphrodite-disguised-as-"Agnes" nodded.

"You might also want to look a little more closely," Aphrodite said. "Goddesses have tasks that usually relate to the world of women. Hera, for example, was responsible for the welfare of women and children, including weddings. Ever been to a wedding that wasn't sheer madness? When would she have had the time to chase after her crazy husband?"

The class tittered with uncomfortable laughter.

"One last thing to think about before we get started," Aphrodite-disguised-as-"Agnes" said. "The HIStory of men is easily found. It was written by men, usually about men, certainly from a male perspective. How else do we know what men did?"

"They built monuments?" Charlie asked.

"Exactly," Aphrodite-disguised-as-"Agnes" said. "Anything else?"

"They waged wars," Ivy said. "So you get arrows and flint and... They even hunted big animals. I mean that was before the Greeks, but..."

"Seems like *men* leave lasting monuments to their existence," Aphrodite-disguised-as-"Agnes" said. "What do women leave behind?"

No one said anything. The silence lagged.

"Nothing," snorted a boy in the back.

Everyone laughed. Aphrodite-disguised-as-"Agnes" grinned.

"Thank you for sharing this common perception," Aphrodite-disguised-as-"Agnes" said. "I will counter your point by saying very simply this — men build monuments out of stone. Women build people."

No one said anything for a moment. Even the teacher seemed a little stunned.

"You are the monument to the women of ancient Greece," Aphrodite-disguised-as-"Agnes" said. "You are the end result of generations of women's hard work and resilience."

"Women don't have to build obvious monuments out of stone or steel," Heather said. "Every single person is an enduring monument to some of the achievements of women."

"Yes," Aphrodite-disguised-as-"Agnes" said. "Your birth is only one part of a woman's achievement. Only a part."

Aphrodite-disguised-as-"Agnes" gave a clear nod. No one in the class responded. The teacher cleared his throat.

"After those profound thoughts," the teacher said, "shall we talk about the six types of love as defined by the ancient Greeks?"

CHAPTER FIVE HUNDRED & SIXTY-TWO

SIX TYPES OF LOVE

Thursday afternoon — 3:44 p.m.

Carrying two mugs and a small thermos of hot chocolate, Noelle went out the Castle back door. She crossed the frost-crusted grass to the garage, where Mike had left the door open for her. She set the hot chocolate and the mugs down on the bench and got to work.

Noelle took her work as Mike's apprentice very seriously. She picked up all of his dirty water and paint-thinner containers and set them on the counter next to the big, deep utility sink by the door. Mike was really good about cleaning his brushes at the end of the day, but she liked to check them anyway. She went through his brushes, picking up a few that could use a good scrub. She made a mental note to take a day to clean the brushes.

"Oh," Mike said as he came from the back. "You know, you don't have to do that."

"I know," Noelle said. "But it's my job as your apprentice."

Mike grunted.

"I like to help," Noelle said. "Makes me feel like I'm giving back for all the help you've given me. Plus, I looked it up on the Internet. This is the kind of thing an apprentice *should* do."

"Well, if it says so on the *Internet*,. it must be fact," Mike said.

"It is," Noelle said.

"Hey! What's wrong with these brushes?" Mike picked up one of the brushes she deemed not clean enough.

"Oh," Noelle said with a sigh. "I just thought it could use a little attention."

Mike scowled at her back.

"I can feel you scowl at me," Noelle said with a laugh. She gestured to the bench. "Your scowl won't scrape off this residue of paint."

"It might," Mike said vaguely.

"It won't," Noelle said. "I brought us some hot chocolate."

"To scrape off the paint?" Mike asked.

"Funny," Noelle said brightly.

He poured himself some hot chocolate and watched her work. He'd never been really comfortable with having an apprentice. If he didn't like Noelle so much, he would tell her to stop coming. She was such a nice girl that he enjoyed their time together.

Nothing weird.

Nothing sexual, that's for sure.

He simply enjoyed her company.

And more than anything, her work was improving by leaps and bounds.

To his surprise, teaching her had improved his work, as well.

"How was school?" Mike asked the same dumb question that every adult asks a child.

She laughed at his sarcastic tone.

"Heather and her grandmother came to talk to us about the six types of love," Noelle said. "You know, like the Greeks defined."

"Oh, yeah?" Mike asked, breathing over the hot chocolate. "That must have been weird. Was Aphrodite wearing her usual low-cut, sexy evening wear?"

"Weird is a word for it," Noelle said. "Heather must have gotten her grandmother to adjust her look. She looked gorgeous, of course, but in a normal kind of way. Heather told us to call her 'Agnes.' She said that 'Agnes' had multiple PhDs. Nash looked it up later and she *does* have a bunch of degrees. She's kind of famous in ancient Greek scholarship."

"I bet," Mike said. "Nice to know everything before you take the test."

Noelle laughed.

"She told us this thing about how women make people, and men make monuments," Noelle said. "I'm not saying it right. Our class was blown away."

"Sounds about right," Mike said.

"Uh, huh," Noelle said.

She turned and gave him the containers for paint thinner. He took the jars and went to fill them. She put water in the water containers and started setting them out. Mike was screwing the caps on the paint-thinner jars.

"I was thinking of you," Noelle said. "You know, when Heather and her grandmother were talking about the six types of love."

"Oh?" Mike asked.

If anyone else had said that to him, Mike would assume it was something sexy or flattering. But he knew Noelle well enough by now to know that there was nothing obvious about what she had to say. Better to be open than to assume he knew what she was talking about and get confused.

"They mentioned a type of love that reminded me of you," Noelle said.

"Me?" Mike said with a snort. "Something about love reminded you of *me*?"

"Yes," Noelle said. She looked at him. "There's a kind of love that's called 'Agape.' That's love of everyone. Heather said that Buddhists talk about it as 'loving-kindness.' It's a kind of universal love."

"And that reminded you of *me*?" Mike laughed.

Then he remembered who he was talking to. He turned to look at her.

"Sorry," Mike said. "Did I offend you?"

"No," Noelle said. "I know that you pretend not to like anyone."

"I hate everyone. Equally," Mike said.

"How is that different from loving everyone equally?" Noelle asked.

She nodded and turned back to the sink. He scowled at her back. She turned off the tap and turned around.

"What are we working on today?" Noelle asked.

"Hating everyone?" Mike asked.

She gave him a patient smile. He sighed.

"Come on," Mike said. "Let's get to work."

He went back into the garage studio, and Noelle followed him.

~~~~~~~~~

Thursday afternoon — 3:44 p.m.

Colin Hargreaves touched Nash's shoulder and nodded toward the basement stairs.

"When you're ready," Colin said.

Nash nodded. He watched Colin open the basement door.

"Coming?" Teddy asked.

Nash nodded. Teddy followed Colin down the stairs.

Colin Hargreaves was Nash's martial-arts teacher, his Sensei. One thing Colin hated was people who showed up for practice and weren't ready to be there. Colin would rather Nash didn't attend class than show up distracted and unable to be present.

"That's how people get hurt," Colin had said at least a thousand times.

Nash looked at the door where Colin had disappeared. He would rather be in class than staring face to face at his own problems. Nash opened the back door to the house and went out into the garden. They had turned this entire yard into a small farm. He and Teddy had helped turn compost into this soil to get it ready for winter. The yard next door — where the lawyer Samantha Hargreaves lived in the bottom and basement, while

Colin and his family lived on the top floors — was filled with a forest of winter-dormant fruit trees and three evergreen trees.

Nash instinctively wandered toward the trees. A set of three evergreen trees sat nearest to the back of the house. Christmas lights were still strung among the boughs. He just wanted . . .

He wasn't sure what he wanted.

He just knew that he had to get his head right before he could attend practice.

Today, the goddess Aphrodite and her granddaughter, Hedone — or as they usually called her, Heather — had come to their classroom to talk about the six types of love. When they'd finished the six types of love, Heather had talked about two others – *mania* and *storge*. Heather had looked right at him and talked about "mania " — a type of obsessive love.

Nash took out his blackened, smelly phone.

"Nash?" a woman's voice came from the house.

Nash turned to see Samantha Hargreaves holding her infant, Sasha.

"Oh hey," Nash said. "Sorry, I was just . . ."

"You okay?" Samantha asked.

Nash just looked at Samantha.

"Sasha saw you out here." Samantha looked down at the infant girl. "She wants to know if you're okay."

Nash looked at the infant. She was grinning at him and holding her arms out for Nash. Unable to ever resist a baby, Nash went to the baby. He took her out of Samantha's arms and held the child tight. Sasha laughed one of her spectacular laughs. Her laugh always made him feel better.

"Come in," Samantha said. "We were just having our tea. Would you like something?"

Nash looked through the door. He'd never been in Samantha's part of the house. The door went to a small kitchen. The back wall was mostly double-paned glass windows. Samantha waved him into the house, and Nash looked at her.

"I'm supposed to be at class," Nash said.

"You can't go when your head isn't there," Samantha said mildly.

Nash grinned at Samantha.

"How . . .?" Nash asked.

"The twins' martial arts teacher said it about a million times," Samantha said. "They were so wild. I think it was a way of getting them to pay attention. But . . ."

Samantha looked at him, and gave him a slight smile.

"I've found it to be a really helpful life lesson," Samantha said.

"Did you take classes from Sensei Steve?" Nash asked.

"Mmm," Samantha said. She nodded and looked at him. "It's cold. Come in. Have some tea."

Nash nodded. Still holding Sasha, he passed her and went into the kitchen. The room was a sea of white marble with grey and gold shooting through it. There were marble countertops and even marble on the floor. Everything matched in expensive precision. He sucked in a breath.

"Very nice," Nash said.

Samantha looked at him for a moment. The electric kettle clicked off. She took two mugs from the cabinet. They made a "tink" sound when she set them on the hard marble. She set the cinnamon spice teabags he liked into them. She poured water over the teabags and turned around with the mugs.

"I don't think I had cooked even one full meal before I had this kitchen made," Samantha said. "Jacob warned me that it wouldn't be very comfortable or functional. 'The floor is too hard to stand on.' 'The counters are hard to clean.' 'You'll need a lot of cutting boards.' I didn't care, so I didn't listen."

Samantha gave Nash a lovely smile.

"I just wanted the very best," Samantha said.

She looked at the countertops and sighed.

"It's a cold room," Samantha said. "And not very functional. I mean, when someone gets a wild hair and wants to make croissants or other pastries, they come here. It's great for that."

Nash grinned.

"Do you cook much?" Nash asked.

"Not much," Samantha said.

Nash nodded to the drawers.

"Crockpot?" Nash asked.

"Yes, like all Jacob created kitchens, there's a bread maker on the bottom and a crockpot here," Samantha said. "I use those a lot. Instant Pot."

She shrugged.

"I mostly eat next door," Samantha said.

"I would," Nash nodded.

Samantha grinned at him.

"Come on," Samantha said.

He followed her into the living area. The warmth of this room made the kitchen feel like winter. Near the kitchen door, there was a sturdy antique farmhouse table in the dining area. Samantha's laptop was open. A fire was burning in the fireplace. An overstuffed couch invited Nash to come to sit on it. There was another sitting area against the front wall, creating a third room.

Nash looked at Samantha. She closed her laptop as she passed and went to the couch.

"Raz bought this for me," Samantha said.

She sat down and nodded to Nash.

"I had this ridiculous couch," Samantha said with a grin. "He bought this couch and had it delivered while I was traveling."

She grinned at the memory.

"He completely changed this room," Samantha said. "New rugs. New table."

Samantha nodded to the farm table. Nash pointed to the table.

"That was in the attic of Mike's studio for years," Nash said. "Chairs, too. Jacob got it from those houses he owned by DIA."

"I *knew* he had help!" Samantha said with a grin.

"Did he say he did it himself?" Nash asked.

"No. Never," Samantha said. She squinted. "I haven't I asked. I was just so blown away at how much this seemed like *home*. Suddenly. I left this cold house and returned to all of this warmth. A real home."

She looked at Nash.

"You can set her on the couch or put her on her blanket," Samantha said.

"I like holding her," Nash said.

Samantha gave him an agreeing nod.

"What's wrong, Nash?" Samantha asked. "I've known you a long time, and I've never seen this darkness on you."

Nash looked down.

"It's unnatural for you," Samantha said. "You don't wear it well."

Nash sighed.

"I found out . . ." Nash said. To his surprise, his eyes welled with tears. "I . . ."

Samantha reached over and took Sasha. She set her in an antique mission-style crib along the wall and returned to the couch.

"Noelle and I were in that crib," Nash said in spite of his sorrow. "I think Jake and Val were, too."

Samantha shook his head.

"Jacob must have a warehouse of furniture," Samantha said.

"Yes," Nash said. "He does."

"Well, at least we know it raises great kids," Samantha said with a sigh. "Delphie knitted the baby blanket. Sasha loves it."

Nash nodded. Samantha picked up her tea.

"You were saying something," Samantha said.

"Oh," Nash sighed. "You know what happened to Sandy?"

"I've been to see her," Samantha said. "She seems to be on the mend."

Nash nodded.

"She fell because I wouldn't give up my phone," Nash said.

Samantha nodded.

"Delphie and I talked," Nash said. "I'm addicted to this stupid phone."

Nash pulled the charred phone from his pocket.

"I was going to class, and I realized that I usually tape our classes," Nash said. "I've never even looked at them, but I have them. I . . . I . . . liked *having* them."

Nash sighed.

"Today, Heather and her grandmother came to our class to talk about the types of love," Nash said.

Samantha snorted a laugh.

"You had a lecture on love from Aphrodite and Hedone?" Samantha asked incredulously.

"Yeah," Nash said.

"That's an incredible honor," Samantha said.

Nash nodded.

"And it must have been so weird," Samantha said. "Aphrodite always looks at me like I'm some kind of beetle. I never know if she's going to step on me or . . ."

"How do you know them?" Nash asked.

"Oh," Samantha said. "I don't really know them, and, anyway, we're talking about you."

"You'll tell me?" Nash asked.

"Later," Samantha said. "So the goddesses of Love taught you about . . . Agape?"

"Well, yeah," Nash said. "But it was more . . . well . . . at the end, Heather talked about 'Mania.'"

"Obsessive love," Samantha said.

"She looked right at me," Nash said. "I felt like she could see into my soul. How I almost killed Sandy and . . ."

"Nadia," Samantha said softly.

Nash nodded.

"My mother was obsessed with everything," Nash said. "Right now, she's obsessed with getting money from my dad. Says that he owes her for all that *he* put *her* through. *All he put her through!* What a joke!"

Nash shook his head incredulously. He looked at Samantha.

"I'm sorry," Nash said. "I don't know why I'm telling you all of this stuff."

"Sometimes, it's nice to unburden yourself to a familiar stranger," Samantha said. She smiled. "Plus, I know all of the players."

Nash nodded.

"Well," Samantha said, after a moment. "You know the paths you need to take."

Nash nodded.

"So why are you so upset?" Samantha asked.

"I . . ." Nash said.

Tears started down his face. Unable to speak, he shook his head. Samantha sat with him until he was calmer. When he was still, he looked up at the clock.

"I have to go," Nash said.

He jumped up and started out of the house.

"Would you mind if I come to see you later?" Samantha asked.

Nash stopped in his tracks. He turned to her. After a moment, he gave her a brief nod and ran out of the house. Teddy was waiting with their bikes in front of the house.

"You okay?" Teddy asked. "You missed practice."

Nash grunted. They got on their bikes and rode to O'Malley's house.

Chapter Five Hundred & Sixty-three
Storge — Familial love

Thursday afternoon — 3:44 p.m.

Tres Sierra stepped out of his electric SUV. He turned and reached across the seats to get his tablet computer.

"Hey," came from behind him.

He straightened and turned around to see Blane coming down Race Street toward him. Tres held out his arms, and the men hugged.

"Where are you coming from?" Tres asked.

"Work out," Blane said. "New rec center. I thought I'd walk home."

"I'm looking forward to going there," Tres said. "You'll go with me?"

"Of course," Blane said. "Nice ride."

"I just picked it up," Tres said. "Can you help me later with the car seats?"

Blane gave Tres a wide grin.

"I tried, but they are so confusing," Tres said. "And I really don't want to screw it up."

"I get Jacob to do them," Blane said. "Are they in there?"

Blane nodded toward the car. Tres nodded.

"Give me the keys," Blane said. "I'll get Jake to do them. You're coming to dinner after you talk with Nelson?"

"I think we both are," Tres said.

Blane nodded. Tres gave him the keys. Blane pointed up to Nelson's yard, and Tres turned to see Nelson standing outside his door. When Tres turned back, Blane was walking toward the Castle.

"See you tonight," Blane yelled.

Tres waved good-bye. Smiling, Tres started up the walk to meet Nelson.

"It's kind of tricky to get back here," Nelson said. "I thought I'd just wait out here."

"Glad you did," Tres said.

Nelson held out his hand to shake, but Tres gave him a warm hug.

"You and Blane..." Nelson said when he pulled back. "You..."

Tres clapped Nelson's back.

"That's a tale that deserves a beer," Tres said. "I've spent the last hour at the car dealership and could use something to wash the taste out of my mouth."

Grinning, Nelson led Tres back inside his carriage house. He took two beers out of the refrigerator.

"I haven't really drunk since... you know... Blane and me," Nelson said.

"Why's that?" Tres took the caps off the beers.

"Blane's an addict and an alcoholic!" Nelson said.

"He doesn't want you not to have a beer or two," Tres said. "He's said that to me. He doesn't want to be around alcoholics or addicts. Is that you?"

A tall man, Tres leaned down a bit to look into Nelson's eyes. Nelson shook his head. Tres held out his beer, and they "clinked" the bottles.

"Cheers," Tres said as Nelson said, "*Santé.*"

"This is nice," Tres said looking around the carriage house.

Nelson nodded.

"Jake?" Tres asked.

"Who else?" Nelson asked with a chuckle. "The man has a lock on the remodeling of everyone I know."

Tres nodded. He turned around and then pointed to the door off the kitchen.

"Pantry?" Tres asked.

"Small guest bedroom," Nelson said.

"Nice," Tres said. "Can I . . ."

He waved his hand in a circle.

"Sure," Nelson said.

Tres turned around. He went up the stairs to the living-room area.

"I have that TV," Tres said.

"Listen, you and Blane . . ." Nelson said. "You were going to tell me. I . . . uh . . . I've worried about you, you know. You're the youngest of all of us, the most free. Hetero. How are you going to handle me and Blane and . . ."

Tres turned to look at Nelson. Nelson's face was red. His body language was tense.

"What are you asking?" Tres asked.

"What are you to Blane?" Nelson asked.

"Oh," Tres said. "I don't know. I've never asked. I can tell you what he is to me. Would that help?"

Swallowing hard, Nelson nodded.

"I was fourteen or fifteen when Enrique started dating Blane," Tres said.

"Oh, that's right," Nelson said, visibly relieved. "Enrique is your brother."

Tres nodded.

"I was sixteen when Enrique moved in with Blane," Tres said.

"That was Blane's house?" Nelson asked.

"The condo?" Tres asked. "Celia bought it for him so that he would always have a place to live."

"Enrique kicked him out," Nelson said.

"Enrique and his mob kicked him out," Tres said. "It took Jacob about a year to get Enrique out of it."

Nelson nodded. Tres was silent for a moment. He wasn't a man who shared much. He'd hoped what he'd said was enough.

"You and Blane?" Nelson asked.

"My parents were really elderly when I was born," Tres said. "So old that I've wondered if I was the child of one of my elder sisters."

"And?" Nelson asked.

"I'm told it's not true," Tres said with a shrug. "Most of my older siblings were married, with their own children when I was born. Enrique was at home. I . . ."

Tres sighed.

"There just wasn't much for a young child in that house," Tres said. "I shared a room with my great-grandmother until she died. After she died, I could go weeks without anyone saying even a word to me. I had a roof. I had food. But human interaction?"

Tres shook his head.

"Then Enrique met Blane," Tres said. "Blane has this way of reaching into the dark and . . ."

Tres looked at Nelson to see that Nelson was nodding.

"Anyway, Enrique's 'friend' became my surrogate brother," Tres said. "He'd make me lunches for the week. When he realized I was bored in school, he helped me figure out a way to graduate early. I was two years into college at Metro when my father asked me if I was ever going to graduate from high school."

Tres shook his head.

"But Blane was there the whole time," Tres said. "Enrique, too, but it was really Blane. After the whole Enrique thing, I thought I'd lost Blane forever. I came to the Castle — there weren't gates then — and begged them to let me see Blane."

Tres shrugged. Tears came to his eyes.

"Sorry, I always get a little bleary when I think of this," Tres said.

Nelson gave Tres an empathetic nod.

"He… Blane, I mean, was emaciated, sick, and clearly distraught," Tres said. "The first thing he said was, 'How's school? Did something happen?' He was still my brother, my …"

Tres shook his head and looked over Nelson's head.

"Anyway, Blane was back on his feet by the time I had finished my Masters in Finance," Tres said. "He asked Jake to hire me as the assistant to the CFO at Lipson. The man was elderly, an original Celia hire. He taught me the ropes and when he retired, Blane pushed Jake to hire me. It was risky because I was so young, but …"

Tres shrugged.

"Seems like it's worked out," Nelson said.

"It's been great for me," Tres said. "I've learned a ton. Helping to orchestrate through the employee buyout has set me up for life. Seriously. I could go anywhere and get a job. I'm hoping to retire at Lipson. That's my goal. What about you?"

"What about me and Blane?" Nelson asked. Nelson blushed. "Are you asking about sex or …?"

"No," Tres said with a grin and a shake of his head. "I don't want to know about that."

Nelson looked up at Tres.

"I was asking about what your goals were," Tres said. "Do you plan on retiring from the Denver Crime lab? Going back to Emergency Medicine?"

"Oh," Nelson said. "I haven't thought that far. I like working for Ava, but anything could happen."

Nelson shrugged.

"You still feel close to Blane?" Nelson asked.

"I feel like he's my family," Tres said. "Heather says that Blane calls me his 'little brother.' I think that's about right."

"And Enrique?" Nelson asked.

"I have lunch with him every once in a while when my mother insists that I tell him something," Tres said. "I don't really feel one way or another about him. He's like my elder siblings. They are people I know, relatives, otherwise..."

"So no big-happy-family parties," Nelson said.

"No," Tres said. "I'm a little..."

"Shy?" Nelson asked.

"Introverted," Tres said.

"Me, too," Nelson said with a grin. He made a dramatic sigh. "You can't imagine how relieved I am."

"Why?" Tres asked.

"I just... I don't know," Nelson said. "You're a young heterosexual male. Why move in with some lady and her husband?"

"And you?" Tres asked. Nelson nodded. "That 'lady' is a Greek goddess."

"That's why?" Nelson asked. "To be near a goddess?"

"No," Tres shook his head. "You're very verbal, Mr. Weeks. You're going to have to slow it down for me."

Squinting, Nelson nodded.

"I was just pointing out that Heather is a goddess," Tres said. "Not that all women aren't goddesses in their own rights. They are. It's just that..." Tres sighed. "We are honored to be in her presence. If something wasn't right, she would know it."

"Oh," Nelson said. "I never thought of it that way."

"She has the choice of every man or woman on the planet," Tres said. "She chose Blane and then she chose us. There's a kind of responsibility and honor with that."

"And you?" Nelson asked. "What about raising kids that aren't yours and..."

"I grew up with the children of my older siblings," Tres said. "I like kids, and they like me. I don't care if I'm their biological father. There are certainly plenty of Sierras on the planet. I really only care that kids are happy."

Nelson nodded.

"You know that Tink works for me in the summers, right?" Tres asked. "She's started calling me 'Daddy T.'"

Nelson grinned.

"Yes, you'll get a name too," Tres said.

Nelson's grin grew wider.

"This is really happening," Nelson said under his breath.

"Yes, lonely boy, you are suddenly going to be a part of a big, loud, weird family," Tres said. "The weird part is me. Well, certainly, you know Enrique."

Nelson laughed.

"Have you met Loki yet?" Tres asked.

"Loki?" Nelson gave a confused shake of his head. "From the movies? Thor's brother?"

"He and Hedone have a 'thing,'" Tres said with a nod and a grin. "Something for you to look forward to."

"I guess," Nelson said.

"Hey, Jake said that they've finished the demo on the house," Tres said. "Can we take a look?"

"Yes," Nelson cleared his throat. "That is what we'd planned to do this evening."

Tres drained his beer. He spied that Nelson's beer bottle was empty. Tres gestured to it.

"It was nice to have a beer," Nelson said. "You can just leave that here."

"Is Mari here?" Tres asked.

"No, why?" Nelson asked.

"She was showing me some options for the house," Tres said.

Mari appeared. She grinned at Tres.

"I was listening in," Mari said.

"Yes, who needs an A.I. when you have a nosy fairy?" Nelson asked.

"Exactly," Mari said. "What is an 'A. I.'?"

Nelson opened his mouth, but Tres continued.

"She can show us different options," Tres said. "I've priced out some of our options. She can show us visually what they would look like — you know, most expensive, medium, cheap. She . . ."

Nelson looked confused.

"Let's go into the other house," Mari said.

With that, they left the carriage house. They went through the backyard and into the main house. The walls had been torn down to the studs. The floors were bare wood. The antique wooden stairs had been covered in paper to protect them during the construction.

Tres took a breath and sighed.

"I love a fresh pallette," Tres said. "Has Jill been through?"

"She told me what she was thinking," Mari said. "She wanted you to know that it was just preliminary. She would be here, but she's at the hospital."

"How is Sandy?" Tres asked.

"You were just there," Mari said.

"I was focused on . . ." Tres said. "I'm kind of a one-track guy."

"Ah, yes," Mari said. "Sandy's okay. Stronger. They are going to move her tomorrow morning."

"That's good," Nelson said.

Mari nodded.

"Now, let's get started, boys . . ." Mari said.

The men followed Mari into the house.

~~~~~~~~~

Thursday night — 10:45 p.m.

"Nash?" Noelle whispered.

They were sleeping in the den of Seth O'Malley's house. True to form, Teddy was sound asleep on the floor. Nash was on the big couch, and Noelle was lying on the smaller love seat. Noelle could hear Nash's silent crying.

Samantha Hargreaves had come to talk to Valerie after she'd talked to Nash. Valerie brought Samantha into Mike's studio, where Noelle was working on the miniature painting Mike had assigned. Noelle had listened to these great women worry over her brother. She knew that he was suffering, but Noelle was pretty sure they had no idea what was wrong. Mike had nodded for Noelle to contribute to the conversation, but she'd just remained silent and worked on her painting.

How can these women possibly understand?

Noelle had promised herself that she would talk to Nash when she got back to Seth O'Malley's house, where they were staying. But Nash was moving heavy plants for Delphie in the greenhouse. Teddy was learning how to cook from Maresol, so she wasn't able to talk to him, either. She'd been hustled off to the shower. By the time she was done, dinner was waiting in the big dining room.

Mike had insisted that she take the piece she was working on with her so that she could look at it in different lights to see what it needed. Of course, Seth's Dad, Bernie, had seen her painting and wanted to talk about it.

To Noelle's horror, *she* was the center of attention at dinner. It was a portrait of her mom, Sandy in watercolor on a polished mammoth bone Mike had gotten from Snow Mass. Her painting was a miniature, not more than three and a half inches high and a little more than two inches wide. Noelle hoped to finish it before Sandy got home from the hospital.

Much to her surprise, the adults actually knew a lot about art — even Maresol. They had some really interesting things to say about her miniature. They asked her why she was working on bone. (Because ivory was cruel.) They asked her how Mike had obtained the mammoth bone. (A Lipson construction guy who had worked the Snow Mass site had sold it to Mike. Yes, he had a permit to sell it.) And then they started talking. She'd taken notes. Even Nash and Teddy had listened in fascination.

At Bernie's encouragement, Seth had gotten up to get a small painting that had belonged to his mother. He returned with a miniature masterpiece about the size of her painting. Noelle knew right off the bat that it had been painted by Eulabee Dix. She'd been bold enough to talk about the piece, as if she knew something about it. She'd told them that it was watercolor on ivory — they didn't know any better then — and that *this* was a picture of Ethel Barrymore.

That caused a lot of loud conversation, as no one knew who the woman in the miniature was. The adults made a big effort not to use electronic tools. Bernie had brought out an enormous, heavy book of New York artists from the American Society of Miniature Painters. They were finishing their pie when everyone agreed that it was, indeed, Ethel Barrymore.

Noelle had been so flushed by the attention that she'd lost track of her worry for Nash.

Now, a full forty minutes after they'd gone to sleep, her worry returned.

Rather than whisper his name again, Noelle got up from her couch. As she had done when they were small, she lay on her side behind her brother. They were tall teenagers but still very slim. The two of them fit easily on the big couch. Nash didn't move when she cuddled next to him.

She heard him try to silence his sorrow and control his sobs. She put her arm around him and hugged him. Her actions seemed to unlock his pain, and he sobbed. She just stayed there with him.

They had always been like two lost souls in the rain.

For most of their life, they were shuttled back and forth between their father's stable home and the chaos that was their mother. Some days were a slog from beginning to end. Together, they marched through the heavy winds of their parents' addictions and the insanity of "shared custody."

They were a team then.

They were a team now.

After a while, Nash was breathing deeply. Noelle thought he might be asleep, when he sat up. She sat up. They instinctively moved until their hips and legs were pressed against each other. When he took her hand, she grabbed on with both of hers. He turned to look at her and gave her a sorrow-filled smile.

"I don't know why I'm so sad," Nash whispered to what he assumed was her question.

"I do," Noelle said.

He looked at her.

"You thought maybe you'd get a normal life," Noelle said in a soft tone. "Away from all this addiction crap. You could be with Nadia. You could be safe and happy and have love and . . ."

He teared up to her words. She gave him a kind smile, and he nodded.

"Have you talked to Nadia?" Noelle whispered.

"And say what?" Nash asked in a soft voice. "I'm a loser addict who nearly killed his mom? She'll . . ."

Nash started to cry again. Noelle put her arm around him.

"You won't know what she'll say until you talk to her," Noelle whispered.

Nash shook his head. Tears continued to roll down from his eyes. Noelle held her brother for a long, long time. At some point during the night, he looked at her with heavy, sleepy eyes. He nodded his head at her couch. She nodded.

"It's going to be okay, Nash," Noelle said.

"It's going to *be*," Nash said, an errant tear running down his face.

She gave him a soft smile and went to her love seat. It took her a long time to go to sleep. She wondered if Eulabee Dix had ever hurt so badly because her brother was in pain. As she drifted off

to sleep, she remembered learning about "*storge*" — familial love
— from the goddesses Hedone and Aphrodite.

CHAPTER FIVE HUNDRED & SIXTY-FOUR

THE LOVE OF MONEY

Friday morning — 9:51 a.m.

"So he says…" Jeraine said. He dropped the bag full of dirty laundry onto the floor of the laundry room.

"Yeah?" Heather asked as she came in behind him.

She set down their laundry bag. They turned and walked down the hallway to get the rest of their laundry. Friday morning was designated Heather, Blane, Jeraine, and Tanesha's laundry time. For the last month or so, Jeraine and Heather had spent this unusual, yet oddly enjoyable, laundry time together.

"He says, 'That's the point,'" Jeraine said.

"What's the point?" Heather asked.

"The point was to sign me to a contract and then *not* give me a show," Jeraine said.

"*And* make sure you don't get a show anywhere else?" Heather gasped.

Heather stopped walking and turned to him. He stopped at her side. He nodded, and they continued walking along.

"*Philarguria*," Heather said.

"What?" Jeraine asked.

Heather ducked into her apartment to get the other bag of dirty clothing and a bag of sheets from Blane's acupuncture practice. When she returned to the hallway, she waited a minute for Jeraine to appear from his apartment. They walked toward the laundry room.

"What was that word that you used?" Jeraine asked.

"Philarguria?" Heather asked. Jeraine nodded. "It means 'the love of money' — you know, avarice. I gave that talk to the older kids at the Marlowe School about the Greek words for 'love.'"

"I bet you left that one out," Jeraine said.

"I did," Heather said. "My grandmother thought we should talk about it because the love of money is so common now, but I said that we should talk about the forms of love that aren't such a focus now."

"And she actually agreed to do what you said?" Jeraine asked.

"I know. Weird, right?" Heather asked with a snort.

Jeraine grinned. They walked the rest of the way to the laundry room. For the next few minutes, they dumped out their laundry bags and sorted them into colors. The laundry room had two huge industrial laundry machines and big dryers. So, it made sense for them to combine their clothing to fill the laundry. Heather poured in the laundry detergent and Jeraine set the settings. When the two machines were chugging along, they left the laundry room.

"You want to come to mine?" Jeraine asked.

"Sure," Heather said.

"I made some bread this morning," Jeraine said.

"Ginger?" Heather asked.

"With the crystallized ginger," Jeraine said.

"Sold," Heather said with a grin.

They went to the apartment where Jeraine, Tanesha, and Jabari were living. The housekeeping crew — run by Rosa and paid by everyone who lived in the Castle — had been through the apartment. It was tidy, clean, and smelled lovely. This apartment's kitchen was just a stove, a sink, and a refrigerator.

Jeraine put the kettle on the stove. Heather sat down at the bar.

"Why did you say that about 'avarice' and that Greek word?" Jeraine asked.

"*Philarguria*?" Heather asked.

"What did you mean?" Jeraine asked. "I mean, it makes sense. That guy has loads of money and a bunch of ex-wives and angry kids. I'd believe that he loves only money, but . . ."

He took a bread pan off the cooling rack and turned the pan over so that the bread fell onto a plate. He set it on the bar and went to get the butter.

"I just don't see how it relates to what I was saying," Jeraine said.

Heather nodded when he turned around. He set the butter, a knife, and a couple of plates on the counter.

"We have a certain capacity to love," Heather said. "All of us — fairies, Olympians, even Titans — we can channel our love in a few ways. You should have seen Perses, who loves killing, struggle when he suddenly, for the first time in his entire life, had *Eros*, *Philia*, and *Ludus*."

"What?" Jeraine asked.

"If you focus all of your energy on *Philarguria* . . ." Heather said, slowly.

"Avarice," Jeraine said.

Heather nodded and continued, "you don't have the energy for some of the more fulfilling loves like *pragma*, long-standing love — like your parents' or you and Tanesha's — or even *philia*, which is deep friendships. The love of money clogs up everything else until it's all you have."

"Why is that?" Jeraine asked.

"Some of it is time," Heather said. "If you're the God of Destruction . . ."

"You spend your life destroying things," Jeraine said with a nod.

He cut pieces of the ginger bread, and Heather grabbed a slice.

"What better way to cause destruction than killing?" Heather said.

His mouth full, Jeraine grunted.

"We won't get into people who are addicted to drugs and sex," Heather said.

She raised his eyebrows, and he gave her an acquiescing nod.

"We have only so much time in a day," Heather said. "If we spend all of our waking hours thinking about obtaining money, we don't have time to cultivate these other kinds of love, even inside ourselves."

"I know a bunch of dudes who have a lot of money and a lot of ... uh ... sex," Jeraine said, picking his words.

"Sure," Heather said. "But it's not really 'love' — or even *eros*. You know that better than most people. It's not very fulfilling."

Jeraine shook his head.

"So how does that relate to my situation in Vegas?" Jeraine asked. "I can't work at the dude's casino, and I can't work at Jammy's friend's place. He *lit-er-ally* signed me to force me not to work in Vegas or, really, anywhere."

"Keep the African-American blockade going," Heather said.

"Prejudiced prick," Jeraine said.

"But he *is* rich," Heather said.

Jeraine scowled at Heather. She gave him a shrug.

"It's not fair," Jeraine said.

"But it does make money," Heather said.

"You're starting to annoy the f ... out of me," Jeraine said.

The kettle blared. He turned to make their tea, and Heather grinned at his back. He'd been attempting to stop swearing so that Jabari didn't pick it up. Of course, Jabari swore like a sailor. Jeraine set a mug of tea in front of her.

"Okay — for those at the back of the class ..." Heather said.

"That's clearly me," Jeraine said into his tea.

Heather grinned.

"This man loves money," Heather said slowly. Speeding up, she continued, "From what you say, he loves money more than wives and children."

Jeraine nodded.

"He likely has friends, but a love of money fills up those gaps, too," Heather said.

"So he doesn't really have friends?" Jeraine asked.

"He has people who make him money," Heather said. "Associates. People who work for him."

"People he owns," Jeraine said with a snort.

"Exactly," Heather said.

"So?" Jeraine asked.

"What do you want?" Heather asked.

"I want . . . You mean, like *everything*?" Jeraine asked. "Like my Miss T. and Jabari and . . ."

"In this situation," Heather said.

"Oh." Jeraine thought for a moment before he shook his head. "Doesn't matter what I want. He holds all the cards."

"Chicken," Heather said.

"What are you talking about?" Jeraine asked, his voice rising with irritation. "I am no chicken."

"Then why not tell me what you want?" Heather asked.

Jeraine gave her a dark scowl.

"Before you tell me that I could not understand your plight as a young African-American man in America, I remind you that I am a *half-breed* Olympian, born out of wedlock, and raised in Olympia because my grandmother tormented my mother all over the world."

"I knew there was a reason I liked you," Jeraine said with a laugh.

"And I'm not saying that this situation isn't infuriating," Heather said. "It's racism — plain and simple."

"He tricked me!" Jeraine said.

"True," Heather said. "And it is hard to be an African-American man right now."

Jeraine gave her a sideways look, and she nodded.

"It is hard," Heather said. "That doesn't change the fact that you *want* something — whatever it is. This desire is a wind that you can set your sail upon."

He took a long drink of his tea to avoid looking at her.

"You want lots of money?" Heather asked.

"I thought it would..." Jeraine said. "Before you said it, that guy would never get ripped off because his attention is always on his money. I wanted money because I thought it would get me something I wanted, but I didn't pay any attention to it."

"So someone stole your money, *and* you didn't get what you actually wanted," Heather said.

Jeraine scowled.

"Sucks," Heather said. "So, maybe you should just be honest about what you want."

"I am honest," Jeraine said.

"Then tell me what you want," Heather said. "Lay it out for me."

"What's that going to do?" Jeraine asked. "You're going to *magic* it all away?"

"I won't magic it away," Heather said.

"Agreement with Tanesha," Jeraine and Heather said in near unison.

"Fine," Jeraine said.

"But I might be able to see what you *have* that he *does not*," Heather said.

"What doesn't he have?" Jeraine asked. "He has piles of cash. He has everything."

Heather shook her head. Jeraine just looked at her for a long time.

"Shit," Jeraine said. "You're saying that, because of his... that Greek word."

"*Philarguria*," Heather said with a nod.

"He basically has *only* money," Jeraine said. "I don't have money..."

Heather opened her mouth to speak, but Jeraine held up a finger.

"I don't have a lot of money," he repeated, "but I have friends, good friends. I have Tanesha. And my parents are even proud of me now. I have... I don't know the others, but I have Jammy, and I have..."

He fell silent.

"That lady who invited you on her tour last year?" Heather asked. Jeraine nodded. "What is it that she said? Something like, 'If you ever need anything...'?"

"Shit," Jeraine said.

"What?" Heather asked.

"I know a lot of artists," Jeraine said. "I could put the word out on this situation and get people to boycott his casino. Hell, stop going to Vegas at all. Boycott the place because it's racist toward African-Americans."

"It won't be everyone," Heather said.

"Yeah, but I know O'Malley," Jeraine said. "Or my Dad does."

"It's the kind of thing O'Malley would hate," Heather said. "He hates unfairness of any kind."

"True," Jeraine nodded. "And he knows everyone. And I know..."

"You should check with Jammy," Heather said.

"Good thinking," Jeraine said. "In case I get in trouble for talking about it."

Jeraine nodded and fell silent, thinking.

"You think that will happen?" Jeraine asked.

"I think the man who has eyes only for money is easily blindsided by people who love well and completely in all areas," Heather said.

"*Agape*," Jeraine said.

"Hey! How did you...?" Heather asked.

"Mike," Jeraine said with a grin. "He was a little freaked that Noelle thought he showed *agape*. You know — it breaks up his badass image."

They fell silent for a moment.

"You have to be a badass to truly love everyone," Heather said.

Jeraine nodded. They fell silent for a while.

"You mind if I call Jammy?" Jeraine asked.

"Go ahead," Heather said. She looked at her watch. "We have ten more minutes before we dry. If you're still talking, I'll start the next loads and the dryer."

"You don't mind?" Jeraine asked.

"Ever try to clean a garment with a rock and a stream?" Heather asked.

Grinning, Jeraine shook his head and went to get his cell phone.

~~~~~~~~~

Friday morning — 10:51 a.m.

In the alley behind the Castle, Jacob leaned over and opened the passenger door. Valerie stepped up into his truck. They drove toward the end of the alley and then stopped.

"Where to?" Jacob asked.

"Oh," Valerie sighed. "I mostly just wanted to talk to you."

"Where's a good place to do that?" Jacob asked.

"Well . . ." Valerie said.

"Have you had breakfast?" Jacob asked. "Want to get a coffee?"

"Do you think Dad's done?" Valerie asked.

She turned to look at him.

"With what?" Jacob asked.

Valerie shook her head.

"You're not listening to me," Valerie said.

"You're not saying anything," he said.

He glanced over to catch her mouthing his words. He grinned.

"Let's see . . ." Jacob said. "It's almost eleven. So yes, I think Dad's done reading the funnies to our mom. He's likely on his way to Lipson. Do you want to see him?"

Valerie gave a slight shake of her head. He turned right, and they went up Sixteenth Avenue. He turned on York Street and made his way to Colfax Boulevard. He pulled through the chain coffee shop drive-thru. After getting coffee for himself and tea for her, he started toward where he thought she wanted to go.

They drove in silence for a while. When he pulled up, Valerie gave a soft exclamation.

"Good job, Jake," Valerie said in a soft voice.

Grinning, he pulled into the cemetery and drove to where their mother was buried. She slid out of the passenger side of the truck. He reached into the cab for a bundle of flowers. Valerie was kneeling over their mother's grave when he got there.

"Here," he said.

She turned slightly. Seeing the bouquet, she smiled and took the flowers from him. He went to sit on the bench near her grave to wait for his sister. A few minutes later, Valerie came to sit next to him. The sky was blue. The sun was out. They were dressed warmly, and the day was not too cold.

"How did you know?" Valerie asked after a moment.

She put her arms around her to pull in her quilted jacket.

"I bought those for you," Jacob said.

"Well, you'd better get some more, buddy," Valerie said with a laugh.

Jacob grinned. Whether due to the cold or just the cold reality of sitting at their mother's grave, they shifted closer to each other.

"What's going on?" Jacob asked.

"I . . ." Valerie sighed. "God, it's great to be home."

Jacob knew better than to rein her in. He simply nodded so that she knew that he was listening.

"I . . ." Valerie sighed. "It's just that . . ."

Jacob held out his hand. She grabbed onto him like she would a lifeline. After a few moments, in the still quiet in front of their mother's grave, she sighed again.

"I guess I'm not making any sense," Valerie said.

"What else is new?" Jacob asked.

She punched him with the back of her hand. They laughed.

"Just lay it out for me," Jacob said what their mother used to say when either of them needed to talk. "Take your time. Tell me everything. Don't leave anything out."

"Yes, Mom," Valerie said softly and then stopped talking.

After a moment, she took a breath and began to speak from the depths of her being.

"I honestly don't think that you remember what it was like to be poor," Valerie said.

Not speaking, Jacob raised his eyebrows.

"Okay, that's unfair," Valerie said. "I just hated it. I really hated not being able to have the simple things that my friends had — clothing, shoes . . . lunch money, a red scooter."

Jacob grinned at the reference to his childhood dream of having a red scooter.

"I just hated it," Valerie said. "Mom and Dad worked all the time. If they weren't working, they were talking about work, scheming how to get more work, or taking us to some God-forsaken job site so that they could work. I wanted a *babysitter* — not a backhoe."

Valerie nodded.

"I swore that I'd never be poor," Valerie said. "I swore that my children would have every little thing they wanted — trips to the beach or Milan or . . . Of course, my children just want to be at home, which is the Castle, so that they can hang out with their cousins. My gorgeous daughter rarely even brushes her hair, let alone worries about her shoes."

"She's kind of young for shoe worry," Jacob said.

"I was her age when *I* was furious that Becky Juslip had these lace Mary Janes," Valerie said. "Pink. I pestered Mom relentlessly for those stupid shoes. When I finally owned a pair — my big present for Christmas — Penny had already moved on to a shoe with a heel. Of course. And I was still the lame one."

"I wonder what happened to Ms. Juslip," Jacob said, mildly.

"Fine, you're right," Valerie said. "I have my revenge against Becky and all of the other Becky's of the world! I *know* that."

Jacob bit back a reply. He waited for her to continue. She took so long that he wondered if the moment had passed.

"That's just it," Valerie said. "I wanted money so much that . . ." She sighed.

"I made a mess out of everything," Valerie said. "Then Mike and I were back together, and we had Jackie and . . ."

"You never gave up your love of money," Jacob said.

Grunting, Valerie nodded.

"Don't tell Mike that I told you, but I was furious at him for giving so many of his best paintings to the Denver Art Museum," Valerie said. "We could have *sold* them and made *a lot* of money."

Jacob didn't say anything.

"I was in the basement yesterday," Valerie said. "The kids were playing in that great room you made for them. 'The Wild Bunch.' Such a great name for them. I found Jackie's perfect, pink, lace Mary Janes in a pile with Mack's filthy soccer shoes. I couldn't believe it! The perfect shoes, and she . . ."

Valerie looked at Jacob.

"I asked her why she'd just thrown her shoes there," Valerie said. "She said that they weren't very comfortable."

Valerie shook her head.

"Very comfortable," Valerie said.

"And?" Jacob asked.

"They are not very comfortable," Valerie said with a snort of a laugh. "I was about to lecture her that women of class wear uncomfortable shoes when I realized that I was just being stupid. Why would I want my daughter to wear uncomfortable shoes?"

Valerie lifted her hands and flopped them back on her lap.

"I've wasted my life on *philarguria*," Valerie said.

"The love of money," Jacob said. "Yes. I've heard all about the Greek words for 'love' as well."

Valerie smiled. What few teenagers who weren't sequestered at O'Malley's house had been talking non-stop about love and the definitions of love. When Valerie didn't respond, Jacob thought it might help if he said something.

"If I may . . ." Jacob said.

CHAPTER FIVE HUNDRED & SIXTY-FIVE

DEEP FRIENDSHIPS

Valerie nodded.

"I understand what you're saying," Jacob said. "I even remember those pink shoes. Do you remember what happened to them?"

Valerie shook her head.

"You got terrible blisters," Jacob said. "You had to see Dr. Bumpy and got a lecture from Nurse Dionne about taking care of your feet. 'No fashion is more important than caring for your feet, young lady.'"

Valerie grinned.

"She's right," Valerie said.

"Of course, she is," Jacob said.

When she didn't say anything else, he continued.

"I don't think that you have a love of money," Jacob said.

"I was furious with Mike over those stupid paintings," Valerie said. "He was like: 'What? I'll paint more. The Denver Art Museum has helped me a lot. They need to raise some money. What's the big deal?'"

"Of course, he's right," Jacob said.

"Hrmpft," Valerie said.

She crossed her arms over her chest.

"I don't think you have a love of money," Jacob repeated. "I think you wanted to be safe."

Valerie turned to look at him.

"Social safety was always important to you," Jacob said. "You didn't want to be made fun of or be bullied or taken advantage of. You felt small. I don't know why, but it still comes over you now.

It's crazy to me, but you feel small, sometimes. Overlooked. Money seems to make that go away."

"Seems," Valerie said. She shifted back to look at her mother's gravestone. "Money steals away everything else."

Valerie sighed, and Jacob waited.

"I'm thinking of leaving acting," Valerie said, firmly.

Jacob laughed. She hit him again, and he laughed harder.

"Why are you laughing?" Valerie asked.

"You love acting," Jacob said. "You love everything about it. You've already signed contracts for two more movies and a commercial and whatever's next."

Valerie scowled.

"Whatever you do, you're not quitting acting," Jacob said.

She sighed.

"Maybe now that the money thing is not such a big deal, you just need to add more of the things you love into your life," Jacob said.

"Like what?" Valerie asked.

"Like hanging out with Samantha," Jacob said. "She is your best friend. Like taking really great care of yourself for a while. Or just playing."

"*Philia. Philautia,*" Valerie said. "*Ludus.*"

"Oh, God — not you too," Jacob said, mock groaning. "Mike's been whining about being 'charged with *agape.*'"

"He wants someone to pay!" Valerie said with a laugh.

They laughed for a moment.

"Actually, I can't think of anything better than focusing on the different kinds of love," Jacob said. "We need them so desperately now. The world seems to have a shortage of love. As Aristotle said..."

"All friendly feelings for others are an extension of a man's feelings for himself," Jacob and Valerie quoted their mother, with Jacob saying, "woman" and Valerie saying "man."

They sat in front of their mother's grave in silence. They missed her so desperately and, yet, somehow, she was still there with them. Valerie sighed.

"Is Mom here?" Valerie asked.

Jacob shook his head and sighed.

"I haven't seen her in a while," Jacob said. He gave a soft shrug. "I assume she's needed elsewhere."

Valerie gave a soft nod. After a few more minutes, Valerie stood up.

"Love you, Mom," Valerie said.

"Now and forever," Jacob added.

Valerie hooked her hand through his elbow, and they walked back to his truck.

"Buy me lunch?" Valerie asked when they were in his truck.

"'Famous' lunch or just lunch?" Jacob asked.

"Just lunch," Valerie said.

"Good," Jacob said.

He started the truck and they slowly drove from the cemetery.

~~~~~~~~~

Friday afternoon — 1:31 p.m.

Sandy opened her eyes.

While she had no idea of where she was, she knew the sound she was hearing — her girlfriends were here.

"Look," Heather said.

There was movement in the room. Jill appeared in front of her.

Sandy smiled — or *tried* to smile.

"Don't smile," Jill said in a soft tone. "Your jaw is wired together."

Sandy's left eyebrow dipped for a moment as Sandy tried to remember what had happened. Jill opened her mouth to tell Sandy. Sandy tried to nod, but she was restrained by a neck brace. She remembered.

There was more movement in the room. Heather sat on the other side of the bed.

"Tanesha was here early this morning," Heather said.

"S-k-l," Sandy said gutturally.

Jill and Heather nodded in agreement that Tanesha was at medical school. As if Sandy had just left the room to get something from the kitchen, Heather updated her on their conversation.

"I was just telling Jill that Jeraine is having trouble in Vegas," Heather said. "Seems like Hecate found him a place to play, but the guy he signed a contract with . . ."

Heather stopped to see if Sandy remembered. She gave a slight nod.

"He's now saying that he never intended on having Jeraine in residence there," Heather said.

"He signed Jeraine only to lock him into not playing anywhere," Jill said.

Sandy made a guttural sound of disgust.

"I said the same thing," Heather said with a grin. "What a jerk."

Sandy nodded. Sandy gestured to her ring finger.

"Aden's been here at night," Heather said. "He's at Lipson now. Would you like me to call him?"

"He wanted to save his sick time so that he could be home when you get there," Jill said.

"He seems okay," Heather said. "He's worried and misses you terribly, but, otherwise, he seems okay."

"Jsssst," Sandy said. She drew a question mark in the air to indicate that she was just asking.

Jill and Heather nodded. Sandy put her arms in a gesture of "baby." Jill shot Heather a look. Sandy hadn't asked about the children yet. They'd argued over what to tell her. Heather nodded to Jill.

"Rachel misses you terribly," Jill said. "Mack and Jack have kind of taken her under their wing. Maggie has been great. She has so much experience with her father being gone. They are amazing."

Jill lifted her shoulders in a shrug.

"Valerie's home, so she's helping with the kids," Jill continued. "It's nice to see her enjoy some family time. The kids adore her, of course. The doctor won't let the kids come to see you yet."

Sandy made a "Why?" face.

"You're fairly bruised and swollen," Jill said.

"You don't really have the strength yet to take care of them," Heather added.

Sandy tried to make a fist. When she was unable to she lifted her hand up to see. Her hand was in a full cast, fingers and all. She groaned.

Sandy made the "baby" gesture again.

"Do you . . . ?" Jill looked at Heather.

Heather shook her head.

"N-sh, N'll?" Sandy asked. "Ch-rly. S-ssy?"

"Sissy is good," Jill said. "She calls every night to see how you are."

Jill nodded her head to Heather.

"You probably remember that the other kids are staying at O'Malley's," Heather said.

Sandy nodded.

"I've heard that they are having a great time," Heather said. "Teddy is learning to cook from Maresol. Katy said that Noelle sat in with them at their piano class. Nash is helping Delphie in the new greenhouse they built."

"N-sh?" Sandy asked.

"He's very sad," Jill started.

They fell silent.

Sandy held her arms out in a "Why?" gesture.

"He feels responsible for what happened to you," Jill said.

"Abi destroyed his and Teddy's phone," Heather said.

Sandy nodded and gestured that this was why Nash was sad. Jill and Heather shared a look. Jill nodded to Heather.

"I think he genuinely feels bad," Heather said. "I went to school to talk about the six kinds of love according to the Greeks. He was almost non-responsive."

"Delphie talked to him about his phone addiction," Jill said.

"G-d," Sandy said. She gestured to her ears.

"Oh," Heather said with a sigh. "I think he heard her. He is very upset. Won't speak to Nadia. Cries in his sleep. He's very . . ."

"He loves you," Jill said.

"But T-d," Sandy said.

"Well, Teddy admits that he was why you turned to look back," Jill said. "He feels badly, but it's really destroyed Nash."

"Teddy has been through so much that he's a little more resilient," Heather said.

"Or he's putting on a strong face because Nash is so upset," Jill said.

"Either way, we have eyes on him," Heather said.

Sandy gave a little nod. She paused for a minute. She couldn't write because of the injuries to her hands. She pointed to herself.

"You . . ." Jill said.

Sandy pointed to her eyes.

"See?" Jill said.

"She wants to see herself," Heather said.

The women shared a look across Sandy's bed.

"I don't know, Sandy — it's not a great idea," Jill said.

Sandy gave Jill and then Heather her intense look. The women looked at each other for a moment. Heather acquiesced, but Jill was firm.

"Pl-ssss," Sandy said.

Jill's resolve broke. They took out a small mirror from Jill's backpack. They leaned in together and held up the mirror.

Sandy's eyes welled with tears as she assessed the damage.

Sandy had two deep wells of dark purple under her eyes. Her eyelids were thick pads of black and blue. Her nose had been reset by the plastic surgeon. It was covered in a kind of a cast. The rest of her face was a mottled display of yellow, purple, and red. She put her hand to her neck.

"You have cracked a vertebra," Heather said. "They believe it will heal without intervention. The neck brace will help with that."

"You broke your ankle and then your leg," Jill said. "They were set in surgery. The doctors think they should heal easily."

"The biggest worry at this point is infection," Heather said.

Sandy nodded that she understood. She continued to look at herself in the mirror for another moment before dropping it into her lap. Sandy's eyes closed.

After a moment, Heather and Jill moved away from the bed. Sandy had been alternatively awake and asleep for the last few days. They had some concern about her memory, as Sandy often asked about the same things over and over again. She didn't always remember what they'd said the last time.

But for now, she was resting.

And that was good.

~~~~~~~~~

Friday afternoon — 2:01 p.m.
Marlowe School

After tapping on the door, Dr. John Drayson leaned his head in to the classroom.

"Now!" an adult man yelled.

The room was in the middle of some kind of experiment. A medical doctor, John tried to figure out what they were doing. The students had been in two tight groups together. When the science teacher had yelled, they began to spin in place out of the group. The groups began to mingle.

"Create a third group!" the man yelled.

"Second law of thermodynamics." were John's first words in the classroom.

The students continued their spinning until the entire room was full of spinning, giggling students.

"Can you feel it?" the man who was clearly the science teacher yelled. "More energy in the third group."

The students were so intent on laughing and spinning that they continued, despite the science teacher's words.

"Okay, let's stop now, so we have time to talk about what happened," the man said.

Caught up in their adventure, the students kept bumping into each other and laughing.

"We have to stop!" the man said.

John let out a very loud whistle. Everyone in the classroom turned to gawk at him. Charlie started walking in his direction.

"Who are you?" the man asked.

"I apologize. John Drayson," John said, in his clipped London accent. "I was just trying to help."

"Yes, well," the man said. "I'm their science teacher."

"Yes, I noticed — Second Law of Thermodynamics?" John asked.

"Exactly," the science teacher said. "We're all together here, so I try to find fun ways for the older kids to engage with the younger kids."

"It looked very fun," John said. "I wish you were my science teacher."

The science teacher blushed and looked back at the room. With a break in the conversation, Charlie hugged John.

"How are you, Charlie?" John asked.

"I'm good," Charlie said. He stood a little straighter. "I'm getting through high school."

"Great job," John said. "I'm proud of you."

Charlie looked at the science teacher and back at John.

"This is Dr. John Drayson," Charlie said. "He saved my life."

John modestly waved his hand in "No" and shook his head.

"He seriously did," Charlie said.

"How did you save Charlie?" the science teacher asked.

"Charlie had been badly beaten," John said. "He had an artery that began to bleed. I was his surgeon."

"In the ICU," Charlie said. "While I was awake. He was making jokes with his wife."

"I think that she was making the jokes," John said. "To keep you cheerful."

Charlie nodded.

"That *is* impressive," the science teacher said. "Are you here for Charlie?"

"While it's always nice to see Charlie. And Noelle...;" John smiled at Noelle. "I am actually here for Nash Norsen."

"How's Sandy?" Noelle asked in quick, anxious language. "Have you been to see her?"

"She's healing," John said. "It's just going to take time. I know she was hoping to go home tonight. With any luck, that will happen. She is still in early healing."

Everyone in the classroom knew what had happened to Sandy Norsen, the wife of Lipson Construction's CEO and their friend's mother.

"Do you need to see the note as well?" John asked the science teacher.

"Note?" the science teacher asked.

"For Nash," John asked.

"Oh, no," the science teacher said. "You checked in with the office."

"I did," John said. "A security guard brought me here, but he was called away for a lack-of-toilet-paper emergency in another area of the building."

The science teacher gave John a quick grin before nodding.

"I understand that Nash will miss the wrap up of this lesson," John said. "I will endeavor to do my best to help."

"It's okay," the science teacher said. "We really just try to give them a taste of this stuff now. If they're interested, they will pursue it."

Teddy ran up and hugged John.

"Where did you come from?" John asked. Looking at the science teacher, he said, "Teddy lives in my household sometimes. His father is in the military, so Teddy lives with Nash in the summer and with us part-time during the school year."

"What are you doing here?" Teddy asked.

"I came to talk to Nash," John said.

Teddy blanched and looked back at Nash.

"You should be nice to him," Teddy said. "He's really upset."

"I was nice to you," John said mildly.

"Were you?" Teddy asked. "It didn't seem very nice to me."

"So says the one who should be in federal prison," John said quietly.

"That was a *long* time ago!" Teddy said, indignantly.

John laughed openly, and Teddy looked a little embarrassed. Recovering quickly, John turned to the science teacher.

"I will return him to where he's staying," John said.

The science teacher nodded and turned to Nash. The boy shuffled to the door. He grabbed his backpack out of his locker and followed John out the door. John put his arm over the boy's shoulder to guide him out of the school.

They drove up Smith Road until they reached the Sand Creek Greenway.

"The dogs will hate us for not bringing them," Nash said when John parked.

"It's okay for us to spend some time talking," John said. "If Maggie or Buster — or even Sarah —were here, we'd play with them and never get to the heart of the matter."

"What is the 'heart of the matter'?" Nash asked with a sigh.

"That's what we need to figure out," John said. Softly, he added, "Come on."

They walked across the bridge and into the greenway.

"Did you ever come here before the cleanup?" John asked.

"I'm fifteen," Nash said.

"That's right," John said with a laugh.

Nash glanced at him. John had a beautiful laugh. Nash had never heard it before. In fact, Nash had never spent any time along with this man. Even so, he was one of Nash's ideal men. John was gorgeous, fit, and muscular. He was tall like Nash was going to be tall. His best friend was gay, and he had no problem with that. But mostly, John Drayson had been married to the same woman for a long time.

"*Happily married,*" Nash heard, as M.J.'s voice jumped into his mind. "*It's mind blowing how happy they are. So, when John talks, I listen, because, man — who else has credentials like that?*"

Nash smiled at the memory of M.J..

"What are you thinking?" John asked.

"I was remembering M.J.," Nash said. "He says that he always listens to your advice about marriage because you're so happy."

John nodded.

"I'm a little surprised that you aren't wondering why we're out here," John said.

"Murder me and leave me here for the coyotes?" Nash asked.

"What?" John asked in a horrified voice. "No. I . . ."

Nash laughed. John gave a rueful shake of his head, and they kept walking. They reached the Sand Creek River. Golden-red in color from mine run off, the sand- bottomed river was a haven for big birds. John pointed as a red-tailed hawk flew overhead.

"I figured it was because I had this weird conversation with Samantha Hargreaves," Nash said. "She came over to talk to Val, and they talked to Noelle."

"Who said nothing about you," John said.

Nash grunted.

"My sisters are like that," John said with a smile. "To this day. Someone says, 'Oh, are you John's sister?' and they are like 'Who wants to know?'"

"IRA training," Nash said.

"That's the PIRA to you, young man," John said with a laugh.

"What's the 'P' mean?" Nash asked.

"Nothing," John said. "I'm sorry I said that. It was a long time ago and won't help you feel better."

"I don't think anything will help me feel better," Nash sighed.

"I wanted to tell you a story," John said. "I think it might help."

Nash glanced at him.

"Do you mind if we walk and talk?" John asked.

"I'd like that," Nash said. "Is it about Alex?"

"It's about me," John said.

"Okay," Nash said. "But how . . .?"

"My wife and her twin decided that I could help you," John said.

Nash grinned.

"They are usually right, so I agreed," John said. "Although, if I'm being truthful, I usually agree to what they ask because I love them, and they truly ask for very little."

"Sounds like them," Nash nodded.

"Of course, if our chat doesn't go well, they will know," John said.

John pointed up into the air.

"Satellite," John whispered.

Nash laughed out loud. It was the first real laugh he'd laughed since Sandy had fallen. The laugh turned into a cough, and his eyes welled with tears. John put his hand on Nash's shoulder.

"Would you like to hear my story?" John asked.

"Please," Nash choked.

John looked at Nash for a second and began.

CHAPTER FIVE HUNDRED & SIXTY-SIX
THE PLAN

They walked along in silence. After a while, Nash gave a little cough.

"Yes," John said with a smile. "I'm sorry. I was trying to decide where to start. How old are you now?"

"Fifteen," Nash said.

"When will you be sixteen?" John asked.

"Six months," Nash said

"Ah, that is helpful," John said.

"O-kay," Nash said.

John smiled.

"Things we have in common," John said. "That's what I was thinking. When I was your age, I was living with my sister and her husband in London. Even though you live with your father, you live with a stepmother, who is as much older than you as my sister is to me."

"What happened to your mom and dad?" Nash asked.

John winced and raised an eyebrow in Nash's direction.

"I can handle it!" Nash said.

John sighed.

"My father died when I was ten. He had a heart attack after a bomb he'd set went off before he was ready," John said. "My mother . . . My father had just gotten out of prison when he killed my mother."

"What?" Nash asked.

"She had me when he was gone," John said. "He was sure that I wasn't his child. He would have killed me if it weren't for my brother, Ciaran."

"Ciaran?" Nash asked. "Mr. Jackie's friend?"

"That's right — you know our Jackie," John said with a smile. "Ciaran and Jackie were in prison when my father died."

John gave Nash a soft smile.

"It's a fairly ugly story," John said.

"So's mine," Nash said. "My parents are alive, but . . ."

Nash nodded.

"Yes," John said. "You and your sister have had a tough time with your mom's addiction."

"And my dad's addiction," Nash grumbled. "But my mom's still alive. Unfortunately."

When John didn't respond, Nash snuck a glance at him. He gave Nash a kind smile.

"I know what you mean," John said.

Nash felt a rush of relief at not being judged for his angry feelings about his mother and his fear that he was just like her.

"I was a year and a half older than you when I left Scotland and went to college at UCLA," John said.

"Scotland?" Nash asked. "I thought you lived in London."

"That was another big mess," John said. "If we get to the end of this, and you want to hear it the story, I will be happy to tell you. But, I think the part that will be interesting to you happened when I was at UCLA."

"Did you meet Max there?" Nash asked. "He went there."

"How did you know?" John asked.

"We've been talking about colleges," Nash said. "Max told us about going to UCLA. He said that you guys lived in the dorm for a year and then got your own apartment."

"That's right," John said. "We moved to this lovely duplex when Alex and I married."

John nodded.

"What I thought I'd tell you about started on the plane between England and Los Angeles," John said.

When Nash didn't respond, John marveled at this interesting young man. He continued.

"I had had this crazy life," John said. "Northern Ireland troubles, my mother's death, the drunken horror that was my father, living with Rita in London, and then in Scotland. All of these things had happened *to me* — most, if not all of them, had *nothing* to do with me. I was the youngest. My father was in prison when my mother fell pregnant. He killed her. He was so horrible that my elder siblings were either in jail, active in the PIRA, or the girls in the convent."

John shrugged.

"I decided that my life belonged to me," John said. "I wasn't going to get caught up in some ancient politics or some drunken mess. I was going to have a *real* life, a *good* life. In order to do that, I needed my very own plan."

Nash glanced at John.

"I have a plan," Nash said quietly.

"I thought you might," John said. "Or I should say that *Alex* thought you might."

Nash nodded. Embarrassed by hearing an adult talking so familiarly about someone he admired, he fell silent again.

"Right there, on the plane, I wrote down the outline of *the plan*," John said. "Would you like to hear it?"

Nash nodded.

"I would go to university in America," John said. "I would focus on three things — working out, bedding women, and being the best in my class."

"Bedding women?" Nash burst out.

"All of them," John said. "Often a different woman every night. Always using contraception, of course. I couldn't let some disease or a pregnancy get in the way of *the plan*."

Shaking his head, Nash grinned.

"I would be the top of my class at UCLA," John said. "Then I would either — go to business school and become a business mogul, all the while bedding all the ladies . . ."

"Of course," Nash smiled.

"Or possibly a doctor," John said. "Maybe a realtor. Something where I could make loads of money and still have time . . ."

"To bed all of the ladies," Nash said.

"Exactly," John said. "I would make so much money that I'd never have to ask anyone for anything. I could do whatever I wanted, whenever I wanted. No one was going to tell me what to do. I just had to . . ."

"Work *the plan*," Nash said.

"No time for drugs . . ."

"Or friends?" Nash asked.

"Well, young Nash, that's the first situation that caused *the plan* to be adjusted," John said. "I met a kindred spirit in Max."

"Max bedded all the ladies?" Nash asked, his voice rising in surprise.

"Of course," John said. "Women. Men. Whoever he was interested in. He liked them all."

"And you didn't mind?" Nash asked.

"Why should I care?" John asked. "I had *the plan*!"

John punctuated the word "plan" by pointing his finger up at heaven. Nash chuckled.

"I adjusted *the plan* for Max and carried on," John said. "Max also wasn't into drugs. He is mind-blowingly smart, so he wanted to be the top of his class as well. We studied. Hard. We partied when we were done with studies. We bedded everyone. Only women for me, in case that's of interest to you."

John nodded.

"Life was good," John said.

They walked along in silence. They stopped on the dirt path near the creek that gave the greenway its name. Nash gestured up onto the embankment.

"That's where the St. Jude Killer kept a lair," Nash said. "Between some old concrete from the airport."

He looked at John.

"So I guess I was here when they were doing some of the cleanup," Nash said.

John gestured to the dusty path and general disorder of the open space.

"Clearly, it's a work in progress," John said. He nodded. "I'd forgotten that you were in on that satellite- stealing mission."

Nash blushed and glanced at John.

"What did you do to Teddy?" Nash asked.

"I took him to the morgue," John said. "There's always someone who is killed falling down the stairs after a long weekend. I made him look at the body. Talk to the families. See how easy it is to die."

Nash grunted.

"No phone is worth that," John said.

Nash nodded but didn't respond.

"What happened to your plan?" Nash said finally.

"I met Alex," John said. "For two years, my entire life revolved around *the plan* I'd written on the back of an airline napkin. It was my friend, my family, my conviction when I needed it. *The plan* was everything. I never wavered. Not even once. It's weird to think about now, but those few lines meant everything to me."

Nash stuck his hands into his pockets and started shuffling down the path again. John walked beside him.

"Everyone who knew me knew about my plan," John said.

"Even the women?" Nash asked.

"Especially the women," John said. "I was the guy they could bed and not expect to hear from again. I was really clear."

"They didn't mind that?" Nash asked.

"I told them up front," John said. "So if they minded, they couldn't complain to me."

"Does Alex know?" Nash asked.

"Oh, yes," John said, with a rueful laugh. "Alex has a background check on every single woman I slept with."

"Every one?" Nash asked.

"Mmm," John said in affirmation.

"It's a lot?" Nash asked.

John nodded.

"Why would she *do* that?" Nash asked.

"For her work," John said. "They presented a possible liability to me and, so, to her."

Nash didn't respond. They walked for a while before he said, "God, how awful."

John laughed. Nash was once again so taken by John's laugh that he couldn't help but smile.

"The moment I laid eyes on Alex, I knew that she was a threat to my plan," John said.

"Because she was so much like Max?" Nash asked.

"Because of how I felt," John said.

"How did you feel?" Nash asked.

"Whole," John said. "Complete. Like this missing hole that I knew *nothing* about had suddenly been filled. I met her, and suddenly . . ."

"You felt the hole," Nash said.

"*The* empty space, my empty space," John said. "It was a space that *the plan* had filled, and suddenly . . ."

Nash nodded.

"Yes, I thought you knew what I was talking about," John said.

Nash grunted.

"I spent the entire day talking myself out of having anything to do with her," John said. "She wasn't very fond of me, either. Oh, she knew all about my 'slutty ways.' That's what she calls it. She didn't like the fact that I was not an American, either. I was off limits as far as she was concerned."

"What did you do?" Nash asked.

"You mean how did we end up married the first night after we met?" John asked.

"Really?" Nash asked. "The first night?"

"I'd known her for twelve hours." John nodded. "And no, we hadn't gone to bed together."

"What? Really? How?" Nash asked, not hiding his disbelief.

"It just happened," John said. "It wasn't even a conscious thought. I just knew that I couldn't survive without her."

Nash made a kind of "tsk" sound. The boy looked down to cover his emotions.

"We were married and then shared this intensely glorious week," John said. "And then she left."

Nash snuck a glance at John. He was so caught up in his thoughts that he didn't notice Nash's look.

"It was awful," John said. "For me. I was alone again. My plan was broken. My voicemail filled up with women who wanted a date. I couldn't go out. I couldn't party. My workouts were messed up because I knew a lot of women at the gym. I . . ."

John looked at Nash and saw that he was privately weeping. John put his arm around Nash's shoulders.

"I was angry," John said. "Really. Truly. Deeply angry. My life was finally my own, and this person came and . . ."

"Fucked it up," Nash choked out.

"Exactly," John said.

They walked under the highway and continued along in silence. After a while, John tugged on Nash, and they turned around to go back. They'd made it to the spot across from St. Jude's lair when Nash wiped his eyes. He looked at John.

"What did you do?" Nash asked.

"I was an asshole," John said. "For more years than I'd like to admit. I probably would be still if Alex hadn't almost died. I mean, have you seen the men she spends her days with?"

Nash nodded.

"But when she was shot . . ." John sighed. "I don't know. I guess I just got over it. She lost her team. I lost these men who were . . . You never met them, but they were truly the best human beings I had ever met. Funny. Friendly. So smart. They were such a great support to me in my schooling and in *my* life. Me. The husband. They were family. *My* family. And then they were gone. Alex was so broken that . . ."

John shook his head.

"That's the problem with a plan," John said, so softly that Nash had to strain to listen. "It makes you lose focus on what's real, and all that's real is very transient."

He fell silent, and they walked some more.

"I was so focused on *getting* somewhere that I didn't really value where I was," John said. "I didn't realize that I had been *there* the entire time until I almost lost everything. I couldn't have survived Alex dying. I couldn't survive it now — and we have children! I have the career *the plan* built! Money! Friends! Status! Everything *the plan* got me!"

John shrugged.

"It wouldn't matter one lick if Alex wasn't there," John said.

They walked in silence for a while. The day was getting cold, and daylight was beginning to wane.

"Fin says that I have to become a better person," Nash said. "Because she's a better person than I am."

"Fin?" John asked with a snort. "The Prince?"

Nash smiled at John's derision.

"Last I checked, you were no prince," John said.

"He was talking about becoming good enough to be with Abi," Nash said.

"In your opinion — is *he* good enough to be with Abi?" John asked.

Nash burst out laughing. John nodded.

"They pick us," John said. "That's how it is. We'll never be as good as them. I will never, ever be as amazing as Alex is. She loves me anyway."

John shrugged.

"That doesn't mean that I stop trying to be fit, smart, educated, and the best person I can be," John said. "I do that for her *and* for *myself.*"

Nash nodded.

"Bernie tells me that you're trying to learn a bunch of languages," John said.

"How do you . . .?" Nash asked.

"He lived on campus at the University while I went to school there, residency, fellowship," John said. "He used to clean the floors in building 500. I was there late one day; Alex was who knows where in the world, and he started talking to me. We're sort of friends, if you can be friends with someone as unique and brilliant as that."

"Small world," Nash said.

"You have no idea," John said. "So, languages?"

"Nadia speaks at least five languages," Nash said. "She easily jumps back and forth between English and Spanish. She speaks Arabic and Ukrainian, and I don't know what else."

"Hmm," John said.

"I should be able to speak with her!" Nash said. "At the barest minimum."

"You have to do one thing at a time, Nash," John said. "Learn one language. Then another. I was twenty when I met Alex. If I'd learned one language every five years, I'd be close to what you're talking about. You have time!"

"I don't have time to be good enough for her!" Nash said. "And now I'm addicted! Game over! I may as well just kill myself!"

Nash angrily shook his head.

"I had a plan!" Nash said, his voice filled with rage. "It was going to work! I was going to be . . . and now . . ."

"Alex told me to tell you that she picked *me* because of *me*," John said. "She didn't know about *the plan*. When she found out, *my* plan became *our* plan. Our plan was so much better, smarter, and more practical. Alex was making a salary, so we were able to purchase a home. From there, together, we grew safety and security, and, eventually ,financial freedom, or relative financial freedom."

"You believe that she picked you for you?" Nash asked.

"Not really, but it *is* what she says," John grinned at Nash. "My guess is that Nadia feels the same way. I know that it's different for the two of you because of your ages and the distance, but . . ."

John scowled and looked at Nash.

"Not much," John said. "We had a lot of obstacles that you wouldn't understand. Lots. They might have been bigger than yours or smaller than yours or easier or harder. We also had our plan."

John looked at the boy, and Nash nodded.

"One thing I think . . ." John said.

John pressed his key fob, and his car unlocked. Nash got into the passenger seat.

"One thing I think," John repeated as he started the vehicle. "Love is . . . magic. Plain and simple. I don't know about past lives. I've had dreams about Alex and me in different situations and different times. She has too. Maybe we've loved each other in many lifetimes or maybe this is it. What I know is that it's sheer magic."

John started driving down the street.

"Everything I wanted happened because I knew Alex," John said. "Things I didn't even know I wanted happened because Alex loved me."

"What do you mean?" Nash asked.

"If you'd asked me when I was twenty years old if I would want my life partner, my beloved, to have a work partner who was smoking hot, smart, intelligent, and someone she loves deeply," John shook his head. "I'd say that was crazy. But you know Raz? He's amazing. He's been such a great friend to me and to Alex. A real brother when I had none. More than that, he loved Alex so much that he found her and saved her life."

John nodded to Nash.

"Love has a wisdom of its own," John said. "I'm not going to tell you to trust it because you're never going to do that. People like us don't trust anyone or anything. We know life is not a romance novel. What I'm saying is that this *thing* has happened to you."

"Sandy being injured?" Nash asked.

CHAPTER FIVE HUNDRED & SIXTY-SEVEN
THAT THING WE CALL LOVE

"What I'm saying is that this *thing* has happened to you," Dr. John Drayson said.

"Sandy being injured?" Nash asked.

"Being in love," John said. "You may as well settle in and see where it takes you. You can always get out if you need to. But you should stop torturing yourself to try to make it happen. It's happening."

Nash nodded.

"Now, I have something serious to talk to you about," John said.

"*This* wasn't serious?" Nash asked.

"Oh, it is," John said with a smile. "Just a little different, I guess."

"What?" Nash asked with more force than he intended. John raised his eyebrows, and Nash laughed.

"Sandy can't make you feel better," John said. "Not right now. She's too sick."

"What do you mean?" Nash asked.

"She is your mom," John said. "The most natural thing in the world would be for you to go to her and want her to forgive you or help you with all of this... angst. If she were well, you'd strategize what to do, talking it over, get some yummy baked goods, and eventually feel better. But she cannot do that right now. She's too sick."

Nash nodded.

"That's why you haven't been able to see her," John said.

"Oh." Nash looked down at his hands. "Noelle and Charlie, too?"

John nodded.

"You need to be happy and light around her," John said. "Nash, you must know that she is not mad at you."

"I do?" Nash asked.

"Of course, you do," John said. "*You* are mad at you. She's not mad at you. You *know* that."

The silence became heavy, and the car filled with pressure. Nash snorted and shook his head.

"She *cannot* help you with this stuff," John repeated. "Not right now. Later, maybe, but not now."

Nash looked at him.

"Did you tell Teddy that?" Nash asked.

"I did," John said. "Teddy is just as upset as you are, but he's trying to accept that he made a mistake."

"I made a mistake," Nash silently mouthed the words.

After a minute, he nodded.

"I made a mistake," Nash said. "It's certainly not the first one."

Nash sighed. Nodding his head, he added, "I can live with that. I can do it."

"I know you can," John said. "And Nadia?"

"I think it's over," Nash said. "She doesn't want to be with an addict."

"Maybe you should talk to her," John said. "Share your plan with her. Give her the opportunity to talk to combine her plans with yours. Work it through with her."

"Trust the magic?" Nash asked.

"*Use* the magic," John said. "You didn't ask for this to come into your life. But it's here now. So you may as well deal with it, because, even if you spend a lifetime with Nadia, it will be over and done with soon enough."

Nash gave a little grunt. They drove the rest of the way to O'Malley's house in silence. Nash thanked John and got out of the car. He'd almost reached the door of the house when Nadia came out of the house. Nash smiled at her and held out his hand.

From the stop sign near the house, John watched Nash invite Nadia for a walk. He grinned as they started off down the street.

~~~~~~~~

Friday evening — 6:56 p.m.

"You're not eating?" Noelle asked Nelson.

Nelson had come home with Ava. He was sitting at the bar between the kitchen and the den with his laptop open. Ava was standing in front of him, making a salad.

"I have a date," Nelson said, without looking up.

"He has a date with *Blane*," Ava said in a sing song voice. "They are going out for a fancy dinner."

Nelson turned in his seat to look at Noelle. His eyebrows pinched with concern.

"You know that Blane and I are together," Nelson said.

"Really?" Charlie asked as he came through the room. He picked up a stack of plates. "You mean the two of you making out in Arizona wasn't a fluke?"

Nash and Teddy laughed as they came into the den. Charlie left with the plates.

"When were we making out?" Nelson's face flushed with color. "You . . ."

"They're just giving you shit," Tink said as she came in from the dining room.

She put her hand on Nelson's shoulder.

"The only thing you should know is that we are on 'Team Blane,'" Tink said to Nelson. Looking at Maresol, she said, "Tortillas?"

Maresol pointed to the tortilla holder. Tink picked it up and left for the dining room.

"Says who?" Nash asked. "I'm on 'Team Templar.'"

Nash started slashing at the air with the knives and forks in his right hand.

"'Team Blane'?" Nelson asked, just a step behind. "There's a 'Team Blane'?"

"You are not on Team Templar," Noelle said. "You're on Team Blane."

"Says who?" Nash asked.

"Me," Noelle said.

"You are not the boss of me," Nash said, pointing at her with the silverware.

"So you think," Noelle said with a laugh.

Ava set the bowl of salad on the bar, and Noelle picked it up.

"Dressing?" Noelle asked.

Ava pointed to the refrigerator.

"I'll get it," Teddy said, his hand full of cloth napkins.

"What about Team Nelson?" Nelson asked.

Maresol opened the refrigerator and took out the dressing. She shook her head at Teddy.

"I'll come back," Teddy said.

"Better thinking," Maresol said.

Teddy left for the dining room. Charlie reappeared, and Maresol gave him the salad dressing.

"I'll be on your team," Nadia said.

She came in from the exercise area, where she'd been swimming.

"And not Team Blane?" Ava asked with a laugh.

"Oh, there's a Team Blane?" Nadia asked.

Ava and Nadia laughed while Nelson tried to figure out what was going on. There was a knock at the door.

"Shower?" Maresol pointed Nadia to her room. "Be quick."

Nadia nodded and jogged off.

"I'll get it," Noelle yelled from the other room.

A few minutes later, Blane appeared.

"You sure you don't want to stay?" Maresol asked.

"We're off to have much inferior food," Blane said.

"'Inferior food'?" Nelson asked.

Blane looked at Nelson.

"What?" Nelson asked.

Laughing, Ava put her hand on Blane's arm.

"We've been messing with him," Ava said.

Nash came back in. Holding out potholders, Maresol nodded to a serving plate of New Mexican-style enchiladas. Nash took the potholders from Maresol, picked up the enchiladas, and left the room.

"Boy, that looks good," Blane said.

"Smells divine," Nelson said.

"You can stay," Maresol said.

"You might have to fight for food," Bernie, Seth's father, said as he entered the room. "These kids eat more than their weight in food. Hi, Blane!"

Bernie held out his arms, and Blane hugged him.

"Where are you off to?" Bernie asked when they stepped back.

"Capital Grill," Nelson said.

"Is it nice?" Bernie asked.

Blane nodded.

"Shall we?" Blane asked.

Nelson closed his laptop and stuck it into his backpack. Blane picked it up.

"I can carry it myself," Nelson said irritably.

"See? That's why we're not on Team Nelson," Charlie said in a loud whisper. "So cranky."

"'Team Nelson'?" Blane asked.

"Just go," Maresol said.

Charlie looked at Maresol and asked, "Anything else?"

Maresol nodded to the pitcher of water. Charlie picked it up and went to the dining room.

"Have fun!" Ava said.

Blane nodded and followed Nelson out of the room.

"Capital Grill is very nice," Seth said when they were in the entryway.

At the door, Nelson turned to Blane.

"Did you know they had 'Team Blane' and 'Team Nelson'?" Nelson asked.

From where he was standing, Blane could see into the dining room. Nash and Teddy were laughing. Tink was shaking her head, and Noelle looked worried.

"Of course," Blane said with a straight face. "Everyone's on Team Blane."

"What?" Nelson asked, incensed.

Blane laughed. He opened the door, and they left the house.

"You think they'll work that out?" Bernie asked the laughing kids.

"Nelson's so gullible," Nadia said, coming into the dining room after her shower.

"What do you mean?" Charlie asked. "There really is a Team Blane and a Team Nelson."

"What?" Nadia asked. "Really?"

She looked at Nash and, then at Teddy and Noelle. They nodded in unison.

"No, there isn't," Ava said when she came into the dining room. She pointed at the teens. "Sit."

They found their seats and sat down. Seth came in and took his place. Maresol brought a covered casserole. For a moment, they were silent as Maresol said her prayers.

"There is so a Team Blane," Noelle said.

"Is not," Nash said.

"So," Noelle said.

"Enough!" Maresol said. "This is dinner. We don't fight at our meals. We use them for enjoying each other's company and learning about our days."

Appropriately embarrassed, everyone fell silent. They began to fill their plates with the amazing-smelling food.

"'Team Blane'?" Seth asked when everything was quiet.

Everyone started to laugh.

"No," Maresol said. She pointed at Seth. "We are not starting this again."

"Starting what?" Aden asked at the door to the dining room.

"Nash, make a place for your father," Maresol said. She turned to Aden. "I wasn't sure if you were eating with us."

"She's asleep," Aden said.

"What's asleep?" Charlie asked.

"Sandy," Aden said.

The teens turned to gawk at him.

"She's in the hospital room here," Aden said. "You didn't know?"

Aden looked at Maresol, at Ava, and then at Seth.

"We figured you could use some private time," Seth said.

"Mom is here?" Noelle asked, standing up.

"Sit," Aden said. "Eat. Sandy is asleep."

"How did she end up here?" Charlie asked. "Where were we?"

"It's something John Drayson worked out," Aden said. He was passed the enchiladas. "She arrived while you were in school. John didn't tell you, Nash?"

"No," Nash said.

"We had no idea!" Noelle said.

"I came with her," Aden said.

"She's resting now," Seth said.

"It's unlikely that she'll wake today," Aden said. "Moving from the hospital took everything out of her. Was Blane here?"

"They just left," Seth said.

"He's coming back here after dinner," Aden said. "He's going give Sandy a treatment. Jill's brother Steve is coming over after that to get her settled in for the night."

Everyone fell silent. For a few minutes, the only sound was of them eating.

"So when *can* we see her?" Noelle's voice broke the tension.

Everyone laughed.

"Tomorrow," Aden said.

Noelle cheered.

"What about Rachel Ann?" Nash asked.

"She'll be here tomorrow," Aden said. "She's having a sleepover with Katy and didn't want to miss it."

"She blew off being with us for Katy?" Noelle asked.

"You would have," Nash said.

"Yeah, but . . ." Noelle said with a grin.

Everyone laughed.

"Today was my day volunteering at the Museum of Nature and Science," Bernie said. "I'm helping to clean some of the bones from the Snow Mass site. And I can tell you — those mammoths? They were really . . . mammoth."

Everyone laughed at his well-timed joke, and their usual, weird dinner atmosphere returned.

~~~~~~~~~
Friday evening — 7:36 p.m.

"I swear, I will never get this," Valerie said under her breath to Jill.

Valerie held up a tangle of yarn and knitting needles. Jill nodded in agreement.

"Now, Valerie," Jill's mother, Anjelika, said. "Human beings have been knitting since the beginning. You will surely learn."

Valerie rolled her eyes to Jill, and Jill grinned. Anjelika looked at Jill. Her smile dropped immediately.

"You're doing better," Anjelika said.

Jill smiled at her mother.

"That's the piece Delphie knitted, right?" Valerie whispered to Jill.

Jill nodded, and the women laughed. They had had an early dinner and were upstairs in Jill's loft having a "girl's night." Delphie was making an effort to teach Katy, Jackie, Maggie, and Rachel Ann how to knit. Of course, the little kids were making potholders on little plastic looms. Oddly, Rachel Ann picked up knitting right away.

Delphie came over to look at what Valerie had done. She scowled at Valerie.

"You used to be able to knit," Delphie said.

"When?" Valerie asked.

"Pre-Mike," Delphie said. "You knitted me a scarf."

"I did?" Valerie looked off into space for a moment. "Huh. I'd forgotten that."

"You don't apply yourself," Delphie said. "Why don't you try a bit?"

Valerie gave Delphie a patient smile, and Delphie grinned. Delphie turned and looked at Jill's work. The Oracle shook her head.

"Is there a craft that you enjoy?" Delphie asked.

"I'm hopeless?" Jill asked.

"Child of the Titan God of Destruction," Delphie shrugged. "It's not hard to see why creating things might require that you make some extra effort."

"I make great kids," Jill said with a nod to Katy.

Katy had been working with Delphie almost since she'd moved into the Castle. Katy was working on a shawl made out of blue alpaca wool she'd bought at a yarn festival.

Delphie gave Jill a long look.

"You're trying not to say that it's because of Celia," Jill said.

"I would never discount you that way," Delphie said with a grin.

Having listened to the entire exchange, Valerie burst out laughing. Jill grinned.

"Get to work," Jill said to Valerie.

"You know what else you make well . . ." Delphie said.

"Brownies?" Jill asked.

"If you insist," Delphie said with a grin.

Laughing, Jill got up. She went to see how Maggie and Jackie were doing. They both showed her the beginnings of lovely potholders. In spite of her young age, Rachel Ann was knitting with some fat needles and thick grey yarn. She held hers up for Jill to see.

"I'm making a blanket for my Mama," Rachel Ann said in her soft, sweet voice. The child's eyes welled with tears. "She's very sick."

"I bet this will help her get well," Jill said.

Rachel Ann gave a quick nod of her head. Jill touched the child's face, and she smiled.

"I get to see her tomorrow," Rachel Ann said. "My brothers and sister, too. But not Sissy."

"Sissy is in France," Jill said.

"I talked to Sissy tonight," Rachel Ann said with a nod. "On the computer."

"How fun," Jill said. "I talk to my brother on the computer when he travels."

Rachel Ann gave Jill a bright nod and returned to her work. Jill checked in with Katy, who was thoroughly enjoying being the expert.

Just another wonderful night at the Castle.

Jill grinned at her daughter and went to make brownies.

~~~~~~~~~
Friday evening — 9:36 p.m.

Honey awoke when M.J. came into the bedroom. He went into their bathroom before taking off his clothing. He crawled into bed.

"How did it go?" Honey asked.

"Good," M.J. said. "Everyone seems in good spirits. I think it will be an interesting trip."

"Are you mad that you aren't going?" Honey asked.

"Mad?" M.J. asked. He leaned up on one elbow. "Not at all. I mean, it's always hard to see them go. I hate missing out. You know? My team is off to Poland to look into an old mine, and I want to be there."

"Because that's more fun?" Honey asked.

"Because they are my team," M.J. said. "I also want to be here for you. You're just getting strong enough to actually spend more time out of your chair. We need to keep working on your strength and coordination. I wouldn't miss that for the world. Especially for an extra trip. I'm gone enough as it is."

"You're sure?" Honey asked.

"I'm a complicated guy," M.J. said. "I can want to be with my team and want to be with you at the same time."

"Sure, but . . ." Honey said.

"No 'buts,'" M.J. said. "Plus, I'm sure they'll need my help from here. It's only me and the White Boy. We need to keep things running at home and deal with all of the technical stuff."

"You'll be able to monitor from here," Honey said.

"Right," M.J. said. "They are ahead of us, so it will be some late nights and early mornings."

"Is Chris coming here?" Honey asked using White Boy's given name.

"Probably," M.J. said. "Or we'll go to the Factory."

"When's his surgery?" Honey asked.

"Tomorrow," M.J. said. "I'll go with him, but really he should be fine."

"And you're sure he told Yvonne that he was getting a vasectomy?" Honey asked.

"She's been pushing him to do it," M.J. said. "Alex said that she's the tiniest, bossiest person she's ever met."

Honey smiled.

"Every time she says that, I wonder how much time she's spent with you," M.J. said.

"Hey!" Honey laughed.

"You're mostly running that job site. Another month, and it will be all yours," M.J. said. "You're going to college and raising Maggie while I'm off playing soldier."

"I have a lot of help," Honey said.

M.J. looked at Honey for a long moment.

"People ask me what it's like to live with my wife's family," M.J. said.

"And?" Honey asked. "What do you say?"

"It's really great," M.J. said. "Sometimes, I think I'd like to have my own home. But . . ."

"There's no way we'd have all of this on our salaries," Honey said. "Fresh, organic food from the gardens. Free daycare almost anytime we need it. Someone to help me. People who clean the house once a week without fail."

M.J. nodded and leaned back.

"It's just that idea of 'making it,' you know?" M.J. asked.

"Oh," Honey sighed. "I honestly think we have it made. No need to make it."

M.J. smiled.

"Why are you unhappy here?" Honey asked, her heart racing with anxiety.

M.J. was asleep. Honey scowled at him.

She wondered how many times a man had awoken his woman with some issue that only left her awake and worried about whatever bullshit he'd brought up. She pushed him on the shoulder, and he awoke.

"Wha . . .?" M.J. asked.

"Are you seriously thinking of moving?" Honey asked. "Getting our own house?"

"Moving?" M.J. asked. "Why? Are you saying you want to move? Really, Honey, this is a great place for us. We have everything we need."

Honey groaned and lay back. When she looked at him, he was grinning.

"You're a jerk," Honey said.

He laughed.

Chapter Five Hundred & Sixty-eight
Healing Power of Love

Saturday morning — 6:04 a.m.

"What are you doing?" Teddy whispered.

"I'm going to see my mom," Noelle said in a whisper. "Dad said I could see her today. It's today."

"What time is it?" Teddy asked.

"Early," Noelle said. "But it's still today! And Dad said."

She was standing on the den floor in her pajamas.

"Shh," Noelle said. "Don't wake Nash."

She gestured to the figure on the other couch. Teddy nodded.

"I don't know if I should . . ." Teddy started.

"Come on!" Noelle said. "You'll wake Nash."

Noelle made a dramatic show of tiptoeing toward the door where Sandy was staying. Teddy rolled his eyes at her efforts. She had to stop and hold her mouth to keep from laughing. He shook his head and pointed to Noelle's socked feet. He slipped his feet across the hardwood. She nodded.

They slipped over to the door.

"What about your Dad?" Teddy whispered.

"He sleeps through anything," Noelle said with a nod. "He won't wake up."

"You're sure?" Teddy whispered.

Noelle nodded.

"I don't know," Teddy said. He looked worried.

Noelle hugged him tight. He sighed out his intense emotions.

"Where's the dog?" Teddy whispered.

"She went up with Ava and Seth," Noelle said. "Come on. He said we could see her *today*."

Teddy nodded. Noelle cracked the door open just an inch. She stuck her nose into the room. Turning back to Teddy, she nodded.

She pushed the door open a crack wider. She slid into the room. Teddy slid in behind her. Sandy was lying in the bed near the middle of the room. She was still hooked up to machines, and there was an IV dripping, but her cheeks held a little color.

Noelle noticed that Cleo the cat was asleep above Sandy's head, on the edge of her pillow.

They continued their slide into the room. Noelle pointed to her father, sound asleep on a smaller daybed. A tall man, his feet were off the end of the bed.

Teddy held his finger to his lips to remind her not to talk.

She nodded.

They slid silently toward the bed.

"Oh," Noelle said out loud when she got there.

Nash was asleep on his side with his arm over Sandy's stomach. His face was puffy and red, as if he'd been crying. Nash didn't wake up, but Sandy did. She tried to reach out to Noelle and Teddy but wasn't able to with her broken fingers. Tears streaming down her face, Noelle fell over onto Sandy. Teddy was so overcome with emotion that he just stood there.

"She can't speak," Aden said from the daybed behind where Teddy was standing. Teddy looked at him. "I know she wants you to hug her."

Teddy began to cry. He leaned over her legs.

"Good thing we didn't wake up the kids," Seth said with a laugh.

Everyone turned to look at him. Maresol came in behind him.

"You okay, Sandy?" Maresol asked.

Sandy's head went up and down in a nod.

"I'll get breakfast," Maresol said. She pushed Seth into the room. "Your dad would like to see you."

Sandy's eyes flicked to Seth. He took three steps and joined the kids in hugging her.

~~~~~~~~

Saturday morning — 9:14 a.m.

"Are you in terrible pain?" Sissy asked Sandy.

They were talking on a computer program via the Internet. Because Sandy's jaw was wired shut and her fingers broken, she was only able to tap out messages on the keyboard. Sissy would ask a question and then wait while Sandy answered via text.

"On lots of meds," Sandy tapped out.

Sissy nodded.

"You look horrible," Sissy said.

"Gee, thanks," Sandy said. She made the effort to do a big wink.

The absurdity of Sandy's wink made Sissy laughed. Sandy gestured to Sissy.

"Please," Sandy typed. "Tell me about you."

"Me?" Sissy asked. Her hand went to her chest and she shook her head. "I didn't just almost die!"

Sandy's head moved from side-to-side.

"I'm just worried about you," Sissy said.

Sandy's braced hands went together in a prayer position. Her blue eyes plead with her younger sister. Sissy nodded.

"Well . . ." Sissy sighed and looked down as she tried to think of what to share. "The term is winding down. Can you believe that I've been here a whole year?"

Sandy as big of a shake of her head as the neck brace would allow.

"Me too," Sissy said. "I've decided to stay an additional year, even though I'll be older when I leave. Do you remember that we talked about that?"

Sandy gave a restricted nod. They'd spent hours in video Internet calls going back and forth about Sissy staying or going. She'd finally decided to stay.

"Almost no one in my class is staying," Sissy said. "Just the head male and head female. They said that they wanted to refine their skills, but really they are looking at the best companies in the world. Another year will allow them to be a little more choosey. I've wondered if they'll stay the year."

"Is ... that ... what ... you ... are ... doing?" Sandy tapped out.

"I'll stay the year," Sissy said.

"Better offer?" Sandy tapped out.

"Maybe. I mean never say never, right?" Sissy asked. "Mostly, I'm not sure if I want to stay in Paris at the *Ballet de l'Opéra national de Paris* or come back to the US to work or wherever."

Sandy didn't respond so Sissy continued.

"I guess you know that," Sissy said. "I think that I have to be honest and say that I'm a little scared to be done with school. I mean, I love being here. In Paris, sure. At school, of course. I know that I went to school in New York, but here it's just ... le vie."

Sissy blinked at Sandy and then translated, "the life. Ballet is life here not just something I do for school."

Sissy nodded to herself.

"Ivan says that being a part of a company is like being in school but more intense because everyone has their level and is competing to move up. I don't know if I'd like all that competition, you know?"

Sandy's eyes seemed to laugh at Sissy.

"Okay, I know," Sissy said. "It's not like I'm non-competitive or anything."

Sissy sighed.

"Maybe it's just me," Sissy said. "After almost a year of ballet school in New York, getting shot and almost dying, and then coming here ... Maybe ballet is my life now because my *life* is ballet, and has been ballet for a long time."

Sandy's mouth shifted to a kind of grin for Sissy. She shrugged.

"I think it's the right choice," Sissy said. "I still love living with Claire and Ben. It's a crazy place. You never know who's going to be at dinner. That's some of the fun. They've been incredibly kind to me. Supportive. Even with Ivan. That's a reason not to rush out of school."

Sandy nodded.

"You think you'll still be able to come to our final performance?" Sissy asked.

"If I can," Sandy wrote out while Sissy waited.

Sissy nodded.

"I know what that's like," Sissy said with a sigh. "Dinner tonight is with Alex and her team. I guess they are heading to do that thing for Nash."

Sandy gestured to herself.

"That's right," Sissy said. "It's your book."

Sandy gave a slight nod.

"Anyway, it's madness when they come," Sissy said. "Fun, but completely insane."

"Summer?" Sandy typed.

"I'm still not sure what I'm doing this summer," Sissy said. "Ivan's been invited to help with those mass graves near the prison he was in. He's not sure he wants to go, but Ivan and Jill's grandfather are the only ones who were there and are now still alive. That alone seems like a reason to not go, but he also wants to make sure that people get home to their families."

"O'Malley," Sandy typed.

"So much like O'Malley," Sissy said with a laugh. "Do you think Ivan got that from Seth?"

Sandy lifted a shoulder in a shrug. Sissy nodded.

"Anyway, I might go with him to Siberia," Sissy said. "I might come home."

Sandy brightened, and Sissy laughed.

"New York City," Sissy said.

"Come see me," Sandy typed.

Sissy grinned.

"Rachel Ann says that at the end of every conversation," Sissy said. "Noelle and Nash too."

"Not Charlie?" Sandy asked.

Sissy laughed.

"Charlie wants to come here for the summer," Sissy said. "He and Tink want to come here."

Sandy shook her head.

"You're right," Sissy said. "That's not going to happen."

Sandy smiled. Her smiled began to fall as desperate fatigue overcame her.

"Listen," Sissy said leaning forward. "Heal up. You have a big life ahead of you. Heal up."

Sandy nodded.

"Do you remember saying that to me when I was in the hospital?" Sissy asked.

Sandy's hand went to her chest. Sissy nodded.

"Now, it's your turn," Sissy said. "Heal up."

Sandy gave Sissy an exhausted nod.

"I'll call tomorrow," Sissy said.

Sandy gave a vague nod.

"Love you, Sandy," Sissy said.

Sandy's hand went to her chest and Sissy nodded. When the screen when black, Sandy fell back against her pillow. She was asleep when Aden picked up the laptop and set it aside. He kissed her cheek and went back to sit on the couch.

~~~~~~~~

Saturday morning — 12:14 p.m.

"I spoke with your doctor," Maresol said as she walked into the room.

Not quite asleep but not awake, Sandy blinked at her. Maresol put her hands on her hips.

"He was very clear that you needed quality nutrition," Maresol said. "Soups, stews — things that are easy to digest since your system is still coming up."

Sandy closed and opened her eyes.

"Oh, don't give me that," Maresol said. "You've been playing the whole 'I'm asleep, why are you bothering me?' game since you were a little girl."

In spite of the discomfort, Sandy grinned.

"I know my girl," Maresol said. "So soup?"

Sandy shook her head. She touched her stomach and said, "Sth-ick" through her wired jaw.

"What about a smoothie?" Maresol asked. "Some fresh spinach, protein powder, that fruit you like."

Sandy lifted a shoulder in a shrug. Maresol scowled at her. They stood like that for a full minute.

"What are you up to?" Maresol finally asked.

Sandy pointed to herself and feigned innocence. The door opened behind them. Tanesha, Jill, and Heather came in. Tanesha was carrying an extra-large Styrofoam cup with the name of a local hole in the wall diner. She set it on Sandy's tray.

"Just how you like it," Tanesha said.

Shaking her head, Maresol did her best not to laugh.

"You girls haven't changed much since you were ten years old," Maresol said.

"We're bigger now," Jill said.

"Not by much," Maresol said with a snort in Jill's direction.

Everyone laughed.

"Would the rest of you like some soup?" Maresol asked. "I made some for the Princess of the Chocolate Shake."

They laughed again.

"You know, I could have made you a chocolate shake," Maresol said.

Sandy pointed to the shake and Jill said, "Not like this one."

"You girls never change," Maresol said with a rueful shake of her head.

"We would love some of your amazing soup," Heather said. "Sandy will too. Can we help at all?"

Maresol looked at Heather. She smiled at Heather and shook her head.

"Just love our girl," Maresol said. "It's what she needs the most."

"Always," Jill said.

Heather nodded, and Tanesha hugged Maresol.

"I'll be back to check on you," Maresol said, wiping her eyes.

She nodded to the women and left the room. Jill put a silicone straw into the shake and held it up for Sandy to eat. For a moment, they watched Sandy drink to shake. Sandy nodded, and Jill set the shake down.

"Wh' hap-ng?" Sandy asked.

"Well . . ." Tanesha started.

They chatted about nothing for the next half hour until Sandy was sound asleep again. They each kissed her forehead and left the room.

"Lunch?" Maresol asked.

Tanesha, Jill, and Heather looked at each other before laughing.

"Come and sit," Maresol said. She tapped the bar at the kitchen. "Tell me how you are."

For the next half hour, they ate vegetable soup, homemade bread, and talked to Maresol about life.

~~~~~~~~~~

Saturday afternoon — 2:04 p.m.

"Have you been here before?" Nadia asked in a low voice as if someone could hear her.

She pulled into a parking and turned off the car. Nash sat in the passenger seat and Teddy was in the back.

"I've only heard about it," Nash said. "You?"

Teddy shook his head.

They were sitting in the parking lot of a three floored historic brick factory. There was a small unassuming sign that said "The Factory" on the winter dead lawn. The red brick of the building was only interrupted by large double pained windows. The receiving bays were now windows.

"It's so . . ." Nadia started.

"Small," Nash said.

Nadia turned to look at him.

"See that building?" Nash pointed to a cinderblock structure in that took up the back half of the city block.

Nadia and Teddy looked at the building.

"It's a parking garage," Nash said.

"How do you know that?" Nadia asked.

"Raz has a parking sticker with the lot address on it," Nash said. He pointed to a sign. "That's a Park-N-Ride sign."

"So those people are . . ." Nadia started.

"They're not taking the light rail," Nash said.

"Where did they go?" Teddy asked.

Nadia looked at Nash, and then glanced at Teddy. They stared at the historic factory.

"It looks too small for all of those cars," Nash said.

Nadia nodded. As they watched, they saw Colin Hargreaves come out of the door of the building. He waved to them. Uncomfortable, they followed his summons by getting out of the vehicle and walking over to where he was standing. Colin shook Nadia's hand and grinned at Teddy and Nash.

"I or someone from the team will meet you out here anytime you're scheduled to be here," Colin said. "If it's someone you do not know by sight, do not go with them."

"Why?" Nadia asked.

"You never know what could happen," Colin said with a shrug.

"Why didn't you go to Poland?" Teddy asked. "I thought you were going?"

"I'm kind of big for a small tunnel," Colin said with a grin. "Plus, it's my anniversary."

The boys nodded and Nadia smiled.

"Anything fun planned?" Nadia asked.

"We're going to the beach for the weekend," Colin said.

"Which beach?" Nadia asked.

"That's still up for debate," Colin said with a grin.

He held open the enormous wood door and nodded for them to enter the building.

"Hey, I know that door," Nash said.

"Yeah?" Colin asked.

"It was in Jacob's shop for about a year," Nash said. He stepped inside the door. "So was that. And that . . ."

Nash pointed to the open stairwell and the banister. Teddy pointed up. There was a gorgeous wooden frame around the second floor.

"This is stunning," Nadia said. She looked at Nash. "You say that Jacob did this?"

"Sam did that," Nash said pointing to the row of round wooden tables set around the old receiving bays which now were large glass windows.

"Jake's dad is a carpenter too," Teddy said.

"I imagine that there was enough work for both of them," Colin said.

"They have a team of guys too," Nash said. "They're from Mexico. Carpenters too."

Nash looked down at the floor.

"He had a few of these beams in his workshop, too," Nash said.

"Do you spend a lot of time in his workshop?" Nadia asked.

"Not really," Nash said. "I like to watch him work. He's really fast and well . . ."

Nash gestured around.

"He makes beautiful things," Nadia said.

"Order out of chaos," Teddy said. "At least that's what he says."

"We love this building," Colin said. "It was designed by the Army Corps of Engineers and put together by Jake and a couple of his teams. There are these amazing little details that you can see, kind of, everywhere. It's amazing."

Nadia, Nash, and Teddy could do nothing but nod in agreement.

"Come on," Colin said. "I'll take you down."

He went to the left elevator. Before they got on, he scanned his retina and punched in a code.

"If you're thinking of hacking this," Colin said, giving a strong look to Teddy and then Nash, "the code changes daily as do the biometric feature. Today, it's retinas. Tomorrow, it will be something else."

The elevator door opened and they got on.

"Like what?" Teddy asked.

"Is this a purely academic interest?" Colin asked with amusement.

"It was a long time ago that we hacked that satellite!" Teddy said.

"We didn't know any better!" Nash said.

"You hacked a satellite?" Nadia asked.

Colin groaned and pressed the number 7 and the number 2 at the same time. They started to drop. Excited and more than a little nervous, they watched in silence as the numbers above the elevator door changed. They reached the floor and the door opened.

"You are entering a secure facility. Here is a locker for your items," Colin said. "If you step through the door with them, they will be fried, even if they are shielded. Before you enter the floor, you'll be scanned for metal and other noxious items."

"Really?" Nadia asked.

"You are welcome to leave anything in your locker," Colin said. "But enter the floor with it and it will be destroyed."

"Good to know," Nash said.

The boys emptied their pockets into lockers while Nadia put her purse inside. She also took off the USB drive that looked like a flower that she wore around her neck.

"Anything else?" Colin asked.

The boys patted themselves down while Nadia shook her head.

"Let's go inside," Colin said.

He stepped up to the door and pressed his hand against the reader. The door clicked open. They passed under an x-ray scanner and onto the Fey Team floor of the Factory.

CHAPTER FIVE HUNDRED & SIXTY-NINE
NOTHING TO SEE HERE

Saturday afternoon — 2:25 p.m.
Elyria Swansea area of Denver, Colorado

Redacted
Information regarding events is classified.

~~~~~~~~

Saturday afternoon — 3:15 p.m.

Sandy woke up with a start from a horrible nightmare about being stalked by her abusers. She moaned. Her pain from her injuries had reactivated her PTSD. She was having real trouble getting rest.

She was lucky, though.

The people around her knew that she was struggling, so they never left her alone. Every time she woke up, she would see someone else that she loved. She just had to turn her head.

She tried but gasped with pain.

"Okay, okay, okay," Charlie's voice came from beside her. The sound of hard pills knocking against plastic pill bottles filled the air.

"Ch . . . Ch . . ." Sandy tried to speak.

The next thing she knew, a young man who looked like someone she knew was sitting on her bed. Gasping in horror, she pulled away from him.

"Wh . . ." Sandy said.

Her dream was still vivid before her eyes. This young man was going to . . . She couldn't bear to watch. She slammed her eyelids closed. Even the act of squinting her eyes tightly closed caused her pain. She let out a sob. A tear streamed down her face.

"Look at me," the young man said.

She was too obedient not to open her eyes.

"It's me, Sandy," he said. "Charlie."

Sandy shook her head, and then he smiled. His mouth was full of braces on his beautiful, gleaming-white veneers. His eyes folded in the way that her dad, Mitch Delgado's, did. She tried to touch his face, but her hands were bound in casts. He pulled off her covers and lifted the shirt Maresol had put on her when she was unconscious.

Like he had done when he was tiny, he pressed his face into her skin. When he was little, he used to hide his head under her shirt when he was afraid. There was no way that anyone in the world would know that. She put her hand on the top of his head.

"Ch'r-ly," she said.

He rubbed his chin on her belly, and she felt the stubble of his new beard. She laughed and squealed. For the briefest moment, she was herself again — whole and happy, in the company of one of her favorite people.

The pain returned.

Unaware that she did it, she moaned. Charlie moved fast. He pulled down her shirt, put the covers back, and disappeared for only a quick moment.

"Here," Charlie said when he returned. "Take this."

He held out some pills. She put them in her mouth. He held the water for her to drink.

"I wanted to ask you . . ." Charlie said. "Well, really Bernie wanted to ask you. Your grandfather. You remember him."

Now separated from the nightmare, Sandy made a quick nodding motion.

"He's made some THC patches," Charlie said. "He gave me one when I came in. He thought that it might help."

Sandy shook her head. Charlie knew how much she was against marijuana use.

"I'm not going to argue with you," Charlie said. "I'm only going to say that these chemicals all have a use. One of the uses of marijuana is for pain relief. It won't make you a dope head. It just might help your pain. Bernie said that there are some studies about the use of it for people with PTSD."

Sandy's eyes flicked to look at Charlie directly.

"Not that you have PTSD or anything," Charlie said.

Sandy tried to grin at him but was mostly unable.

"Now, none of that," Charlie said. "Do you want to try it?"

Sandy looked at the ceiling for a moment before giving him a slight nod. He pulled back the covers again.

"Bernie said on your thigh," Charlie said. "Maresol put you in pajama bottoms."

"'s-OK," Sandy said.

Charlie pulled down her pajama bottoms and put on the patch. He pulled up her pants and pulled the covers back on.

"He said he made these himself," Charlie said. "Watched a YouTube video or something like that. Do you think he did?"

Sandy lifted a shoulder.

"Yeah. I don't know, either," Charlie said.

She lay back and hoped that the pain meds or the patch would start working.

"In the meantime," Charlie said. "I brought a book."

"C-nt rr-dd," Sandy said.

"Ah, yes, my lady," Charlie said in a bright voice. "You cannot read, but I can."

Sandy looked at Charlie. He held up a copy of *The Witches* by Roald Dahl. Sandy made an effort to clap, which caused her to gasp in pain and her hands went "thump." It was one of her favorite books.

"I also have a copy of *The Hobbit*," Charlie said. "And, if you'd like to branch out, we could start *Harry Potter*."

"I-v r'd Hrry," Sandy said.

"Well, I could always get you *Little Women*," Charlie said. "Or should I call it by its official . . ."

"L' B-tchz," Sandy said.

Charlie laughed and then became serious.

"Tink and I are staying here at Seth's, along with Nash, Teddy, and Noelle," Charlie said.

Sandy gave him a slight nod.

"Nash, Teddy, and Nadia are talking to the Fey Team," Charlie said. "The team is on their way to Poland but won't be there for a few days. Hopefully, you'll be better to watch when they go into *your* mine."

Sandy didn't respond, so Charlie pressed on.

"Teddy and Nash, even Noelle, have a lot planned, but I'm not going anywhere," Charlie said. "I'm not working this weekend, so you sleep when you need to. I'll read when you're awake. Next week, after school, I'll be here."

Charlie gave a nod.

"Wrrk?" Sandy asked.

"I'm taking family leave," Charlie said. "We all talked, and it seems like I have the most freedom. I think everyone would rather be here. I am just lucky enough to be able to."

"A-D'nn," Sandy said.

"He's at work now," Charlie said. "But he'll be back. He was going to try to work here, but Seth talked him out of it. You know — Seth's rule for everyone else."

"Wr a' WrK," Sandy tried to say as Charlie said, "Work at work."

"Of course, he works all the time," Charlie said. "Are you sorry Aden's not here?"

Sandy moved her hand across her forehead as if she were relieved.

"So you have the second string," Charlie said with a big smile. "Shall we start?"

Sandy nodded. He took his reading-glasses pouch from his pocket. With great flourish, he pulled the glasses from the pouch and put them on. He gave her a kind smile and started to read.

~~~~~~~~~

Saturday evening — 7:15 p.m.

"It was like . . ." Nash put his fists to the side of his head and then pulled them out. "*B-quew.*"

Nash shook his head.

"Mind totally blown," Nash said.

"Have you been there?" Ava asked Seth.

He gave a quick nod of his head. He looked at Nash.

"Now, you have to be careful not to discuss anything that might be sensitive in nature," Seth said.

"I didn't really understand that," Nadia said. "Why did we have to swear to secrecy and all of that?"

"The Fey Team is an intelligence team," Seth said. "Just *knowing* about them is classified."

"You mean people don't know they exist?" Teddy asked.

"A lot of people," Seth said with a nod. "When was the last time your dad was on the front page of the newspaper or on CNN?"

"Never," Teddy said. "I've seen him back up when reporters are around. He kind of slips away."

Seth nodded.

"That's what they are like," Bernie said.

"'They'?" Seth asked his father.

Bernie laughed.

"You were one of them?" Teddy asked, his voice filled with awe.

"Define 'them,'" Bernie said.

"A 'G-man,'" Nadia said in a mock 1950s gangster voice. "A spook. A spy."

Everyone turned to look at Bernie.

"I would answer that question, but it might incriminate me," Bernie said.

Nash and Teddy squealed with laughter. Everyone laughed either at Bernie or at the boys.

"I worked for my country when my country needed me," Bernie said. "In those days, there was a lot more need for a lot more men. It wasn't like it is now, where only 2% of the population is in the military. Then, it was almost everyone. My father went to the Great War. When I was a kid, my friends and I went to Guadalcanal to fight. My son went to Vietnam with his best friend."

Bernie nodded to Seth.

"Everyone you knew went to war," Bernie said.

"Except rich people," Noelle said with a sniff.

"Nadia's father went." Bernie nodded toward Nadia. "He was already well on his way to his second million when he signed up to fight. Most men would have been ashamed to not sign up. It was considered 'un-American.'"

"And to be a Government-man?" Maresol asked.

"Well, that was much less cool," Bernie said with a big smile. "It was mostly for the freaks and geeks."

"Which were you?" Teddy asked. "A freak or a geek?"

"Freak," Bernie said with a laugh.

Everyone laughed with him. When their laughter died down, Bernie became very serious.

"I lost good friends at war," Bernie said. "My eldest son didn't come home from Laos. I'm glad that there are fewer wars and fewer soldiers. I hope to live long enough to see a day there are no wars and no call for young men to give up their lives."

Bernie gave a curt nod, indicating that he'd said all he would say on the topic. Everyone fell silent as they ate their meal. Aden cleared his throat.

"I've never been in the military," Aden said. "And, I cannot imagine the pain of losing a child to the atrocities of war."

Bernie looked over at Aden, and Aden gave him a nod.

"I appreciate your service," Aden said. "If there are fewer wars, it's because your generation fought to make that so."

Embarrassed, Bernie looked down at his meal. Maresol leaned over to kiss his cheek.

~~~~~~~~~
Saturday evening — 7:15 p.m.

"When do you think they'll come back?" Ivy asked.

She was standing in front of Delphie with her back turned to her. They had had dinner early, so Ivy took the chance to shower. Ivy's hair had grown out into long curls that tangled easily. Every night, Delphie carefully combed out Ivy's hair. Tonight, Delphie was braiding it into a series of small braids.

"You mean, Charlie and Tink?" Delphie asked.

"Nash and Teddy, too," Ivy said. "I get to see Noelle every afternoon after she paints. I don't get to see the others."

"Except at school," Delphie said.

"Right," Ivy said.

Delphie let the silence lag. When Ivy had something important to say, she usually started with a neutral topic and waited until she was sure someone was listening. When Ivy didn't say anything else, Delphie replied to the question.

"I think Sandy's still pretty sick," Delphie said. "She's staying at Seth's so they can be together as a family there. You can really tell that they aren't here, huh?"

"Uh-huh," Ivy said. "There's still lots of people to talk to; it's just that they are more my age."

"Would you like to stay with Seth, too?" Delphie asked. "I'm sure Seth wouldn't mind. They certainly have room."

"Oh, no," Ivy said. "Not at all."

Delphie stared at the back of the girl's head and willed her to speak her mind. After a moment, Ivy sighed.

"I was just thinking about how they all have a 'thing,' you know?" Ivy's head jerked around to look at Delphie. "Charlie loves basketball. Noelle — painting. Teddy and Nash are always geeking about something or another."

"Tink doesn't, really," Delphie said.

"Tink's like me," Ivy said. "She's just getting over everything. Plus, she's been talking about learning to swim. I guess she had lessons when she was a kid, so, it would be *re*learning."

"Do you know how to swim?" Delphie asked, hoping she'd picked the right topic.

"Uh-uh," Ivy shook her head.

Every time she moved her head, the braids flew out of Delphie's hand.

"Would you like to?" Delphie asked, grabbing the braids again.

Ivy didn't respond. After a minute, Ivy sighed again.

"We can get you lessons this summer," Delphie said.

"I would like to swim, but . . ." Ivy said. "I think that maybe I'd like to have my *own* thing."

"Oh," Delphie said. She felt enormous relief that she was finally clued into what Ivy wanted to talk about. "What kind of thing?"

"That's just it," Ivy said. "I don't know. I just think that . . . You know, I'm not going to therapy as much, and I have more time and stuff. I'm going to work this summer but I also could learn something new or get a passion."

"'A passion'?" Delphie asked.

"You know, like they have," Ivy said. "Did you know that Katy had 'horsey bags' years before she'd ever been on a horse? That's . . . I want to have something like that — that's not just about my trauma and loss."

"Ah, yes — makes sense," Delphie said.

"Katy loves horses. Noelle loves art," Ivy said. "Even Tink loves sewing and she's going to be swimming and . . ."

"Charlie," Delphie said.

"That, too," Ivy said.

"What kind of thing do you think you might be interested in?" Delphie asked.

"I don't know," Ivy said. "The only other thing I did was help to find you. And, well, that's done."

Delphie wondered for a moment if Ivy felt that it was her fault for Ivy not having a "passion." She shook off this ridiculous thought. Instead, Delphie decided to take Ivy at her word. Delphie began to ask about a variety of things. Ivy was too polite to do anything other than answer Delphie's questions. So they began a verbal dance.

"Do you like art?" Delphie asked.

"No," Ivy said, emphatically. "I *really* suck at that."

"What about playing a musical instrument?" Delphie asked. "Do you like those lessons you're taking with Bernie?"

"Not really," Ivy said. "I mean, I think it's good to do. I mean, I like being around Bernie. I just don't love the piano, you know?"

"I do," Delphie said. "How about something physical like running or martial arts or . . ."

Ivy shrugged.

"I take martial arts with everybody once a week," Ivy said. "I know that Nash and Teddy go every day, but I don't like it enough to get *that* interested in it."

"Running?"

Ivy shook her head.

"How about archery?" Delphie asked. "Mr. Max would teach you."

"I love Mr. Max, but . . ." Ivy shook her head.

Delphie wracked her brain. She tried to think of the skills that people she knew had.

"What about smart stuff like rockets?" Delphie asked.

Ivy shook her head.

"Maybe math? Or computers? Or writing?" Delphie asked. "You do love to tell stories."

Ivy shook her head.

"Would you like to be in a play?" Delphie asked.

"They don't have those at my school," Ivy said.

"Not now, but they would if you asked for it," Delphie said.

Ivy sighed. Delphie glared at the back of Ivy's head in frustration. Delphie kept carefully combing Ivy's hair and braiding it.

"Have you ever . . ." Ivy started.

Delphie looked up from her work with hope. She waited. Ivy didn't continue.

"Have I ever . . ." Delphie said.

"Um," Ivy said. "Remember those photos I showed you?"

Delphie scrunched up her face and tried to remember which photos Ivy was talking about. She took a breath to ask if Ivy was talking about the baby elephants when Ivy spoke.

"You know, of that nebula?" Ivy asked. "You know — the stars?"

Of all the things Delphie was going to say, she was not going to guess that Ivy was talking about a photo of a nebula. Delphie made a vague noise to avoid sounding relieved that she hadn't said the wrong thing which would have launched another round of verbal dancing.

"I was thinking that maybe I would like to look at the stars," Ivy said.

"Oh?" Delphie asked.

"Uh-huh," Ivy said, nodding. "Kind of expensive."

"Expensive?" Sam asked from the doorway. "That sounds like my cue. What's expensive?"

CHAPTER FIVE HUNDRED & SEVENTY

VIEW OF THE STARS

"Looking at the stars," Ivy said.

She blinked at Sam as if he should know exactly what she was talking about. Sam looked at Delphie.

"I think she's thinking about getting a telescope," Delphie said.

"You know who knows everything about telescopes?" Sam asked.

Ivy shook her head, releasing the last braid from Delphie's hand. Delphie managed to catch the braid before it unraveled. Delphie quickly wrapped a hair band on the braid.

"Who?" Ivy asked, her voice rising with interest and hope.

Delphie tapped Ivy's shoulder to let her know that she was done braiding.

"Mr. Nelson's father," Sam said. He looked at his watch. "It's still early. Why don't we head over to Nelson's to see if he can ask his father?"

"Okay," Ivy said brightly.

Delphie gave a rueful shake of her head. Sam held out his hand, and Ivy took it. With that, they were off. They went down the stairs and out of the Castle. They had walked only half a block before they crossed the street to Nelson's. The big front house was dark and silent, but the light was on where Nelson lived in the back.

Sam knocked on the door. Nelson opened the door. He had a huge bowl of popped popcorn in the crook of his arm.

"What's up?" Nelson asked.

He looked at Sam and then at Ivy. With his look, Ivy's eyes went immediately to the ground, taking her head with them.

"We were wondering if we could talk to your father about telescopes," Sam said.

"Are you interested in telescopes?" Nelson asked. He squinted at Sam and then looked at the top of Ivy's head.

"We were thinking about maybe getting one to play with," Sam said. "We haven't looked through telescopes before."

"Why don't you come in and play with mine?" Nelson said. "I have it all set up. I was going to watch the transit tonight. Did you want to see the transit, Ivy?"

Ivy's head nodded. The men stared at the top of her head for a moment.

"We would love to come in," Delphie said from the pathway up to his house.

Ivy turned to look at Delphie. She gave her aunt a big smile. Ivy then looked back at Nelson and nodded.

"It's a Saturday," Delphie said. "We can stay up late. We can sleep in tomorrow."

"Great," Nelson said. "I was just settling in to watch. It finishes around 4 a.m. Is that okay?"

"Where should we go?" Sam asked.

"I have a porch that's set up for star gazing," Nelson said. "You know what? Why don't I call my dad? I bet he'll come over. He always has some experimental, super fancy telescope on loan from NASA."

"Would it be too much trouble?" Sam asked.

"Not at all," Nelson said. "I'm sure he's getting ready to watch this transit too. Plus, he loves to introduce people to the stars. Since there's four of us, we may as well get his equipment. We'll get his advice whether we want it or not."

Laughing, Nelson stepped aside to let them into the house. When Ivy passed, he dropped the bowl of popcorn into her arms. Nelson and Sam went into the house to call Nelson's father,

Pierre. Ivy carried the popcorn inside the house, and Delphie shut the door.

~~~~~~~~

Sunday morning — 3:14 a.m.
Paris, France

"So what do you think?" Lieutenant Colonel Alexandra "the Fey" Hargreaves asked.

"I still don't understand why you're doing this," her biological father, Benjamin, said.

He had been her mentor until he'd retired some number of years ago.

"It needs to be done," Alex said. "And done well."

"Why you?" Ben asked. "Why your team?"

Alex turned her head to look at him. They had been poring over maps of Poland on his ancient wooden table in his private office in the basement. The fire blazing in the fireplace didn't cut through the cold seeping in from the miles of limestone below. They were now sitting in armchairs around the fire. They spoke in quick Parisian French.

"Why you?" Ben asked in a near whisper.

She opened her mouth to speak but he held up a finger.

"And don't say, 'Why not me?' because I taught you that bullshit answer," Ben said.

She gave him a wide grin.

"Why . . .?" Ben started again.

"Hold your horses!" Alex said with a laugh. "Give a girl a moment to get a word out."

He grinned.

"Okay, why me?" Alex asked. "Why my team?"

"It's the first non-US military project that you've taken since . . ."

"I promised John I would stop saying 'everyone died,'" Alex said.

"How long has it been?" Ben asked.

"He bet me that I couldn't go a month," Alex said. "That was three months ago. I haven't . . ."

She shook her head, and Ben laughed. She smiled.

"Yes, this is our first civilian contracting since everyone died," Alex said.

"My lips are sealed," Ben said.

"Until you decide to rat on me," Alex said.

They laughed. He took a sip of his cognac before continuing.

"You own a portion of a military contractor," Ben said. "You sit on the board."

"I am aware of that," Alex said.

"Why not send them to do this?" Ben asked. "Why take the Fey team? It's not like you don't have enough on your plate with your children and home, not to mention the Factory."

Alex nodded. She fell silent as she dove deep into herself to come up with something honest that he would accept. She shook her head.

"I don't believe that you don't know," Ben said. "I *won't* believe it."

"I can tell you what I told the team," Alex said. "And, you should know that we voted on it. The entire team chose to take on this project — every single vote a 'yes.'"

"Fair enough," Ben said. "Let's start there."

"I told them that there were three reasons to take this job," Alex said. "The first is personal. We all know and love Sandy. We would help her in any way we possibly can."

Ben grunted and nodded his head.

"I am concerned about the rise in white nationalism in Poland," Alex said. "Sites like this are protected by people not knowing they are there. That's bound to end. The site survived the Nazis. It would be awful if it was looted by this new brand of Nazis. The families deserve more than that."

Ben grunted.

"There are still more than a hundred thousand missing works of art that were stolen from Jewish people by the Nazis," Alex said. "According to the journal, as well as the records Sandy and Bernie have found so far, this tunnel is bound to be full of it."

"Is that reason number three?" Ben asked.

"Still two," Alex said. She paused for a moment. "The third and most obvious reason is that the money is good. Sandy was one thing, but now Nadia is pitching in. There's a lot of money on the table. They are going to hire someone. It may as well be us."

"What will you use the money for?" Ben asked.

"Body armor," Alex said with a nod. "Recent changes to our budget have cut our body armor budget in half. The fee from this job will more than support new body armor."

Alex nodded.

"Body armor," Ben said softly. "How plush."

Alex grinned.

"Depending on what we find, we may get a finder's fee or two," Alex said. "We'll use those to repair some of our gear."

"Makes sense," Ben said.

"The Fey Team's budget's been slashed," Alex said. "We need to make up the difference or stop our cushy lifestyle."

Ben grinned at her. They fell silent. Ben got up from his seat to refill their glasses with cognac.

"What's *your* reason?" Ben asked when he sat back down.

"I think it's cool, in an *Indiana Jones* kind of way," Alex said. "*We get* to enter this mine. No one has been inside since it was sealed and the owner shipped to a concentration camp. *We get* to right a true wrong. Bring justice to some people as well as ease the mind of a dear friend who happens to be injured right now."

Ben looked away from her for a moment before he nodded.

"Relieve some of your guilt," Ben said.

Alex sighed, "Honestly, I have so much guilt that this thing does little more than nudge it a bit."

"You shouldn't," Ben said.

She took a breath to speak but he continued.

"I understand. You've been asked to do difficult things in horrible circumstances," Ben said. "You feel guilty because you're not a psychopath."

"Maybe not a very good psychopath," Alex said with a grin.

Ben laughed.

"You forget that I've seen your tests," Ben said.

Alex shrugged.

"I will accept your answer to all of this under on one condition," Ben said.

"Oh yeah?" Alex asked. "What's that?"

"That you take me with you," Ben said. He gestured to himself. "I am an original Indiana Jones."

"Bernie said the same thing," Alex said of Seth O'Malley's father.

"He taught me," Ben said with a laugh.

They laughed.

"You are welcome to come," Alex said. "It should be fun. Honestly, it's a great training exercise for the team. We've mixed it up so that the people at home haven't worked that side of things and some of our weaker members get field time."

"In an Indiana Jones kind of way," Ben said.

"Exactly," Alex said with a laugh.

She smiled at him, and he grinned back. They finished their cognac in silence.

~~~~~~~~~

Sunday morning — 6:01 a.m.

In her drug-induced slumber, Sandy heard the door open. She roused to near waking. Whoever or whatever had opened the door hadn't moved.

She fell back asleep.

There was a sound of quiet scratching across the floor. Cleo lifted her head to look at whoever had entered.

Sandy stirred.

There was a jumping sound.

Once.

Twice.

The third time a small body landed at the end of the bed. A short woman, Sandy could just feel something at the end of her feet. She opened her eyes.

There was a kind of scrambling on the bed. There was a weight near her feet at the end of the bed.

Unable to look because of the neck brace, Sandy attempted to say, "Hello?"

She heard Aden get up off the smaller bed.

"Rachel!" Aden said. He walked to the bed. "How in the world?"

"But Cleo can be there!" Rachel said, her voice choked with tears. "I won't bother her."

Aden lifted their daughter off the bed. The little girl stayed in her curled up form. Sandy tried to smile.

"I just want to be close," Rachel said. She sniffed back her sorrow. "Noelle and Nash and Teddy and you and everybody, Charlie, but not me . . . I *won't* be a nuisance! I *won't*! I just want to be close!"

Aden's eyes caught Sandy's. She nodded. Aden set the little girl back on the bed.

"Stay away from her broken foot or ankle," Aden said. "Even the slightest movement causes pain."

"I will," Rachel said. "I promise."

"I was going to show you," Aden said, leaning over so Sandy could see his face.

He held up a chunky knitted blanket and draped it so that Sandy could see it.

"*Rachel* knitted this for you," Aden said.

"W-aaw," Sandy said.

"Uh huh," Rachel said. "I love you, Mommy. It was made with love!"

Sandy's hand stroked the soft blanket.

"Delphie blocked it," Aden said.

"Be-ti-fl," Sandy said. "S' Sfft."

She stroked the blanket.

"Th-nk yu," Sandy said.

Rachel sniffled. Her head nodded against the bed. Sandy's eyes drifted shut.

"Let's rest a while," Aden said. "Breakfast will be ready soon enough."

Sandy was asleep. Aden touched Rachel's shoulder. He pulled the new blanket down a bit so it covered his daughter and went back to bed.

He rolled on his side to watch Sandy.

Their daughter was tucked in a ball at her feet. Her cat was tucked in a ball above her head. He smiled. She was well protected, well loved. He drifted to sleep with that thought on his mind.

~~~~~~~~~

Sunday morning — 6:21 a.m.

When the apartment door closed, Tanesha rolled onto her side. She squinted at the clock and then got up. She wandered into the bathroom.

Since they'd lived in the Castle, Jeraine took Jabari so that Tanesha could have time on Sunday morning to herself. Initially, the idea was that Jeraine would have time some alone time with Jabari. But living at the Castle, Jeraine had bragged to Jacob, Blane, and Aden about being such a great husband for creating this space for Tanesha. Sure enough, the other men refused to be left behind. Soon, the men and their younger children joined him in these early morning adventures. When M.J. found out, he refused to be outdone by the other husbands. Mike followed suit as soon as he saw the men leaving together with their kids.

Her girlfriends, including Honey and Valerie, each had quiet Sunday mornings now. Of course, that wasn't as true for Sandy now, but Aden would get on the ball soon enough.

Tanesha liked to spend the time reading the goodies and extras in the weekend *New York Times* and the *Los Angeles Times* over a few pots of tea and something yummy. She peered into her freezer to see what she had this week.

It had been Heather's turn. Heather had promised to ask her grandfather's cook to make them something out of the honey from Ares' hives. This thing had sat in Tanesha's freezer for the last few days. Smiling, she took the treat out of the freezer. She filled and turned on the electric kettle.

There was a knock on the door. That was Jacob psychokinetically sending her newspapers from the front of the house to outside their apartment door. She waited a moment and then opened the door.

There was no one in the hall.

She tossed the newspapers on the couch and went to make her tea. Jeraine had cleaned her ceramic tea pot and filled it with fresh tea leaves. Smiling, she made a mental note to thank him for helping her quiet time. She filled the pot with water and carried it to the couch.

She sat down in the glorious middle of the couch.

The room was completely silent.

She opened the *New York Times*. The top story was some other chaos created by the Nonsense-Maker-in-Chief.

"Tsk," Tanesha said.

She flopped the paper over so she could see below the fold and sucked in a breath.

The headline read: "Casino owner found dead late last night."

There was a picture of the casino owner who'd refused to release Jeraine from that ridiculous contract. The article's second paragraph mentioned Jeraine and the threatened boycott of Las Vegas.

Her mind ran circles around the news. Just because this man was dead didn't mean that the contract would be voided.

"Shit," Tanesha whispered.

It meant that the entire Vegas thing was a big mess.

Her life had just become a lot more complicated. She tossed down the paper and went to get her phone. She needed to check Black Twitter to see what this was about. It took her a moment to log in.

Black Twitter was abuzz about the death of this man. Jeraine and his friends had enlisted the prominent African-American thought leaders on Twitter to help promote his threatened boycott of Las Vegas.

Everyone had an opinion about this billionaire's death.

Some said he'd died because of the pressure he felt from the boycott. Some white nationalist said that Jeraine should be in prison for "murdering" this man.

"As if," Tanesha said.

She continued reading Twitter. The general consensus was that no one was going to miss this jerk.

She saw a clip of his forty-year-old wife teeter around on five-inch heels and skin-tight clothing while dragging their two young children into the hospital last night.

"Someone's going to miss him," Tanesha said out loud.

She pressed on the video of the Police Chief press conference and tried to glean the details.

They believed the billionaire had died of natural causes.

He was 84 years old. His arteries had more stents than pins in a pincushion. The heart attack wasn't a surprise to anyone.

Because he was so wealthy and influential, they were going to do an autopsy.

Tanesha sighed.

"What a mess," Tanesha said out loud.

She looked at the phone for a moment and wondered if she should call Jeraine. She instinctively shook her head.

This was the kind of thing that could send Jeraine into one of his anxiety-induced freak-outs. His brain would blink out. He would completely fall apart.

Her phone pinged.

She looked to see a photo of Jabari and the other children chasing Sarah and Buster at the dog park. She smiled at the photo.

He didn't know. Yet.

She was pretty sure that Jeraine's agent, Jammy, would know better than to call him. She bit the inside of her lip.

Maybe she should call him.

Her phone rang. She was so lost in thought that she did what she almost never did — she automatically answered her phone.

"Hello," Tanesha said, her mind still focused on the death of this billionaire.

"Is this Miss T?" a woman's voice asked.

Tanesha pulled the phone away from her ear to look at the number. It was blocked. She thought for a second and then shrugged.

"Some people call me that," Tanesha said.

"I always liked you," the woman said. "You were grace under a lot of crap."

"Okay," Tanesha said.

"These men," the woman's sorrow came through the line. She sniffed. "They put us through hell, and then they..."

"You've got that right," Tanesha said. "Is there something I can do for you?"

"I just wanted you to know that..." the rest was lost as the woman began to sob.

"Is there someone I can call for you?" Tanesha asked.

"No." The woman took a breath. Her voice was laced with rage. "That bastard died on top of some floozy. I should have expected it, but . . . I . . . and now I'm humiliated."

"I know what that's like," Tanesha said.

"I know you do," the woman said. "This is between you and me."

There was a sound of paper being ripped.

"That's Jeraine's contract," she said. "Fuck them. You tell Jeraine that Jeanie took care of it."

"Wait — what?" Tanesha asked.

"I've got to go," the woman said. "I'm going to buy out the front row for a year. You tell Jeraine that."

"Who is this?" Tanesha asked.

The woman said the name of the young wife of the billionaire.

"I don't get all of it," she said. "But I get a lot."

She blew out a breath. Her emotions were packed away.

"Now starts the rest of your life," Tanesha said.

"Damn right," the woman said and hung up the phone.

Tanesha looked at her phone. She went back to Twitter to see if any of the things the woman said were on Twitter. The first thing that came up was a photo of shredded paper from the wife of the billionaire.

The post said: "Jeraine's contract. Setting things straight. Love you, Miss T. #Jeraine #Freedom"

Tanesha clicked the heart and retweeted the post. Grinning, Tanesha poured herself her first cup of tea for the day.

Denver Cereal continues . . .

Aaron Alvin:
Father of Ava; also called "The spider" by Yvonne Smith.

Abi the Fairy:
General in Fairy Corps; great-grandmother of Tanesha; Fin's partner; First mother

Aden Norsen:
CEO at Lipson construction; single father of Nash and Noelle; husband of Sandy.

Alma Fontaine:
Mother of Heather Lipson; Psyche.

Alexandra Hargreaves:
Identical twin to Max Hargreaves; 'The Fey;' the leader of the Fey Team; wife of Dr. John Drayson; sister to Colin and Samantha Hargreaves.

Anjelika:
Megan, Mike, Steve, Candy, and Jill's mother; infact-toddler teacher at Marlowe School; wife of Perses.

Andrea Menendez or Andy Mendy:
Mother of Sandy; Seth's love & lover from the time he was 14 until he lost her when he was 30.

Annette:
Reality television star; mother to Jabari; Jeraine Wilson's ex.

Arthur "Raz" Rasmussen:
Member of the Fey team; boyfriend of Samantha Hargreaves.

Ava — Amelie Vivian Alvin:
Denver Police Crime Lab Technician; wife of Seth O'Malley; daughter of Aaron Alvin.

Ben Red Bear, Detective:
Denver Police Detective in charge of investigation of rapes; involved in the distribution of child pornography; murderer of Sandy's mother.

Bestat Behur:
Partner to Zack Jakkman; stepmother to Teddy; dragon.

Beth Baker:
Ava's best friend; Child Psychologist; murdered by Saint Jude.

Blane Lipson:
Jacob's cousin; assistant to Jacob Marlowe at Lipson Construction; Chinese Medicine doctor; husband of Heather; father of Mack and Wyn; bone marrow transplant ended his HIV infection.

Bob aka 'Blood spatter Bob': Former expert forensics instructor with the FBI; currently a laboratory technician in Ava's Denver Police Department lab.

Bumpy Wilson:
Good friend of Seth's; medical doctor; father of Jeraine Wilson, husband of Dionne, born Leroy Wilson.

Buster the Ugly Dog:
Seriously ugly, but awesome dog; adopted by Aden Norsen

Candace or Candy Roper:
Daughter of Anjelika; sister to Jill; lesbian; mother to ex-partner's children.

Charlie Delgado:
Stepbrother of Sandy; street kid; drug addict; moved in with Sandy and Aden in *Cimarron*.

Mr. Chesterfield:
Rodney Smith's large black dog, which he was given in prison from the Puppies for Prisoners program; best friend of Jabari.

Cleo the cat:
Asteria, mother of Hecate, wife and cousin to Perses.

Delphium or Delphie:
True oracle; once called Oracle Taber; dear friend of Celia and Sam Lipson; owner of the Castle.

Jabari Wilson: Young son of Jeraine Wilson and Annette; biological child of Tanesha Smith and Jeraine Wilson

Jacob Marlowe:
Son of Sam Lipson and Celia Marlowe; husband of Jillian Roper; brother of Valerie Lipson; president of Lipson Construction; owns his own rehabilitation business; carpenter; hockey player, teller of Denver Cereal.

Jeraine Wilson:
R&B sensation; husband of Tanesha Smith; son of Bumpy; recovering drug and sex addict.

Jeraine Wilson, Junior: Young son of Jeraine Wilson; not in Jeraine's life.

Jillian or Jill Roper:
Daughter of Anjelika and Perses; healer; mother of Katy Roper and twins Tanner and Bladen; wife of Jacob Marlowe; ex-wife of Trevor Mc Guinsey.

John Drayson, MD:
Vascular surgeon; husband of Alex Hargreaves.

Julie Hargreaves:
Mother of Paddie and Connor Hargreaves; wife of Colin Hargreaves.

"Ivy" Anna Marie McDonald:
Street child; friend of Tink and Charlie's; youngest assaulted in rape case with worst injuries; Delphie's niece; lives at Castle part-time.

Katy or Katherine Anjelika Roper Marlowe:
Daughter of Jillian Roper and Jacob Marlowe; bestfriend of Paddie Hargreaves; current possessor of Vanquisher sword.

Leslie: A laboratory tech in Ava's Denver Police Department lab.

Leslie Roper:
Wife of Steve Roper; mother of infant Elisa Roper.

Levi Johanssen:
Won Delphie in a card game when she was 5-6; held her as a slave/The Oracle Tabor; attempted to kill Delphie; deceased.

Liban:
Queen Fand's "twin" sister; looks like Cleopatra.

Lizzie O'Malley:
Daughter of Seth O'Malley; Biological mother to Conner Hargreaves. Wife of James "Jammy" Schmidt V.

Mack Lipson:
Toddler son of Heather and Blane Lipson.

Maggie Scully:
Toddler daughter of Honey and M.J. Scully

Margaret Peaches or Sergeant Margaret Peaches:
Fey team member; partner of Sergeant M.J. Scully; niece of Gando Peaches; member of the Diné people.

Manannán:
A Celtic sea deity; possibly first ruler of the Isle of Man; husband of Queen Fand; father of Prince Finegal and Princess Marigold and Edith; ancestor of Jacob Lipson

Maresol Tafoya:
Seth O'Malley's housekeeper; mother of Bonita's Seth's second wife; friend of Delphie.

Max Hargreaves:
Identical twin to Alex Hargreaves; brother to Colin and Samantha Hargreaves.

Megan Roper:
Daughter of Anjelika and Perses; healter; partner of Tim; mother to Ryan and two other boys.

Mike Roper:
Son of Anjelika and Perses; museum quality classic art painter; healer; husband of Valerie Lipson; art mentor to Noelle Norsen; hockey goalie.

Michael Bladen Roper Marlowe:
Infant son of Jill and Jacob Roper-Marlowe; identical twin of Tanner.

Mitch Delgado:
Sandy's stepfather who she called 'Dad'; father of Charlie and Sissy; Seth O'Malley's best friend; died of lung cancer about 8 or 9 years ago due to sarcoidosis from Vietnam.

M.J. or Sergeant Michael Scully Jr.:
Fey team member; partner of Sergeant Margaret Peaches; husband of Honey Lipson.

Molly:
Bookkeeper for Jacob Marlowe's rehabilitation business; wife of Pete.

Nadia Kerminoff, MD
ER doctor, head of Kerminoff Industries, a global corporation; ex-lover of Ivan, Russian mother, wealthy American father; "dark arrow" soulmate of Nash Norsen.

Nash Norsen:
Son of Aden and Nuala Norsen; brother of Noelle Norsen; "dark arrow" soulmate of Nadia Kerminoff.

Nelson Weeks, MD: A technical analyst in Ava's Denver Police Department lab; ER doctor; love interest of Blane Lipson; Templar Weapons Master.

Noelle Norsen:
Daughter of Aden and Nuala Norsen; sister of Nash Norsen; girlfriend of Teddy Jakkman; artist.

Nuala Norsen:
Ex-wife of Aden Norsen; addict and alcoholic; biological mother of Nash and Noelle Norsen.

Patrick "Paddie" Hargreaves, Jr.:
Best friend of Katy Roper; nephew of Alex and Max Hargreaves; son of Colin Hargreaves; current possessor of the Sword of Truth.

Patty Delgado:
Mother of Sissy and Charlie; pretended to be Sandy's mother; wife of Mitch Delgado.

Pete:
Husband of Molly; father of her children; friend of Aden Norsen; co-site manager at Lipson Construction.

Perses:
Paid assassin; rescuer, Titan, and biological father of Jillian Roper.

Pierre Semaines:
Father of Nelson Weeks; survivor of train bombing; works in missile development; Templar Weapons Master.

Rachel Ann Norsen:
Young daughter of Sandy and Aden.

Rodney Smith:
Father of Tanesha; imprisoned for 26 years for a murder he didn't commit; husband of Yvonne Smith; site manager at Lipson Construction.

Ryan:
Oldest son of Megan Roper and Tim.

Sam Lipson:
Husband to Celia Marlowe; married to Tiffanie Lipson; boyfriend of Delphie; father to Valerie and Jacob Marlowe-Lipson; step-father to Brianna, Becky, Honey and the 'step-whore.'

Samantha Hargreaves:
Sister to Alex, Max and Colin Hargreaves; girlfriend of Art Rasmussen; best friend of Valerie Lipson; mother of Sasha; criminal defense attorney.

Sandy Delgado Norsen:
Best friend of Jillian Roper; one of Jill's group of best friends; wife of Aden Norsen; mother of Rachel Ann; hairdresser.

Sarah:
Yellow Labrador belonging to Jacob Marlowe.

Seth O'Malley:
Godfather and biological father of Sandy; best friend of Sandy's step father; Denver Police Detective; gifted composer and prodigy pianist

Stepsister or Stepwhore:
Eldest daughter of Tiffanie Lipson; sister to Honey, Briana, and Becky Lipson; step-daughter of Sam Lipson; second wife of Trevor McGuinsey.

Steve or Stephen Roper:
Son of Anjelika; middle child of Roper family; medical nurse to Honey Lipson; husband of Leslie.

Sissy Delgado:
Stepsister of Sandy; anorexic; talented ballet dancer; currently in Paris studying at the Opéra national de Paris.

Tanesha Smith:
One of Jillian Roper's best friends; wife of Jeraine Wilson; daughter of Rodney and Yvonne Smith; grandchild of Urial; medical student.

Tanner Handy Roper Marlowe:
Infant son of Jill and Jacob Roper Marlowe; identical twin of Michael Bladen.

Teddy Jakkman
Son of Fey Team member Captain Zack 'the Jakker' Jakkman; best friend of Nash Norsen; dates Noelle Norsen.

Tink or Tiffanie:
Street kid; friend of Charlie Delgado's; attacked and beaten by gang of rapists, Heather and Blane Lipson's adopted daughter.

Tim:
Partner to Megan Roper; father of Ryan and two other children.

Tres Sierra:
Lover of Heather Lipson; CFO at Lipson Construction; brother to Enrique, Blane's ex-lover.

Trevor Mc Guinsey:
Deceased ex-husband of Jillian Roper; assumed father of Katy Roper; fiancé to the step-whore.

Valerie Lipson:
Daughter of Sam and Celia Marlowe; brother of Jacob; wife to Mike Roper; soap opera and movie actress; mother of Jackie and Eddie.

Wanda (Wade) Le Monde:
Met Sissy at Eating Disorder Inpatient Treatment; transgender child; daughter of Erik and Edith; girlfriend of Frankie Aziz.

Wes or Wesley Kapanski:
Hollywood producer; Was engaged to Valerie Lipson at the beginning of Denver Cereal.

Wyn Lipson:
Son of Heather and Blane Lipson; "little Greek God."

Yvonne Smith:
Mother of Tanesha Smith; forced into prostitution after her husband was imprisoned; daughter of Ne Ne and Urial.

Zack 'The Jakker' Jakkman
Father of Teddy, Britanie, and Samuel Jakkman; 'The pilot' to Sissy & Charlie; Sandy's childhood pen pal; friend of Sandy's.

THE STORY CONTINUES AT
DENVER CEREAL.COM

FIND US ON FACEBOOK:
FACEBOOK.COM/DENVERCEREAL

**If you like *Denver Cereal*,
please take a moment and leave a review. Your
review helps *Denver Cereal* continue.**

MORE ABOUT CLAUDIA AT:
CLAUDIAHALLCHRISTIAN.COM